O'HARA'S CHOICE

Also by Leon Uris

A God in Ruins
Redemption
Mitla Pass
The Haj
Trinity
QB VII
Topaz
Armageddon
Mila 18
Exodus
The Angry Hills
Battle Cry

O'Hara's Choice

A Novel

LEON URIS

HarperCollins*Publishers*

Note from HarperCollins Publishers Inc., New York:
Leon Uris passed away in June 2003, shortly after reviewing
his copyedited manuscript. Throughout the remainder of
the editorial process, we have attempted to maintain the
integrity of Mr Uris's original words and intentions

HarperCollins*Publishers*
77–85 Fulham Palace Road,
Hammersmith, London W6 8JB

www.harpercollins.co.uk

Published by HarperCollins*Publishers* 2003
1 3 5 7 9 8 6 4 2

A catalogue record for this book
is available from the British Library

ISBN 0 00 717618 X
TPB 0 00 717619 8

Set in Fournier and Spartan

Printed and bound in Great Britain by
Clays Ltd, St Ives plc

Dedicated to
my cousin
HERSCHEL BLUMBERG
"the finest ever seen"

It takes enormous support. God bless and everlasting gratitude to Marilynn Pysher, researcher, Jeanne Randall, assistant, and Cassandra Bliss and Kathy Mulcahy, caregivers.

1

PADDY'S WART-HOGS

1888—Prichard's Inn

The Royal Society of Paddy O'Hara's Wart-Hogs were the ugliest and most vile men to ever wear the uniform of United States Marines. They were molded out of old, stiff, cracked leather.

The Wart-Hogs were an exclusive brotherhood with no provision at inception for perpetuation. There were about eighteen charter members, no one knew the exact number, all men whose lives had been saved in battle through the gallantry of Paddy O'Hara in three, maybe four, separate Civil War actions.

For many years after the War, all who could gathered for an annual donnybrook. As time moved on, many of the reunions took place at graveside and the society grew more exclusive. But no Wart-Hog ever died in the poorhouse. They were bound by the most powerful of all ties, that of men and their comrades in a war.

The Wart-Hog doors were always open to other Wart-Hogs, but they were scattered and burdened with family life and other

1

traumas, so that meetings became occasional and by chance. Only
three remained in the Corps. However, it appeared that the rendezvous at Prichard's was by design.

Prichard's Inn & Tavern stood on the Post Road in Virginia,
across the Potomac from Washington, a most convenient watering
hole.

Master Gunnery Sergeant Wally Kunkle was first to arrive by
horseback from Quantico down the pike. The Corps had a piece of
land there and had established a small, convenient station near the
Capitol, where they formed up new units, or housed an overflow
from Washington. Quantico had become a nice rest spot and transit center.

Master Gunnery Sergeant Kunkle had been on sea duty and a
member of the contingent that ran the Germans out of Samoa.
Kunkle had not been home in three years. Well, he actually didn't
have a home.

The Gunny wore his forty-odd years well and he cut quite the
figure as he rode up to the inn at Prichard's. When the stable boy
had seen to the horse's comfort, he came to the Gunny's room and
poured buckets of hot water over him in a big galvanized tub to
wash away the road dust. Kunkle then repaired to the common
room with the large fireplace in the pub and allowed himself to be
overtaken by nostalgia.

1840s—Philadelphia

Wally was the middle child of nine kids, son of a German immigrant who worked as a blacksmith in the Philadelphia police stable.
The family lived on a cobblestone alley in a squeezed row cottage
in South Philly. During one particularly dirty winter, Wally's
mother and an infant sister died of the throat disease.

The children, save Wally, were scattered to relatives, mostly on
farms in western Pennsylvania. Wally was a quiet, ornery, angry,

fierce kid, and when the authorities came for him, he hid. He was finally taken to a humorless Lutheran orphanage, where his failure to bend to discipline led to corporal punishment.

Wally had a fight a day, sometimes more. After a year of it, he ran away from the orphanage and begged his father to let him remain hidden in the cottage to which he had returned.

The tiny house no longer had the siren lure of baking bread, as it did when Ma was alive, but had deteriorated into a home for rats drawn by the smell and taste of beer.

Wally spent his time near the navy yard on the Delaware River, where street urchins hung out, and picked up penny work doing laundry and running errands for the sailors. It was a highly territorial environment, where one used his fists to stake a claim to work a particular barracks. Wally fought his way to the barrack housing a Marine platoon.

Some of the Marines had been heroes in the wars against Mexico and the Seminole Indians. There were shoes and brass buttons and buckles to be shined and fresh hay to be changed in the bedding and a potbellied stove to be fed and cleaned. And clean he did. The Marines had far fewer bedbugs than the sailors.

Corporal Paddy O'Hara, an Irish immigrant who had survived the terrible potato famine, became Wally's big brother and protector. Wally made it the best job in the navy yard. The Marines were generous with smokes, the currency of the day.

On payday, illegal boxing matches were held beyond the main gates. Marines, sailors, shipyard workers, and visiting crews all had their champions in bare-knuckle pugilism. Before the men went to the pit, kids held preliminary fights for pennies tossed into the ring, and an occasional nickel. For Wally Kunkle at thirteen, this was a bonanza. After a particularly bloody match, there was sometimes as much as a dollar to be divided, seventy–thirty.

As a fighter, Wally Kunkle was cursed with a special gift. He could absorb punches and never go down. His talent, born in the alleys of South Philly and honed at the orphanage, won a lot of beer money for the Marines who bet on him. Wally ran out of competition his own age and size and had to take on bigger kids. "Young Ironsides," the Marines called him, and "Boilerplate" and "Kid Granite Jaw." Even Paddy O'Hara was unable to get Wally to stop fighting heavier and heavier opponents.

Then the inevitable happened. Wally took on an opponent thirty pounds heavier than himself. He showed the courage of a little bull, but absorbed a fearsome beating.

Corporal O'Hara pleaded, in vain, for him to throw in the towel when a sudden change of fortune occurred. Wally's opponent became so exhausted throwing punches that he could no longer lift his arms or catch his breath. And that was that. After laying out the bullyboy, Wally collapsed.

Corporal O'Hara lifted Wally in his arms and carried him back to the barrack and declared his boxing career over. The Marines patched him up and carved out a bed space for him on the floor near the stove, where they laid a sack stuffed with hay for Wally's comfort.

When the juvenile constable came looking, Wally was kept hidden and the Marines advised the constable not to come looking again.

Well, they had pet dogs and such, but Wally presented a different problem. The platoon commander, Lieutenant Merriman, was a right fair guy and, noting the men's affection for Wally, had some documents fixed up to state that Wally Kunkle was actually sixteen years of age, and he was sworn in as a Marine. At thirteen, he became a Marine drummer boy.

Paddy O'Hara had lost his family—four brothers and two sisters— in the Irish potato famine ten years earlier. The sole family survivor other than himself was his sister Brigid, who became a housemaid in New York. When Paddy was sixteen, he joined the Marines.

Against all odds, Paddy had been a prolific reader as a child, and under his brotherly watch, Wally entered the world of reading and writing. There were always books and magazines circulating in the barrack, mostly about girls and sexual situations. There were

also barrack readings of poems by Paddy O'Hara, which gained an
unusual popularity among his fellow Marines.

By the year of 1860 . . . eleven Southern States had formed a coali-
tion to preserve the institution of slavery and threatened to secede
from the United States if Mr. Lincoln was elected president.

In November, Abraham Lincoln won . . . and as his inauguration
grew close an ominous cloud was descending upon the land.

Southern States called up their militias. Southern-born officers
resigned from the army and headed home to organize the Rebels'
army.

Wally Kunkle's platoon, designated as the First Philadelphia
Marines, was ordered from the navy yard and boarded a troop train
that swept down from Boston and New York, taking on militia and
reserve units at every stop.

The train was met by dignitaries on stands covered with
bunting and bands hustling up profound patriotic music and cheer-
ing citizens.

The dignitaries spoke fierce language about the traitors in the
South and women wept and the newspapers blared headlines reeking of war fever.

By the time the train reached Washington, there was no anger
to compare. The pending war changed the way people saw the sun
rise and set. All focused on this new specter. In Washington, all
other forms of life had been numbed by war cries.

March 1861

Wally Kunkle was a drummer boy under the speaker's platform as
Mr. Lincoln held his hand on the Bible, then spoke in words that
reiterated the righteousness of the Union cause and sent forth a
surge of confidence in the Northern States. Within the month,
seven Southern States seceded.

The Confederacy demanded that the federal fort guarding Charleston Harbor be evacuated. When Lincoln refused, Fort Sumter was shelled and captured, and thus began the great American tragedy.

The zealots in the North demanded quick and decisive punitive action. The brazen Confederate act, they said, was no more than a dare. Quick victory was the demand. And the Union battered itself into a frenzy. It will be over by the Fourth of July! Great time to hold a victory parade.

The press wrote front-page editorials and the generals and Congress promised instant victory.

But Lincoln was not so sure. As he hesitated, the Confederacy and Union moved two forces toward each other, mostly of untrained or poorly trained militias. Now that the armies were on the move to face off, the instant-victory camp promised to smash the Rebels and march on their newly declared capital of Richmond. *End of war.*

The Confederate States, knowing the fight would come, had a more skilled officer corps and put the better force on the field.

Despite that, Washington was in a state of premature celebration. Everyone knew exactly where the battle would take place. The newspapers printed maps of the coming battlefield. Congressmen, civil servants, and thousands of the civilian population of the capital packed picnic lunches, loaded their wives into carriages and omnibuses, and took to the turnpike, already clogged with troops marching to the front.

Each side would field thirty thousand ill-trained, ill-equipped troops commanded mostly by men who had never seen combat.

Thirty miles from Washington and a hundred miles north of Richmond, sitting in a gap of a northern Virginia mountain range, sat the town of Manassas, unexceptional except for the rail junction that went off in all four directions.

For the Union forces to capture the Manassas Gap meant splitting the Confederate forces in half and opening the gates to Richmond.

On green rolling hills overlooking Manassas, spectators from Washington spread their picnic lunches and cheered their lads moving down into the fray.

The First Philadelphia Marines was led by Lieutenant Merriman, who kissed his wife and daughters as they marched past. The First Philadelphia was attached to a quickly assembled Marine battalion whose members had fewer than three weeks' training.

The army's guns moved on horse-drawn caissons and drummer-boy Kunkle had to beat quick time to keep up with them. At a creek named Bull Run on Jerome House Hill, they set up near a stone bridge. The plan was to cross Bull Run, secure the bridge, and bring the artillery over.

The guns and picket line around Jerome House Hill seemed in right fair position overlooking the creek.

Behind them, the First Philadelphia could hear hurrahs echoing from the onlookers.

Hurrah! Hurrah! echoed up the valley and the gap.

Hurrah! Hurrah!

Prichard's Inn

Master Gunnery Sergeant Kunkle's reverie faded to a wisp. Mr. Prichard stirred the embers of the fire, added a pair of logs, and prepared the bar and tables for evening drink and fare. As the grandfather clock chimed, the innkeeper adjusted the cuckoo clock behind the bar then drew a couple tankards of ale and came to the fireplace in hopes of some conversation.

"It's early yet. Your mates will be along."

The Gunny nodded in thanks for the ale.

"A reunion? Celebration?" Mr. Prichard pressed.

"Bull Run," Kunkle grunted.

"Bull Run, indeed! I was just ten years old. This was my old man's place then. I see you've known glory."

"If Bull Run be glory, then fuck glory."

*   *   *

As Wally Kunkle drummed the First Philadelphia onto Jerome House Hill, they could hear the popping of musket fire. A distant cheer from the spectators' vantage point behind them drifted past.

Lieutenant Merriman set up a defensive picket line peering down at the creek and stone bridge as the army artillery unhitched and set up a battery of cannons. If the Rebs showed up and made an attempt to cross, the First Philadelphia would repulse them, rise and lead the Marine battalion over the bridge, secure it, get the artillery across, and help open the road to Richmond.

That was the plan.

Bursts of Rebel cannon stepped up to the creek, then up the hillock to Jerome House.

The federal artillery responded, and the bright day turned an instant gray and the air shrieked with shells going out and shells coming in. The sound became unbearable despite the wads of cotton stuffed in the soldiers' ears.

The Confederates were on target first with a violent shaking of the earth. Wally Kunkle was struck by a flying object that smashed him to the ground and sent him crawling on all fours in search of his drum. He screamed as he saw the missile that had struck him was Lieutenant Merriman's leg.

It shocked him from his fear as he crawled to the officer, took off Merriman's belt, and made a tourniquet on his stump.

Paddy O'Hara knelt beside them and stared at the sheet-white fast-dying officer.

"Can you hear me, sir?"

"Aye," Merriman croaked.

"They got two of the cannons and the artillery officer. We've lost both sergeants!"

Another burst and Wally and Paddy threw themselves atop the lieutenant.

"Shit, man!" Paddy yelled. "Some of our people are breaking rank!"

Merriman gasped out, "We're on the far flank, O'Hara! We

have to hold this hill or they can break through to the turnpike!"
Then he said no more.

"I need an officer! I need a sergeant!"

Wally saw his smashed-up drum and gagged next to the bloody
lieutenant's body.

"I'm it, Boilerplate. Can you get useful?" Paddy yelled.

"Aye . . . aye . . ."

"All right now. Crawl about, keep low. Pick up every musket
and powder horn you can find and carry them to the big boulder
behind the tree! Go!"

Paddy took command, shoring up his picket line. There were
plenty of guns to be found because, to his horror, O'Hara had seen
the Union troops scatter and throw down their muskets.

The balance of the Marines were caught in a draw alongside
Jerome House Hill. Instead of digging in, they wavered and some
broke off.

A cannonade blast fell within scratching distance and choking
smoke blotted out the hill. When it passed over, most of the
Marines were in flight. Paddy took Lieutenant Merriman's saber,
got behind the First Philadelphia, and threatened them to stand
fast. He slashed the head of a fleeing coward.

Paddy allowed himself a brief smile as he saw Wally Kunkle
dive behind the big rock with four or five muskets in his arms and
load them with powder.

Rebel cannon hit close again. Wally Kunkle choked on the dust
and saw his arm go bloody from a shock of concussion. He was
frozen with fear, dead men all around. At the instant of decision his
fear ebbed. He felt thirst, eyes stinging, unable to see more than
blobs, and it was the toil of battle and it was Paddy O'Hara keeping the Marines of the First Philadelphia on the line . . . and now it
all went ethereal . . . ethereal, like he was an angel looking down
watching himself move through time and space.

The Marine line held a good position, looking down the knoll
from Jerome House to Bull Run Creek and a hill beyond it.

The crest of that hill soon filled with enemy. Artillery gone.

Marine battalion broken. One choice only. Muskets were of short range, so Paddy would have to let the Rebels cross and come up the knoll to within sixty or seventy yards. It would take a steady hand.

The cannon fire stopped and Johnny Rebel let out terrifying screams as they poured down and over Bull Run Creek, certain that their artillery had cleared out Jerome House. Capture! Consolidate! Then organize a breakthrough to the turnpike itself! The Rebel yell became a single earth- and sky-shattering scream.

"Fire!"

Remnants of the First Philadelphia held off the first charge and took up new-loaded muskets. From the slope, some of the Confederate wounded crawled forward and picked off two Marines, three . . .

Another wave of Rebels charged and were again beaten back, and now another, but they were coming with less determination. Paddy's line became thinned out pitifully when a breakthrough came.

The drummer boy caught a flick of a look into the wild eyes of a Southern soldier. Wally fired a pistol as the Rebel boy plunged his bayonet home.

In one of the few places of Union valor that day, the knoll before Jerome House Hill was littered with Southern dead. The attackers took covered positions, not eager to charge again.

The strength of the First Philadelphia's numbers had dwindled to a half-dozen men. If the rebel captain had known, all he had to do was sneeze hard and break through.

Wally Kunkle's side bled, his hands and face blistered, but he kept his position until the pain in his shoulder became so terrible he could not fire.

Paddy got to him, tore open his shirt, said something foul, and went to work. Wally hung in . . . hung in . . . He screamed. Paddy put the ether to his nose and Wally began giggling . . . "Good boy, good boy, there you go, lad . . . I think we got the bleeding stopped . . .

"Come on, darkness, come on," Paddy said. "God, Mary, I'm

praying to every Catholic saint . . . come on, darkness! Please, blessed darkness, please fall!"

A peek of the moon over the hill. The Rebels were pulling their wounded back to the creek. The firing stopped. Thirsty men drank and dried up their blood, and soon Paddy could see their campfires over the way.

He had four men left, including a somewhat helpless Wally Kunkle and himself. Kunkle was a burden, badly messed up and flying high but still salvageable.

What to do? Crawl down to the rebel line and try to shoot them back across Bull Run? Never work with three shooters. Paddy reckoned the rebels had taken a large number of casualties at Jerome House and would not make a night assault. Night assaults were a barbaric way to fight a war. Their energy must be as low as ours. And water . . . they'd die of thirst halfway up.

However.

The Rebels would probe with patrols. They might harass all night. Come the dawn, this position was done in. Two choices, maybe three.

Send the other two lads back to get reinforcements. He'd stay with Kunkle.

All three go back and leave Kunkle.

Go back as a unit and carry Kunkle, but that would eat up time. Jesus and Mary, what's a fucking corporal to do?

Wally Kunkle became conscious as a bit of daylight flitted through the trees. Oh Jesus, it hurt! Paddy O'Hara's face came into view above him, hard to recognize.

"Hey, Paddy, where are we?"

"On the turnpike."

"How'd we get here?"

"Patiently."

He propped Wally against a wagon wheel. Wally clutched the corporal. The turnpike was clouded and dirty with specks of dust showering down like rain. The wounded were stretched at roadside and being removed to wagons. The rest of it was a mass of caissons and men marching, dragging, and carriages of civilians all struggling for their piece of road back to Washington.

"We held fine," Paddy said directly into Wally's ear, and Wally nodded that he understood. "Delaney and Marconi came through. They've been evacuated."

"Wha . . . happen—"

"We got the shit kicked out of us, that's what. The living shit. We held till dark, then had to weave through Rebel patrols all the way back. We've moved a company of Delaware militia onto Jerome's in case the Rebels wish to continue this brawl."

Wally jerked away from him and began crying and slurring. "Our fucking battalion broke and ran," he garbled. "Hey now, Boilerplate, a doctor gave me something to give you in case the pain gets too bad."

"I don't want no—"

"You'll take what I give you. We got a long war to fight."

Prichard's

The grandfather clock tolled. Mr. Prichard whipped out his pocket watch. Twenty seconds passed before the cuckoo clock responded. The innkeeper made an adjustment.

Kunkle had one eye open. "What's it?" he asked.

"Ah, you was having a peaceful doze. When my clientele comes in to have a few jars in the evening, the cuckoo clock has to sound within fifteen seconds of the big guy. Over fifteen seconds and I have to sport a round. Under fifteen, I collect two pennies from every man at the bar."

"I'll bet with you," Kunkle said, and closed his eyes again.

·· 2 ··

BENJAMIN MALACHI BOONE

1888—Union Station—Washington (the Same Day)

Major Benjamin Boone knew by rote the instant the train slowed on the big curve before its entry into Washington. He snapped his eyes open as Monroe, the porter, who had made Boone's friendship over dozens of trips to the capital, entered the compartment and filled the water basin.

Ben dunked his face and took a towel from Monroe, after which the porter assisted the major into his jacket. The empty bottom half of the right sleeve was folded up above the elbow and sewn shut. With the arm stump in place, Monroe buttoned the major's jacket and brushed it off.

The engine sounded its ceremonial hissing, whistling, squealing, and farting to proudly herald an on-time arrival.

Monroe buckled the major's belt and declared him fit for debarking. Ben Boone's grade was impressive—only one rank below

Lieutenant Colonel Commandant Tom Ballard—particularly considering Boone had one arm, a limp, and limited sight in his left eye.

The train braked, rudely pitching the two men together. Private Lamar Jones, the major's Washington orderly, entered, snapped off a sparkling salute, and took the major's carpetbag from Monroe. Boone slipped a silver dollar into the porter's hand.

"You sure about this, sir?" Monroe asked.

"I got lucky in a poker game last night."

"Thank you, Major, and I hope to catch you on the way back."

The two Marines made their way from the terminal to a mash of carriages. Traffic into Washington these days was heavy, drumming up talk in Congress of building a grand terminal. When they reached the carriages, Jones whipped out an envelope and handed it to the major.

> *Dear Ben,*
> *I will not require your presence at the meeting with the*
> *Secretary of the Navy tomorrow. Be at my residence for dinner*
> *on Wednesday at seven bells. Dress informal, men only.*
> *—Lieutenant Colonel Commandant Thomas Ballard, USMC*

Ben got into the carriage hissing beneath his breath. He had been aced out of an important—no, vital meeting. What chance would Tom Ballard have across the table from Horace Kerr, the shipbuilder, and Commodore Chester Harkleroad, chief of naval design? Less than none. Damned!

Boone grunted at the reality. He and Harkleroad in the same room could blow the lid off the building. Harkleroad and Kerr, goddamn sons of bitches. They'd already got the secretary in their pocket.

"Jones!"

"Sir!"

"Take me directly to Prichard's Inn. I'll be staying for a night or two."

"Aye, aye, sir. When shall I fetch you?"

"Wednesday afternoon will be fine. Is there a clean uniform in my closet?"

"Yes, sir. Got all the stains out. Your brass is polished to snuff."

"Jones!"

"Sir!"

"Do you know how I want this ride?"

"Yes, sir. In silence, sir."

Ben looked with awe at the expanding alabaster grandeur of the Capitol building as they made their way through the congestion. The new monument to Washington, now open to the public, soared over it all. High, slender, reeking of majesty—its four corners were like a powerful lighthouse beam streaking out to the entire planet, announcing that this would become the center of the earth.

Ben fretted about being left out of tomorrow's meeting until they crossed the river, then let the countryside lull him.

Lord, had it been four years since the remaining Wart-Hogs had seen one another? Him, Captain Tobias Storm, the mustache that supported a man, and "Boilerplate" Kunkle. Would they accept the new assignment? Both of them had so much service time they could just up and resign. After too many years you can get the esprit de corps knocked out of you. Were they too weary? Did they still believe? Or had they become feeble?

Ben shifted his position as a pain settled in his hip. One thing or another hurt a fair part of the time. He had been wounded in battle on numerous occasions, but his limp and stump were not a result of enemy fire. During maneuvers several years back, Ben thought he was still a rider in the Horse Marines and got low-bridged by a tree branch and his mount rolled over on him.

Though seriously maimed, Ben Boone was too valuable to discharge. He resumed his career and became one of the few remaining Marine officers with influence.

He had evolved into a brilliant maverick military theorist, so much so that his voice and papers had long reach and he was a regular consultant to the army as well as the navy and often called upon to advise the president.

After he lost the confrontation with the tree, Boone ultimately ended up as the lone Marine officer assigned to the Naval War College at its inception in 1884.

The army tried to lure Ben with colonel's epaulets and the navy dangled a commodore's stripe if he would transfer to their services. He chose to remain a one-armed Marine who would probably never be promoted higher than major.

Ben's mind fell into cadence with the horse's beat and he dozed and let the memories in.

1845—Lynchburg, Virginia

Benjamin Malachi Boone's memories started when he was a boy in his home in Appalachia. Every year, feuding clans declared a local peace for a glorious Fourth of July in Lynchburg. This particular year, a uniformed Marine sergeant had come recruiting.

Although the Corps was a tiny outfit, it was able to attract exceptional recruits because it had the capacity to draw its strength from past valor and present patriotism.

The first source was the sons of immigrants in three or four large East Coast cities that had ports and naval facilities.

Of equal importance were the farmlands.

Dedication to the Corps was above the norm. The navy also recruited heavily from immigrants, but these were men apt to be going to the sea as a last resort, where one depended only on officers for loyalty. The navy had always drawn their crews from grungy places. A seaman in the lower ranks had a mean, often brutal life.

Marine contingents aboard ship were its police force. Punishment of a crewman could mean a lashing or being brigged on rations of bread and water or an inhuman keelhauling beneath a ship. Navy desertions were commonplace and mutinous whisperings were as much a part of most voyages as the disgusting food and cramped quarters.

The elevated status of the Marines led to a distinct dislike between them and the sailors. Although they shared much misery and the same flag, each stayed with their own.

In Lynchburg on the Fourth of 1845, the Marine recruiter had eagle's eyes, and claws as well. Generally speaking, hillbillies made first-class troops. All of them were skilled hunters and mountain men, tough as jerky and used to hard work on slim rations.

Eighteen-year-old Benjamin Malachi Boone won the musket-shooting contest by a wide margin against some very fine opponents.

Ben Boone was prime meat for the Corps. Moreover, the recruiter found out that this one could read and write, having learned by memorizing the Bible. The recruiter offered him an eight-dollar bounty, a sum that Ben had to take seriously.

The Boone clan consisted of a dozen families and allies who dominated a swath of mountain from Preacher's Hollow clear to Glasgow in the Blue Ridges.

Ben Boone's grandfather, Enoch, the family patriarch, had spent that winter of horrors with George Washington at Valley Forge and was there at the final battle at Yorktown. He was a Christian zealot and a fervent abolitionist in a state where slaves, numbering almost half the population, upward of a half million, toiled in the tobacco fields. It was an open secret that the Boone "territory" held underground-railroad stations. Not all of the clan agreed with Father Enoch's preachings, but no one would betray their kin, abolitionist or not.

Fortunately the Boones held their piece of mountain without much challenge. They were deadly riflemen and fiercely loyal to one another. Their pride was great in the men from their clan who had fought in the country's military.

Benjamin Malachi Boone was the best among the coming generation, but it was his time to serve and he went off with his family's blessing. So great were Ben's skills that he was commissioned to brevet second lieutenant less than a year after he joined the Corps.

March 1847—Aboard the USS Lafayette

America had burst forth on an expansionist binge, lopping off huge territories from Mexico and reaching from ocean to ocean. Texas had been annexed. California was hoicked from Mexico on the rationale that if America didn't hoick it, France or England would.

For the better part of a year the navy blockaded Mexican ports on the Gulf under the command of Commodore Perry. Small landings, raids, sieges of wavering forts called for an increase in the size of the Marine Corps.

The Corps recruited, trained, and spread aboard ships an undersized regiment. A Marine liaison was required by both Commodore Perry and General Winfield Scott.

Perry was astonished to be sent young Ben Boone, a brevet lieutenant scarcely twenty years of age, but Scott welcomed him. They were both abolitionists from the same area of Virginia and Boone quickly earned the commander's respect.

The invasion of Mexico was on! Winfield Scott surveyed his magnificent fleet of seventy ships with twelve thousand soldiers aboard. The fighting was all over in California with the fall of the villages of San Diego and Los Angeles. Now, to hit Mexico in the center and march to the capital!

A six-foot four-inch bear of a man, "Old Fuss and Feathers" exuded confidence to his staff as the fleet deployed for the bombardment and siege of the stinkhole of Vera Cruz. He did not believe that a Mexican army of peasants impressed into service would offer a serious fight.

Not only did the Mexicans acquit themselves well, but heat and dysentery and malaria and swamps and yellow fever wrung the juice out of Scott's army.

By September, a war-hardened and wiser army reached the plain of Mexico City, domain of the ancient Aztecs and the fortress of Montezuma.

Ben Boone had been at the general's side during the entire campaign, displaying hillbilly cunning. With the Marine unit down to

battalion size, their swift, controlled movements and courage
gained in reputation. Boone was at last released from Scott's staff
to command a company.

September 13, 1847, became the greatest battle in Corps history.
Ben Boone's company was the first to reach and storm the Halls of
Montezuma.

After the war, General Scott, seemingly in permanent command of
the army, sent Boone to West Point for advanced schooling. Scott
shadowed Boone's progress and then had him stationed in Washington.

The general tried to cajole Ben into transferring to the army and
Ben skillfully rejected entreaties, demands, and commands. Ben
remained the Marine Corps liaison. After three years of it, the general finally let him go to sea, to all those shitholes Marines seemed to
adore.

By the time the Civil War loomed, Scott was ill and exhausted
and broken by time. He realized he was too old and without the
energy to command such a conflict. He set about feverishly to create a grand strategy for the Union, if Lincoln were elected. Ben
Boone, still a brevet second lieutenant in the Marine Corps, was
ordered back to Washington.

1861—Washington—the United States War Department

By the time Ben's ship docked in Baltimore, Lincoln was inaugu-
rated and the Confederacy had fired on Fort Sumter. War was
inevitable.

General Scott wore his years badly now. He was saggy and sad-
dened when Lieutenant Boone reported.

There were two or three sentences of small talk. He tapped Ben's
record book on his desk and Ben nodded that he understood.

"I can no longer give my best," the general said, "and I doubt if
I'll live through this war."

"I understand, sir," Ben said.

"You're losing your goddamn accent. You been reading?"

"Two years in London and lots of time aboard ship, sir."

"We are both Virginians, Ben. How is this going to sit with you? Many of our finest officers are heading south. Longstreet, Pickett, Jeb Stuart, Tom Jackson, Robert E. Lee. It was Beauregard who ordered the bombardment of Sumter."

"I do not choose to be among them," Ben answered.

"Nor I," Scott replied. "I'm glad to hear you feel the same."

"It took mighty courage for my grandfather to be an abolitionist in the Blue Ridge Mountains. I heard him preaching, but it was those times I got to sit on his lap and feel his big hand stroke my head. 'Slavery is evil, it's wrong, boy. It's the worst thing that ever happened to the human race.' "

"And that's still your feeling?"

"My family still has a station on the underground railway, sir. And I am rather disgusted with the British. They gave up slavery, but they want us to continue on and on to supply cotton for their mills. Maybe not openly, but they'll support the Confederacy."

"Then we agree that the curse of slavery must be eradicated."

"General, I was born with a squirrel gun in my hand. By the time I was ten, I was helping runaway slaves. Our job was to get them to the Allegheny stations in West Virginia. From there they had a shot at Ohio."

"No wonder you're such a good tactician."

"Not quite good enough, sir. I would make one or two, maybe three, runs a year. One time we got ambushed by the Virginia militia. They lynched all six of the slaves, two men, two women, two kids. My uncle Hackett was strung up in Roanoke with a 'nigger lover' sign on him. My kin rescued me."

"I know your grandfather was a powerful shadow over you, but tell me why? Why did you do it?"

Ben Boone, who had the best poker face in the Corps, bit his lip.

"I saw how much black men loved their kids and women, as

fiercely as we did. And, I know, sir . . . in their agony they was speaking to God.

"General Scott, you know my hills and my county. When you're indentured to your pitiful acres of tobacco, you're no more than a half step better than a slave. I was born hungry, lived hungry, and when I hunted, I hunted hungry. Shoot straight or eat collards. It was damned near famine year-round with us and never a year passed that we didn't bury some kid, died of pellagra. In some ways we were worse off than slaves. A slave was fed enough to be kept alive. Greed knows no color. It was the same system keeping us crushed, but as woebegone as we were, no one would change places with a slave, even one who ate chicken every day."

That was a lot of talk in one breath for a man from the Blue Ridge Mountains. Ben patted his jacket pocket, feeling for his pipe, looked at the general, who nodded that the smoking lamp was lit.

"After this war is done—well, I don't expect to be here, but, Ben, you will. The South will be very sick. I hope you'll return home and help govern them. Many Southerners detest slavery, but not enough of them. It is going to take decades, generations, maybe a century for them to even come face-to-face with the evil they have inflicted." He grunted and shifted his large body.

"They call me 'Old Fuss and Feathers.' They can start calling me 'Old Aches and Pains.' I've reached the time that the aches in your body come to a confluence with the aches in your heart.

"Well, I didn't recall you from London to exchange bullshit. We either win this war or America will wind up as a fleeting comet in the story of man."

They stared at each other through pipe smoke and cigar haze. "In the coming months," the general said in measured words, "the Union is going to go through the painful experience of learning we are not fighting a corrupt Mexican army or chasing down Indians. Half of our officer corps is gone. That has created new openings for Union officers with more ambition than skill and courage. Mr. Lincoln is going to be looking at some terrible incompetence before he is able to get a handle on this war, and no small part of it will be his generals.

"As my last important duty, I feel bound to give the president my best ideas for a Union strategy. There's a lot of blather about a quick victory, but you and I both know that is unlikely. I want you on my transition team to turn the military over to Lincoln in the best possible shape. I know you've been thinking all the way back from London. What kind of grand strategy should we develop?"

"Blockade," Ben answered without hesitation.

Scott broke into what resembled a smile.

"That's it, son."

"You're most generous, sir."

"We have to train an officer corps and enlisted ranks to fight a long, hard war. That will take time. The linchpin of this design must be an immediate blockade of the Southern ports along the coast as well as the Mississippi River.

"You're going to like this part, Boone. Every vessel must carry a Marine unit to board blockade runners on the seas and land and capture Confederate forts. I am going to recommend that we triple the size of the Corps immediately and I want you to remain as my liaison with your commandant."

"I understand, sir."

"Good. The Marine Corps will have value, but the war will be won by huge armies fighting titanic land battles. And once the war is over, no one is going to want to fight and the Corps will again have outlived its usefulness. Ben, for God's sake, resign this pukey little Corps and transfer to the army . . . now."

"Sir, I can't agree."

"Dammit! What will we be saving? An archaic institution? What for? Christmas-tree decorations?"

"Sir, I can't agree."

"Fucking tell me why, Lieutenant Boone!"

"When we lifted Texas and California from the Mexicans we did not go from sea to shining sea, sir, in order to rest on our laurels. We were saying, 'Hello, Monroe Doctrine, here we are, overlords of the hemisphere.' Since the Mexican War we have landed units in Buenos Aires, Nicaragua, Uruguay, Paraguay, Fiji, the isthmus. When this war is done, the United States will enter as a world power and have a world-power two-ocean navy. As our commerce spreads, along with the idea of democracy, there will be many more landings and expeditions, larger rather than smaller. One day the United States is going to find itself having to land on an enemy beach defended by two brigades. We'd better know what the hell we're doing. Choke off the Corps and this country, in hindsight, will realize it went and shot off one of its nuts, and not in a pleasant way."

Brevet Lieutenant General Winfield Scott stared at Boone and then thought, Well, what the hell, nobody can change a hillbilly's mind.

"The Brits are way ahead of us with their Marine Corps and nobody in England is trying to abolish them. Maybe an old power like the British can see the future more clearly than we can . . . Sorry, sir."

"Like hell you're sorry," Scott answered. "I'll be briefing President Lincoln tomorrow night. I shall require your presence."

· 3 ·

THE RETURN TO
FORT SUMTER

Winfield Scott's master plan for conducting the war was adopted, giving Lincoln time to shake out his senior officers and create a great army.

Keels of ships of every class were laid and launched, from ocean-ranging men-of-war to paddle-wheel gunboats reporting for duty on the Mississippi River.

There was not one spectacular victory, but the blockade resulted in a daily, relentless wearing down of the enemy. The South required vast supplies from the outside and blockade runners poured out of the European ports to get in on the bonanza of the black market.

Every so often the Union fleet caught or sank a blockade runner, but most of them got through.

There was enough money involved for profiteers to keep a steady line moving across the ocean. Yet, for every vessel that failed and for every cargo lost, the noose on the Confederacy grew slightly tighter.

Odds heavily favored the North with thrice the population, thousands more miles of railroad, and twenty-fold the industrial might. The Union had farmlands, the raw materials, and a highly skilled labor force.

Given time, the Confederate States would run out of everything from soap to gunpowder. Given more time, the Confederate States would be pulling up their rails to melt them down for metal and ammunition. There were hundreds of thousands of angry and desperate slaves to be held in check, and they were desperately needed, for the export of cotton and tobacco crops had to pay for everything.

The will of the South was a story of sacrifice on the home front and courage on the battle front that told the Union it was in for a long and bloody haul.

Although the Confederacy might never defeat the Union, it could drain the will of the Union and bleed the war to a standstill in order to win at a bargaining table.

Would Union resolve cave in, in the face of years of wanton slaughter? The Union cause had to be mighty enough to stand behind their battle cry of "unconditional surrender." A leader of boundless greatness was able to instill a commandment into the soul of the nation that slavery was against God's will.

And so, a tragedy for the ages was on.

Winfield Scott retired and a war that was supposed to be over in a blink entered its third year. Early in 1863, Ben Boone was assigned to the mighty frigate USS *Tuscarora*, a stalwart of the mid-Atlantic squadron.

He was to take command of a newly formed company, made up of 102 marines pulled together from a variety of ships and posts.

The USS *Tuscarora* was a sight to behold at its berth in Baltimore, double decked with cannons and spoiling for a fight. K Company was ready and waiting as Lieutenant Boone came up the gangplank and was piped aboard. First to greet him was Sergeant Paddy O'Hara.

Ben renewed his friendship with old hands and acquainted himself with the new men. He was assigned an area on the aft deck and, with his sergeants, crafted vigorous exercises, drills, and inspections to keep his men alert and ready for action.

K Company was soon thinking as a unit, with each man and each squad catching the others' rhythms. By the time the bark-rigged beauty set her sails and cruised serenely down the Chesapeake, Ben had a handle on what to expect from his people.

On the ocean beyond sight of land, the *Tuscarora* made rendezvous with two dozen warships, and rumors leaped from ship to ship. It was apparent that something huge was in the offing.

The armada sailed and steamed west, then made a huge turn and circled south, where it was joined by a half-dozen more ships from the mid-Atlantic squadron.

On the dawning of the twelfth day, land was sighted.

Lieutenant Boone left the officers' wardroom and hastened to find Sergeant O'Hara.

"Sergeant!"

"Sir!"

"Assemble K Company in our deck area with full combat gear."

"Aye, aye, sir."

"It's a big one."

K Company was topside in minutes and a roll call was taken.

"All present or accounted for, sir."

With his sergeants trailing him, Lieutenant Boone checked every man's kit, ammunition, and water, and his potential courage.

"Stack your rifles and packs and gather around."

The men fanned the sweat from their faces with the newly issued broad-brimmed campaign hats. The company dog, Ugly, panted with thirst, but knew it was time to be silent.

"The land yonder," Ben said, "is the entrance to Charleston Bay. At dawn tomorrow the Marines of K Company have been honored to lead the invasion to recapture Fort Sumter."

The cheer was piercing and in a few moments they could hear rally cries from ship to ship.

Ben went over the drill one more time . . . naval bombardment . . . we are restricted to quarters . . . keep your ears plugged at all times . . . aweigh all boats at 0300 . . . whalers row to portside so our ship will give us protection from enemy fire . . . steam launch will hook up all *Tuscarora* whalers . . . we will be towed to a place behind the breakers . . . we will unhook from steam launch when naval bombardment lifts . . . most crucial maneuver is rowing through the surf . . . unload, secure whalers, form a perimeter, move toward Lizard's Gate, stop out of rifle-fire range . . .

. . . ammunition and water will not arrive for over an hour, so fire and drink with great care . . .

. . . bear in mind that thirst and exhaustion are as much the enemy as the Rebels . . .

. . . and fucking remember that the noise will be like a herd of bulls getting their nuts cut off . . .

. . . we will have to depend greatly on hand signals . . . keep plugged . . . I don't want any deaf Marines coming out of this battle . . .

"Letters for home will be collected at seven bells tonight," Paddy said. "Kindly help any brothers who have difficulty writing. Anything else, sir?"

"Get Ugly a hatful of water and gather around close."

Ben took an envelope from his pocket, opened it, and read it.

To the officers and men of the mid-Atlantic squadron:
Our armies are performing gallantly inside Confederate territory. Fort Sumter is where this conflict began. Its recapture will sound a clarion call to rally the Union toward our inevitable triumph, as well as sounding a clarion call to our

*citizens in the South to forsake their odious cause. May God
keep you and return you safely to the arms of your loved ones.*
                                                    —*A. Lincoln, President.*

In the stillness that followed, Ben handed the letter to the men
to be passed around.

"I am a Virginian," Ben said, "but remember that one-third of
all slaves brought to our country passed Fort Sumter on their way
to the slave block in Charleston."

The company was dismissed, but the midday heat clung tight. It
became still, so very still, as the ships deployed and land loomed
larger. Paddy found a wistful Ben Boone staring hard at infinity.

"How is it?"

"Looking good, Lieutenant. Some of the men are even manag-
ing to nap. Rest of them are writing letters or having old letters
read to them. May I smoke up here, sir?"

"Please, with care. Bloody *Tuscarora* is a floating bomb."

"How's it going to go tomorrow, Lieutenant?"

"Depends on how much damage the navy can inflict." Ben
looked away, but Paddy's curiosity was sharp on him. "Navy has a
propensity to believe that their gunfire will devastate any given
target. A few pissy-ant forts have surrendered without resistance,
but Sumter is not a pissy-ant fort."

"We'll be shooting a hell of a lot of guns at them. There's got
to be three or four hundred cannons in the flotilla," Paddy said.

"Yeah, and if I was the Rebel commander, I'd just evacuate the
fort during the bombardment and come back tomorrow, assess the
damage, and make the defense from there."

"We going to reach Lizard's Gate?"

"Paddy, I argued all morning for scaling ladders. They said
there won't be a Lizard's Gate left and there will be a dozen
breaches in the wall to choose from."

"Yeah," Paddy said, "maybe a little too optimistic."

"Well, before the war is over maybe somebody upstairs will recognize just how difficult and tricky a landing is."

All the hatches, doors, and portholes had been opened to allow any breezes that might happen by to circulate. From the bowels of the *Tuscarora*, several decks down, came the clear and beautiful voice of Corporal Luigi Pastore.

> *Just before the battle, Mother,*
> *I am thinking most of YOU,*
> *While upon the field we're watching,*
> *With the enemy in view . . .*

and he was joined:

> *Comrades brave around me lying,*
> *Filled with thoughts of home and God,*
> *For well they know that on the morrow,*
> *Some will sleep beneath the sod . . .*
> *Farewell, Mother, you may never*
> *Hold me to your heart again,*
> *But oh, you'll not forget me, Mother,*
> *If I'm numbered with the slain . . .*

❦ · 4 · ❧

THE USS *TUSCARORA*

Ten brigantines moved into Charleston Bay, followed by a hodge-
podge of barks, schooners, sloops, and steam-powered gunboats,
until sight of the redoubt came clearly into view. A rocket flared
from the command ship, now arrayed with sails clewed up but prepared to get under way.

One girds for battle with fear and fantasy.

The reality of the coming hell split the air with the first salvo.
Thunderclaps and lightning flashes rose to a level of unreality.
Pain of the crackling concussions mixed the real and the unreal
into a quagmire of noise. Recoil of cannon bucked the ship and it
rose and dropped on swells. On and on and on and on it belched
and powed and snorted until ship and man creaked from the twists,
until a numbed dream state took over.

A bosun's whistle pierced. "Now hear this! Marine Company,
man your stations!"

"Okay, rats! Let's get out of this hole!"

Up the ladder, guns and kits banging bulkheads and Paddy's whistle pierced.

"Fucking Rebs are catching it tonight!"

"Man the whalers!"

A swell spray at waterline and the *Tuscarora* leaped on the water, popping and jumping and dancing and rising too damned high and tilting too damned low.

"Aweigh all boats!"

Seven boats were lowered from their davits, fourteen to sixteen men to a boat.

A cable popped on number three, hurling the men into the sea, leaving the whaler dangling miserably, helplessly. Men were fished from the water; some were drowned by the weight of their load.

Men in the six remaining boats rowed hard to get around to the safe side of the *Tuscarora* and rendezvous with their steam barge. Working by flashes of cannon light and rockets, one after the other passed and hooked to the barge, but the final boat rode a chop right across the others' lines.

Ben Boone made an instant decision to untangle. He barked through his megaphone, "Number four, cut your line!"

Number four replied and began to row in behind. The steam launch was like a dog walker holding five leashes.

Shouts of confusion in the water were heard between bursts. Eight steam launches pulling fifty whalers arrayed and chugged slowly toward the shore.

Paddy tapped the lieutenant's shoulder. "Rocket from the beach! Sergeant Layton has landed with the recon squad!"

As the launches moved in, the bombardment finally quit, but there was too much filth in the air to see.

At break of day, the launches detached and the whalers rowed into a surf turned nasty by the night's bombardment.

Shit!

The number two boat twisted on a high wave, its bow plunged, and the boat broke. The lieutenant's boat rode in hard and waggled onto the sand.

Boone and his first sergeant were in knee-deep water. Ben took quick count. "Looks like about half the company got in. Number four is still out there rowing in!"

A company of sailors had no better luck getting their people in. It was chaos in their area, half the sailors stumbling and being washed in afoot.

Ben saw a small inlet, bank and brush to his right. "Paddy! Have four men pull one of these boats over there and secure it, then survey the beach."

At that moment it all hit Ben Boone in the guts. The sound of his own voice made him realize that Sumter was deadly quiet. What the hell did it mean? Abandoned or laying ambush?

Some fifty yards inland, Ben caught Sergeant Layton signaling him. He crawled up alongside . . . and as an ill wind blew the smoke away, Fort Sumter stood, unbreached. And the massive iron door at Lizard's Gate was bolted shut.

Behind Layton, the sergeants had assembled what was left of their squads and, with the company of sailors, moved up toward Lizard's Gate.

In came Paddy O'Hara, carrying Ugly, who had last been seen battling to stay afloat in the surf.

"I told Pastore to leave that animal on the ship!"

"Ugly jumped off the deck of the *Tuscarora*. I've got a boat stowed behind the bank. Best I can figure, we've got forty of our people in and twenty sailors."

And Paddy said: "Oh, Jesus! We got no breaches! You told those idiots to give us scaling ladders!"

The invaders froze in their shell holes as Sumter rose up like a wounded carnivorous dinosaur and fired a volley of musket and cannon.

Boone, Paddy, and Sergeant Layton huddled tightly. "We are fucking trapped! The fort has hardly been damaged. Rebel artillery has a clear view to the water! Our people in the landing boats will be slaughtered."

"Sure looks that way to me, sir," Layton agreed.

"We'll never storm through Lizard's Gate with less than a couple hundred men," Paddy said. "And we don't have them."

"Got a multicolored flare?"

"Yes, sir."

"Fire it toward our ships, high and clear!"

The warning signal arched up and burst. Its message: "All landing boats turn around and go back to your ships."

There was so much fire from Sumter pounding the water, scoring a hit, and another, that no one needed encouragement to retreat, and those rowing in fled back to their mother ships.

"They'll attack us from Lizard's Gate! Layton, move your squad into place to cover a retreat. Paddy!"

"Yes, sir."

"I'm taking a dozen men to help Layton hold a rear guard. You get the rest of the people to the water and back into the whalers and the hell out of here!"

"Sir! You take them back, I'll stay!"

"Git!" Ben snarled.

As Paddy O'Hara tried to make an orderly retreat, Boone and Layton set up a fifteen-man picket line near Lizard's Gate.

Most of the Confederate artillery was trained on the retreating whaleboats, but some now switched to the confusion on the beach.

Heads with gray caps popped up on Sumter's parapets.

"*Yowohee . . . Yowhee . . . Yowheeeeee,*" the Rebels yelled. Lizard's Gate cracked open and out they came.

Ben's people waited, waited, waited . . .

"Fire!"

A half-dozen Johnny Rebels went down and the rest wheeled back into the fort. With luck, it would give Boone and Layton a few minutes to get down to the beach, and this they did, into a scene of mayhem. Getting the remaining whalers to go back over the surf would be more difficult than riding it in on the landing.

"Over here! Over here!"

Jesus, it was Paddy! He had maneuvered himself and five men back near the tiny inlet. Paddy signaled that the whaler was intact and put some of the wounded in the boat.

Paddy quickly darted out, kneeling, turning over fallen men, found a pair of wounded, threw one over his shoulder, and dragged the other back to the scant cover, then went out and got another wounded, then another.

Ben screamed and was blown down hard. He tried to rise to his knees, but the pain was unbearable.

"Lay still!" Paddy commanded. Ben tried to get up again, but no, no way to make it.

"Can you hear me?"

"Yes!"

"Your shoulder is separated. Your arm is busted and full of grapeshot." Paddy cut the end of Ben's belt off and shoved it into his mouth. "Bite down, hard!"

Paddy feverishly applied a tourniquet and, thanks to Jaysus and Mary, stemmed the flow of blood from Ben's arm, then pulled the jacket off a dead man and used it to wrap the torn shoulder tightly against Ben's body. Ben Boone willed himself to his senses.

"Stand me on my knees, Paddy!"

Oh Lord, what a mess. Shit! Piss! Corruption! Fuckall! How can anything be salvaged? The water was red with the blood of floating dead. Only the still and the moaning were left on the beach. In a few moments the Rebs would come out again and this time they'd reach the water. A few sailors were behind cover. They'd have to surrender or be slaughtered.

"How many good men do we have?"

"Five are in condition to row."

The wounded on the beach would be doomed to die in their own pus if the Rebs didn't bayonet them first. Some would be captured alive. Ben would stay with them.

"Put those wounded lads in the boat and get out of here, I'm staying."

"Sorry, sir, I have to disobey you," and with that Paddy opened a vial of ether, sprinkled it on a cloth, and sent Ben Boone to sleep.

Paddy O'Hara crawled out on the beach time and again, dragging back more wounded and ordering the healthy men to throw them into the boat.

And again he went out for wounded, and again . . .

. . . until the Rebels came screaming once more through Lizard's Gate . . .

He threw an unconscious Ben Boone into the whaler, threw the wounded in one after the other until twenty of them lay in the bottom of the boat quivering like netted fish.

The boat was too heavy to row. Paddy and the rowers sloshed and slipped in the blood and vomit, finding newly dead and heaving them overboard until the whaler lost enough weight to move, then pushed along, tightly hugging the bank for cover.

Sea grass kept them out of the firing line of the Rebs, who were too busy finishing off the wounded and shooting those retreating into the surf to look for fresh targets.

The whaler stayed thus until darkness, the healthy men quieting the wounded and sending dead ones over the side. Four rowers and twelve wounded remained.

The four rowers moved out with a wounded Marine at the rudder and Paddy leaning over the bow to count and measure the severity of the surf.

And good black darkness clamped in.

It took three hours to find a steam launch. Paddy was the last man able to move, near dead from thirst. War makes bad sights, civil war makes worse, but there was never a sight to match the bottom of that whaleboat on that night.

Having saved three men at Bull Run and fourteen survivors at Sumter from massacre or prison, Sergeant O'Hara was well on his way to becoming a legend.

He became the second United States Marine to be awarded the

new Congressional Medal of Honor and was ultimately promoted
to sergeant major.

1888—Prichard's Tavern—Late Afternoon

Private Jones wheeled off the highway into the roundabout of
Prichard's Inn. Jones retrieved Major Boone's carpetbag as Master
Gunnery Sergeant Kunkle emerged from the inn and saluted.

"Ah Christ, Gunny, give us a hug!"

They clanked against each other.

"Kunkle! You're uglier than you were four years ago."

"Hell," the Gunny said, "nobody's that ugly, not even me."

❧ · 5 · ❧

AMANDA BLANTON KERR

1888—Washington—the Following Monday

The waiting room of Navy Secretary Nathaniel Culpeper's office was efficiently quiet. Three male clerks, civilians, and a naval attaché scratched away at the papers on their desks with an air of importance. In a small foyer, an unblinking statue of a Marine private guarded Culpeper's door.

Amanda Blanton Kerr wiggled restlessly, trying to get into her book. She opened her necklace watch. Her father had been inside for nearly an hour. Amanda's eyes drifted from her pages. Her alert glance took in everything about her.

The attaché gave a small smile and nod of sympathy as he checked out Amanda's enthralling beauty. She gave him a slight curl of her lip, hinting of a flirtatious engine inside her.

Her eyes went up the Marine guard and down the Marine guard with scarcely a glance. The attaché sniffed another smile. The Marine continued looking forward, unblinking.

*   *   *

Beyond the mighty door, Secretary of the Navy Nathaniel Culpeper pondered. He was a great ponderer. On one side of his desk sat Horace Kerr, the shipbuilding titan, and beside him Commodore Chester Harkleroad, chief of the navy's massive building program.

The pair of them stood foursquare against Lieutenant Colonel Commandant Thomas Ballard, referred to snidely as the Marine Corps' "Uncle Tom." The old warrior was desperately trying to salvage his Corps, but he was in for another lacing today. Moreover, those two bastards opposite him had managed to keep his major, Ben Boone, out of the meeting.

The commodore's naval architects and Horace Kerr's engineers had proffered advance blueprints for a new class of armored cruisers. No quarters, mess, or provisions had been drawn for a Marine unit, not even to man secondary guns.

Final approval by Secretary Culpeper would further deplete the Marines. Two nights earlier, young Theodore Roosevelt, a rising star in the Republican Party and naval circles, urged Culpeper to sign off on the plans.

"The Marines," Roosevelt argued, "breed animosity aboard ships. Sailors can, most certainly, police their own vessels. The Marines went out of style with grappling hooks and cutlasses. They don't even shoot well anymore."

Though there was some sentimental feeling for the Marines from past fights, the Corps had become a redundant, obsolete unit of candy soldiers. Culpeper was bending under the demands of the party, the admirals, and a most vocal Horace Kerr.

The story goes that Horace Kerr's ancestors had landed south of Plymouth Rock two days earlier than the *Mayflower*. His great-grandfather was an hour ahead of the Minutemen at Concord and his shipworks won the war for the North.

Indeed, Kerr had made his initial fortune building ships for the Union fleet. He was a rising star among the entrepreneurial barons.

Now, over two decades after the war, Kerr was in the center of the new steam-and-steel navy. He himself was a man of steel, helping craft the new American fleet, an imperial fleet, for the nation's great leap into world commerce. A hard-edged genius, Kerr was a real power in the power rooms of Washington.

Four presidents had heard him out, carefully. He could not be intimidated by anyone . . . except, perhaps, by his daughter, Amanda, who at that moment burst into the office and headed for the cloud of cigar smoke.

The Marine on guard followed on her heels.

"Amanda," Horace Kerr roared, "what the devil is going on here?"

"Sorry, sirs," the Marine said. "I told the lady the meeting was closed."

"You might have restrained her," Commodore Harkleroad grumbled. "You people do have training on how to stand guard?"

"Sirs, I did not think there was anything in the manual that directly applied to this situation. I felt that shooting her or threatening her with my saber or physically placing her under arrest was not appropriate to the situation, inasmuch as she and Mr. Kerr had the same last name, *sirs!*"

"You were standing guard against a girl!" Harkleroad snapped.

"She used trickery to get past me," the Marine answered.

"You are impertinent! I demand a reprimand!" Horace Kerr feigned a rage that caused the potted plants to tremble.

Secretary Culpeper joined them, turning to Commandant Ballard to see what "Uncle Tom" had to say. The commandant scratched out a note and slid it over the desk.

Culpeper glanced at it and passed it to the others. It read: *Paddy O'Hara's son.*

Silence.

"Amanda, how lovely to see you," Culpeper crooned.

Commodore Harkleroad said something in mangled French on the order of "beware the femme fatale." What might have been considered a laugh found its way around the table.

"I really don't think this calls for bread and water, does it, Miss Amanda?" Tom Ballard asked softly.

Amanda, who had gathered which way the wind was blowing, turned to the Marine and said, "I was very rude and I apologize."

The others nodded in unison.

"Colonel Ballard," Amanda said, "I'd like you to command . . . Private . . . er . . ."

"Zachary O'Hara," Ballard said.

"I want you to order Private O'Hara to attend a post-debutante charity dance at Inverness," she said, referring to an event that was to be held at the Kerrs' Baltimore mansion. "Saturday, next."

"I can assure Miss Amanda that Private O'Hara will be guarding your door, properly."

"No," Amanda corrected. "I wish to extend my apology by having him as a guest." She turned. "I'll wait, Father," she said, and burst out of the office as suddenly as she had burst in. Ballard nodded for Zachary to leave.

Horace Kerr softened. "She's a handful. Just turned sixteen, you know, made her social debut in Baltimore a few months ago. She's feeling her oats. Stepping into her charity duties, all that."

"He does have a proper uniform for the occasion, does he not, Tom?" Kerr asked, referring to the private.

"I can't do a hell of a lot for the Marines these days, but I can see to it he has a dress uniform."

In the 110-year history of the Corps, it was the only time that a commandant ordered a new dress uniform for a private. It included a white sash belt, a gleaming brass buckle, a white spiked hat with pom-pom, and the loan of an officer's ceremonial sword.

❧ · 6 · ☙

CAPTAIN TOBIAS STORM

The senior Wart-Hog, Tobias Storm, received his commission into the Marines through the established system of political patronage.

His father, Marcus Storm, a Bostonian, had been among the ranks of Andrew Jackson's troops when they handed the British a sound defeat in the War of 1812 at New Orleans. The war had been over when the battle was fought, but the victory was celebrated, nonetheless, as one of a David over a Goliath.

Marcus Storm took his discharge there, overwhelmed by the allure of New Orleans and its French heritage. The fancy goods and tawdry way of life were of a sort not seen in Boston.

He returned to Boston two years later, with a dozen trunks of silk and wines and aromas and ornate gems. Marcus Storm became a smashing success as a purveyor of luxury imports from France, which filled a hole in the staid Bostonian existence.

His marriage was blessed with four sons, more than enough to carry on the family enterprise; in fact, there was one too many. Marcus selected sons numbers one, two, and four. Number three, Tobias, was odd man out.

Tobias was a spirited young man more given to chasing skirts than to selling the material to make them. He was a contender in every saloon he patronized. It would be best, Marcus thought, to ease him away from Boston, but neither the army nor the navy would take him. As a last resort, he was imposed on the Marine Corps and went on to have an undistinguished career, notable only for the fact that he was present with Admiral Dewey when the latter entered Tokyo Bay to introduce Japan to the glories of Western civilization.

Tobias was left in Tokyo to put together a small railroad, one of the gifts to the Japanese emperor. He had a way with iron and machinery.

On returning to the States, Lieutenant Storm's value to the Corps came in his assessment of military ordnance. There was no standard for procurement of weapons and Storm's job was to try to see to it that his little Marine Corps was not handed down everyone's obsolete cannons and muskets.

In the final months of the Civil War, the Union had cracked through at Vicksburg, Farragut was in Mobile Bay, and the Confederacy was cut in half along the Mississippi.

On the coast side, an enormous fleet of over a hundred Union warships, packing more than a thousand guns, moved toward Cape Fear. Wilmington, North Carolina, one of the last operating Confederate ports, was the objective.

Fort Fisher, twenty miles downriver, stood between the Union armada and Wilmington. This assault plan was to achieve the obliteration of Fisher, by naval gunfire; then an invasion would be led by an entire battalion of Marines.

Second Lieutenant Tobias Storm had remained Second Lieutenant Storm throughout the war, but had been part of the creative planning that improved the accuracy and destructiveness of artillery firepower.

With the war going the Union's way, Storm needed his piece of it and nagged his way onto the USS *Algonquin* as commander of a company. The men loved Storm. He was of medium height but powerful build, and jolly comments came through his great mustache. He had, by doubling a navy requisition illegally, gotten a new rifle-bored, single-shot, lever-action gun to replace their pitiful muskets.

More good fortune was his when Sergeant Paddy O'Hara was assigned to him. O'Hara had been seething to avenge the disaster at Sumter, and from the looks of this fleet and a Marine battalion to lead the assault, Fisher would fall.

Fort Fisher was earth and sandbags and logs, surely no match for the Union's thousand-plus guns.

A Confederate shell hit the powder stores of the *Algonquin*, blowing Tobias Storm off the bridge into an inferno on the deck below.

Fortunately, he landed at the feet of Paddy O'Hara, who carried him to the ship's rail, held him, and leaped into the water and swam for another ship a moment before the *Algonquin* exploded.

Fort Fisher did not fall that day. The Union, no longer as squeamish about casualties, made another assault later, and this time was successful.

That is how Tobias Storm became a Wart-Hog. After the conflict was done, the nation wanted war no more. Stationed mostly in Washington, he was promoted to first lieutenant and married a robust lady, Matilda Morris, whose inheritance allowed them to establish a home and a family.

Storm loved the military and refused to resign to open a branch of the family importing firm in Washington. He also thought less of himself for not having seen a single action in a war in which he was tossed overboard just as the battle had commenced.

*   *   *

The Marine Corps was now scraping around, looking for some sort of mission to help keep it relevant, when they were brought in to solve a domestic problem.

There was growing concern in the government regarding happenings in the territory of Alaska.

Alaska had been purchased for a pittance from a bankrupt Russian czar. Locked in and frozen a good part of the year as it was, only the most daring adventurer attempted to traverse the uncharted northern passages. Death pointed an icy finger at courageous but ill-advised men who penetrated too far north.

The current source of riches around the Bering Sea was being plundered by Russian poachers. The Aleutian Islands formed stepping-stones between Russian settlements in Siberia and the Alaskan mainland. The Russians had devastated the fragile Indian civilization, imposed a system of serfdom, and otherwise ravaged the region under their mangling rule.

Seals, otters, and other fur-bearing animals were the life-support systems of the natives and the victims of savage commercialism by the Russians.

During nesting season, Russian poachers came over the Aleutians to Alaska, though it was now an American possession, and slaughtered seals by the tens of thousands, often by club, to save ammunition and prevent damage to the valuable skins.

As with the American buffalo, the massacre of the seals brought the Indians close to ruin. The hunter received a half-dollar or less for a pelt. Three dollars was the rate the Russians got from the fur-hungry Chinese market.

The Hudson Bay Company was having the same problem with Canadian poachers who sold their pelts for four to five dollars in the exploding London fur industry.

The tribes who depended upon the seal for survival were in a dire condition and feared that the seal was being slaughtered to extinction.

Lieutenant Tobias Storm sailed north from San Francisco with a platoon of Marines. At the same time a company of British joined forces with them. Autumn quickly closed them down in their post on Unalaska Island, where they waited out the long winter's night for the spring thaw.

That springtime, their joint operation stemmed the flow of seal blood and bagged two prison ships filled with poachers.

After twenty-two years in the Corps, Tobias Storm received his second promotion, a medal of commendation, and a soft cruise aboard the USS *Kansas,* which was doing a goodwill tour to open markets in the South Pacific and Asia.

· 7 ·

THE GUNS OF NANDONG

1878—Nandong Province

Emperor Wu Ling Chow, as he insisted on being addressed, looked down from his hillside palace to the spellbinding harbor known as the Blue Pearl of the Orient. The USS *Kansas* skimmed into the bay at eventide with all ceremonial pennants aflutter.

The clever, dangerous warlord and self-proclaimed emperor had kept the breakaway province of Nandong and its population of twenty million as an independent state despite being hemmed in by contentious neighbors.

Wu Ling Chow had survived royal court treachery, provincial enemies, and forays by foreigners and had made the price for invading armies too high. The emperor's hard-fisted rule had kept Nandong free of the opium scourge. With a master of artful pacts as its leader, Nandong had endured only a controlled smattering of Western intrusions.

But the guns of the foreign fleets were growing larger. Unvarnished greed of the foreigners, now including Japan, all sought his prize. How long could he keep the noose from choking Nandong?

Wu Ling Chow reckoned that the Americans, the newest silk-seeking player in the Orient, would be less of a threat than his neighbors. There was a marked difference about the Yankees. Or was the emperor deluding himself? At any rate he would not be drawn in by homey American gregariousness. Scratch their lacquer and they would most likely be the same color as the British and French and Portuguese and Germans and Dutch and Japanese.

To satisfy himself, Wu allowed a goodwill visit. The twenty-one-gun salute from the *Kansas* whetted his appetite and he was greeted by a trio of Yankee salesmen from the State Department and the trade and government establishment.

After an unbearably pompous round of welcomes, meetings began with the Americans and Wu personally.

Wu Ling Chow was cautious, but the Americans' open friendliness kept discussions alive. In Nandong City, Lieutenant Tobias Storm did a crack job with his Marine detachment in keeping lusty sailors from the *Kansas* under reasonable control. The ladies of Nandong long knew sailorboys' needs and were likewise pleased that the pleasures of the crew ashore were attained without wrecking the place.

At the end of the first week, Wu Ling Chow came aboard the American warship for an evening of entertainment.

A chorus of sailors serenaded him and soloists did their bit and the band played a lovely concert. Sharpshooters put on a daring exhibition.

The final act of the night was Lieutenant Tobias Storm performing with a pair of pet seals named Stars and Stripes. The lieutenant had saved them from slaughter when he was on duty in the Bering Sea and raised them from pups. Stars and Stripes both held the rank of sergeant, although Stripes had been busted several times for his sopping-wet appearances in the bunks of Marines, scaring them half to hell.

Stars and Stripes carried the evening with juggling and balancing feats never before seen even in a land of acrobats.

When the emperor invited the officers and performers to a dinner and requested a show at the palace, maybe the foot was in the door, the Yankees thought.

The following day, Tobias Storm received a summons to come to the palace.

At the end of their meal, Wu Ling Chow had a magnificent chessboard set up with chessmen adorned with gold and jewels. The pawns alone were three inches high.

Storm, who considered himself a damned good player, pondered. Does one whip an emperor in his own palace? Tobias won two games without drawing a deep breath. He was surprised that one so wily as Wu Ling Chow would play so poorly. Or was he getting into some kind of Chinese maze? Perhaps Wu was testing the Marine's honesty. On the other hand, had his court and concubines been throwing games for years just to please him?

In the third game, the emperor annihilated Storm's board in quick, masterly fashion. The message did not go unnoticed.

Storm would never win another chess game against the emperor, but he sensed the tide of trade negotiations running in the Americans' favor. The American delegation gave him great latitude to deal and held their collective breath.

It did not take long for the lieutenant to sniff out what was ailing Wu Ling Chow, who eased their discussions toward weaponry, Storm's strong suit. Nandong required modern artillery to replace its ancient blunderbuss cannons, which could not hit an elephant point-blank. With only mild hills and a few deep gorges, the province was a tempting target for foreign incursions. Her sweeping coast was, likewise, open to pirate forays. Wu Ling Chow needed dug-in emplacements and the ability to man them properly, and the guns he needed were simply too large and cumbersome to get in undetected.

Feeling rather secure about a confidence with Lieutenant Storm, Wu Ling Chow popped the question. Could Nandong manufacture its own rifle-bored, breech-loading cannons and the shells to feed them?

"I don't want you to go into consultations with your people, just give me your opinion."

Tobias had seen brilliant bronze castings in the city and about the palace, but they were Buddhas and bells and made of the wrong metal.

"Does the province have an operating iron mine?" the Marine asked.

"Yes, and of excellent grade."

"And the Chinese certainly know what there is to know about gunpowder."

The emperor nodded.

A day later a secret protocol was drawn up between the emperor and the State Department official with Lieutenant Storm and one palace minister witnessing.

America would provide blueprints and manufacturing methods of the most modern artillery, from 5 to 14 inches and from 75 to 105 millimeters.

America would likewise provide the know-how to make shells and auxiliary equipment.

America would provide a team of civilian experts, under contract to Wu Ling Chow, to set up and operate a clandestine factory.

America would assign Lieutenant Tobias Storm, legally, under international precedent, to train officers with a specialty in artillery.

Lieutenant Storm would retain his Marine Corps rank as well as legally hold the rank of colonel in the Nandong military.

America had no financial obligation except for Lieutenant Storm's Marine Corps salary and allowances.

There would be no further American military presence. When guns were tested successfully, the American civilian team would turn over manufacturing matters to Nandong personnel.

In return:

Wu Ling Chow would grant exclusive trade concessions as
listed on the attached pages.

It was a very quiet deal so as not to send off alarm bells all over
China. Few would even know of its existence.

Beyond that, Captain Dinkel, commander of the *Kansas,* had a
heart-to-heart with Tobias. The navy was extremely liberal about
pets aboard: dogs, of course, cats, monkeys, an occasional goat, but
Stars and Stripes were eating enough fish every day to feed half the
crew. Emperor Wu sensed that the gift of the seals was not Lieutenant Storm's idea, but he most gratefully accepted.

The endgame was that Tobias Storm was promoted to captain
in the Marines and commissioned a colonel in the Nandong military as superintendent of the new academy.

After returning to the States to collect his family and receiving a
heavy briefing by the State Department and military, Tobias
returned to Nandong with his dear wife, Matilda, their sons Norman
and Jason, and their youngest, a daughter, Brenda.

In 1879, Storm founded a small military school that, over time,
rose to a very high level of respect in the region.

It seemed so celestial in the beginning. Surely heaven's gates had
swung open for the Storms. They were housed in one of the lesser
royal compounds—an ebony- and redwood-carved, ivory- and
jade-decorated domicile of Oriental splendor—wrapped in gold-
and silver-threaded silk brocades, and served on Ming porcelain.

The first bucking of heads between Tobias and Wu came almost
immediately. Tobias planned an initial class to consist of twenty-five
cadets to go through a very hard two years' training.

The normal way of doing things in Nandong would be to draw
the candidates from the most important families and loyal relatives.
Inner-circle patronage was the ancient system and was not to be
toyed with.

Colonel Storm reckoned he could abide with, say, three or four such cadets but insisted on open recruiting from the general population and countryside.

Wu Ling Chow halted the argument quickly. The loyalty lineage could never be tampered with.

"Okay, Your Majesty, it's your fucking army," Storm said . . . way beneath his breath. Twenty-five cadets were selected and underwent the displeasures of a brutal training regimen.

Within a month, eighteen of the twenty-five candidates had limped off in horror.

The colonel got a royal summons and learned that court shenanigans were being played by men of devious character and cowardly bent.

"Your Majesty, I cannot do what you want me to do with candidates who have soft hands and softer backbones. I am not here to play toy soldiers with a bunch of spoiled rich kids. And, Your Majesty, if you want to play with fourteen-inch coastal guns, you had better find me men who would be capable of being Marine officers."

Easily said, but the interlocking privileged families were the source of the emperor's power, along with the old generals who had done the ruthless work to keep Wu on his dragon throne. An influx of commoners would create jealousy in his military, and how would the important families accept the failure of their sons? Could he keep them in check?

On the other hand, Wu Ling Chow was Wu Ling Chow for good reason. He had survived since childhood with an omnipresent scent of conspiracy and, from his teenage years on, defended his throne without pity. He realized that court intrigue was bound to escalate and let it be known that he needed the new weapons and officers no less than he needed his old entourage.

Furthermore, it did not go unnoticed by Wu that the new corps would be heavily indoctrinated to ensure super-loyalty in the matter of the household guard. Wu shored up his base and assured his court that the academy was in their long-term interests.

"Otherwise our way of doing business will be carried on as usual," he promised his retinue.

The emperor then took the plunge and issued a unique decree for open recruiting, which brought thousands of applicants from the underclass: merchants, common workmen, and peasants.

Storm sifted out those of high intelligence who passed tests of personal courage and who had the ability to travel a long way on very little rice.

Starting over with two dozen handpicked cadets, Storm saw twenty-one of them survive this training from hell, have the English language crammed into them, and learn to place honor above corruption. The academy became "The House of Illustrious Glory."

A few more years saw the new officer corps rise to forty men. Around the hills, with sweeping lookout vistas, deep bunkers, with arsenals and connecting tunnels, the artillery went into place.

One if by land and two if by sea. A bandit gang from the south ran into Gatling-gun fire, and shortly thereafter, two privateer vessels were blown out of the water from nine-miles' distance. The coastal raids dwindled. Since all of this had been accomplished covertly, surrounding neighbors trod carefully.

Matilda and Tobias stopped to take a deep breath, and when they did they sniffed the trade winds leading back to America. Homesickness crept in, particularly for the boys, who were approaching young adulthood, a time for setting up their future.

Back in Boston, Marcus Storm, patriarch and founder of the family's small import empire, with one son in Boston, another in London, and a third in Paris, went with hat in hand to Tobias.

For as long as he could remember, he had felt only a remote affection for Tobias. But his third son's success had changed the manner in which the family regarded him. He now held the keys to their Oriental ambitions. Nandong's artisan work was among the most magnificent in China.

Communications by ship from America were long in reaching

China, but when his letters arrived, they were filled with Marcus's pleas for Tobias to establish a trading company.

Matilda and Marcus proposed that Norman and Jason return and be completely educated into the firm and thoroughly trained in the evaluation of European artwork. At the end of two years they were to be given full partnerships, and one or both would return to operate a Nandong export company.

Round-trip communications took several months, but the ship finally came in with a contract of agreement from Marcus Storm. Wu Ling Chow guaranteed the franchise on the condition that Captain Storm remain in his service till the Asian branch was established . . . and that the emperor receive a reasonable percentage of its profits.

Matilda and Tobias agreed to stay in Nandong till their sons returned, feeling they were creating a rich life for them, culturally even more than financially.

Brenda Storm was another matter. The girl, to all intents and purposes, became more Chinese than the Chinese, thriving on her life. For a blossoming young lady of her ilk, the notion of a future marriage to a ranking nobleman was not out of the question.

The factory was operating smoothly. The academy demanded less and less of his personal supervision, and it was clear that Captain/Colonel Storm was now woven indelibly into the palace fabric, a fact that made him extremely uncomfortable.

"I'm a Marine," he told Matilda in his less happy moments, "and Marines do not make government policy, Marines carry out their duty, however repugnant it may be."

Suddenly he desired nothing more than to be relieved of this command, but then a ship arrived with a diplomatic and military pouch.

Without recourse, he was commanded to remain. His work in Nandong had helped create a much-desired and firm relationship. *Hang in there, Tobias, until you can establish unshakable stability,* he was told.

"Stability," Tobias cried to Matilda, "is an IMPOSSIBILITY!"

But he calmed down and finally formed a justification. "I will stay on duty as long as the Corps wants me on duty here. It is the least I can do for what the Corps has given me."

"I, too, will remain," Matilda answered. "It is the least I can do."

8

THE BIRDS OF PERU

When Tobias felt that the region had attained the kind of stability he had been requested to establish, he once again asked to be reassigned.

The emperor held in his hand a copy of Colonel Storm's request.

"But your sons have not yet returned, and it has been three years."

"We need to speak straight on, Your Majesty."

"We always have," the emperor retorted, "in a somewhat circuitous manner."

"I speak for Madam Storm as well as myself. Although I will hold no interest in the future trading company, it was highly unethical of me to seek profit from my position at the palace—I prefer life as a Marine rather than a merchant. In my eagerness to establish a good life for my sons, I did a corrupt thing. I know Your

Majesty would not hold me hostage until the return of my sons to Nandong, so you are no longer bound by our agreement."

"And your sons? Will they return?"

"That is up to them. The madam and I feel we have afforded them the opportunity, but it is their decision what to make of their lives."

"You speak so strangely. This world would become chaos if fathers did not control the destinies of their sons," Wu said.

"The tradition of obedient sons is not as powerful in America as in China. The value of my mission here has been proven. I am no longer needed."

"You are needed, Tobias."

"The artillery and the academy are on firm footing. That is what I came for. I did not come to be a minister of the royal Nandong court. I long for my own way . . ."

"Tobias, I have seen you look down from your balcony, over the wall to the port. Each time a ship leaves Nandong filled with emigrants—or shall we call it by its true name, substitute slave labor, contract indentured labor, coolie labor . . . the pig trade. My people go out of China as pigs, live as pigs, and most die as pigs."

"I am deep into your history and I understand the conditions under which China has had to evolve. Too much desert, too many magnificent mountains, and never enough bountiful earth. God's wrath has devoured your people through drought, flood, earthquakes, bandits, monsoons, disease, and drought again. Massive starvation and basic existence have been China's curse for the centuries. Sometimes, Your Majesty, I can almost bring myself to understand why you have to throw your people out to the world. What I cannot bring myself to understand, ever, is the lack of human compassion."

"You forgot to mention the recurring cycles of infanticide and the ravages of pestilence, Tobias. Much less the rape of China by foreign nations that drugged our people with opium. And put the coolie trade in suffocating holds. No matter where the coolie lands, he is looked upon as a subhuman monkey."

"And the profits from the coolie trade?" Tobias dared.

The emperor gave a small laugh. "At least the coolie knows he is worth something. We have become a mockery. Compassion ends at the line where we claw out continued existence. Royalty cannot rule with compassion."

Wu thought for a moment, then went on. "The coolies are flung out to a world to work the most dangerous mines, building railroads over sun-scorched deserts, doing the filth and pity work for cruel overseers."

The emperor scratched his signature on the document to approve Tobias's departure, then held his hand on it for a moment.

"There are unusual beaches in Peru," Wu Ling Chow said, "and unusual islands off Peru's coast. For millennia, birds have deposited their guano, building up mountains of bird droppings. Coolies are entombed in these places and pick at the guano and sack it to be shipped to the European fields to fertilize them." His voice quavered, a very rare occurrence. "Are those droppings not our people? Are we not treated by the world as bird shit from Peru? Few coolies survive on these islands and beaches for more than a year. Those who do survive have established colonies and the colonies have taken root and will prosper and they send for their families.

"We will eternally bear humiliation because of our treatment. In your Bible, Tobias, one of the ancient prophets said, 'The survival of the human race depends on human dignity.' Do not speak to me about compassion and democracy until we are granted human dignity. Until then, I shall rule as I shall rule."

After two terms, Captain Storm petitioned to return to America. He and Matilda and crates of opulent possessions landed in San Francisco, where they entrained for the long and exhausting journey across the country.

1888—Prichard's Inn

When Major Boone received the telegraph message of Captain Storm's delay, he dispatched his orderly to the commandant with a letter requesting that he and the Gunny be allowed to remain at Prichard's.

Colonel Ballard, fresh from another put-down at the hands of Secretary Culpeper and Commodore Harkleroad, quickly granted the request.

My Dear Major Boone,

By all means continue your leave. Master Gunnery Sergeant Kunkle is likewise authorized to remain.

You have argued your case splendidly for the formation of an Advanced Military Program. Our recent setback regarding sea duty aboard the new Vermont-class cruisers now makes adaptation of AMP our highest priority.

It seems fitting that this mission fall to the last remaining Wart-Hogs. One could surmise that Master Sergeant O'Hara saved your three asses over a quarter of a century ago for just this purpose.

I pray for your success.

Thomas Ballard
Lieutenant Colonel Commandant, USMC

❧ 9 · ❧

IN THE GARDEN

1888—Baltimore—the Following Saturday

The grand, elegant mansion of Inverness crowned Butcher's Hill. Grand, elegant carriages swept into the grand circle like ornate figures on a music-box carousel and deposited the finest gowns in Maryland at the door.

On this, her first post-debutante event, Amanda stood serenely in a stunning foyer leading directly into the great hall.

Horace Kerr puffed out like a proud blowfish, all toothy in a fixed smile. His wife, Daisy Kerr, carried her middle years grandly.

Amanda was taller and slimmer than the other young ladies, who tended to be plumpish and moonfaced from too much Maryland cooking and a lack of physical activity.

Most debutantes, and those mothers still able to do so, revealed the allowable amount of cleavage and a bosom held in place stiffly by the whalebone in their undergarments.

Not so Amanda Blanton Kerr, whose gown draped like Grecian

gauze. Her breasts, fully but thinly covered, moved delicately with her handshakes and embraces.

God, Horace Kerr thought, she is a knockout!

Good Lord, Daisy thought, what brinkmanship!

The great hall was a wild and bright galaxy of tinkling crystal in the chandeliers above and tinkling crystal at the champagne bar. Amanda nodded to the orchestra leader to start and seemed annoyed for an instant as a thousand yards of brocaded flounce floated up and down to the beat of a waltz.

Private Zachary O'Hara might well have been a Habsburg prince as he approached the reception line with plumed spiked white helmet tucked under his left arm.

"Ah, so we meet again, Private . . . ," Horace said.

"O'Hara, sir."

Then Horace caught his wife's rather dazed expression. Holy Christ, what is this?

"My mother, Daisy Blanton Kerr," Amanda said.

"Mrs. Kerr, thank you for having me."

"For a moment I didn't think you would get here," Amanda said.

"I, uh, waited till everyone else went in."

"How thoughtful," Daisy said.

As Amanda linked arms with Zachary and they entered the great hall, all eyes were on them.

"What a handsome young man," Daisy said.

Horace Kerr growled.

"Miss Amanda," Zachary said, "could I check my sword? I don't think I could manage a polka wearing it."

A polka they did, a wild polka, and the circle grew around them and broke into cheers. It was the most giddy moment of her life, with a partner so perfect, so graceful, so manly. They caught their breath to applause as Amanda took a place near a sagging buffet filled with foods Zachary had never before seen. A line of couples drifted to them for an introduction.

Several plump young maidens allowed as how they had openings on their dance cards, to the discomfort of their escorts.

Thank God he's not a captain, Horace thought as he chomped and chomped from a bottomless bowl of caviar.

After the first blast of Inverness, Private O'Hara gained quick control of himself. He was polite and at ease and so softly charming to the she-wolf pack.

Amanda, who had supposed he would be all thumbs, was having the tables turned on her in her own territory.

Amanda sorted out a few dances with Zach for her closest friends while their escorts sniffed. She more than made up for their discomfort by giving each of them a whirl with her and soon it all settled down to "great fun," really great fun.

Amanda had insisted—no, demanded that her father hire a second orchestra, a band of black musicians who could banjo and blow out the new ragtime craze. It was not quite proper for a high social affair, but Horace Kerr's daughter was not a run-of-the-mill debutante.

When the final waltz, gavotte, quadrille, and polka wound down, the black band took over and soon "Lisa Jane" and "Oh Them Golden Slippers" and "Baby Mine" reverberated off those sacred walls.

By midball, the revelers needed a break while loaded platters refilled the buffet. Horace Kerr was delighted by the thought that the ragtime dancing would be the talk of the town for weeks to come. Actually, he was rather pleased that Private O'Hara had brought out a flair in his daughter. She may have picked a fight she will not win with him. Ah, to be able to listen to their verbal duel, he thought.

Amanda led Zachary through the French doors.

"Time for a stroll in the garden," she said.

They made their way down the broad stairs to the veranda, then down again to the most profound fountain in Maryland.

They passed benches of pecking puppy lovers and moved on

into a dark part of the garden. There was still sufficient light
reflected to really study the white silk flow of her gown. She was
sleek and fine and different from the hoopskirted girls with buckets
of tight, hanging curls. Their show of junior cleavage was poor stuff
alongside Amanda. Amanda was quite freely dressed and Zachary
could see the press of her nipples, right up to the point of impro-
priety.

Her hair flowed easily, commanded by her slightest movement.
Zach knew this girl's eyes concealed a vast trove of wisdom and
strength.

"Well, how does it feel to be the 'belle' of the ball?" she asked.

"I'm not quite sure," Zachary said. "You've been the belle of
the ball all your life, how *does* it feel, Miss Amanda?"

"Please call me Amanda."

"Thank you, Miss Amanda. I'd like to know what whim passed
through you to have me here in Inverness."

"Well," she started, "I was sitting in the waiting room of Secretary Culpeper's office waiting for Father. I could see you in the
foyer but you couldn't see me. My book was very dull and one naturally looks about when one is just sitting there and waiting for
one's father. He had completely forgotten I was even there. So, I
made a game of studying you, standing there so forthrightly. I
grew curious. Can you speak? Could you support a mustache? Do
you ever blink your eyes?"

"I do have a Marine buddy who has trained himself not to blink
his eyes," he answered.

" 'Well,' I wondered, 'can I get past this mighty lion guarding
the gate?' Men rule by raw power. Girls rule by sleight of hand.
How do you find them?"

"Girls of sixteen can be very silly."

"And boys of nineteen even more silly."

"For your enlightenment, I am twenty and can support a
beard," he said.

"So I diverted your attention; it was easy to get past you."

"If you had me ordered to Inverness to make me feel lowly and ill at ease, you have not succeeded."

Zachary delivered his words smartly, not avoiding the intensity of her stare. He seemed to understand and was prepared for the game he knew she made of reducing young men to silly boys.

"Where did you learn to dance so well?" she asked, changing the subject.

"I was born and raised in the Marine Corps. I learned in dance halls. My da first set me on the end of a bar when I was six years old."

"Oh . . ."

"My da was a top-ranking NCO. When we were stationed in and about civilization, we'd join the local church with other NCOs and their wives and we'd dance at . . . charity affairs."

That stung! Quick now, Amanda . . . "And your mother?"

"She died a few days after giving birth to me."

"Forgive me."

"Of course," he said, and smiled. "You know as well as I that if you are a Marine stationed in the capital, half your duty is to know how to dance."

And she smiled and tottered for a moment on the brink of saying something, then decided. "Daddy's garden is filled with couples who couldn't wait for midball to get out here and neck. Most of them have been matched up by their parents at age eight, so that by the time of their cotillion they were virtually engaged. I know every girl here. Every one of them has been felt up. Except me. I have mushed around a little but never really found it to my liking." Her hand touched his face and chin. "I think I've been waiting for someone who can support a beard."

"I know it's fuzzy, but the Marine Corps says I have to shave every morning whether I need it or not. Anyhow, I'm gaining on it."

"Zachary," she said with a new tone, different from her other tones.

"Yes, ma'am."

"I see boys and men look at my bosom longingly, but I've never let anyone touch my breasts." Zachary turned a bit away from her. "Are you afraid?"

"Yes, ma'am."

"Sit here with me on the bench," she said, and rocked back and forth. "I've never revealed them before, not to my brother and hardly to my own mother and sister. Will you be my friend for a minute?"

He nodded.

"When I turned thirteen, something began happening inside me."

"I think I understand," he said.

"I was looking at myself in the mirror one morning and was overcome with the impulse to touch myself. It set off incredible sensations I did not know existed. I tried to speak about them to my mother, but it was not something to be spoken of. So I asked my dearest friend, Willow, but she was completely innocent. I soon learned that I was in a forbidden place. Here, this sudden wonderment was happening inside me, but it made my own mother too uncomfortable to speak about it. Touching myself was not only forbidden, but sinful. Parts of the Sunday sermons that had made no sense to me as a child suddenly made sense. I had gone in league with the devil. I couldn't tell anyone how joyous it felt. I learned what was happening to me and I also learned that becoming a woman was a sentence to suffer. Zachary, I must be making you terribly uncomfortable."

"No, not at all."

"I've never even really enjoyed holding hands with a boy before this. I always had casual boyfriends, but I came to know they had their own stirrings, as well . . ."

Zachary nodded once more.

"When you are dancing and wrestling with boys you can feel them getting emotional beyond their ability to control. You know what I mean?" she asked.

"Yes."

"Boys would always be humiliated. Suddenly it struck me, one day, that it was a time, a moment when a girl had the power."

"I think we are going too far with this conversation," he said.

"You're just like everyone else, Zachary, wanting to keep me locked inside a high square wall."

"Amanda, I'm just a buck private."

"I don't believe that this is what God has in mind, to give us such tender feelings and not be allowed to explore them."

Zachary stood and she stood with him.

"I'm very flattered, but there are some strict regulations against this," he said.

"Then you are afraid . . ."

"Amanda Blanton Kerr and Zachary O'Hara together is rather ridiculous. This kind of . . ."

"Feeling," she said.

"Yes, this kind of feeling is not for us."

"But that's not the way I feel at this moment," she said softly.

They stood there silently and she nodded.

Zachary took off his gloves slowly, moved her dress down over a shoulder, and slipped aside her thin halter. Both of them took his hand to her breast and he felt it beautifully in rhythm with their gasping breath, then he kissed it and wrapped his arms around her and kissed her unconditionally. Before the fury came on, he took a step back and adjusted her clothing.

Zachary, she thought, this is everything!

Her gasps rose to a pant. She reached for him, but he held her off.

"I admire your confidence and candor, Amanda, and I appreciate your affection of the moment, but this is all we can have."

"Touch me one more time."

"No."

"Then kiss me again."

"Please, no."

"Then you are a coward!" she said with sudden anger.

"Have you ever watched a man lashed with a cat-o'-nine-tails and seen what he looks like after a month in solitary on bread and water?"

"That is what it seems like for me to take on the curse of being a female. I exaggerate but I don't look forward to a life of it."

Giggles from the girls on the garden bench reached their ears and a resumption of the waltz flowed out from the great hall.

"Will I ever see you again?" he asked.

"You're stationed in Washington. After your debut here tonight," she said, "we are bound to run into each other. I don't feel we have to go out of our way to avoid each other."

Amanda had been given a dose of her own medicine, finding herself spiraling beyond her capacity to control. She had dared herself into a magic moment and knew instantly that she must continue to own those moments in the future.

But it was so good, a thrill so wild, that the Marine standing before her could well take her over.

Zachary's mouth had gone dry. Fear? No, I'm not afraid, but was anything before ever like this?

"I don't think we have to go out of our way to avoid each other," she repeated.

"I want to hold you again," he said.

"No."

"It feels too good. You're the one who's afraid, Amanda."

"Damn you, Zachary!"

"And damn you, Amanda!"

❦· 10 ·❧

AMP

1888—Prichard's Inn—the Next Night

The night was blustery and vile by the time Captain Storm arrived. After exchanging greetings, the stable boy brought in logs and renewed the fire as Tobias devoured his meal. Mr. Prichard, in his nightshirt, set out numerous bottles for them on the hearth and bid them good night.

The Gunny and the captain nailed their eyes to Ben Boone, who folded up a letter from the commandant.

"We've been aced out of an entire new class of heavy-armored cruisers. They'll be carrying fourteen-inch guns, but no Marines."

"So, I traveled all the way from China to hear this?"

"The navy set aside some space for us to hang up a few hammocks in case of emergency between the numbers one and two boilers and next to the powder store six decks down."

"With a straw bottom to feed the sea horses," Gunny said.

"How many years you got in the Corps, Gunny?"

He scratched his head and counted some on his fingers. "Twenty-six, maybe twenty-seven."

"What about you, Toby?"

"Forty-four."

"Count me in for forty-three," Ben said. "What's that come to?"

"A hundred and fourteen years," the captain answered.

"You shipping over, Gunny?"

"Shipping out," the Gunny corrected. "I'm looking forward to my thirty-year retirement parade."

"You may be the first man to have the entire Marine Corps pass in review," Ben said. The other two knew what the major was getting around to.

"You've sailed past more ship masts than there are men left in the Corps. Under a thousand, counting the three who mustered out last week."

"I'm going to be seventy in a few years," Tobias said. "I know you men think I'm loaded with rare jade, but running a Chinese military school was a form of water torture. My back has a hundred and twenty stab wounds in it, all anonymous. Thank Christ I had Matilda with me. You've heard the term *going native*? That's me."

Ben blinked in sudden realization that Tobias Storm's mighty mustache had turned white.

"All we got left is John Philip Sousa and that Marine band in lion-tamer-red uniforms and a Marine anthem lifted from an Offenbach operetta. All we do is guard shipyards."

As though on cue, the wind lashed in, swinging open a window, which the Gunny closed as Ben refilled his cup.

"Up in Newport in the war college, I can smell the tidings. Our military planners have set the table for the coming century and there's no place at it for the Marine Corps," Ben said.

"I'm ready for the farm anyhow," the Gunny said.

"And I'm ready to become a respectable importer of yin-yang ebony tables and to introduce Washington to chopsticks and fake Ming dynasty vases," said Storm.

"The Corps is bogged down with relics," Ben pressed on, "a bunch of old farts hanging on to feeble ranks, getting bench sores on their asses, waiting for rigor mortis to set in. I can think of over a dozen officers I'd like to put to pasture . . . present fucking company excluded."

"I heard you, Ben," Storm said.

Kunkle laughed. "Remember old Captain Penrose? Hell, he was sitting in his chair dead for five days before anyone noticed it."

"What's the difference?" Storm said. "We can't replace them with new people anyhow."

"Maybe we can," Ben said.

"Let's have it, Major, in English," the Gunny said.

"Commandant Ballard is a hell of an officer. He's kept us alive, but he spends these nights counting Marines. Senator Foley, one of our own, thank God, got some pork attached to the military budget. We're authorized now up to a strength of seventy-five officers. That's fifteen more than we have now. A dozen retirements on top of that would open up the possibility of two dozen new young second lieutenants."

"To what avail?" Gunny Kunkle asked. "Who wants in, anyhow? We're already the shithole of the military."

"You'll only get dregs through the patronage system. Look at me, all the way up to captain in nearly a half century. Fucking good thing I gave that Chinese warlord a pair of seals."

"Gentlemen," Ben said, "you have just made my point."

"Hark, there's a raven looking in the window," Tobias said.

"Evermore." The Gunny burped.

"Let the man talk, Gunny, we've traveled far."

Ben was out of his chair with a sudden burst of excitement. He stretched and cracked his body into alignment. "See, the problem is . . . Let me tell you what the problem is. Once we had a doctrine. We rode American vessels and kicked ass on pirates and we went on kick-ass expeditions, like yours in the Bering Sea and yours, Gunny, in Montevideo, and mine in Panama and Seoul. Now the navy has a real fucked-up notion that they can cruise into any bay, anywhere, and the king and all his people will kneel down, shivering. One day we're going to have to put a battalion down in some swami balmi island and swami balmi island has got a German regiment defending it, waiting for us, and the navy is going to look around and say, 'Where the hell's the Marines?'"

"You're out to save the Corps, again," Storm said. "How many times does this make?"

"It's an ongoing process," Ben retorted. "We've had no doctrine since the Civil War. We've never made a clear statement since the debacle at Fort Fisher."

"I remember it well," Storm answered.

"And I remember Sumter," Ben said back. "Our doctrine has been sitting there, staring us in the face. When the Civil War was done, the country said, 'War no more,' but a generation has passed and now America wants to play with the big boys. The big boys send in big expeditions and there will be more expeditions as we plant our flag, hither and yon."

"Sir," Kunkle said.

"My fucking name to you is Ben, Ben-the-fucking-hillbilly."

"Ben-the-fucking-hillbilly, you're talking about amphibious warfare, again."

"I'm talking about the future of warfare."

"Let me remind you that we got the shit kicked out of us."

"Because we had no doctrine!" Ben cried. "We've never been able to train men *our* way. We've never been able to school our own officers. Big expeditions are going to happen in this world in our times and we start right here to create a doctrine."

"How?" the Gunny asked pointedly.

"Yeah, Ben, how can we make naval gunfire work? How do we get boats in through breakers on a rocky bottom?"

"How do we carry enough water?" Gunny asked.

"How do we get the wounded off?" Storm fired.

"How do we shoot a bull in the ass with a banjo with our piece-of-shit rifles?"

Ben took the commandant's letter from his pocket and a pencil. On the back of the page he wrote the nonword *AMP*.

"I give up," Storm said.

"Advanced Military Program. We quietly start our own school. Someday it might be an academy."

"AMP," the Gunny said, "Asshole Marines in Paradise."

"Fool's paradise," the captain amended.

"Paradise," the Gunny said. "Isn't that where we're supposed to be guarding heaven's gates?"

"Streets," Tobias corrected, "streets."

Ben had their heads going. He knew it. He blasted on: "How many chop suey officers did you graduate and get commissioned for the emperor?"

"Maybe a hundred in the eight years."

"Backbone of his fucking army, isn't it, Toby?" They listened. "We get rid of our dead wood. After an intense AMP course, we got fifteen, eighteen new officers and as many top NCOs. We teach them artillery at Meade and ship design at Annapolis and take them to Sandy Hook to learn about torpedoes and send them to me in Newport to learn naval battles. And you, Kunkle, you run them in ankle-deep sand and teach them how to piss squarely by the manual, how to saw off a man's mangled leg in combat, and how to shoot their fucking rifles straight. For the first time in Corps history, we will train Marine officers to do Marine work."

"AMP?" Captain Storm said.

"AMP," the Gunny echoed.

"It's not an academy, not even a training course. It's just a program. We're gaining friends in the Congress and some top officers in both branches are starting to hear us. Make this first program work and we're in. So, take your time and think it over. Gunny, I need your answer now."

"How long will the program last?" he asked.

"Two intense years that would take five years anywhere else."

"My hitch is up in two years, Major. I'll give you my all," Kunkle promised.

Ben patted the Gunny on the back and looked to Storm. "I know you're going to have to talk this over with Matilda."

"Hell, we pretty much figured this out. I'm pressing seventy and we've got grandchildren we'd like to get to know. We'll be in Washington?"

"Aye."

"Well, the intrigue in Washington won't be as bad as in the Nandong palace, and we've got enough Mandarin crap to furnish the White House. I can give it two years, but, Ben, are we really going to be able to change our status?"

"We've got to bust our ass trying. We're down to the last nickel."

"Have you made a roster of this first group?" the Gunny asked.

"Somewhat, but of course I'm open to any ideas."

"We're all still here courtesy of Paddy O'Hara. I'd like to see his son, Zachary, assigned to AMP," the Gunny said.

"He might see that as a handout," Storm said. "Of course I never really got to know the kid between my duty in China and the Aleutians."

"I've thought about the Wart-Hog perpetuation society," the major answered. "He's a fine prospect, but he's just twenty, with only two years in the Corps."

"Not exactly," the Gunny interrupted. "Zachary O'Hara was born into the Corps. He's as sharp as any enlisted man we have. Besides, Paddy saved my ass twice on the battlefield, and that gives me two votes."

"I know how close you and the sergeant major were, Gunny— more than brothers—but do we want to saddle the boy with more than he can handle?"

Storm added, "He does have his old man's shadow hovering over him."

Ben said, "If the first AMP is successful, maybe we can get him in the next class or the third."

"Yeah, maybe this would bust him," Storm agreed.

"Then I'll take my retirement now," Gunnery Sergeant Wally Kunkle said coldly. He was not precisely refusing an order but playing with its fringes.

"There's more to this than meets the eye," Tobias said when he caught his wits.

"Then, think of the other side of it," the Gunny said. "When Paddy O'Hara's son comes through, that really speaks of our continuity."

"What's behind this, Gunny?" Ben prodded.

"Sure, we all owe Paddy's memory. But on my honor, I believe Zachary O'Hara, on his own, deserves this shot."

"And you'd really retire otherwise?"

"Yes, sir."

"That's blackmail."

"Yes, sir."

"Shit," Ben said, then slowly held his hand out. *"Semper Fi,"* he said.

"To the Corps," Tobias said, offering his hand.

"Semper Fi," the Gunny said.

❧ 11 ☙

PADDY O'HARA'S FINE SON

There came a moment in the fearsome and adventurous life of Sergeant Major Paddy O'Hara when the man needed to catch his wind. From the day of his birth, life was in a hard place; in Ireland during the Great Hunger, and in Hell's Kitchen and on bloody battlefields in the Civil War.

Of course he knew the great comfort of singing around the campfire and the bottomless loyalty of comrades as a warrior in a warrior's place.

The rank of sergeant major was the highest enlisted rank of a given unit. There was no sergeant major of the entire Corps, but no one failed to recognize that Paddy O'Hara was the most celebrated of them all.

He served directly at the pleasure of the commandant and was stationed in the Washington barracks. Every year or so, when enough new recruits were sworn in to make up a platoon, Paddy was dispatched to train them, and they were a hell of a lot better coming out of four months with him than they were going in.

Otherwise he was an unofficial ombudsman for the men in the ranks. In addition to visiting the installations in the East, he was a recruiter's joy. Paddy was able to choose the pick of the litters to swear in to the Marines.

Ordinarily, a hero, even of Paddy's stature, would eventually be mustered out, but after the Civil War, the Marines were on the brink of collapse and Paddy was too damned valuable to give up.

Then Paddy got a yen for softness in the form of a woman. With the end of his service on the horizon, he turned his attention to wooing and winning himself a wife.

The lass came in the person of Maureen Herndon, out of County Wicklow, a maid working under his sister, Brigid, in a mansion on New York's Fifth Avenue, belonging to wealthy German-Jewish merchants.

Paddy was many years Maureen's senior, but no measure of man could match up to him, and they wed. Paddy sought out faint memories of the rare moments of gladness he knew as a boy before the famine.

Aye, they did love each other, for sure. He softened at the sight of her, could feel his heart thump when she touched his cheek, trembled when he held her, and he even tried poetry, on occasion.

Maureen continued to work as a household servant in Washington until she became pregnant at the end of their first year of marriage.

Maureen had left Ireland and entered America suffering from a dormant, undetected consumption, a scourge of the Irish.

The disease flared during her pregnancy as she drained her own strength and gave it to the child in her womb. Zachary was born in 1868. Maureen died three days after.

When only a few weeks old, Zachary was given to his aunt Brigid to raise in New York. Paddy's grief was worse than all hungers, all blood in all battles.

In a gesture of eternal fidelity, the Corps sent Paddy on a goodwill morale-building mission to far-flung posts and aboard vessel after vessel.

When the man started coming out of it, he never searched for bliss again. He drank and fornicated to a degree that strangely added bravura to his legend. Sadly, his visits to New York were damned near unbearable; what he saw in his son was the reason for his wife's death.

The Corps tottered on letting him go but always found an excuse not to, until Brigid almost died in a flu epidemic.

The commandant called him in.

"Your sister can no longer care for Zachary. Her employers are willing to give her quarters at their home, but not with a child. We cannot have you on an extended beer bust boosting morale if your son is in an orphanage. Either you establish a home for Zachary or I will regretfully have to terminate your service."

It was language clearly understood. Paddy had enough seniority, extra pay for being an expert rifleman and for winning the Congressional Medal, and for travel per diem, that he was able to establish a cottage not far from the barracks, where there were always wives of NCOs about for nanny work.

What was good about the arrangement was that Zachary, who had made use of his first five years in Hell's Kitchen with his aunt, picked up the pattern of the Corps and wove himself into his father's life flawlessly.

There was generally room for Zachary to tag along on his father's rounds, and he never got into trouble, and learned to make do on his own. These became a place where father and son came together on occasion. Paddy, ever a reader, always had a book or two in his kit and Zach learned them all . . . and then some.

Zach was a little Marine from the beginning, a small drummer boy at first, complete with uniform, who knew the drill, accepted the rigid order of life, smelled out his da's moods.

He also knew the joys of barrack life, the hard language, the knit of the only family he ever had.

At times, when appropriate, Zach was able to join the hikes, in sand and mud, fire live ammunition, sleep in a pup tent, and was super-cut in matters of spit, polish, and Corps preciseness.

And God Almighty, when he did some honorary drumming and bugling for a pass in review or colors, it was pure nirvana.

They buddied in a sort of way. Zach was no stranger to the slop chute, though his drinks were soda, or a dance off base, and the boy played good baseball and rode decently.

Although they were in close physical proximity at times, their hearts never really seemed to get together. They were like a pair of planets on flashy elliptical orbits that came within touching at times—but then always streaked off in opposite directions.

There were those sudden moments, time and again, when Paddy would be stunned by a flash of Maureen's face in the boy.

Zach was burned from it and led to plunge into a lonely place where he wondered if his da hated him. The pair of them would go into long silent periods that only an Irish father and son could endure. Apart . . . together . . . apart together, never quite touching.

Came that revered day for Paddy O'Hara's mustering-out parade. There were seven senators, double that number of congressmen, the commanders of the army and navy, and the vice-president of the United States in attendance.

Paddy was financed to open a fine Irish pub in Hell's Kitchen and became a ward heeler for Tammany Hall. He still cut a fine figure behind the long bar as well as in the back bar, where a glass case held his Medal of Honor, his sword, and other sacred memorabilia.

Paddy's loneliness for the Corps was partly filled by Irish adoration. His saloon was a notable meeting place for the growing Irish political and municipal establishment. It was Zach, as much as Paddy, who hungered for the tidy life and staunch friendships of the Corps, and the boy counted each birthday as one year closer to enlistment.

Zach developed a life of being very useful in the bar, seeing that his da was well fed, got some decent sleep, and dressed like a dandy. They had a right decent flat above the saloon, but often was the night Paddy entertained a lady and needed the space.

Zach carved out a place for himself in the storeroom adjoining the bar; a chair and a light for reading and straw-filled burlap bags to snooze on.

There's no lack of humor in an Irish pub and there was no lack of it in the deceptively gentle boy who, only God knows why, enjoyed girls more than the smell of stale ale.

Zachary was a walking boy, all caught up in the wonderment of the neighborhoods. Bearing no ill will and always ready with a handshake and smile, Zachary was comfortable down there with the Italians and Germans opposite Hell's Kitchen on the East Side. There were the strange wonderments of the Chinese and the Jews all staking out boundaries and their own peculiar aromas and singsong talk.

He had a black friend, a teamster's assistant who took him to the Black Continent on the Upper West Side.

Zach understood something tremendous was happening. They all wanted a piece of America. Something grand was going to emerge from the confusion.

But in truth, one would be hard put to say who missed the crisp air of the parade ground the most, Paddy or his fine son.

Had not that terrible night happened, burying them both under a rubble of secrecy, they might well have drifted into a stable relationship. But what happened was bound to happen and it did, and the foulness of it all ripped their hearts out.

Zachary O'Hara was sworn in before his eighteenth birthday and Paddy died a little over a year later from stomach cancer, taking that terrible night to his grave.

1890—Two Years Later—Washington

From day one Zachary O'Hara was fully aware of the name he carried into the Corps, but he also knew he could never be his da, despite their terrible ending.

No doubt the Corps was damned glad to get O'Hara but more proud that O'Hara never tried to get a free ride. He was dedicated, decent, well read, and well mannered, a solid Marine on his own.

After his short tour of duty in the Washington barracks, Private O'Hara was assigned to two years in the new AMP course being launched.

He devoured his studies, had a penny in his pocket, buddies in the barrack, girls at the Riverside Amusement Park on the Potomac, and Washington seemed like cherry blossom time all year round.

Despite his low station, Zach's ballroom prowess became known and his services were constantly sought. The presence of a mere Marine private at the more formal affairs caused eyebrow-raising contretemps among the charmingly dull but ambitious officer cadre in the capital.

The charmingly dull daughters of the establishment, age sixteen and beyond, were breathless to be able to snare him for an evening.

Charmingly stern fathers and chirpy mothers gave their daughters leeway when it came to Zachary O'Hara, considering that his late father was one of the most celebrated heroes in the nation's history.

Although the AMP studies were severely demanding, Zachary had acquired military knowledge from birth, and it gave him a leg up. He did what any good Marine would do under the circumstances, ran the clock out on very little sleep and mastered the fine art of sleeping while eating breakfast. He thrived on it, even when Gunny Kunkle leaned on him.

As Amanda Kerr had surmised, they ran into each other now and again.

Horace Kerr realized that his daughter Amanda was too intelligent, too adventurous, for any of the young men in her circle. He also recognized that Private O'Hara seemed to be the only young man who could keep up with her.

Horace went into a soft strategy. He made his own appraisal of

Zachary O'Hara and was impressed. Damned shame, Horace thought, he didn't have a proper pedigree.

Amanda was now past seventeen. Her important life decisions lay ahead. The father and daughter were well into their first true era of peace. From the cotillion onward, they seemed to feel each other's rhythms. He had given her a lot of room to rove in and she in turn had seriously taken on her family duties.

Now this Zachary fellow, he reckoned, was very attractive and Amanda had never been so taken by a boy. It was only a matter of time before she would want to invite him again. If Horace made a fuss, it could lead to another rebellion.

Rebellions rarely happened, once when Amanda was a child, and once before the cotillion, but she could knock down the walls of a city, she was that bold and determined. Horace knew not to draw a line, because there would be hell to pay if he crossed it.

He had awarded his daughter what he had given to very few— respect. Her words were never to be taken frivolously and her wishes never brushed aside. It was a civil relationship now, a relationship of equals.

Horace had the wreckage of his relationships with his son and older daughter to haunt him. Likewise, a long line of disappointing relatives—father, brothers, nephews—feeding at the trough of his success, themselves riddled with mediocrity.

Amanda was it. She was the endgame. From the time she was six or seven when she had first stood her ground against him, Horace trod with care, but Amanda had finally come to understand that she would not gain her desired end unless she carried out her half of the bargain.

Bedrock? Amanda knows what she wants in life, Horace realized. In the end, it won't be a Marine. Horace trusted her behavior and instincts. She'd not go overboard and lose her inheritance. She was too ambitious, too clever, and too spoiled to throw away what lay ahead for her.

So, Horace, he told himself, don't rush in like a bull. Handsome

Marines come and handsome Marines go, but the Kerr family is forever. Don't squeeze her on this, trust her poise and control.

"Why don't you invite Private O'Hara to join us for Sunday brunch at the Willard, our next time in Washington?"

He could feel his words give her pleasure, but she also understood that this was a gesture with limitations.

"He's a decent chap," Horace went on, "and this is America. After all, his father saved half the Marine Corps at one time or the other."

"That's very nice, Father. I'll think about it."

Horace did not tack on an addendum of warnings. Amanda already knew what they were, and knowing them, she rationed her time with Zachary delicately. Nor did she ever let Zach know of the stabs of jealousy she had endured seeing another and then another girl show up on the arm of this blossoming Irish rover.

1889–1890

Zachary loved seeing Amanda. There was more to see of her each day. He never told her of the stabs of emotion that he had felt as well.

No one would mistake Private O'Hara for a fine Irish tenor, although he sang the aching lyrics with perfect soul, if not perfect pitch. He and Amanda had gone off on a picnic and he serenaded her as he paddled their canoe toward shore. He eased the vessel onto a shallow beach, took off his boots and socks, stored them carefully, rolled up his trousers and jumped out into calf-high water, tied the boat, then carried her ashore, piggyback.

Their picnic was in soft shade and grass by a field of wild black-eyed Susans. Amanda wasn't feeling hungry, so he ate for the two of them. She was intoxicated by the beauty of the day.

She stood up suddenly. "Turn your back," she ordered. In a moment he was allowed to turn back around. He saw her pantaloons and underskirts folded on the ground. She still had her dress on but it was close to transparent in the light. Amanda lay back down and stretched and groaned with pure delight.

"I'm free!" she cried.

"Well, don't get any more free," he said, telling his heart to quit thumping.

"I hate all those clothes they make us wear."

He could steal a peek or two, but not to touch, he warned himself. They cooed for a bit, then dressed in proper swimming costumes, dared to dive into the river, re-dressed, and she leaned back against an oak as he fished around in the bottom of the picnic basket.

Amanda's mood changed, just like that. "I was looking over the blueprints of the new class of armored cruiser my father is going to build."

Zach offered her a bite of apple, which she took. Her eyes told his eyes that she was going to jab him about something.

"You can read blueprints?"

"What you meant to say is that girls aren't smart enough to read blueprints."

Zach knew she was picking a bloody argument. He clicked on his warning button to remain placid.

"I'm impressed, Amanda, okay? I'm really impressed. I guess I won't be serving sea duty on one of your father's boats."

"Why do you want to stay in the Marines?"

Zachary knew her question had been long in coming. The afternoon became serious.

"It's my home," he answered.

"Somebody always telling you what to do?"

"There are rules, and if you follow them, it's a good thing. It's a good structure and I have a thousand brothers."

"You couldn't have joined to please your mother, Zachary. You did it to please your father."

"Probably," he answered. "It all came in a natural order of things for me."

"Then you would be someone else if it hadn't been for your father," she said.

"Who would you be," he shot back, "if it weren't for *your* father?"

"But I like who I am," she said, "and where I am, and I know where I am going."

"So do I."

"Then you must like being a private sleeping on a straw mattress in a barrack."

"I haven't had time to sew my stripe on. I've been promoted to private first class."

"You mean prisoner first class."

"Sometimes I wonder, Amanda. Who is the prisoner? You or I?"

Amanda came to her feet, irately, meaning to say something rotten. "Doesn't it become demeaning to you to always be patted on the head as Paddy O'Hara's boy?"

Zach gave her a smile in return. "I like being Paddy O'Hara's son just as you like being Horace Kerr's daughter."

Amanda softened her tone, probing to find a way to break his skin, a paper cut, not deep but one that hurt. "What do you owe Sergeant Major O'Hara?"

"You're trying to irk me, Amanda. Why?"

"Because I think you feel you owe your father too much. Someone with your ability and promise shouldn't be slopping around at the bottom of a sty."

"You're rough, Amanda. You don't want to hear about anything good because the only good is what you think is good. Nobody else's good means anything if it isn't exactly like yours."

"Then let me know what you think is good," she huffed.

"Amanda," he snapped, "you are the commanding officer of the entire world except for me."

"Then tell me," she said.

They sat among the black-eyed Susans as the sun lost its power. They cared. Amanda wanted to understand why an orphan boy found such contentment with so low a station. Even if he became an officer, he'd still be somewhere near the bottom. Is it laziness that holds him back? she wondered. Or fear? How can anyone accept such low status in the midst of all the glitter?

Zachary felt her searching, to turn the two of them into more grand than it was.

"My da left me with a number of wondrous things," Zach began. "I owe him enough to try to understand what these things are."

"And you've found them, then?"

"I had my problems with my da's greatness, with his name. I had to fend off a lot of envious people, but I also understand what he gave me."

"I think you've created a fantasy about both your parents. You've set them on lofty thrones."

"I know what you want to hear, Amanda. Paddy O'Hara could be a mean son of a bitch. He oftentimes ran his men by fear and he could intimidate officers as well. But he got them through alive. He became a tinhorn politician in a saloon bunted in red, white, and blue swirling in a sea of corruption. He made himself believe he loved my mother like a saint, but he was a lying bastard to other women and he drank hard and always had a game of poker running."

Zachary grasped both her arms and held her fast.

"And he read me Shakespeare and he wrapped his big hand around mine and trudged me to the playhouses on Broadway and museums where only the mighty trod. But what I really remember was when he was the great sergeant major of the Corps. I'd ride on his shoulders when we were passed through the sentry gate and we'd march out to the parade ground and hear the song of bugles and the roll of drums as the color guard lowered our flag. I watched five hundred Marines with tears streaming down their cheeks as they passed in review on his last day. Proud officers had tears in their eyes, as did the vice-president of the United States. They mourned and keened for a month in Hell's Kitchen when my da died, and they mourn to this day. He could do foul deeds, but they loved him. They loved Paddy O'Hara because he was an Irish champion when the Irish had poor few champions."

He turned Amanda loose and stepped back. "My da left me his sergeant major's buckle, not much more, and he probably thought I'd never grow into it."

"Maybe he left you a cruel, false dream of the Marines."

"I know you think we're a pack of wharf rats with a high desertion rate and swilling in a sea of booze, but I own no more ambition than for a life in the Corps."

They packed the picnic basket wordlessly. He helped her back into the canoe, and before twilight, they paddled back to the world.

❦·· 12 ··❦

DAISY

From her widow's walk at Inverness, Daisy Blanton Kerr watched her daughter being paddled to the dock. She saw Amanda and the O'Hara boy walk hand in hand lazily toward the stables, bumping each other playfully with their shoulders and hips, then disappear into the barn.

It was a time before they emerged, brushing hay off each other. In a moment the stable boy came out with Zach's buckboard for his long ride back to Washington. Both horse and carriage showed Marine Corps vintage. It will take him all night to reach his barracks, Daisy thought.

Zach slung his pack aboard, hopped onto the driver's seat, and helped Amanda up. Daisy turned the corner of the widow's walk to see them move at a slow gait to the circular drive.

She looked through her spyglass. The watchman in the gatehouse opened the massive guardians to Inverness. Daisy blanched as her daughter and the Marine went into a long, lingering embrace.

Daisy saw her daughter become distraught and half swoon off the driveway and hold both hands to her face. Was Amanda crying? Amanda never cried.

The Kerrs had waited half an eternity for Amanda's time to come. The Constitution Ball would be their finest social conquest, an affirmation of the place they had reached among the nation's mighty families. It had been dreamed of with pulsating anticipation by both parents. As the calendar announced the year of another "Constitution," a sense of near hysteria bubbled up inside Daisy.

The ball, held every fourth year, beginning a decade after the Civil War, was initially meant to be a gesture of reconciliation. Unmarried postdebutantes from the ages of eighteen to their early twenties came together from every city in the nation: the proper girls from Boston and the honey-drawling Southern belles and such and such, invited by secret committee, "commanded" to the Potomac Mansion House Hotel.

They'd swoop in on the red-and-gold carpet with their escorts on their right and their patrician parents behind.

The ballroom filled with military flag officers, cabinet secretaries, and rarely anything lower than a senator. All parties in position, the Mansion House was a place for the celebration of treaties and mergers.

Forty-three girls were invited to this year's ball, more from Boston and New York, fewer from Philadelphia and Baltimore. More from Virginia, only two from Alabama. The daughters of families from growing city empires, Cleveland or Memphis, found their way in, but hardly ever anyone from Mississippi or west of it. Hurrah, this year oil and cattle won recognition with the invitation to a girl from Texas. And two from California, where blue blood was on the rise from mining and railroad fortunes.

Amanda Blanton Kerr was the only Marylander to be so called, and it was up to her to choose a worthy escort.

*   *   *

Amanda came to the main door. Daisy met her on the stairs. As Amanda passed her mother, she briskly brushed the hay off her shoulders.

"Zach and I were necking," Amanda said.

Amanda knew by her mother's nervousness that picket lines were being formed for battle. Daisy took her arm, led her to the conservatory, and rang for tea.

"I sense a problem that I think best to face now," Daisy began.

"What do you mean?"

"Many is the time I wished I had your wings. Your toughness also frightens me, but all things considered, I have never taken you for stupid."

Amanda was startled by Daisy's sudden show of purpose.

"It has been two years since you and your father came to your understandings, but I can see the wheels in your mind once more in motion. You are about to test the waters again, aren't you, my dear?"

Amanda reddened.

"When one is eighteen," Daisy said, "there is nothing to compare to the awakening. A roll in the hay against a boy's strong body, a canoe ride over the lake and down the river."

"That's enough, Mother!"

"There's nothing like first love, I agree . . . I almost remember."

"Zachary is shanty Irish, an enlisted, Marine-barrack-raised Catholic, the lowest class of *merde* in the realm," Amanda snapped, coming to her feet and knocking over her teacup. "Don't bother!"

"Sit down!" her mother commanded.

She did, with aggravated stiffness and tightly locked teeth.

"Bank your rage, young lady. Do not use the Constitution Ball as a challenge to Horace Kerr."

Daisy could tell by the look on Amanda's face that she had read the situation accurately. "You are spoiling for a fight you cannot win. Horace Kerr has too many weapons in his arsenal, too much artillery, too many regiments, too much firepower."

Amanda slipped back into her chair and tried to pour herself tea, but was too shaky. Daisy did it for her, calmly, and her mother's calm ruffled her.

"You were, what, seven when you made your first stand?"

"I hardly remember it," Amanda said.

"Like hell," Daisy retorted. "You remember every moment of it and you have found and mastered ways to hold Horace at bay ever since, but while that was happening, he lost the family game badly."

"Are we going to—"

"Yes, we are going to," Daisy interrupted. "You are clever and you are courageous and I believe quite ruthless, like your father. Over the course he's had to pasture out an entire clan fit for nothing but racing boats and cashing checks. And, your brother and sister as well."

Even though she was a female, Amanda felt, early on, that she held the future of the Kerr family. She'd never seen her mother quite like this and it was disturbing.

"As I said, Amanda, I do not take you for stupid. It's all yours, unless you push him too far. You will lose the game, endure cruel punishment and the precious freedom you've carved."

Amanda fought back. "All my life I've watched the daughters of all our proper friends bounce out on the stage like painted puppets being manipulated by their parents working the strings. All of them too frightened to rebel against a system that stamps them out like so many dolls from a doll factory."

"How very sad for them," Daisy mocked. "But even bound by the rules, maybe there are five girls on this planet as fortunate as you are."

"What about you, Mother?" Amanda threw out defensively.

"Huh, I was served up by my family to consecrate the banking end of the business. I learned, very early on, your father was driven by more ambition and lust than any one woman could cope with."

"And you let him have his doxies?"

"Hell, he probably left the bed of a mistress to marry me. There were times I was delighted to discover that he was too used up to try to get close to me."

"If this is my welcome to the way things really are, aren't there some things we need to share?"

"Amanda, you are cleverly tilting this conversation away from its subject."

"Mother," Amanda started slowly. "Six months ago, you and I were going into the city for fittings. I waited for you in your apartment, as always, and I idled through your bookshelves. I happened on a book of poetry with a rose pressed in it, nothing more, except it lay on a page of desperately declared love."

Daisy lowered her eyes.

"Well?"

"Your father is a bit of a brawler in bed and I had never really known a gentle man before. He was English, actually. I met him on my first trip to England. He was, of all things, a theatrical producer with a wife, children, and later, grandchildren. He passed away a few years ago."

"Oh, Mother," Amanda said compassionately.

"Obviously we carried out our trysts with extreme discretion. He knew of islands off England or up north in Scotland where no one knew us or gave 'tuppence ha'penny.' I don't believe your father would have really cared. Perhaps it would have been a small blow to his ego. But how could the man complain with his string of mistresses, and a wife who ran his home and social life flawlessly?"

"Are you certain?"

"Yes. The only thing that Horace Kerr fears is public ridicule. So long as the news never reached his clubs or banks or the press, he wouldn't give a damn. Just his fine name matters to him."

"Was it worth it?"

"Hard to say, Amanda. After a while you stare at the rose pressed in a book of poetry and hardly remember what he looked like. What I do know about Horace Kerr causes me to shiver on your behalf. He was beyond cruel to your brother Upton, his only son."

"And Emily, hidden away for none to see?"

Daisy sagged. "We won't talk about your sister."

Amanda arose deliberately and began to walk off.

"You'd be a fool to underestimate this man. He'll stop you. He'll stop anyone. The way your father adores you, he'll destroy you before he lets you go, even if it means he must destroy himself in the process. Do you hear me, for God's sake?"

"I hear you."

"Hang on to this place you've won and learn to live in it. Don't test him. Do not test him!"

❦· 13 ·❧

THE PLEASURE GARDEN

Two Weeks Later

Something tickled Zachary's nose. His hand rubbed it as he opened his eyes and yawned. He saw Amanda kneeling over him and smiled.

She had teased him to awakening with a stem of hay. Zach propped on his elbows. He was in the barn of the Inverness stable.

"I wasn't expecting you to arrive till noon."

"I got off duty early yesterday. Captain Storm loaned me his chaise. Anyhow, I got here in the middle of the night and didn't want to make a grand entrance. The guard and his wife invited me to sleep in the gatehouse, but after I got the horse fed and watered, I decided to open a bale and bunk in here."

"You must be hungry."

"Always," he said.

"Are we going to Chesapeake Park?" she asked. "You promised."

"You got permission?" he asked.

"Of course," she said.

"Let me grab my pack and clean up."

Zach followed her to a kitchen as large as the one in his barracks. There were several servants' tables, according to rank. A platter arrived with a Maryland breakfast, including fried chicken. "Sawyer will show you to the washroom. I'll be back in a bit."

He could not eat the platter clean. Zach gave off a happy stretch and followed the servant to a washing room and showers.

Zach returned to the kitchen and saw Amanda waiting at one of the tables with a black girl, of her age, sitting beside her, and assumed she was a member of the household staff. On closer look, the girl was dressed in a lovely way, with a stunning hairdo and a smart little bonnet perched on her head. She was altogether quite pretty.

"I want you to meet Willow Fancy," Amanda said. "You heard me speak about her."

Zach caught his bearings instantly, smiled and held out a hand gallantly. "Very pleased to meet you, Miss Fancy," he said, and slipped onto the bench opposite them.

"Willow is my best friend," Amanda said. "She was dying to meet you. Isn't he gorgeous?" she asked as she turned to Willow.

Zachary blushed and became shy.

They made a half hour of banter, enough for Zach to realize that Willow was obviously educated and extremely well spoken. And finally . . .

"Zach, I had your chaise cleaned and your horse put out to pasture for the day. He might as well roll around and get a grooming later."

"That's nice."

"Then off we go," Amanda said.

Zachary felt a moment's clumsiness, realizing Willow could not be asked to join them, but clearly the two girls had many such awkward moments and handled them with ease, embracing and bussing cheeks.

"He is gorgeous," Willow whispered.

*   *   *

Down Butcher's Hill they rode, pulled by a magnificent Hamble-
tonian trotter. They skirted the docks, then went bayside until
they were lured by the siren call of a calliope belching out "The
Yellow Rose of Texas," and soon smelled the mixed aromas of
bratwurst and popcorn through the archway which announced
CHESAPEAKE PARK.

Zach excused himself and unhitched the horse and tied him in a
reasonable stall, helped park the carriage, and spoke to the attendant, who held up his hands and scraped and bowed.

"Goodness, what did you tell him, Zach?" Amanda asked.

"I told him I'd better get the same horse back," Zach answered.

Zach had never seen Amanda's eyes so wide and sparkly. She
squeezed his hand as they made their way down the midway.

Hawkers and balloons and cotton candy and windmills whirled
on sticks and they tripped through the fun house and clung through
the haunted house and then the house of mirrors. Amanda shrieked
as she matched friends and family to the distortions.

"This one is Father!" she cried at the huge long head and stubby
body.

Now a wiry, moose-jawed image. "Gunny Kunkle about to run
us through ankle-deep mud!"

They skipped the freak show but were awed by fire-eaters and
knife throwers and jugglers. The magician was awesome.

Zach wasted three nickels trying to knock down a pyramid
of iron milk bottles with softballs. And another two nickels were
blown to beat the man guessing their weight. They each sat in
the weighing chair. The barker guessed them right on, as his
little hidden foot pedal froze the chair at 170 for Zach and 119
for her.

"Too bad, Marine, better luck next time."

"I'm really much lighter," Zach whispered to her.

"So am I," she said.

They rode the carousel, she on a unicorn and he on a fiery

dragon. He collected a brass ring on the third ride, to win her a baby doll.

Any Marine would have to step up in manly fashion, doff his jacket, take the heavy, long-handled mallet, and try to pop a weight up the scale to hit the gong. After three "ughs," Zach gave up.

"Ohhh," moaned a gathered crowd.

"Little lady?"

Amanda whacked the treadle and the bell bonged. The man gave her a chirping toy canary on a stick.

"Rigged," Zach grumbled.

On they went down the midway, blowing a dollar and thirty cents, a deep whack in a month's pay, but Zach had come prepared to spend! When hunger overtook them they devoured mutton on a stick, licked their fingers clean, and settled for a moment to enjoy sarsaparilla-flavored ice cones, which dripped through the thin paper cup.

"Sure is messy!" Amanda said, her hair bouncing in concert with her mood. "How many girls have you brought here?"

"None."

"Oh . . . boo!"

"Well, none here. There's the Riverside Park in Washington. It's kind of a hangout for the guys at the barracks."

"And a place to pick up girls," she prodded.

"Yes," he agreed, "but never anyone like the one who is with me now."

"Zach," she cooed, and kissed his cheek.

"How many times have you been here?" he asked.

That quickly, Amanda's mood turned somber. She shook her head no, took a breath, and said, "We pass this on the way to Father's shipyard. I begged him to take me and he finally broke down. Unfortunately I was dressed like a princess going to a coronation. Chesapeake Park was much simpler then. A pleasure garden. As we passed and people passed us, the gaiety around us seemed to become subdued. I realized Father's Pinkertons, detectives from the yard, were trailing us to guard us, and men began tipping their hats and saying 'Evening, Mr. Kerr,' and the women curtsied and everyone sort of moved away from us. Even the house of mirrors wasn't funny."

An evening breeze off the bay was blessedly warm and tender.

"And?" Zach asked.

"Despite it all, there was enough wonderment here to want to come back and I asked to bring Willow. Zach, I was only six or seven and had been completely shut off and sheltered from everyday people and public glances. It was my first lesson in the world of black and white."

"I didn't really mean to . . ."

"No, let me finish. Negro servants were such a part of what was normal in my life, it never occurred to me that I couldn't bring Willow.

"After that," she went on, "Father would hire a carnival or small traveling circus complete with a merry-go-round and bring it to Inverness. Of course Father fixed all the con games, and the prizes handed out were magnificent. I threw mine away."

Her sour memory evaporated when the band started the evening concert at the big gazebo. Zach and Amanda stretched out on the lawn near the benches with a hundred other couples, who were soon in the mood to spoon. Neither of them had ever felt closer to anyone than they felt at this moment.

When a medley of John Philip Sousa's marches was played with spirit, it made Zach feel grand. He sat up and clapped in time and then offered her his lap as other spooning couples did, and Amanda put her head on it and he touched her hair and traced her face with fingertips feeling of down until her breath became so uneven she had to hold his hand still, lest she cry aloud with joy.

Later she gave her lap to him and both groaned beneath their breath.

The concert ended with a thumping "Stars and Stripes Forever" as the bay mellowed up for the evening. He tugged her gently to her feet. Nighttime was coming. Chesapeake Park glowed with a merry mixture of a thousand gas lanterns and electric lights.

They strolled, just another pair of sweethearts, and stopped at the tunnel of love. The waiting line seemed endless, but their patience was not. They wanted some moments alone. The song from another calliope caught their attention and soon they were standing before the first Ferris wheel in Maryland, only the third in the entire country. It had been in the background all day, but now it loomed and seemed to be a thousand feet high, lifting open seats into a giant circle in the sky.

Amanda felt Zach's hand go moist with sudden sweat and his lips paled. The wheel stopped for another couple, and another, leaving those on top dangling and swaying.

"We don't have to go on it," she said.

"Yes, we do," he answered.

The attendant clicked the bar over their seat and the great wheel zoomed up counterclockwise, hurling them into space.

Now, over the top their chair went, and they could look down to the blizzard of lights and hear the cacophony of sounds of girls' screams and barkers' beckoning and the croaky toots of the calliope.

As they started to come down, the Ferris wheel stopped and their seat swung hard, as another couple was loaded on below . . . move a bit, stop and wait as another couple . . . and another . . .

She looked at him and she was alarmed by what she saw. Zachary was not quite together with things, his face glistening and his hands holding the bar in a death grip.

"Zach!" she cried.

He did not hear.

Four Years Earlier—Paddy O'Hara's Saloon—Hell's Kitchen

Any man who had been a Marine sergeant could read trouble on another man's face. One of the nice parts about living with Zachary

was that he rarely showed such feelings. On this occasion the boy
was giving off a telltale signal. Something had been gnawing at him
for several days.

It was deep into the night, heading for three o'clock. Paddy sat
on a bar stool opposite Zach, who was clearing the cash register.

"What's on?" Paddy asked.

Zach tried to weasel out, but to no avail.

"I'm confronting a problem."

Paddy leaned over the bar, poured himself a mug, and waited
for Zach to unfold his words.

"I dream I'm falling and try to reach for a hand to grab me, but
it's never there. It happens all the time now, every night."

Paddy grunted. "How much do you remember about getting
stuck out on the fire escape?"

"It's only been spoken of in drifts and whispers. I don't really
know."

"You was three and a half, living with Brigid up on the fourth
story, and you crawled out on the fire escape. The counterweight
rope broke and the window slammed shut. You remember any
of it?"

"Not truly."

"We always thought it best, me and Brigid, not to talk about it
in front of you. Anyhow, you was hanging on to the rail screaming
and she busted the glass to get to you, but you wouldn't let go, so
she wrapped her arms around you and hung until the fire laddies
coaxed you in. We should have spoken to you, but you were pretty
much a tough kid and I figured you'd outgrow it."

Zach snapped rubber bands around the stacks of bills, placed
them in a sack and into the safe.

"After my last birthday, I realized that given another year or so,
I'd be sworn into the Corps. If I can't go up a ship's mast, I can't be
a Marine, Da. I'd disgrace you, and the Corps as well."

"Why the hell didn't you tell me!" Paddy growled.

"For the plain and simple reason that I saw how you came
down on men who were afraid, because you were the one man

in the world who had no fear. And you couldn't stand fear in others."

"Oh, Jaysus," Paddy moaned. He signaled for a bottle of Irish whiskey. "That is my game in life, Son. Do you have any idea how many times I confessed battle fear to the priest? Fear is the monster that has to be stilled at birth and you never had the comfort of your mother's breast. Flies hanging from the flypaper are filled with fear. Violets bending to the sun are frightened, to say nothing of the rats in Hell's Kitchen."

"I've never known you to be afraid."

A hardy shot of whiskey slowed Paddy and he rounded up the nerve to pat his son's hand and stare, his eyes looking a different way.

"We are all riddled with fear. It is how you are able to cope with it which makes you the manner of man you become."

"You were scared at Sumter?"

"I'm still scared of Sumter," Paddy said, and his son understood that his da wasn't telling him this in order to make him feel good.

"You've always handled yourself so well, Zach, I thought it was you who had whipped fear. Small fucking wonder you dream of falling. I had the same kind of nightmares."

"Did they ever go away?"

"Aye, when I went into the Corps. I knew that if I fell, some Marine would grab my hand and help me get up."

"Did prayer help?"

"I never had much luck with the Virgin. She probably figured I was too rowdy. All right, then, let's sleep on it."

Zachary knew his da's inner wheels were grinding, but unless he warned his da that he couldn't make it as a Marine, it would all become too shattering later.

The next day Zachary made himself scarce, walking the neighborhoods till after dark. When he returned to the saloon, one of the bartenders told him Paddy was waiting down on the river at Pier

Four, where a worthy schooner, the *Beatrice K*, was docked. The skipper, Mike Ryan, was a longtime patron of the bar.

A moment of terror came upon Zachary as he approached the ship. That would be Paddy O'Hara's way of solving things, like those night marches through the dark swamps, daring anyone to fall. Zach looked up the mast and fought off a surge of vomiting. His da met him at the top of the gangplank.

"Must be a hundred feet to the crow's nest."

"A hundred and twenty-two," Paddy said sans mercy.

"It's no use, Da."

"I'm not ordering you to go up the mast, but I'm saying words you must hear or carry a stone in your guts the rest of your life. I cannot make you do what you can't do, but before you can't do it, you are going to have the benefit of my advice."

"I'm a coward!" Zach cried.

"Having said that, listen up. This moment is here, now. It can't be changed. It will never go away. The ship's mast is going to tell you where you are going to settle on the human scale. No matter what you do, you are still my son."

"In name only."

Paddy wanted to kneel and plead, but it was beyond his way of doing things. "I've enough lead in me to forge an anchor. I can handle another wound. It is the wound you will have to endure that frightens me."

Please God, Zach prayed, make this moment never have happened! Please God, make it go away! But it didn't.

"You are the advance scout for your platoon," Paddy began, "and your men are entering a blind ravine. There are sheer rocks up there that you have to climb to get observation, the only place from which you can spot an ambush. You have to climb up to be able to warn them or they are dead meat marching in—"

"Stop it, now. I've seen the sergeant-major tricks."

"NOW . . . HEAR . . . THIS. There is no greater glory than the moment a man makes his decision that death is preferable to yielding to fear!"

Paddy backed away, somewhat frightened himself. "You're still my son," he said harshly, and went down the gangplank.

1891—Chesapeake Park

The Ferris wheel stopped and the operator unhooked the bar.

"We'll do another few rounds," Zach said.

And away they went, backward, up and up, into a patch of darkness, and the wheel was braked and it stopped and the passengers dangled.

Amanda kissed him with a tongue full of adventure and he met her in midfield.

Let's fly like this forever and ever! We'll never run out of kisses or most subtle ways to touch each other here and there in a most decent manner.

There you are, mighty Paddy O'Hara, standing on the dock, hands raised and shouting, "Hip hip hooray!"

Well, I went up the *Beatrice K*'s pole three times, Da, and I'm a fucking Marine! And then an afterthought . . . I don't know whether I love you or I hate you, Da.

Can you imagine? The operator of the Ferris wheel wouldn't even let the Marine pay for his extra rounds.

They walked, him somewhat weak-legged, back toward the midway. Amanda knew full well that Zach's father had been there with them. As they left the Ferris wheel, they were hanging on to each other in a new and different way.

At the dance pavilion, the blue-plate special was fifty-nine cents, within reason, and consisted of a combination of Maryland fried chicken, a Maryland fried crab cake, and a side of oysters with mashed potatoes, string beans, and "various," to be concluded with a quarter of a watermelon.

Amanda wanted desperately to slip Zach a five-dollar bill but knew it would cut him to the quick and perhaps dampen the most wonderful day of her life.

Zach had come fully financed for the excursion. He had ironed sixty-two shirts for his buddies at the barracks at a nickel each, added four dollars and ten cents in a poker game, and drew a few dollars from what he had riding on the paymaster books.

"What will you have to drink, Marine?"

"Beer."

"What year were you born?"

"Eighteen twenty."

"And you, miss?"

"Beer, 1824," she said, looking straight at him.

"I'll bring you a pitcher, it's cheaper."

They held hands and cruised with their eyes around the pavilion.

"Who all is here?" she asked.

"A lot of Irish," Zach observed. "Steel-mill workers from Sparrow's Point. Lot of Germans," he continued, "teamsters and dockworkers. See those midshipmen lining the bar?"

"Uh-huh."

"A Norwegian training ship is in port. Over there, maybe trouble, two tables of single ladies."

"What do you mean by *trouble?* Good trouble?"

"Bad trouble. Notice, when the music ends the Norwegians go back to the bar."

"They're probably bashful with the language and all."

"No, that's not it. They came together and they're leaving together. They're taking care of each other."

"Look, Zach, one of them is leaving with a girl," Amanda said.

"Let's hope he doesn't wake up tomorrow on a Greek freighter heading for Montevideo."

Amanda's mouth went agape.

"I draw shore-patrol duty sometimes. We've gotten more than one sailor out of a mess."

"Are you teasing me?"

"We fought a war in 1812 about the British borrowing our sailors without consent."

"Would you agree if I went to the bar and asked one to dance?"

"No."

"*You* wouldn't be jealous, would you?"

"Oh sure, a little bit. That's not it. I am responsible for you."

Amanda felt incredibly protected. On to more mischief. He challenged her to a glass of beer. It had a disgusting taste, but her curiosity was aroused. Why is beer so sacred? It's really not all that bad. Hmm. Hmm.

"Hey, there's a buddy from my platoon. He and his girl are being seated at a table of strangers. Would you mind?"

"Ask them over."

Zach zinged out a whistle and shot over the floor. "Hey, Varnik! Over here, man!"

The two Marines fell on each other as long-lost cousins, not as two men who spent all their living hours together.

"Hi, ma'am. I'm Zach."

"I'm Beth Shaughnessy."

"Amanda," Amanda said.

"Casper Varnik," the corporal said, shaking Amanda's hand and bowing. "Hey, we got lucky, huh, Beth?"

The party was on. They recounted their daring adventures down the midway. Casper Varnik was thick of neck and shoulders and Beth was thin but deceptively pretty, with Irish-colored hair and skin and a pert nose.

"I work at Müeller's," Beth said to Amanda.

"I don't know that one," Amanda said.

"Cotton-finishing factory. I do the fancy stitching on bed linens. My sisters work there as well. Where do you work, Amanda?"

"My father has his own business. He has a shop, outfits boats."

"Lucky you. It took me a long time to get lacework on the third floor, but they're very strict on us. I'm on a wait list for a nanny's job," Beth said, crossing her fingers for luck.

Beth lived in Pottstown, an Irish enclave of Baltimore.

Casper Varnik came from halfway across the country—Chicago!

"How did you two meet?" Amanda asked.

"I was visiting a cousin in Baltimore," Casper said, "and there was this here social event at the Sacred Heart Seamen's Mission."

"I'm a Baltimorean, too," Amanda said. "You poor fellows should have found yourselves a couple of birds at Riverside Park near your barracks."

The corporal patted his girl's hand with sincere affection. "Not on your life," he said. "You know it ain't all that bad. We get a forty-eight-hour pass every month. Catch a train to Baltimore, hop the trolley to Pottstown, and hey, we still got Sunday, huh, Beth? Zach, how's about you and me taking the late train back to Washington tomorrow?"

"I pulled guard duty. I've got to be at the barracks early."

"But last train to Washington's in an hour," Casper said.

"I did some extra work at Captain Storm's house, and in exchange, he loaned me his horse and rig."

"Jesus, 'scuse my language, that Captain Storm is more like, you know, a father than an officer. His wife, Matilda, throws a spread for us every month, Chinese food. She's got this big pan in their galley, and as fast as we can eat it clean, she's throwing more stuff into it."

"What does your dad do?" Amanda asked Beth.

"After the eighth kid he went west with the railroad, an old Irish tradition," she answered, and switched the subject, admiring Amanda's doll. "Casper never wins the brass ring." She held up a velvet cushion with a glittering CHESAPEAKE PARK and a painting of a mostly nude woman dancing the hoochie-koochie. "I have one of these already."

"It's beautiful!" Amanda said, giving Zach an imploring look. He nodded.

"Let's trade!" Amanda cried. "My doll for your pillow."

"Gracious!"

A straw-hatted quartet attired in vertical peppermint-striped jackets gave out with "Ta-Ra-Ra Boom Der-E."

The Marines took their girls to the dance floor. Casper Varnik

and Beth Shaughnessy were no slouches at ragtime. They traded
partners, stepping wildly. Now a quadrille with a Norwegian sailor
and his girl and a soldier boy and his girl. They danced till their
sides ached.

Zach put his hand over Amanda's glass as Casper poured a
round. She'd already had two.

"It's quite all right. I have a very fine escort," she said, taking
his hand away.

All too soon their witching hour fell.

Oh, to drive a dandy phaeton pulled by a magnificent Hamble-
tonian trotter with the most beautiful girl in the world cuddled up
against you.

Amanda ran her hand over the garish velvet pillow. It would be
two weeks before Zach got a forty-eight-hour liberty. Maybe she'd
slip over to Washington? That would not be wise. She told herself
not to fall into a state of sadness.

The carriage turned onto the road up Butcher's Hill. They could
make out the lights of Inverness on its crown. As the carriage passed
through a dark stretch of road, she told him to pull over.

"Aye."

He tied up where the horse could nibble at a patch of tall grass.
Amanda asked him to snuff out the carriage lamps and they were in
total darkness.

"We're still early," she said. "I love this pillow. I really liked
Beth and Casper."

"This was the first time I've met her in person, but I've been
looking at her picture on the wall by Varnik's bunk for a year. She's
a soft little thing, like an Irish nymph. Varnik isn't too articulate,
but you should see how he takes charge and controls men, and his
tactical sense. He's going to be a great Marine officer."

Amanda chose her next words cautiously. "I could get Beth
onto the household staff at Inverness," and added quickly, "It
would be better than the job she has now."

Damn! His silence said everything.

"Zach, I'm sorry."

"Varnik and I are equals, buddies for life. Lord, my da was a sergeant major when he and my mother married. She did the Irish washerwoman's chores and carried out the chamber pots in someone's fine mansion."

"And it angered your father, badly."

"No, they knew the drill when they married. What riled him was the everlasting low station of all the Irish. Varnik serves at the pleasure of his country. They love each other and can maybe make a go, but it's a hard life to be the wife of an enlisted man."

"I am sorry," she repeated, then shivered, although it was warm. "It's been such a beautiful day, I want to hang on to it a little longer."

"Did your parents really know you were going to Chesapeake Park?"

"There is that possibility."

"You told me you had their approval."

"I did, in a manner of speaking."

"But you didn't, specifically."

"It falls under the terms of a treaty with Father." Amanda could feel Zach smiling through the darkness. She sighed. "You aren't the only one who has to live up to regulations. Before I was sixteen I always had a couple of Father's Pinkertons with me or following me everywhere. I've made a lot of different kinds of different friends, some who made my father's hair bristle. It was difficult to keep them, so I decided to take a stand."

"How'd you do that?"

"In my parents' world, daughters are presented to society when they're sixteen. Well, the Baltimore Cotillion was coming up and I told them I would not attend unless he gave me some freedom. A year of Mother's noble scheming would go down the drain. Father and I did not exchange a word for over a month. Then he yielded. Father agreed that in the future I could leave Inverness without his Pinkertons and I could keep my friends on the condition that I was properly escorted and home before midnight."

"But it was still difficult for you to keep Willow?"

"It may be hard for you to understand. There are no black people in the Marine Corps," she said.

"I tried to sort some of that out going into all those contrary villages in New York. Once the suspicion of difference is overcome—it has to come about or otherwise we're just replanting warring countries in America."

"Then you can understand that we are like sisters, and I love her."

"And there were times today, you wished she was with us."

"I am very happy about who I was with today." She pulled back from him, now only touching by voice. "I want to be able to take Willow to Chesapeake Park, just once before we're very old."

"Tell me about it, Amanda."

She felt for his hand again, and it felt so good to be touched by him and to say words to him that she had always kept secret.

❧· 14 ·❧

THE HALLS OF INVERNESS

1858—Inverness

War drums along the Potomac became yet louder. The industrial establishment knew that war was going to happen and set forth to feather their nests.

Horace Kerr had already relieved his father and older brothers, Malcolm and Donald, of the ranking positions in the family shipyard. They were too rooted in the past. Their shares of stock would see them and their heirs through life with great wealth, and the family members magnanimously continued to speak to one another, realizing Horace held the keys to the vault.

Horace had grandiose plans to expand the facility at Dutchman's Hook fivefold and placed his bet on the Union in the event of war.

Baltimore's first banking family, the Blantons, fit the bill. In the beginning, the Blantons' hearts leaned toward the Confederacy, but never their money. The Blanton bank also sought investments that would reap a golden harvest from a war. Horace Kerr filled that order.

Daisy Blanton's marriage to Horace Kerr sealed the loan. Inverness was still in a building stage when Daisy moved in, bringing her personal slave, Laveda Fancy. Laveda's husband, Matthew, a top-notch household slave, was thrown into the bargain.

Daisy and Laveda were both twenty years of age, arriving at Inverness with forty steamer trunks belonging to Daisy and one belonging to Laveda. The new Mrs. Kerr became heavily dependent on her slave. All of the building taking place and the staff and management of a fifty-three-room mansion were beyond Daisy's capabilities.

That was fine with Horace. Daisy was lovely to behold and a social wizard, well tutored in the arts, and with a great eye for quality. There was also her mighty family. She'd grow into her other responsibilities, budgets, personnel, and such. For now, Daisy was a fabulous hostess and charmer.

Mr. and Mrs. Howard Leamington were imported from England as majordomo and head housekeeper, positions they had held for the late Earl of Harlingham. Professional and polished, proper speck-of-dust hunters, they were a class act who knew their place.

Yet . . .

Daisy soon realized that the Leamingtons would run Inverness *their way* and was uncomfortable with them from the outset.

Inverness was largely staffed by slaves, not typical fieldhands but well selected and slightly elevated household, grounds, and stable workers. None was employed in a supervisory capacity, although some held rank and privileges, such as the chefs and horse trainers.

The Leamingtons did not find them near the caliber of English and Irish servants. Their manner was curt and authoritative.

The Fancy couple annoyed the Leamingtons the most. Matthew had been an all-around assistant to the managers of the Blanton estates. He had learned numbers, could count, add, and subtract, and recognized a hundred or so written words on sight. He was also an unofficial liaison between slaves and supervisors.

Laveda's position was the major threat to the Leamingtons' authority, for she had the ear of Daisy Kerr. Inverness glided along smoothly but with no sense of joy. The Leamingtons' noses were constantly sniffing and the distant sounds of spirituals from the Negroes' cottages became more mournful.

True to their professional skills, the majordomo and his scratchy wife played up to Mr. Kerr and deftly insulated him from household problems. Horace remained oblivious of the mounting tension. He was too consumed with his business and those other things a man of his station needed to be consumed by.

When he entered his home, all he wished to see was serenity, efficiency, and sparkling banisters, and he prided himself on his brilliant move of bringing the Leamingtons over from England!

Daisy dared not complain in light of her husband's satisfaction with the British couple. She was masterfully cowed by them and often left their presence trembling in Laveda's arms.

Leamington was unable to enlist Matthew Fancy as an informer. Intrigue was whispered through the Inverness corridors, past the closet doors. As enemy camps formed, Daisy became more dependent on the Fancys.

So, there it was, one big happy Inverness, with crisply cut lawns, highly polished silver, magnificent horses, prize roses, and impeccable service, all sailing on whispers.

Down the ways into the bay at Dutchman's Hook, the Kerr shipyard sent hulls as fast as they could be pegged together. Horace's wealth was becoming immense.

Horace was able to pay off his loans early to the Blanton bank. While things looked nearly perfect, a damned crisis was brewing in Baltimore. Although Maryland would probably remain in the Union, it had a nasty mix of sympathies. From a dead-on practical point of view, Maryland had the largest number of slaves, aside from Virginia. Maryland's tobacco fields required as much hand and stoop labor as the cotton fields farther on down south and were as backbreaking to keep up as the sugarcane plantations in the Deep South.

A fair number of Baltimore public places had begun having separate entrances for Northerners and Southerners, and a good part of the press railed against Lincoln.

Horace came under pressure from the Washington establishment and particularly from his Republican Party to make a bold, clear statement to help keep Baltimore and Maryland loyal.

The Kerr fortune and future would depend on a Union victory. He pondered the question of what to do. His decision was suddenly hastened, in the middle of the night, when Daisy sat up in bed, weeping.

Oh, good Lord, what the hell? he wondered.

Daisy had been a loving bride who was quickly being molded to fit into his scheme of things. He was totally unaware that she faced her first, crushing defeat in life when she realized she could not manage Inverness.

Daisy had cooed her way through with Horace. But she was still a Blanton and the Blantons were mighty, and an heiress of her stripe was entitled to a tantrum.

"Why are you crying?" he asked.

"I'm pregnant!"

"What news! Oh, my precious girl. Weep no more. You've made me tremendously happy!"

The sky opened. "I hate the Leamingtons!" Daisy shrieked.

He was unable to reason with her or console her. He calmed her enough to lie back on her pillow, and she sobbed softly while he put on a dressing gown, lit a cigar, and paced the floor.

First the secretary of war, then the Republican Party, now this! Well, truth be known, he really didn't like the Leamingtons either. So, then, now a pregnant wife and Inverness still being completed.

"Horace," she called, "please put out your cigar. It is making me very nauseous."

"Sorry, dear."

He patted her to sleep, then repaired to his office and concentrated.

First problem. The Union had to win the war, outright. The

Confederacy had revealed its strategy: the South could never win it on the battlefield so they had to keep their army intact, bleed the Union, and suck their will until the enemy allowed the Confederate States to establish their own nation at the conference table.

This condition would change only when Lincoln found the generals who would take the casualties necessary to smash the Southern army.

He was stuck with the Union.

Problem number two, Baltimore and Maryland. The Republicans, through Kerr, had to make a bold move to support the North. What?

Problem three, getting rid of the fucking Leamingtons. They had an ironclad contract and probably were not above blackmail, through cunning innuendo and lies about Inverness. Above all things, Horace Kerr could never take a threat to his social station.

At that moment he was struck by an epiphany!

The next evening Matthew and Laveda Fancy were summoned to the master's apartment, where Horace and Daisy awaited them.

One and all agreed that they were pleased that Daisy was with child. Horace started to light a cigar, broke into a smile, and deferred gallantly to his wife's condition.

"Today, I have spoken to my legal staff and they are going to prepare documents," he said, leaning forward, "to grant freedom to all people in servitude at Inverness."

The Kerrs were puzzled by the lack of reaction. There was a weird expression on Matthew's face, and his eyes were like stony agates flashing out, piercing them.

Horace immediately got the drift.

"I never have fully reconciled myself to the institution of slavery," Horace blurted, "but if you are living in a system, you go along with it. Good riddance, I say."

The Fancys seemed unmoved.

"I've never used field slaves," Horace continued. "It's always been a household matter. Even so, I admit slavery is flawed." His words skidded to a stop before their wall of silence.

"You don't seem overjoyed," Daisy said.

"Darling," Horace retorted, "this is a sudden and imposing moment for the Fancys. I'm certain that Laveda and Matthew are simply overwhelmed and speechless."

"We accept our freedom," Matthew said.

"Good," Horace said, racing on. "Before we call all our . . . workers together and inform them, there is a separate matter that the four of us should try to remedy, a problem with the Leamingtons. Will you shed some light on it for me?"

Another nonanswer. This was not going so easily.

"Laveda knows my feelings toward them," Daisy said.

"We'd like to be able to go on our way," Matthew said.

"My God!" Daisy cried. "We've just given you your freedom. You can't just up and leave."

"I go with my husband," Laveda answered.

"In my condition?" Daisy asked.

Horace jumped in quickly. "Even though everyone will be freed, they will have their jobs here and their housing and a salary to boot. You all can come and go to Baltimore as you wish, carrying proper identification papers."

"You said we would be free. Just how free is free?" Matthew asked.

"You and Laveda will be promoted to very good positions here."

The Fancys still remained unmoved.

Horace understood that he was losing the day. Daisy's face was bloodless. Something was happening here, now, that was going to change the way life was lived. Horace needed to be astute with his answers, perhaps even drop the slave-and-master banter.

"I would like to have a serious talk with Matthew. Would you mind, Daisy? Laveda?"

Matthew's wife looked to her man for an answer. He wavered for a moment. "All right, Laveda," Matthew said to his wife.

"See that Miss Daisy lies down and gets some rest," Horace added.

They left haltingly.

"Let us talk, man-to-man," Horace began.

"May I sit down?" Matthew asked.

Horace's face reddened. Something was happening! He held his arm open to a chair never before sat in by a black person and he unpeeled a cigar.

"Cigar?"

"Thank you, no."

"This is a damned good one."

"I worked the tobacco fields for one of the Blantons in Virginia when I was a boy. Spending my whole life around tobacco seems to make it hard for me to breathe right."

Horace lit up, alone. "Feel completely free to speak, even though I might not like it."

No answer.

"Look, speak up. What you say will never leave this room."

"What do you want me to say?"

"I'm granting you freedom. What's on your mind?"

Matthew spoke quite softly. "I tread now carefully, but I do not believe you can bring yourself to say 'I need you' to a black man and his wife."

Horace gauged his adversary. He was one smart black. Of course the question of need had never occurred to Horace. All right, then, let's play the game.

"Suppose I am willing to grant that we may need you. I need you to do a big favor. I need you to help me get rid of the Leamingtons."

"I'm not starting out a new life by turning on a white major-domo," Fancy answered.

"Listen up, Matthew. There are powerful people in Baltimore who are going to jump all over me for freeing my slaves. Believe me, it takes balls to do what I'm doing. The Leamingtons are masters of their game. They can spread rumors and see to it that we are smeared in the press. I need to pack them off to England, quick. Now, can you help me?"

No answer. Switch the appeal. "Mrs. Kerr is in a very delicate

condition. A social scandal would damn near kill her. Do you realize how the Leamingtons could spread lies? I'll back you up, on my
honor."

"Not to offend your honor, but I don't see any black man testifying against any white man."

"Testifying to what?" Horace pressed.

"Study your damned estate ledgers!" Matthew cried.

"What!"

"I'll say no more."

"How can you possibly know about such things, Matthew?"

"I knew I had to learn to count and add and subtract to get out
of the fields. I learned a hundred words by sight so I was able to go
work in the stables. Mr. Kerr, I know how to order a dozen bales of
hay and I know when only eleven are delivered."

"And how'd you learn to speak so well?"

"From a white man named Mr. Fancy, who ran the big Blanton
horse farm in Virginia. He'd come from England, like the Leamingtons. Every day he'd paste up a new word for me to learn in the
tack room."

Horace had found the weak spot and slipped an ace up his
sleeve to be played at the proper moment. The ash on his cigar
grew longer and could have been knocked off with the blink of his
eye, yet grew longer still.

Because of the extent of the building and inflated war prices, the
Leamingtons had obviously found ways to pump up the estate
budget. Horace cursed himself for not doing his homework. What
else would he find? Double entries, inflated bids, kickbacks, short
deliveries? Those sons of bitches.

"So they've been stealing my white ass off."

Matthew cracked a smile. "Once they felt they were trusted and
would not be subjected to monthly audits, the larceny began."

"What about Miss Daisy?"

"I took the ledgers to Miss Daisy every month to sign off on
them. She didn't want to be bothered. The Leamingtons didn't fig-

ure I could read, but I watched the expenses balloon. I didn't say anything because I never wanted my black ass whipped again."

Jesus!

Horace stared at the new Matthew Fancy, seeing an entirely different . . . well, person . . . yes, person. Horace had a finely honed ability to spot mediocre talent, as he had in his brothers and nephews. He had kept them in mediocre positions, but Matthew Fancy was better than the whole lot.

Conversely, when he came across that rare bird with brilliant feathers, he'd win his trust and reward him. Horace never thought of Matthew in normal terms. Matthew could be developed into a first-class piece of personnel. Horace was not going to lose him, despite his color.

"I envision a bright future for you here at Inverness, beyond your wildest dreams."

"Mr. Kerr, you cannot possibly know what my dreams are."

Horace was talking, not listening. "This will be a big job, maybe without an official title, but I will send over a top executive from the yard to assist you. You're perfect, folks will listen to you. They respect you."

"I do not wish to be a black overseer."

"Manager, Matthew, manager. Overseers are for fieldhands. We have no disciplinary problems here and you can keep it that way. What do we have at Inverness, sixty or so full-time people, butlers, maids, cooks, gardeners, laundry workers, stable hands, security? These are not agricultural people. Make that a hundred folks including the nonworking children, pregnant women, ill and injured, old folks. Slavery was no good, but I have been on the decent side of it. I've allowed families to live together. I've never gone in for whippings. I will continue to house everyone, enlarge your personal plots, et cetera, et cetera, et cetera. These benefits will come to a rather staggering sum."

"Up to seventy-eight dollars a slave, a year," Matthew said quietly.

"What about wages?" Horace countered. "Four to eight dollars a month per worker."

"Mr. Kerr, if you paid all of the people at Inverness for the rest of their lives, it would be more than covered by seventeen days' profit from the shipyard."

Jesus!

Matthew Fancy's calculation came to within a whisper of what Horace and his chief accountant had figured.

"It could seem a little strange to you now, but once you get your induction—," Horace began.

"I've had my induction," Matthew interrupted. "Permanent stripes over my back. Let me ask you one question, does freedom mean that free Negroes will be able to work at the Kerr shipyard?"

Horace squashed his cigar in an alabaster ashtray and folded his chubby fingers together in the style of a high boss.

"The first time I give a Negro a job at Dutchman's Hook, the Irish workers, thinking I freed the slaves to get cheaper labor, will riot. God knows how many Negroes will be killed, lynched, burned out, whatnot. I am freeing your people to say that Horace Kerr believes in the Union, and Baltimore and Maryland must remain in the Union."

"What are your true reasons, Mr. Kerr?"

"This war is being engaged to preserve the United States. As time passes, it will take on the real and most powerful meaning, abolishing slavery in America. Bear in mind, white boys are dying on the battlefield every day and the scars will take years, decades, to heal and can only be healed by the cooperation of enlightened men."

"The white boys who are dying for the Union hate us."

Horace Kerr had never seen a fiercer negotiator. The stink of slavery would not conveniently flow away on the next tide. The time has come to quit the bullshit, he thought.

Horace's eyes teared. "I need you, Matthew, and Daisy needs Laveda."

Matthew was stunned. He never believed such words would find their way out of a white man's belly. Horace played his ace.

"If you stay, I will hire the finest teacher money can buy for the exclusive job of tutoring you."

"Every day?"

"Every day."

"Laveda as well?"

"Yes."

"You must be doing this for your own purposes."

"You're damned right," Horace agreed.

"What do you want?" Matthew asked.

"I'll give you the help you need. Learn what there is to learn. Only one thing I'd ask is when I call all the folks together, I'd like you and Laveda standing at our side so they'll know this isn't a trick."

"I won't do that."

"Why the fuck not?"

"What you are giving us may not exactly be slavery, but it won't exactly be freedom, either. You may be exchanging systems because slavery is bound to die. What you're giving us may only be slavery by another name and four dollars a month."

No use railing, Horace told himself. He knew he'd only touched the tip of their suffering. He'd better not lose Mr. Fancy.

"I agree," Horace capitulated. "How old are you, Matthew?"

"Twenty-five."

"Huh," Horace mumbled. "Would you care for a drink?"

"I sure wouldn't mind."

Horace did not spare his finest Napoleon brandy. Something wild and incredible, something monumental, was unfolding, and he thanked God Matthew Fancy was with him.

"Anything you need or want, right off?"

"Yes."

Horace nodded for him to continue.

"When we are in private, you and Mrs. Kerr can address Laveda and me by our first names, provided we may address you by your first names. When we are in the company of others, we wish to be addressed as Mrs. Fancy and Mr. Fancy."

Gulp!

Horace arose and very slowly extended his hand. "Mr. Fancy," he said.

Matthew took his hand. Both of them stared at the handshake.

"Thank you, Horace," Matthew said.

❧ 15 · ❧

WILLOW

Matthew Fancy bolted off the starting line and never looked back. Horace Kerr was entirely pleased by his own keen judgment. Matthew's capacities broadened on a daily basis and brought about a painless transition.

By the time of the Emancipation Proclamation, the Kerrs had gained a reputation for being compassionate and farsighted in freeing their slaves early, though they personally had ended up as the true beneficiaries of their decision.

A decent executive from the shipyard, Mr. Compton, had been brought in to assist Fancy, but in truth, Fancy needed no assistant. By the end of the war, Matthew all but managed Inverness.

He became the "man," the buyer who filtered all bids, read all household contracts, and ordered everything from French wines to grass seed, and did so without corruption. When he had deflated the Leamington budget by a third, he pressed Kerr into a salary raise for the entire staff until they became the best-paid domestic help in Baltimore. No day's end ever found Matthew Fancy away from his studies.

One night nine years into the relationship, Kerr brought home a contract that had been drawn up between his shipyard and an insurance company and asked Matthew to scrutinize it. It was a jigsaw puzzle. Fancy's legal mind proved far beyond the ordinary.

Kerr offered him a closet-sized office at Dutchman's Hook with its own sink and toilet so he could be kept on hand as an adviser, but Matthew refused and did the work at his own desk at Inverness.

This was fine with Horace. If Fancy had come to the yard, it would have been under the subterfuge of being a personal butler or such. As it was, Horace had painted a nice anonymous background so no adversary saw or heard Fancy—but surely they felt him.

Never with a title, never at board or banking meetings, and never in a courtroom, Matthew was shifted, as if by sleight of hand, from slavery to Jim Crow, almost unnoticed until . . .

. . . the Baltimore and Ohio Railroad came to Matthew Fancy to retain him as a consultant on a major right-of-way controversy.

This shook Kerr, immeasurably. Unless Mr. Fancy were given a title and a contract, Horace could not forbid him from taking outside work. To do so would be to lose him. The B&O retainer was soon followed by a Who's Who of Maryland industries—importers, distillers, insurance companies.

It was all done without public note.

Matthew Fancy's lifelong agenda was now able to come into play. From the beginning, he had spent hours showing Daisy how the operation worked, and she seemed to come out of a lifelong intellectual stupor. Daisy came to enjoy her expanding knowledge . . . and power. She was, at last, becoming the mistress of Inverness.

Matthew set about training an executive staff, half black, half white, giving Daisy further decision-making ability. Matthew promised to always remain in a supervisory post so Daisy knew she had backup, and she grew quite comfortable with her supervisory duties.

*   *   *

For several years, Matthew traveled to Washington on a bimonthly basis to lecture at the Howard University Law Department, the first Negro institution of its kind in America.

And now, to be free, at last.

He moved off the Inverness grounds to a small colony of successful Negroes in Skerryton. They had a lovely modern home, and in its rear, he opened a legal consulting firm, manned by two Negro apprentices from Howard University. None held legal certification, but they were sought out by the mighty and the lowly alike.

Giving more and more corporate work to his staff over time, Matthew plunged into a salt mine of labor, taking case after case pro bono to define the rights of former slaves.

Between Inverness, his wealthy clients, and a never-ending line of the disenfranchised petitioning him, it happened. He worked himself to death by heart attack in his late thirties.

There was never the likes of his funeral. Horace Kerr walked in the cortege behind Matthew's mule-driven coffin, undraped by any flag, with two other white dignitaries and a thousand blacks.

Matthew Fancy was short remembered outside of Inverness. He left no landmark legal decisions, no righteous speeches, no promising sermons. He was just beginning to do what he wanted and too soon died, doing it.

When all the accounts were settled, it was learned that Fancy had given every penny of his earnings to help former slaves. He left a pregnant wife and a great deal of debt.

Horace Kerr paid off the Fancys' mortgage and pensioned Laveda with a touch of magnanimity, including some shipyard stock, which would see her through her days in comfort.

Matthew Fancy never really left Inverness. His ghost dwelled in one of the closets in the long corridor and the memory of him infected Horace Kerr's days.

During her husband's tenure at Inverness, Laveda played a role nearly as major as his own. While assisting Daisy in the day-to-day running of the home, Laveda also became the nanny to the first two Kerr heirs, Emily and Upton. Twelve years passed until Daisy became pregnant a third time.

During the years that the Kerrs had their children, Laveda had four miscarriages and no children. A recurring disaster seemed to strike her at the beginning of her second trimester and she'd miscarry.

The best white doctor, Daisy's own, examined Laveda but could only speculate on her problem. There was something in Laveda's internal makeup that would not allow the womb to hold the fetus in place to full term.

Daisy had gone into her fourth month without problem when Laveda confided she was pregnant again and desperate to save this child.

A month later, Matthew Fancy died.

When Matthew was set down in the Negro cemetery in Skerryton, Laveda was brought back to Inverness, where she could be given bedrest and constant attention.

This fit into Horace Kerr's scheme of things. He certainly owed that much to the late Matthew Fancy. Moreover, Horace was constantly trying to convince God that he was truly sorry about slavery. Laveda was installed in the finest of the servants' quarters, an apartment belonging to a departed chief butler.

Amanda Kerr was born first, followed in two months by the screaming, healthy Willow. Laveda was the nanny of one of them, the mother of the other, and wet nurse to both.

The girls played in the same playpen, napped in the same crib, and nursed from the same black breasts. In the germless isolation of Inverness, no special attention was paid, at first. After all, in the old days, many white owners' children grew up with slaves as friends, until they were trained to consider them differently. In almost all cases, the friends came to learn that the black friend was there only to serve the white friend.

Daisy allowed Laveda a fairly free hand to run things, fearing that otherwise she might leave. Horace was a bit twisted about the matter, but it was women's business, so long as peace prevailed in his kingdom.

However, his concern soon deepened. He became disturbed when Willow spoke or acted as if she did not know her place or when he saw Amanda at home among the Negroes. The longer the situation went on, the worse it grew.

A growing number of awkward moments came when the girls needed to be separated on social occasions. They sensed and learned where the lines had been drawn, yet remained inseparable friends, believing most of the world was rather silly.

One day, a realization hit Horace like a bombshell. He was reading the paper on the veranda in his rocker, with the girls playing nearby. Horace blinked, shocked that Willow was so bright, actually better with words and keener with logic than Amanda. He observed Willow for several days and realized she was as intelligent as her late father.

How could this be? Wasn't Matthew Fancy the exception ... for *all* Negroes? It was not so, then. Fancy's daughter was the brightest child he had ever seen. Good Lord, what could such a thing mean?

Separation, here and now, was in order. Horace came up with a splendid idea. Daisy was interviewing tutors so Amanda could begin her proper education.

At the same time he had a one-room school set up for the half-dozen Negro children on the estate. The two girls might fuss in the beginning over their separation, but it would soon become normal for Willow and Amanda to go to their own teachers.

Amanda was nearing seven when she was advised of this by her father. That night, she and Willow disappeared. Though desperate, Horace did not want to bring the authorities in too soon for fear it would trigger a scandal, but an all-night search proved fruitless.

The girls had run as far as their legs would carry them, then climbed up a tree and clung to each other.

By dawn's light, bloodhounds were brought in, damned good

trackers, the heirs of sires and bitches who had run down a thousand runaway slaves.

Amanda and Willow were soon found, still on the manor grounds, two miles from the main house. The dogs clawed at the trunk of the tree where the girls were hidden, and yowled crazily. When the hounds were removed, the girls threatened to hurl themselves to the ground from thirty-five feet.

By late afternoon, hunger and fear had overtaken them and some firemen were able to snatch them and safely bring them down.

Amanda was placed in her apartment, doors and windows guarded. She locked herself in a closet and refused to come out. The door was broken down, she was dragged out, restrained, then force-fed.

As quickly as the food and water was put into her, she'd spit it out. By the third night, Amanda lay quite ill and listless, but her will was unbroken.

Amanda was only the second person ever to make Horace Kerr totally capitulate. Matthew Fancy had been the first. Horace allowed that the girls could be tutored together.

Amanda stood fast for her freedom, and was a clever and stubborn force when provoked. An armistice prevailed. Horace was having enough problems with his failing relationships with Emily and Upton.

Daring her father as she became a teenager, Amanda carved out a second life, studying art, music, and poetry away from Inverness in the small but thriving cultural salons of Baltimore and Washington. She was often in the company of writers and intellectuals, many tilting toward the "bohemian."

A long time had passed since Amanda climbed that tree with Willow, but Horace Kerr was not blessed with a short memory. He yielded reluctantly to her whims, always aware that someday there had to be a showdown.

For the time being, his Pinkertons shadowed Amanda whenever she left the grounds. Amanda made a sport out of ducking them.

By sixteen, she was extremely composed, extremely beautiful, and extremely mature. She fit in well in her lively circles.

Back to the affairs of Inverness, the Baltimore Cotillion was coming up. Daisy prepared for the high social season and even flirted with the idea of having Amanda make her presentation in both Baltimore and Washington.

That would triple the juicy intrigue, but the idea bogged down when Amanda refused to select an escort. Amanda knew all the eligibles, but the only true desirables were far outside of the intrigues of Inverness.

Willow Fancy would also have a presentation, a small and limited black imitation-white cotillion in Skerryton. At least she and Amanda could prepare certain things together. They'd be lonely for each other on their big nights, but separation had now become a more common occurrence.

To swear eternal friendship, they pricked each other's finger and sucked each other's bloody fingertip.

Willow and Amanda were having a fitting in Amanda's apartment. Their white silk gowns were near matching. Weren't they the only sane ones in the world? The black and white of it had gotten them rocking with laughter as they stood before the long mirror while the dressmaker pinned them, when Horace entered behind a single knock.

"Get these fucking niggers out of my home!" The words were never spoken but his expression said everything.

Laveda left Inverness, forever. Willow was deeply scarred. Amanda was placed under lock and key again, and this time she felt compelled to eat and drink to keep herself alive and keen of mind.

The siege of Inverness wore on. Daisy became frantic that Amanda still had no escort. Horace quit his raving and became frighteningly calm. He sent out urgent word to his Washington office, which quickly found and hired the penniless son of a Scottish earl who earned his keep doing a royalty charade as a fill-in at secondary embassies and parties. Horace's move was kept secret.

In fact, it would create quite a stir when Amanda appeared with such a "catch" on her arm.

The days ticked on. When Amanda did not appear at the first of the precotillion affairs, Daisy pleaded with Horace. Forty-eight hours before the debut, Amanda was brought to her father's apartment.

He was icy.

"What is it you want, Amanda?"

"An apology to Laveda and Willow."

"That has already been made, many days ago. What else?"

Ah now, those eyes of Amanda Kerr glared point-blank into the eyes of Horace Kerr.

"Go on," he said.

Her voice shook, not from fear but with determination. "I want to be able to leave Inverness without being spied upon and be with friends of my own making."

"I will grant that so long as you are escorted by a proper male who can defend you."

"An escort of my own choosing, Father. If you don't find him welcome in the house, I shall meet him at the gate."

"And be home at a decent hour?"

"Yes."

"You will keep out of trouble?"

"You will have to trust me, Father."

"I'll promise that," he said, "in exchange for your promise to carry out your social responsibilities to Inverness and to the family."

Horace felt the acid glow in his belly, stood, and clasped his hands behind him. Although his relationship with his other daughter and son had been extremely bad, he had never given in to them.

"Well?"

"I agree," she answered.

"Due to the lateness of the hour and the urgency of the situation, I have brought in a neutral party of sufficient heritage to escort you to your presentation. Lord Dunsmore."

She cracked a wee smile. "Yes, that's fine, he's harmless."

"See your mother now, for she's desperate."

"Why did seeing Willow in my room trouble you so much, Father?"

"Certainly you know why. Maybe you don't."

Amanda wasn't going to end it here. "No, I don't," she challenged.

"It just struck me hard seeing you and a black woman dressed in the same silk gowns. I'm a victim of my generation."

"Generations," Amanda said, "centuries."

"I should never have taught Matthew Fancy how to play chess. I loathed the fact that he could pick up inconsistencies in clauses in contracts that had blown right past me and my lawyers. I did not love him. I did, however, give him a great deal of respect and I compensated him very well."

"What price this confession, Father?"

"There is no one else I can speak to of these things but you. I thought surely, Matthew was a total anomaly, like a counting mule. Then I watched Willow grow up alongside you. It eroded my last defense of slavery. I have come to realize that there might be as many smart black people out there as smart white people. I see a fearsome price to be paid. Yet I still harbor bigotry."

"That must be difficult for you to say."

"You are a great heiress, Amanda."

Horace Kerr would always try to craft a bargain. Amanda felt a truce was in place, but one not built on bedrock. The difference of their "reasons" was going to come back time and again. Would he ever truly let her exist beyond Inverness?

After Chesapeake Park—1891—on Butcher's Hill Road
to Inverness

Chesapeake Park and the splendors of the day seemed a long way off.

Amanda was drained from telling the story of the Fancys. Zach seemed stunned, personally affected, as if he had been hit by something. He got down from the carriage and steadied the dandy horse for the trot up the hill. As he relit the lamps, Amanda saw that her Marine was sorely shaken.

Did he really understand about Willow? She believed he did. The loving side of him was what made her swirl.

Certainly no other boy had ever understood. They were all so damned condescending. Only now and again in her circle of artists and writers was there some sort of compassion.

"What's disturbing you, Zach?"

"It's nothing."

"It is something."

He shook his head.

"Is it Willow?"

"No, I think your friendship with her is beautiful."

Her kerchief wiped his brow.

"Zach."

"I have a problem with heights. It struck me strangely, tonight."

"Did you ever have a black friend?"

"Maybe . . ."

He released the brakes and gave the reins a tug and hung on to his haunting secret.

"Will I see you in two weeks?" she asked.

"Yes," he said.

It was a bittersweet end to the glories of the day. They knew they each had a penchant, for better or for worse, for looking into the other's dark corners.

⟨ 16 ⟩

NOW HEAR THIS

1891—a Month Later—USMC Barracks—Washington

When the grid for Washington had been laid out in 1800, President Thomas Jefferson and Marine commandant Major Nicholas took a horseback ride together for the purpose of selecting an area to house the Marines.

A lot was chosen, bounded by Eighth and Ninth and by G and I streets in the southeast part of the grid. The barracks and commandant's house became the oldest building in continuous use in the capital.

Newly remodeled enlisted quarters of 1891 held fifteen-man squad rooms with iron bed frames, hair mattresses, white sheets, blue service blankets, and well-filled pillows. Linen was laundered at government expense.

The Advanced Military Program moved deep into its second year.

Major Ben Boone and navy captain Richard X. Maple were old

friends who had served on the command staff during the Civil War. Both were posted to the Naval War College in Newport when it commenced in 1884.

By 1888, Captain X, as he was known, was promoted to second in command of the United States Naval Academy in Annapolis, largely in charge of curriculum.

While so many of his military peers found the Marine Corps superfluous in times of peace, Maple had always leaned toward keeping it. As the first AMP class was moving to completion, Major Boone had a middle-of-the-night brainstorm. Winning the support of Captain X in this crucial period could mean the difference between the end of the program—and thus the Marines—or a future for his beloved Corps.

Ben came down from Newport regularly to lecture at Annapolis and chewed on Maple's ear until he prevailed on him to bring a group of midshipmen to the Washington barracks for a seminar on the Marines. Maple agreed, reluctantly, to see what AMP had wrought.

Captain Tobias Storm came up with the next unlikely idea. Storm could compare this first AMP class to the cadets he'd trained at his academy in China.

"Ben," Tobias said, "we'll be teaching these sailors ten different classes. I want two or three of them taught by some of my enlisted people."

"Out of your fucking mind, it could be a disaster," Ben retorted strongly.

"AMP was your idea and it has always been your thesis to train every Marine so he can take over for any other Marine."

"Within limits."

"Your Chinese are now the best young officers in Asia and I say these lads here are even better trained. They know artillery from slit trenches."

Ben mulled. Rather a glorious, dangerous idea. Captain X would be in attendance. Some kid could get up in front of a class and start stuttering and blow AMP out of the water. On the other hand . . .

"When are the penguins arriving from Annapolis?"

"In time to see colors on the parade ground today. The Gunny will conduct the first session after evening chow, a he-man's history of the Corps."

"Storm . . . ," Ben whined.

"What's this crap of the last two years been about?"

"God save the Corps," Ben mumbled, surrendering to the idea of enlisted lecturers.

"Excellent decision, Ben."

Early that night, after the midshipmen had partaken of a meal somewhat better than standard Marine fare, they were herded into the big classroom. Major Boone and Captain Maple took seats, inconspicuously, in the rear.

The white-clad peach-fuzzed plebes buzzed a little nervously. They had heard the monster stories about their little sister service and this was a very strange place.

Master Gunnery Sergeant Wally Kunkle entered and barked, "'Ten-shun!"

The midshipmen scrambled to their feet as Captain Storm, now deferring to a walking stick, entered.

"Be seated, at ease, and hear this." The Gunny's voice crackled off the walls. "You people are here to learn as much about the Marine Corps as we can cram into your gullets in the next few days." He went on to point out the stack of binders on each man's desk, state the purpose of AMP, and introduce the commanding officer, Captain Tobias Storm, whose credentials in Asia and the Bering Sea were spellbinding.

"In the next days you will come to know us," Storm said, "and a few of you of sound bodies and unsound minds may even think of a career in the Marines."

Storm flashed a quick smile to Ben Boone and surveyed the thirty-five plebes before him. Christ, he thought, they sure don't look any better than my Chinese cadets. He cleared his throat heartily.

"The United States Marine Corps is the oldest military organ-

ization in our nation, predating the Declaration of Independence."

He had everyone's attention.

"Old enough," he went on, "for me to grow this mustache."

End of merriment. The plebes were settling in comfortably as
Tobias explained the loose confederation of the colonies whose
delegates met in Philadelphia at the Continental Congress.

"There was no standing army. Each colony had its own militia
to deal with policing problems and to keep the Indians at bay.
However, the open sea was a plundering ground for pirates. Moreover, European navies, particularly the English, boarded our
unarmed merchant vessels and impressed our seamen.

"Therefore," he continued, "the Continental Congress of 1774
authorized the formation of a Marine Corps to place armed detach-
ments aboard our merchant ships. The actual covenant was agreed
to in a saloon called Tun's Tavern."

Storm turned the class over to Master Gunnery Sergeant Wally
Kunkle after a fairly stunning introduction and took his own place
in the rear with Ben and Captain X.

Wally Kunkle, showing the effects of much warfare, was not all
that puzzling a selection to begin the seminar. The plebes had
before them a living creature who had been the drummer boy at
Bull Run, and they were enthralled.

The Gunny intoned a literate but salty rundown of Corps history from its swashbuckling days to the storming of the Halls of
Montezuma. The Corps' minor role in the Civil War blockade was
told and the tragedies at Fort Sumter and Fort Fisher were not
omitted.

The middies gathered around the living Gunny at the finish to
get a closer look, perhaps a word, a nod, a handshake.

The next morning, as everyone took their places, Ben Boone could
hear Tobias Storm's belly rumbling in tune with his own. The
coming lecture would be delivered before a judge of high rank,
Richard Maple, and a jury of curious plebes.

"'Ten-shun!" Kunkle cracked. As the midshipmen scrambled to their feet, Private First Class Zachary O'Hara entered. Maple leaned forward, wondering what kind of ambush these lousy Marine bastards had set. The midshipmen were no less astonished.

Captain X looked sternly at Ben and Tobias, but could nearly hear their thoughts: Let us train our people our way for our job and we'll deliver the finest ever seen.

"Now hear this. Private First Class O'Hara will conduct this class. You will accord him the same respect you would accord an officer. Be seated."

A beardless wonder standing before thirty-five other beardless wonders. Zach showed calm presence and poise. He knew what this moment was all about and liked where he stood.

"Anyone here who doesn't know what this is?" he began, pointing to a map of the world behind him that stretched nearly the width of the room. The flitting of doubt that had hopped from plebe to plebe abruptly stopped under the sure tone of his voice.

"As Marines, we take enormous pride in our training and discipline. As the first underclass of AMP, we have also been encouraged to express diverse opinions. We demonize our enemies. They demonize us. It is standard procedure to hate each other in order to be able to obliterate each other. Yet the intelligent officer does not let demonization get in the way of clear thinking. The enemy must also be regarded as a human being as intelligent as you, as courageous, and as believing. Knowing his point of view will enhance your ability to make better decisions."

Zach had grown a beard before their very eyes.

"What we have to examine here now is the probable course America will follow in this decade leading up to the twentieth century. The papers on your desk will give you every point of view in government and military thinking and planning. It's mostly boring reading but relevant."

The room was very quiet now as Zach perched on a high stool and allowed that he could be interrupted at any time for a question.

"Who had fathers and grandfathers in the Civil War?"

Nearly everyone raised a hand, including Captain Maple.

"Their generation has passed since the war. America buried upward of a million dead, the South was a wreck, and the need to heal our most urgent priority . . ."

There was a sudden scratching of pens dipped in inkwells as he went on.

"Before the war we had already annexed Texas and California through force as a national ambition. We justified our expansion on the premise that we were more entitled to the land than was a failing, corrupt European regime . . .

"Today, in 1891, there is no danger from either of our neighbors. There is a strong sense that we will see war no more on continental American soil.

"Therefore, there is no reason to burden ourselves with a huge army. The main mission of the army, led by its magnificent cavalry, has been to subdue the Indian population. Your first binder of papers pertains to the writings of our best minds on the pros and cons of the Indian question. I think it's safe to say that the navy is not going to play a major role in the future of Nevada. However, we do find disturbing parallels between certain views on the Indian question and earlier justifications of slavery, namely the notion that the Indians are subhuman savages incapable of adaptation to our version of civilization. Therefore, it has been reasoned, it is no sin taking them down in battle and herding them onto reservations. There is also a very strong minority opinion that in doing this, we may be setting ourselves up, if not for another Civil War, then for decades of misery."

"Sir!"

"Yes, stand and give your name."

"Midshipman Darlington. What is the Marine Corps' position regarding the Indian question?"

"I've asked my instructors that question," Zach said. "The Marine Corps has no position. America is a democracy, ruled by civilians. There will be many times in every man's life when he disagrees with his government."

"Is there a way that a military officer may recuse himself?"

"No," Zach answered firmly. "You are officers of the Constitution. You must carry out the nation's policies and the law whether you agree or not . . . with the following caveat. If an order is so heinous and against every moral fiber of your being to obey, then you must get out. We hope we will never again find that conscientious objectors outnumber officers of the Constitution."

Jesus, let me think about that, Richard Maple thought. How cleverly the Marine had laid out a controversial thesis. It was becoming heady stuff and the lad was right about one thing. Thank God the navy was not involved with the Indians.

". . . Back to the Civil War, which was our national crossroads. We came out of the war with an obsolete navy ranked fifteenth in the world, behind Austria. During your fathers' generation, wind-driven sailing ships had been vanishing, giving way to powerful vessels of iron, fired by steam. In this period, our factories belched in prosperity, our agricultural abundance became the envy of the world, and our natural resources seemed bottomless. But we have become the victims of our own greatness . . .

"By design or otherwise, a great nation must engage in international trade and commerce. A two-ocean nation must have a two-ocean navy, respected in every port of call . . .

"Let's have a go at this map and focus on the gigantic landmass and geographic location of America. Our size plus our inevitable growth has made us into a world power. Nearly seventy years ago, President Monroe understood that our future included becoming the dominant nation of the hemisphere. The new American navy will carry out the vision of the Monroe Doctrine. What gives us this right? Our hemisphere was colonized and looted by European powers which still control parts of it . . .

"Coming up on history's calendar will be the collapse of the nefarious and corrupt Spanish empire. Unless we have the will and power to impose the Monroe Doctrine, the Europeans will attempt to rush in to fill the vacuum left by this colllapse. We will accept no more expansion in our hemisphere. Hands off. That is the name of the game."

This was digested as Zach went over the British, Dutch, Spanish, Portuguese, French, Swedish, and Danish incursions and possessions.

"Outside of this hemisphere, there exist choke points where a navy is the vital player. What are some of them?"

"Gibraltar," a midshipman called out.

"Suez."

"Aden."

"Dardanelles."

"Correct," Zach went on, "but we have the choke point to end all choke points." His pointer touched Central America.

"The Isthmus of Panama," he said, "is the most important piece of land for the future commerce and defense of this nation. The isthmus is this thirty-mile strip of land dividing the Atlantic and Pacific oceans and it is the possession of Colombia. The French have gone belly-up attempting to build a canal across the isthmus. We feel that America must step in and try. If there is to be a canal, it must be under our control."

"Mr. O'Hara, doesn't that come directly under the Monroe Doctrine?"

"We believe it does. In your fourth binder, there are papers detailing our case. I think that the most compelling justification is that for an American ship to go from the East Coast to the West Coast, it must make a fearsome voyage of up to fifteen thousand miles around Cape Horn, a passage known as sailing from hell. The canal would be a priority for our national self-interest."

"But, sir, would that not make us an imperialistic nation?"

"Well, let's see," Zach answered. "Colombia owns the isthmus, but Colombia is unable to govern itself. That becomes a threat to our future."

He pointed out a number of military and political arguments regarding spheres of influence.

"Democracies, of a kind similar to our own, are going to be very, very slow to emerge from Spanish America, which includes Brazil, all built on the backs of slaves. America's hands are far from clean when it comes to this issue. We will support democratic movements where we can, but we are also going to be dealing with dictatorships, self-styled liberators in the mountains, religiously dominated governments, bandits. We will knock bridges down. We will build police forces and put bridges up. Sure, we're going to bet on the wrong horse some of the time, but America must be the main force of stability as well as a protector from future foreign intervention.

". . . Let's take a look at the Pacific. The British, Dutch, Germans, and Portuguese are all over the place. Japan is an emerging imperial power, casting her eye toward the Philippines and Hawaii. That means we will need forward bases, coaling stations, dry docks, and friendly treaties all over the planet."

"Sir, what about our future relationship with England?"

"Yes, England. We've had our shakedown cruises with the British in the Revolution and the War of 1812 as well as dealing with much British sympathy with the Confederacy. We have evolved to realize that, in many ways, England is our most natural ally, as much or more so than the French, without whom we could not have won our independence. The bottom line is this: Both England and America will benefit far more from an alliance than from an adversarial relationship. We need them, they need us. You will see close cooperation in the future, and, we believe, we will never go to war with England again."

"But, Mr. O'Hara, England is by far the greatest colonizer. Won't we be just like them, sort of picking up some of their droppings?"

"We share a common language, common heritage, and many common bonds, but there is a difference. America is different from any nation created in the history of man.

"More powerful than fourteen-inch naval guns and stronger than any massive army is the unique place America holds in the minds of man. We won our freedom with ideas more powerful than arms. We set a precedent in the eyes of the world by daring to engage in a bloody civil war because of an ideal. We enter the new world not so much to plunder, to crush people, or to rule . . . All mankind whispers our name . . . America . . . with reverence. So long as we maintain our basic human decency, the world will behold us as the keeper of man's most noble flame."

When all was said and done, Major Ben Boone gave the final lecture, and it was a rouser.

". . . There is a national military imperative that separates the Marine Corps from all other services. We will need a unique body of men at the ready on both coasts, aboard our naval vessels and stationed wherever we fly a flag . . . a unique force, small, highly skilled, and enormously dedicated, that will be able to move on a moment's notice to any trouble spot in the world. Further, this force will continue to develop a hybrid skill, establishing a doctrine for amphibious warfare. The United States Marines has grown into its future role. If we had no Corps today, we'd have to invent one tomorrow."

All the lessons of the AMP seminar were brought to a delicious boil as the President's Own Marine Band marched down the barracks parade ground before Captain Maple and the midshipmen.

Formed nearly a century earlier, at the end of the Revolution, from the remnants of the fife-and-drum lads, the band had inducted a group of Italian musicians to fill in its ranks. The commandant assessed every Marine officer ten dollars to buy instruments for the band.

The President's Own debuted at the inauguration of John Adams, the second president, on the lawn of the new presidential mansion, later to be known as the White House. They played at Gettysburg when Lincoln delivered his famous address.

They played the hell out of it this day. John Philip Sousa and his lion-tamer-red-uniformed men struck up "Semper Fidelis" as they passed the review stand, a moment never to be forgotten.

In their grand lacquered, ebony-furnished home, with its mandarin-red-and-gold drapes, the Storms held an informal reception and dance where the plebes were seduced by their first experience of Chinese cooking. Beer was served judiciously. Marines of the AMP came with their girlfriends, provided their girlfriends brought an extra girl for a middie.

Captain Storm held down a table on the garden lawn with Major Boone and Captain X.

"You have thoroughly charmed my men," Maple said. "A number of them have already inquired about service in the Corps."

"And what did you tell them?" Ben asked.

"I told them these past four days were pastry. Get up at four-thirty in the morning and drill with these sons of bitches till midnight just one day and you'll need no further convincing to remain in the navy."

Tobias and Ben smiled, cats licking their chops.

"Your instructors are pretty blunt," Maple said. "Has Commandant Ballard attended any of these classes?"

Tobias scratched his jaw. "He kind of gives us a wide berth."

"He should. Some of what was said was borderline treason."

"He knows what we're up to."

"I must say I was impressed by that O'Hara kid," Maple said.

"You know who he is," Ben said.

"Yeah, I know, Paddy O'Hara's son. Those words, I'll remember them." Richard Maple pressed his fingers together, closed his eyes, and tried to remember. " 'A great new emerging world power need not invoke fear among nations so long as it remains guided by a noble idea.' "

"Fucking poetry," Tobias said.

"He's a pretty good kid," Ben agreed cautiously, for he sensed a little quid pro quo coming up.

"Any chance that if I sent over two or three promising plebes to take your next AMP course in its entirety, I might chat with O'Hara?"

"Somewhat less than none," Storm answered.

"We'll shoot him first," Ben added.

"How long before you complete this first AMP course?" Maple pressed.

"It's our initial class. We don't know exactly what our cutoff date is. A second group is being formed now, at least on paper."

"Where are your people going to be stationed when they graduate?"

"About half of them haven't had sea duty. They'll automatically have to do a cruise aboard ship," Storm said. "O'Hara hasn't done sea duty yet."

"And you know how hard we're fighting to keep Marines aboard the ships," Ben added quickly.

The near-empty gin-and-tonic glasses were given short shrift when reinforcements arrived. Maple realized he wasn't going to budge them.

"All right, you bastards," Captain X said, "I want to bring the entire upper class of midshipmen over here for the same seminar. Satisfied?"

"Are you satisfied?" Ben asked.

"You're mavericks, both of you. Some of your zeal needs to be tempered, but your case is infallible. You see our future with clarity. You speak the truth and I have to support you. Try to make it a little easier for me."

Maple looked up to see Zachary O'Hara approaching with Beth Shaughnessy between him and Corporal Varnik.

"Excuse me, sirs," Zachary said.

"Yes?"

"My best buddy, Corporal Varnik, and his sweetheart, Beth Shaughnessy. Varnik and I don't waltz very well, Captain Maple, and she wondered if you would do her the honor of a dance."

"The honor would be mine," Captain X said gallantly.

The band resumed and Maple whisked Beth to the dance floor with dash.

"O'Hara, how the hell did you know waltzes were coming up next?" Storm asked suddenly.

"I requested them from Warrant Officer Sousa," Zach answered.

❦ 17 ·❧

EMILY

Three Weeks Later—Inverness

When shadows crossed Emily's apartment, it gave Horace a bit of the shivers. A purplish hue and blinking lights from the dancing aspen leaves outside and the medicinal smell, not unlike an undertaker's, all made him uneasy.

Emily sat in the purple light, hair knotted tight, pallid, grown spinsterishly ugly. The eyes were glazed now. She wandered, *pitpat*, this that. A giggle.

The nurse indicated to Horace that Emily was very tired from the visit and he'd best go.

"Good-bye, Emily," Horace said.

She looked at him curiously, then held up her hand to be patted and kissed.

"We will see each other again soon, Emily."

"Yes, it's Mother's birthday, or is it Upton's . . . I have a new dress. Miss Lowry thinks I'll be quite able to attend the party."

When Horace closed the door behind him, he leaned against the wall and wiped the perspiration from his upper lip, then scrambled to get a cigar going. Its aroma followed him out of the seldom-visited north wing.

He found his way to his upstairs parlor, slumped into his leather armchair, and one more time sailed through the litany of justifications.

No one could accuse him of being an unloving or indifferent father. Emily was his firstborn. She had come at a splendid time, although, truth be known, and he never showed it openly, he was miffed that the firstborn had been a girl. No damned way to start a dynasty, but what the hell, this was only the beginning of child siring.

Horace was a jolly father, joker, bearer of gifts for Emily. Dinners were pleasant, as were social engagements. The family, bumblers though they were, could be great fun.

When did the drift begin? With Daisy? With Emily? Horace and Daisy were an exemplary couple, altogether civilized, settling into both married life and times apart, in the traditional mold. They continued to share a bed, and soon enough, Daisy was pregnant again.

She lost that one, and another, before his prince was born. A male was on the scene and the Kerr name secure.

Yet sweet Emily was a precious child to be fussed over. However, it was soon apparent that she would be exceedingly plain and even dull-witted. The Kerrs were all handsome people, sturdy blond Scottish Celts. There was mumbo jumbo in the Blanton line. Yes, Daisy's mother and grandmother were rather plain women. That would certainly account for Emily.

Emily's plainness seemed to express itself by a growing shyness. The more shy she became, hiding behind the skirts, the more shovels full of attention she required. It was a bottomless pit, with attention barely soothing her hurt of the moment.

Horace grew fidgety over the whole business and tried to bully his way through to her, while Daisy heaped on the art of coquetry, obedience, and awareness of the splendor of her family and heritage. Emily played the piano fairly well, her only smidgen of talent. The one place she could communicate as the center of the family was at a sing-along.

But Horace Kerr wanted more lively songs and not all those Stephen Foster moanings about 'tater fields and dead massahs.

Emily's fingers began to strike off notes, which never failed to bring a remark of displeasure. "God, child, you've played it a thousand times. You'd think you'd be getting it right."

Sing-alongs about the piano, no matter how well intended the participants, always ended now with sour notes. With each new endeavor, the girl felt it was going to end in failure . . .

As when Emily fell off her pony three times in the practice ring and Horace slammed her back into the saddle and only stopped when Laveda Fancy carried off the child, who was screaming hysterically, while Daisy said nothing.

. . . And Emily's tutoring went slowly, nerve-rackingly. She developed a stutter, triggered most often by her finger-pointing father.

Daisy remained passive and compliant, even as she knew her daughter was going to be a limp limb on that proud family tree.

Daisy created a daily routine that would satisfy Horace, mainly through permitting him to avoid Emily. When Emily's weeping and Horace's outward frustrations had been dulled, one and all made themselves believe that Inverness was in shipshape.

Required to attend a minimum of social events, the girl used calculated loneliness as a shield from all that bouncing business out there beyond her apartment and beyond Inverness. Loneliness meant peace among dolls who could not talk back.

When Emily's fifteenth birthday clicked on past, Daisy Kerr came face-to-face with the unpleasant truth: In another year, her daughter's cotillion was coming up. It would be no easy task to obtain an escort of note or rank, or any escort, for that matter.

Nonetheless, the cotillion had strong meaning, far beyond the walls of Inverness, and Daisy, in order to save unbearable humiliation, had to fish around at the bottom of the barrel.

The Sheldon Jollys were a family of tattered aristocrats who had fled Georgia after the Civil War, settled in Baltimore, and were able to get in, just on the fringe of proper circles.

The melody of the Old South flowed from Sheldon Jolly's mouth, as did the scent of bourbon. As a lawyer he served a useful role in the movement of funds of questionable origin and cargoes of goods that had circumvented customs taxation. Whatever a man had to do to live a proper life, he did. By God, he even elbowed his way into a number of clubs, to find kindling for his fires.

Norbert Jolly, Sheldon's son of eighteen, had gathered enough ne'er-do-well charm to get in under the wire with less demanding young ladies. He was prevailed upon to become Emily's escort.

Emily and Norbert, in tails slightly tattered, were among the last to enter the cotillion ballroom. A pair of Pinkertons and their wives watched their every breath while Horace Kerr looked over his shoulder to make certain that Jolly did not make any unwonted efforts to show himself as a pretender to the throne.

They caught Emily's burst of hysteria and confusion in time to whisk her out of the ballroom and save Horace public humiliation.

Emily Blanton Kerr lost whatever she had been hanging on to and woke up in a netherworld and was placed in quasi exile in the cold north wing of Inverness.

After Horace's visit to Emily's quarters, Daisy came to their upstairs parlor with a drink long and strong enough to take the enamel off his teeth. He sipped and he sighed. He had tried to see Emily every fortnight, more or less, but knew going to the north wing and coming out of it would fill him with futile sorrow. He never wished Emily dead, of course.

"How was it today?" Daisy asked perfunctorily.

"Emily is trying to get up for a birthday party. She doesn't realize that it is her own birthday. She'll be thirty-two years old."

"We can have a family gathering," Daisy said. "Some of her cousins will come as well as her uncles."

"That's about all they're good for," he mumbled.

Horace stood and walked to the large bay window, from which he could see the stables. He was certain he saw Amanda and held a pair of field glasses to his eyes. There she was with that bloody Marine! Horace would never get used to the men's-cut riding britches that Amanda had had tailored for herself. No sidesaddle rider, she. There was a magnificent new Arabian stallion being broken in the ring. Huh, she'd be riding him in short order.

Actually Horace got a kick out of it when Amanda invited a young man to ride with her, then scared the hell out of him. She was a wild rider. Well, what the hell . . . what the hell.

"What the hell," he said, "Amanda is riding old Banjo and she's putting that O'Hara person on Miss Godiva. Those two nags only have three good legs between them."

"Perhaps they are just in for a pleasant canter, my dear. Doesn't always have to be a cavalry charge, you know."

"And maybe she doesn't want to bruise O'Hara's pride with a real horse." He grunted, then grunted again. In addition to her riding britches, Amanda wore a floaty silk blouse with the top button open. Hardly a proper habit.

"Men's britches," he said, setting the glasses down.

"I wish I could have ridden that way."

"Why? Sidesaddle is perfectly lovely."

"Well, Horace, the britches could well tickle her fancy!"

"Daisy, bite your tongue." He walked away, then snatched up the little pillow Emily had given him. "Where the hell did Emily get this garish thing? Chesapeake Park with a hoochie-koochie dancer."

"Amanda gave it to her. She sees her sister every few days. I'm certain her Marine beau won it for her at the amusement park."

"Her beau! I'll beau him!" He sighed massively. "You said at breakfast there was something we had to talk about."

"It will hold," Daisy teased deliberately. "You are quite upset now."

"Don't do that!" he demanded.

"Thad Vanderbilt has accepted Clara Lustgarten's invitation to the Constitution."

"What! That German cow! What the hell do the Vanderbilts want with the Lustgarten brothers' breweries?"

"Well, don't ask me, Horace, but the Vanderbilts were the most important family left who had a male available."

Horace drank in the meaning of her words. The Constitution was still weeks and weeks off, but the hens were picking off the stud roosters at a fearsome rate. The Lustgarten brothers were inconsequential in the larger scheme of things, but they were shrewd operators. They had plugged both ends of the Mississippi River with a variety of breweries under different names, then collected every stop on the river. It was a classic monopoly. Could the Vanderbilts be fronting, let's say, a dummy brewery to open in, say, Kansas City?

"Well, Daisy, who is left? Any of the Newport scene?"

"The pickings are getting rather slim, but I have a notion or two. There's no need to panic yet."

"To hell! She's on the verge of staging another of her tantrums. That goddamned Marine."

"Amanda and Private O'Hara are about to crash into a stone wall. I'd wager it must be weighing heavily on their minds today. Horace! Don't make a bull's rush. I know Amanda will come to you."

⟢ 18 ⟢

ELYSIAN

At the Same Time—Deep in the Woods of Inverness

Amanda and Private O'Hara's ride was altogether pleasant. She had left the sporting horses home. Old Banjo and Miss Godiva had senior status, so Zach was spared her usual flaming romp.

They came to a confluence of three streams. Old Banjo took a drink, picked out the right stream, and followed it to a wall of thick brush. The wily critters inched their way through as their riders lay down over their necks.

A passage opened. An uphill climb in pebbly water to a sudden glade, pond, and bank, and free and happy flowers and mystic-scented magnolia and willow branches cascading to the water.

They leaped from their horses and rushed together in a fevered embrace . . . never let her go, never let him go. He lifted her up on her toes and twirled her about, both of them light-headed from the surge of rapture and mumbled "oh Gods" and "hold me's" and "Amanda" and "Zach" and as they called each other's name like angels' kisses.

They had reached Elysian.

It took a time of holding before they'd dare part so they could behold each other, then they touched foreheads, held hands, and let the moment consume them.

With a sudden burst of exuberance Zach let out a cry of joy and dove into the pond and threw water into his face. Amanda followed him, kicked water on him, and he flung himself bodily into the pond again and she flung herself atop him and they rolled around and around like two porkers in mud heaven.

The kisses were soaked as he pulled her to her feet, flung her over his shoulder, and scrambled up the bank. She fell to her knees and wrapped her arms around his knees and she called his name over and over.

Zach looked down at the beauty and what rushed through him now near caved him in. He backed away, telling himself to stop now before his power to resist had flown.

They said something, both of them, about going slowly mad during the absence, about counting minutes, about . . . Now they stared curiously at each other, rather dumbfounded . . .

"I love you, Zach."

His mouth trembled and his voice went awry. "I love you, Amanda."

"I love you, Zach. I never knew that any such person as a Zachary O'Hara existed in this world."

They sat and he held his head in his hands, repeating words he had never spoken. "I love you," he said, and got a bit silly and mimicked himself, "I love you."

Now that, Amanda Kerr, was a real confession by a real man, a Marine man, a man who never existed before. They spoke nonsense for a while, using the conversation to give themselves time to allow what was happening to sink in.

The urge came on them to pour themselves into each other and they clung and slowly became the victims of what they had declared.

They could hold each other until dark like this, but sooner or later they had to come out of the woods, and this knowledge began to scratch at their passion like hard chalk against a blackboard.

Old Banjo, who had whiled many lonely hours here with Amanda, got his nose between them. Amanda opened a saddlebag, shared with Zach a towel to clean off some, then spread a blanket.

"The beauty of it here is overwhelming," he said.

"Old Banjo and I come up here every so often to meditate. He's a thinking man's horse."

Amanda had dried herself, but her blouse remained damp and clinging. Zach stared until he had to lower his eyes.

"When Banjo was younger we'd race through the lower meadow, go off the trail, and jump the fences and ditches and climb rocks so I could shake off father's Pinkertons. I happened on this place. The Pinkertons never found it."

He wanted to ask her about how many boys she had lured into the glade but dared not. She wanted to tell him she had never told a boy that she loved him before this, but she dared not.

Realizing there would be pain in the words ahead, each floundered. There could be no way to make this tender. He was anchored, anchored hard to the notion that he was not going to do her harm.

"I guess we've got some things to figure out," he said at last.

She nodded and watched the wildness of the moment transform itself into one tinged with dread.

Zach said the ancient Marine words: "I'll be shipping out soon."

"How long?"

"Another two or three weeks of classes, and then there's no way of knowing."

"Two or three months maybe?" she asked.

"It's possible. The scuttlebutt is that officers and men who have done sea duty will receive landside posts. The rest of us will do a tour aboard ship."

"How long does that last?" she asked shakily.

"Maybe a year."

"Longer?"

"Sometimes."

A clutch of panic seized her.

"It's a ways off, thank God," she said, "but my family always goes to Newport for the summer. If you're still here, I'll get out of Newport and come to Washington to be with you."

"I wanted you so badly I didn't give much thought of how love was going to fit in with the rest of my life."

"Father has a suite at the Willard Hotel—"

"I'm lying," Zach interrupted. "I haven't been thinking of anything else."

"Zach, we will have time together."

"This is a stupid time for a stupid love that should not have started in the first stupid place, and I'm the one who pushed it . . ."

Amanda clenched her fists and shook. Zach steadied her, then withdrew his touch. She groped . . . "What about Beth and Varnik?"

"He's done his sea duty and he's due for a promotion to sergeant. He'll get a post on a base."

"What about them?" Amanda demanded.

"What the hell do they have to do with us?"

"Ten minutes ago," she cried, "you and I said to each other the most beautiful words I've ever spoken or heard."

"I shouldn't have taken advantage of you," he said.

"Don't you know, I took advantage of you?" she answered. "I have been thinking as well," she continued. "I am asking you to take me to the Constitution Ball."

"Amanda, I'm going far away for a long time."

"No one can force me to love anyone else."

"I don't want to return from overseas and fight my way into a tower, then climb the circular stairs two at a time and burst into your cell . . . and there is the skeleton of Amanda, chained to the wall in the company of tower rats."

"The Constitution Ball is a meat market, just like Butcher's Hill here used to be. Maybe it will take more courage to show up with me than you have."

"I hope that when the time comes," Zach said, "and I'm sent into battle, I'll be my da's son. To show courage simply for the sake of showing courage by falling on my sword would make me an idiot."

"I have the courage to declare our love before the whole world and their meat market."

"Can we talk about this sanely?"

"Of course," Amanda snapped.

"My love for you is as strong as I am capable of at this moment. I don't know how much I love you, but I know I love you enough not to let you piss your life away. Public humiliation of Horace Kerr is war by any name. Tainting your reputation for the rest of your life by gossipmongers is unacceptable. And, my arrogance would mortify the Marine Corps."

She didn't like the way he was glaring at her, probing for compassion, or was he seeing another Amanda?

"I thought I had a man with the courage to declare our love publicly. That is the only way we can make it stand. You've spoken about my father and the Corps. Everyone except you and me. How can it work, Zach?"

"Then write me an ending that isn't tragic. There can be no fool greater than one leading a cavalry charge without a horse."

"Take me, Zach," she demanded.

He wanted to say something about defending her honor, his honor, the Corps' honor, Horace Kerr's honor. But there was something grinding at him from her.

Who was that speaking from inside her? Was she truly that deeply in love or hopelessly infatuated or . . .was this the rage of a spoiled heiress holding her breath till she got what she wanted despite the ruination she would wreak?

"How much of this," Zach said, fearing her answer, "has to do with loving me and how much of it has to do with using me as a pawn in this game, this disease, this plague, between you and your father?"

Amanda had never been spoken to this way. She was exposed and startled.

"How much do you want to beat Daddy?"

"I don't know," she mumbled, not meaning to speak.

"I didn't hear you!"

"I don't know!" she screamed. Then there was the long silence that occurs as one mulls over what one has just discovered about oneself. This young man was as powerful as her father. She had never realized the impossibility of her quest. How do we leave these woods now?

"I guess that in whatever ending we choose for our story, there's nothing so sacred as your Corps," she said, trying to give him one last jab with her emotional sword.

"There is something more sacred," he said.

"What?" she challenged.

"What you let me see and touch on our first night in the garden."

This put her back on earth. She arched her back. "What happened in the garden was my needing to discover something and needing an honorable Marine to do the deed. So I found out. Having one's breasts titillated can be rather enjoyable, but it's not the end of the world."

"But it *is* the end of the world!" he said.

"Tits!" she cried. "Is that all you people think of?"

"Pretty much, when we're off duty."

She cupped her breasts angrily. "Tits, the minute you get out of the trenches. Tits and trenches."

"A woman's breasts are the most beautiful creation God ever made. When they are the breasts of Amanda, they're damned near worth dying for."

A hard breeze hit the glade and the limbs all knelt and shook weeping leaves.

So, how do we leave the woods, Amanda? she asked herself. Love him every minute we have left, knowing your heart will be shattered? Run off to San Francisco? Have him desert and follow you? Go to Shanghai? Hear his fifty-year sentence at the court-martial? This man was all and he was not going to bring her to harm.

They had wrung each other dry.

"Let's go back," Zach said.

"You ride old Banjo back. He knows the way home. I need to be alone," she said.

She closed up with nary a word and took her beauty away from his touch. Both of them deeply, deeply wanted her blouse ripped off, but to hell, let damned fools keep their dignity.

She gave a short whistle for the horse, then handed Zach the reins. He mounted.

"I'll be around for a while, unfortunately," he said. "What do you think we ought to do about seeing each other again?"

"It's done," she said.

Zach jabbed old Banjo in the ribs and the horse headed downstream.

"Zach!" she called.

"Aye?"

"Yes, I want to see you again!"

~· 19 ·~

MONOPOLY

One Week Later—Dutchman's Hook

Did Amanda's call mean peace or war? Horace Kerr, an ultimate master of intimidation, was having the tables turned on him. He walked to the boardroom adjoining his office and stood at the high windows looking down on the driveway.

Amanda's carriage passed through the gate. Amanda closed her parasol and accepted the driver's hand to help her out, then disap-
ed into the building.

orace returned to his office and quickly involved himself in
apers on his desk as his secretary, Mr. Allsop, knocked and
ed, with Amanda trailing behind. Horace Kerr wore his best
, his smiling one, and instructed Mr. Allsop to see that they
not to be disturbed.

manda pecked his cheek. He caught a whiff of subtle fresh-
She drifted to the huge bay window behind his desk that
ded a throne's-eye view of the empire.

The iron crane birds hovered over three massive and three smaller dry docks. A slab of molded steel was being slapped into place. Hot rivets were pitched and the blue flames of the welders' torches hissed. A railcar bearing a house-size boiler squealed to a stop.

The noon whistle blasted and the ship's clock in the president's office tolled. Horace's hand instinctively whipped the gold time-piece from his vest pocket. It was noon, three times over.

In a moment, three thousand antlike workers had come off the scaffolding to open corned-beef- and knockwurst-filled lunch boxes.

It grew quiet, outside.

Amanda turned to face her father's office, an American success story complete with a James Whistler oil of his late father. Disposable Angus Kerr, founder of the yard, still held the place of reverence at the altar, as one would have it in a civilized family.

"What's the grand occasion?" he asked.

"Father, I've had some thoughts about the Constitution Ball," she began.

"Oh yes, that. Your mother has kept me abreast of things." His innards roiled.

"I've come to realize how terribly important it is to you."

"Yes, but more so to your mother."

"It is the only Constitution I'll ever attend. I wish it didn't have to be this yearlong girlie-girlie game in a coven of witches."

"That's rather harsh; however, not without merit." He winked. Who among us, he thought, could follow the trail of a conniving female? Horace willed himself calm so as to see all matters coming up with clarity. He'd not blink if his father's portrait fell off the wall. "Your mother has bemoaned the fact that the list of eligible escorts is growing thin."

Her eyes danced about the room. She adored this office and all beyond that lay at her father's feet. "Who among the crown princes is left?" she asked. "Two, three, maybe four, in a stretch. All of them second-rate Forbeses and Astors."

Down came the gauntlet! Here comes the Marine! How many

hundreds of times had he looked over this very desk to men gone dry with fear, unable to speak because their tongues were stuck to the roofs of their mouths?

Imposing such terror, judiciously of course, was what made a great man great. Ultimately, he held all of the candy in his pocket. He warned himself not to explode, even though she was pumping him up with some kind of queer rationalization.

"We are going to have to engage in some very open talk," Amanda said.

"Go on."

She looked beyond him into the yard again. "With the new Vermont class you're laying the hull for in number one dry dock, it will bring Kerr to within a hairbreadth of being the principal builder of warships."

"What are you prattling about, child?"

"I'm putting things on the table that never have been put there before," she said. "Shall I go on?"

He wanted to balk and demand she stop maneuvering him. "Certainly, go on."

"My father is trying to build ships faster than his yard is capable of doing, and in another year or fifteen months, Kerr will have to stop bidding."

Horace straightened up as though he had been whacked, dumbstruck by her sudden ambush. It was a first sighting of a hidden Amanda. Who was she? She'd come in armed to the eyeballs, perhaps after years and years of her own conniving preparations, until the Constitution gave her bargaining power. Listen up, Horace.

"The story goes," she said, "that it was your brilliant stroke to select Dutchman's Hook, because by the beginning of the Civil War, you'd already smelled the future of steel ships and wanted to be in proximity of the Sparrow's Point steel mills."

"And Mother no doubt told you about the Blanton financing."

"Some of it."

"It is far more complex than mother-daughter gossip over tea . . . or witches' brew."

Amanda kept going, refusing to bite at her father's sarcasm.

"What my father needs now is the final, elusive piece of the puzzle to create a Chesapeake monopoly of warships, cargo ships, and passenger ships so every boatyard on the bay will be under contract to him."

"Stop the babble," he said. "You're extremely clever, Amanda, but this goes totally beyond the scope of your comprehension."

"Dutchman's Hook is full up," Amanda continued. "There's no room to expand. Nor will the state of Maryland allow any expansion. The Maryland Select Commission has filed a confidential but strong report that the waste from Kerr and Sparrow's Point could be endangering the oyster and crab beds for commercial fishing."

"Are you going to tell me how you've come upon all this?"

"Matthew Fancy had a shrewd mind and made a very good teacher," she answered.

Horace slowly poured himself a tall glass of water and asked for leave to light a cigar, then sat back, both enchanted and apprehensive. Then he arose, clasped his hands behind him, and walked away, his back to her. She followed him.

"The Kerr balance sheet has a building surplus. Suppose Kerr were to buy out a solid old yard, one that could put Kerr into the cargo- and passenger-ship business in direct competition with Belfast and the River Clyde in Scotland?"

"You have amazed me today," Horace said. "But I've worked my way through all of this for years. There is no such yard, unless I go to sleep tonight with a molar under my pillow and the tooth fairy gives me one."

"There is one in Hampton Roads," Amanda said.

Horace allowed himself a deep sigh, turned, and patted her cheek. This was a wonderful new Amanda, but thank God this ridiculous game was over. Now let her down easily, he told himself. Do not bruise her dignity.

They ventured to the leather armchair part of the office. "I'm taken in by all this and I see it as an important moment for us. It's going to take a while for it to sink it. You've given me a four-year education in less than an hour. But Hampton Roads is a naval facility, lock, stock, and barrel. There are some small yards still operating under a grandfather clause since the Revolution, but none of sufficient size for Kerr's needs."

"Wouldn't the Constable Works fill the old dinner pail?"

"Hugh Constable has a tradition of building beautiful bay steamers, coastal boats, personal pleasure yachts. And Hugh Constable would never sell or merge."

"They're in trouble," Amanda shot back.

A first drop of real blood fell, and Horace Kerr smelled it. "How's that?"

"Twenty years ago Matthew Fancy worked out an option for Constable on the adjoining South Basin, and although they used some of it as an auxiliary, it's never been really developed. Hugh Constable has gotten a recent itch to go into ocean passenger liners. He renewed the option for the South Basin for another fifty years, but it cost him millions. He started to build a pair of dry docks that would hold twenty-thousand-ton ships, then found himself financially squeezed."

"There is no possible way Hugh Constable could have been seeking financing without me knowing about it."

"That is because they have done the bulk of their banking through England and some European principalities. They bought the South Basin option for several million, took further loans to dredge their channels, and badly misjudged the engineering needed. Halfway through the construction of the first dry dock, they were squeezed so badly they had to put up their private preferred stock as collateral."

"How do you know this?"

"My brother, who is never mentioned here by name, happens to hold a seat in Lloyd's."

"I don't want to hear a goddamned thing about Upton!"

"Fine, then that's it."

"Your mother told you this! Why didn't she tell me?"

"Mother knew nothing of this. When she made her first trip to

England eight years ago, she brought home a letter to me from Upton. We write regularly to each other."

"Where the hell does he send letters to you?"

"To Willow."

"Behind my back!"

"It could not have been otherwise. He is my brother and I have a right to love him."

Horace arose, anguished, unable to speak further.

"Upton has always known how desperately you want the Chesapeake monopoly."

"As long as Constable holds a fifty-year option, they are in a position to drive too hard a bargain," he mumbled, then threw up his hands. "What the hell does all this have to do with the Constitution Ball at the Potomac Mansion House?"

"What if Glen Constable were on my arm?"

"Glen Constable! Hugh Constable's boy?"

Amanda nodded.

"That is disgusting! Glen Constable is a womanizer who has gone through a vile public divorce. He is more than twice your age and has a daughter who could be your sister. How would you enter the Mansion House—in a scarlet gown?"

"He is a charming fellow who finally got free of a drowning marriage."

"And what about his reputation with doxies?"

"That seems to be rather standard tradition for most marriages."

"I am about to strike you!"

"You are being your bully best, Father. However, Glen's reputation will be quite enhanced if he can win me," she answered.

"You think I'll ever kowtow—," he said.

"I think you are going to batten down the hatches, trim off the emotional fat, and come to the conclusion worthy of a man of your stature."

Horace pouted a moment, wanted to laugh, wanted to cry. He'd never been worked over like this, not even by presidents!

At the core it made brilliant common sense. Let's see, Glen

Constable was in his early forties, an extremely good-looking, congenial chap. He was next in line in the Constable hierarchy and he had always been a sharp executive, certainly better than the grungy lot in the Kerr clan.

In truth, Amanda and Glen Constable would make a stunning couple, tall and elegant and blond, like Scottish lairds. What a message they would deliver. THE CHESAPEAKE BAY, ONE AND ALL, BELONGS TO KERR! THE PERFECT MONOPOLY.

A piece of personnel like Glen Constable married to Amanda could end Horace's generation-long nightmare of succession.

They would be a Maryland family! Headquartered at Dutchman's Hook. Inverness! Maryland had never gotten its full share. It was Massachusetts and Virginia always hogging the glory.

"Well," Horace said, "we are all grown up now, aren't we? What about that Marine?"

"He's going on a long cruise of sea duty."

"Out of our lives?"

"I'm trying, Father."

"I trust there won't be a bad aftertaste, like gossip that could cause you embarrassment."

"Not unless it's precipitated by an immaculate conception."

"And you're certain you'd be able to keep Glen Constable on a short leash?"

"He craves my youth and he'd die for the prize. Father, look at me. His days with doxies would be done and he knows it."

This wonderment of a woman emerging before him made him close to teary.

"The Marine boy. How much does this hurt?"

"Enough."

"Tell me, my precious girl, did Zachary O'Hara reject you before you put this long-simmering plan B of yours into play?"

"You'll never know," Amanda said.

"Well, you have learned the first lesson of a queen. Never fall in love with a commoner."

BEAUTIFUL DREAMER

1891—the Marine Barracks—Washington

Beautiful dreamer
Wake unto me
Starlight and dewdrops
Are waiting for thee.

'Tis said, with no prejudice, that if Corporal Daniel O'Moran had not chosen the Corps, he would have starred in every vaudeville house in the country and more than likely ended up on the concert stage.

O'Moran pressed his right hand firmly against his belly and swept the air with his left as his vibrant tenor and longing lyrics filled the chapel.

Beautiful dreamer
Queen of my song

List while I woo thee
With soft melody.

Corporal Zachary O'Hara, now wearing the red stripe down
his trouser legs in memory of the blood of noncommissioned officers shed in the Mexican War, steadied his pal, Sergeant Varnik,
whose new golden epaulets trembled.

The congregation arose as Beth Shaughnessy, on the arm of
Captain Tobias Storm, marched down the aisle.

Varnik took up most of the kneeling pad at the altar and Beth
very little of it while the steam between them hissed like over-
worked boilers.

After vows, they swept from the chapel beneath an archway of
drawn swords.

Zach spotted Amanda in the last row and waited to let the place
empty. In a moment, they were alone. They sat together awkwardly,
not having seen each other since that golden and ugly day in the
glade.

Zach blurted something about going out on field maneuvers and
something about being on standby to ship out because bandits in
the isthmus had raided the train being guarded by Marines, but the
emergency faded and they returned to finish their AMP classes and
one thing or another.

"My mother asked me to accompany her to New York for the
opera season and, well, as you know, one thing can lead to another."

"Sure," he said.

"I see you were promoted."

"Corporal."

"You'll end up with an armful of those stripes."

"Varnik has drawn a great post. The navy keeps a small contingent of about a dozen men in Recife, Brazil. There's a lot of Americans shipping in and out. They keep an eye on things, if you know
what I mean."

"Yes."

"Beth is going to be able to join him. I understand the living there isn't too expensive. Anyhow, Captain Storm gave them permission to marry only a few days ago."

"Recife. Sounds like the end of the world. Oh, you Marines! And yourself?"

"A cruiser is somewhere in the middle of the Atlantic heading for Norfolk."

They ran out of words and slowly, slowly dared to come into eye contact.

"There's to be a Marine guard tomorrow night at the Constitution," Amanda said. "Will you be there?"

"No."

"I've thought a hundred times about seeing you tomorrow. I'm glad we don't have to put each other through that."

A small orchestra culled from the big band could be heard from the reception in a nearby rec hall.

"Amanda," his voice whispered in pain as he reached for her.

"Zach, if you touch me, I'll die," she said.

"I could be around a few more weeks. Actually, I have some leave coming. Please let me see you."

They measured it up.

She reached over and gave him an instant kiss on the neck, long enough to nip him good with her teeth.

"I love you, Zach," she said, and fled the chapel.

Major Ben Boone trained down from Newport the next day for a round of meetings, including an important late session with the commandant. Ben didn't reach the barracks till sunset, where a lone bugler played "Colors" and a four-man color guard put the flag to rest.

Tobias Storm was waiting in Ben's quarters.

"Damned barracks is as quiet as a moth pissing on a weed," Ben said.

"Most of the enlisted personnel have drawn tin-soldier duty at the Constitution Ball. Matilda is going with one of our sons. We get invited everywhere. Everyone thinks I can get them a deal on Chinese imports. So how'd you make out with the boss?"

"Good. This first AMP class has raised some eyebrows. We've picked up a couple of friends at the War College, and guess who, Senator Davenport, has opened the door for us."

"Davenport. Jesus, he's a big one," Tobias said. "Never thought he'd convert."

"You know how it is," Ben said. "Once they convert, they become Holy Rollers. Have you drawn up your list for the next AMP class?"

"Almost completed."

"It's full steam ahead," Ben said.

A nervous moment followed.

"Matilda and I would like to retire; however, we love Washington. I want to stay on and get this next class going. I believe in AMP, strongly."

Ben allowed himself a deep sigh and a deeper drink of relief.

"Of course I've got to promise her a wedding every year. I hear tell there's a couple of merry widows hunting you down in Newport. Now, your wedding could well cap Matilda's career."

"If the United States Marine Corps wanted me to have a wife, they'd have issued me one," Ben growled. "Have you ever noticed that all widows had great marriages and all divorcées had shit heels for husbands? It's my stump they go wild over."

Another nervous moment began.

"Ben, what bad news are you sneaking around?"

"Didn't realize I was wearing it on my sleeve."

"You are, the bad one."

Ben grumbled, then gargled down a shot of rum. "I was hoping to get six, maybe eight, commissions for this first AMP class. We only got two."

"Oh, stew of barking dog. Two!"

"Two."

"What happened?"

"What always happens. We haven't got the money."

"This is some fucking Marine Corps, can't promote eight men to officers," Tobias growled.

"It ain't like in China, where the emperor just goes out and takes it from the peasants. We have a Congress."

"Boy, do we have a Congress!"

"Anyhow, Senator Davenport is putting an amendment on an appropriations bill. It might happen by the end of the year. But for now, we have to choose a pair."

"Platoon Sergeants Kirkendahl and Maynard," Tobias said. "Both of them have put in nearly three hitches."

"Kirkendahl, Maynard," Ben thought aloud, "they'll make fine officers."

The mood was leading to a binge. Two new officers out of such a brilliant class was pathetic. Tobias stared hard at Ben, who had gone rather inarticulate.

"What's up?" Tobias demanded.

"You know all that shit I've been collecting since I've been in the Corps," Ben said.

"Your amphibious-warfare mania?"

"Yeah, that shit. I've got a half-dozen trunks loaded with material dating back to prebiblical history. I've never been able to give them the proper time, and maybe time is running out for me. The commandant agrees that this material has to be collated, condensed, and put into a paper. I petitioned Colonel Ballard to let me take a full-time assistant to Newport for just that purpose."

"And what did Uncle Tom Ballard say?"

"It could well mean our future."

"Ballard say that or did you say that?" Storm pressed.

"What do you say, Tobias?"

"I say you're trying to draw me in."

"All right. There were three commissions, not two. The third man is coming to Newport with me if you sign off on him."

"And who do you have in mind?" Tobias asked with feigned innocence.

"You know fucking A who I have in mind. Is he as good as I think he is?"

"Better," Storm answered without hesitation.

"Does Zachary O'Hara suffer from any kind of long-term problems?"

"You mean Paddy's ghost?"

"I mean Paddy's ghost," Ben said.

"Who can compare with Paddy O'Hara, much less his own son. Zach and his da went through some things we'll never know about, but he's emerged as his own man. In many aspects, Paddy couldn't touch him."

"I wonder, sometimes, what went on between them," Ben said.

"It won't interfere with the work you have planned for him. I think I'd be a little more worried about Zach being a maverick," Tobias said.

"Well," Ben ventured, "is he going to be a fine upstanding maverick like me or a pain-in-the-ass maverick like you?"

Tobias shrugged. "He'll get his ass in a sling same as we do."

"Is he going to have a shit hemorrhage about not being given his sea duty? He's got the right to petition the commandant for it."

"He'll piss and moan a little, but he's a Marine," Tobias said, realizing that Ben Boone was oozing around the heart of the matter.

Ben fidgeted and stormed one-handed through his pockets, his routine for loading and lighting his pipe. Tobias twisted the ends of his mustache.

"Hmm," Ben said, shaking out his match vigorously and deploying it in an ashtray.

"What are you fiddle-farting around for?" Tobias finally asked.

"Okay, okay, okay, Zachary O'Hara cuts a pretty dandy figure and you know how Newport can be. As a commissioned officer, he's going to be invited to a lot of high-stakes functions. Lots of girls are going to be coming with a brass ring to put through his nose."

"Terrible problem," Tobias said. "He had the same terrible problem in Washington and he was only a PFC. Main thing is, can he do the job for you?"

"Tobias, every tinhorn robber baron in America keeps a thirty-room summer shack in Newport. The lawns are festooned with peppermint-striped party tents for their pre-debutante, debutante, and post-debutante girl-childs, all scratching, hounding down some innocent lad for a summer romance."

"While," Tobias interrupted, "de black folk in de peppermint tents all have their hands chopped up shucking oysters for de white folk!"

"I don't want him to waste his life crewing Vanderbilt's yacht or getting plucked off at some string quartet at the Breakers," Ben shot back.

"You are really talking about Horace Kerr's daughter."

That called for a refill.

"That Kerr compound is crawling with Kerrs who envision themselves as the future of the America's Cup. Amanda will be around all summer, and then some. Is there a chance we can lose him by bringing him to Newport? Maybe we should send him to sea duty?"

"How the hell should I know!" Storm defended.

"To hell you don't know, Tobias. You wring out the crying towel for all your boys."

"How well do you know Amanda Kerr?" Tobias asked.

"Between Washington and Newport, fairly well. She is stunning and she is as smart as they come."

"And at this moment she is entering the Potomac Mansion House on the arm of Glen Constable, so put down your seabag and stand at ease. Zachary O'Hara and Amanda Kerr cannot have each other. Her old man is about as friendly to the Marine Corps as Attila the Hun. In addition, O'Hara is a Catholic and we are not exactly living in an age of enlightenment."

"Tobias, she is formidable. She gets everything she has her mind set on."

"Horace Kerr is even more formidable. Glen Constable represents a deliberate and serious announcement."

"She's still a girl," Ben said.

"Ben, you and I cannot outwit those silky thugs. She may be

innocent down there"—Tobias pointed to Ben's legs—"but she also knows what Kerr and Constable mean together. Missy Kerr knows what a monopoly is."

"I wish I knew you to be right," Ben said.

"My educated guess," Tobias went on, "is that Glen Constable is a thoroughly smitten slob over Amanda and hungry for the merger with Horace, even if it means Constable ends up as a minority stock-holder."

"Bunch of maggots," Ben said. "Maybe we'd better send O'Hara to sea duty instead of torturing him. We've seen too many tortured boys . . . men . . ."

"You need him?" Tobias asked.

"Very much," Ben said.

"Otherwise your life's work may never see daylight?"

"Possible."

"Then take him to Newport, for chrissake."

They stared at each other until fireworks erupted outside with close-together *pop-pop-pops*, then whistling explosions. The Constitution Ball was under way.

"You're going to have to trust O'Hara, Ben."

"Can I?"

"He's a Marine, you'll *have* to trust him. That's all we've got, Ben. That's all we've ever had, trusting each other."

The decision now made, time to mellow out, like Wart-Hogs. They sipped and reminisced and shored up each other's courage. Ben pressed the buzzer for his orderly and Private Lamar Jones knocked, tucking in the last of his shirttail.

"Enter!"

"Sir!"

"Is Gunny Kunkle in the barracks?"

Jones hesitated just long enough and peeped an "Er, yes, sir."

"Get him up here on the double."

"Yes, sir."

The old salt arrived three minutes and nineteen . . . twenty . . . twenty-one seconds later.

"Sirs."

"At ease, it's Wart-Hog time. You look like a mile of dirt road."

"I've been attending a sick friend."

Ben poured him a drink, and themselves as well. "To us Wart-Hogs. Gunny, we got news. We're only getting three commissions out of AMP, for the present."

"Shit." Kunkle groaned low.

"Kirkendahl and Maynard, how's that hit you?"

"Good, Major. Third man?"

"I'm taking somebody up to the War College with me."

Kunkle looked over to Captain Storm and back to Ben Boone and back to Captain Storm.

"You mean . . ."

"Yeah," Tobias and Ben said together.

"Is he on that royal guard detail at the Mansion House?"

"No, sir. He got it exchanged for mess duty."

"Get his ass up here!" Storm bellowed as the full measure of the distilled stuff in him hit the gong.

"Sirs . . . fellow Wart-Hogs, sirs . . . he is fucked-up beyond comprehension. We placed him under the cold shower with a puke bucket," the Gunny said.

By the time the Gunny got O'Hara put together, the two officers were singing a jolly chorus of "Dixie." Boone observed Zach. "I've seen better-looking specimens in a slaughterhouse, after they've been decapitated."

"Think we ought to execute him," Storm said, "or maybe we ought to send him to discover the South Pole."

"I appreciate the fact that I'm not as alert as one should be on duty, sirs, Gunny. I'm out of uniform, as one should not be on duty. You see, I've got a fucking hole in my fucking heart . . . *sirs!*"

Gunny helped Zach's spaghettilike body into a chair as Zach, trying to sit erect, gazed glassy-eyed at the three of them.

"Do you know who I am?" Ben asked.

"Yes, sir, Major Boone, sir," the chalky number answered.

"Try these on," Ben said, flipping his old gold bars on the table.

"Somebody lose a lieutenant?" Zach said.

"I said, try them on. I'm taking you to the War College with me in Newport, Lieutenant O'Hara."

Zach reached for the bars, then pulled his hand back. "I should like to request being transferred to sea duty," he said.

"Request denied," Boone said.

"But . . ."

"Tough shit."

Zach cleared the fuzz and nausea and pounding from within, regaining command of himself, studying the three rocks of ages before him.

"This is the greatest honor a Marine could have, working for Major Boone, and I know what you're uncomfortable about."

"It is none of our business so long as you do your duty properly."

"I can't promise that I won't see her again, but I swear on my honor I'll do my best to complete my task."

"That's good enough for me, Lieutenant."

Zach held the gold bars in his hand, then broke down entirely, his head finding its way onto Tobias Storm's chest as he wept.

"I wish my da were here!" Zach cried.

Master Gunnery Sergeant Wally Kunkle pinned a gold bar on each of Zach's collars.

"Through no authority granted in me whatsoever, I do declare you a Wart-Hog!"

> Wart-Hogs will fuck gorilla poon,
> And name their kids for pickles,
> Wart-Hogs' cuisine is broken glass,
> 'Cause going down it tickles.
> Wart-Hogs will bathe in liquid shit,
> And love the grand aroma,
> And drink a pint of buzzard's puke,
> Then sing of home sweet homa.

❧ 21 ❧

AFTER THE BALL

The Next Day—the Willard Hotel—Washington

As noon chimed, not a creature was stirring in the Kerrs' suite. The Constitution Ball had lasted nearly till dawn. Back at the hotel, the Kerrs and the Constables congratulated themselves on the triumph until first light, when Glen and his father and mother retired to their suite two floors below.

Amanda disappeared into her room and Daisy collapsed with exultation. Horace Kerr remained in the parlor, behind the green leather-top desk, staring bleary-eyed into the future. The thudding news had been whispered into his ear as they departed the Mansion House. The fucking Marine had been recommended for a commission and assigned to the Naval War College in Newport.

Horace held the terror of it at bay until he was alone. Daisy and Amanda did not yet know and they would be asleep till midday. Horace realized that he had to be more profound of purpose than at any other time in his life.

Less than twelve hours ago, Amanda's entry into the Mansion House was Westminster Abbey stuff, the arrival of the queen-apparent with her handsome consort, reeking with pride, a delicate half step behind her. Glen's smile was of adoration. Horace didn't realize Constable had so many teeth.

Amanda was attired with Grecian simplicity, gossamer stuff that flowed in rhythm with her fine movement. She seemed the only one among the young women who was not bare-shouldered, her thin straps setting off her only jewelry, a single strand of black pearls that rested happily in the open field near her bosom.

The grand ballroom oozed with diamond tiaras, bombastic cleavage, and enough curls to have worn out every beautician in Washington. They were all pinched and punched up in a rerouting of God's endowments.

Horace Kerr's victory! It had been so ethereal, he remembered. The room was stricken silent and he thought of a little girl stopping a roaring locomotive with a wave of her hand. Calling it a "feast of the gods," Horace mused, might be carrying it a bit too far, but he knew that this Constitution Ball would be long remembered for Amanda's entry and waves of sound suddenly gone silent.

She came in gay and friendly as a balcony of Marine trumpeters heralded. She had hugs and smiles for everyone, particularly those ladies who had come from far away, but somehow she seemed untouchable.

By the time they reached the Kerr table, the statement was indelible. The President's Own Band played a soft background. Horace did see his daughter flinch a few times when Marine guards passed by, ushering folks to their tables.

The glory of the moment would last to his grave, and no doubt beyond. But that was last night and today is today.

The moment he received the disastrous news, that old raven began to circle overhead. Why did his thoughts have to screech back to Upton now? The raven flew in although the window was closed, and it sat mocking on the mantel, staring at him.

*   *   *

The raven had first come that terrible moment two decades earlier, the day he realized his son was different. It was a situation Horace could not understand. When faced with such riddles, beyond human comprehension, he turned to the deep Presbyterian beginnings that his own father, Angus, had pounded into him. This personal connection to God was the only damned thing his family ever gave him. He damn well needed a visit with the Lord before Amanda woke up. He beseeched the Lord to bear in mind that he did not abuse this privilege of personal consultation but only used it in dire emergencies.

Horace Kerr had satisfied himself early in life that he was destined to be a great man and great men are challenged to show their strength by facing down disasters of biblical proportions. Horace told the bloody raven to stop staring. God had already tested him with Emily, and God knows that he had done his best. Then Upton!

It was in the days long ago when little boys were dressed in lace-trimmed velvet and wore curls until they were weaned from their mothers, nannies, and other females and required to step up into the man's world. Fact is, Upton looked too natural in velvet, different from other lads. Playing and sleeping with dolls was supposedly normal, up to a certain point.

Horace watched Upton's behavior grow more in that direction, day by day, year by year, until he had to say to himself, "God has given me a queer son!"

Did he rage? No! Horace made it his mission to try to put muscle on Upton, from self-defense lessons, to seamanship in a storm, to the finest military academy for boys, to pitching hot rivets in the shipyard. Rough-and-tumble, that's the way!

From Upton's sixteenth birthday onward, Horace subtly made highly desirable ladies available to his son and virtually placed a line of upper-rung doxies between Upton's sheets. The results were indifferent.

The father would watch in despair as Emily tripped over the piano keys, accompanying Upton playing the violin, with his long hair passionately tossing and long delicate fingers fluttering over the strings and his long thin body swaying with the music.

God had tested him to his absolute limit with Upton. All of the years of toil, all of the planning and scheming and blocking and manipulating Horace had done at Dutchman's Hook were going to be for naught. It would all be a Pyrrhic victory without a Kerr name to carry forward.

The sad part of it was that Upton showed clever skills in banking and negotiations, but he lacked the inner steel required to make powerful decisions or run a yard of hulking gorillas.

Whom could he speak to about Upton? No minister or bishop of his church, for certain. No physician would see Upton as other than an abomination.

Horace was determined to make an honorable compact. He took Upton on a hunting trip to a lodge the Kerrs kept in the western part of the state. Father and son, straight on. He told Upton he'd realized the boy's behavior was deviant early on and prayed he'd outgrow it. A trick of God. However, all families had secrets and God alone knew how many secret queers had gained fame throughout history. Great men kept great secrets. Now was Upton's chance.

Horace felt that he had come to a decision of Solomon-like wisdom. He learned that fairies were quite capable of fathering children. That was science. If Upton wed a brood mare of Horace's choosing, they could produce the sons to preserve the Kerr name and establish continuity.

Horace would stay closely involved in Dutchman's Hook until his demise. Upton would be kept as a "behind-the-scenes absentee landlord." In case Horace went physically or mentally defunct, there would be a strong set of advisers to hold things together until a grandson took over. This was a scheme that had worked well during slavery times.

God willing, Horace would find a man of Matthew Fancy's caliber to "advise" Upton. Now, if that wasn't an honorable solution, there was no honorable solution!

In return, Upton would be allowed to set up his own pansy garden somewhere out of sight where he could satisfy his abnormal desires.

What the hell else was Horace to do? He'd gone the extra mile. He had flirted with the devil to turn a blind eye to Upton's behavior. How had Upton Kerr repaid his father's incredible understanding?

Without so much as a farewell, Upton moved to London before his twenty-first birthday and ceased all contact with his father. Largely financed by Daisy, Upton carved himself a very successful career and apparently led an unspectacular social life.

Horace plunged to the depths of sorrow. That was when God illuminated Amanda. She was God's gift to compensate for the failure of his other children.

Horace pulled out a stack of Willard Hotel stationery and peered at the mantel warily. The raven was gone!

It was Horace Kerr and God now like never before. Horace's small, neat handwriting indicated that he was focused, concentrating.

THE CONSTABLE MERGER: Fast inside track, most direct solution. From moment Glen was invited to escort Amanda, father Hugh tipped off eagerness to consolidate. His option on the Southern Basin was Constable's ace card, but so long as he could not develop it, it became a case of raw nerves. Cold cash and balance sheets would gain a 75-25 control. AMANDA WOULD ALWAYS CONTROL A MINIMUM OF 60 percent.

HOW WILL THIS MARRIAGE ARRANGEMENT WORK? Arm in arm they reek of power. The Constitution attendees were mesmerized by Amanda. The way she floated from table to table welcoming those other floppy girls into what quickly had become her court . . .

GLEN CONSTABLE, OVER LONG RUN? That dog won't hunt no more. He'll be quite content to lie at her feet before the fire. GC is slovenly smitten. Amanda holds the cards and is too bright and selfish to shoot herself in the foot. It will be a comfortable long-run arrangement, like myself and Daisy.

BESIDES, Glen is going to make a fine executive, properly guided.

BESIDES, Amanda's restlessness is not unlike my own. She has already displayed that she considers a union with GC almost a deal. And, if anyone strays, it will be Amanda and she'd never do it in such a way as to create a scandal.

ETCETERA, ETCETERA, ETCETERA.

THAT FUCKING MARINE: Newport swarms with social maggots. Many families, overly burdened with females, could go for the O'Hara bait. Aside from his father's fame, O'Hara is a clever boy and could fit into some family's scheme.

O'HARA DOES have gold bars on his epaulets now, which give him open access to top-tier "royalty." I've seen many ambitious young lads stake out and impregnate such daughters with marriage as their mutual goal.

GNAWING POSSIBILITY: I'd have to give even money that Amanda and O'Hara engage in a summer romance. Frankly, I admire O'Hara's sense of honor. HOWEVER, Amanda will get her way on that one.

OPTION: Press Glen Constable's case and push for an early merger. Amanda would see right through that. What little gift could I give Amanda to help sway her? Let's look at this further.

BRILLIANT IDEA! Set up O'Hara with a magnificent doxie, a high-class member of the sisterhood. Import her from Boston or wherever, put her in a glowing apartment. The only problem with this is that I've never known a mistress who didn't end up having a big mouth. But put this on hold as well.

ETCETERA, ETCETERA, ETCETERA.

OPTION: Flat-out lay the law down to Amanda. Chances are I'll have to sooner or later. Let us not use this card until we absolutely have to.

LET US LAY THIS ALL OUT ON THE DESK AND SEE IF WE CAN CONNECT SOME DOTS.

OPTION: If it appears Amanda and O'Hara are heading for a roll in the hay, then arrange a discreet accident for him. Now, we have to tread slowly, Horace my friend. It seems that every time an elimination has been called for at Dutchman's Hook, it is never carried off without someone bumbling. If we go this route, a foolproof plan must be made.

IF, GOD FORBID: Amanda becomes pregnant via O'Hara, I do not wish to go through the same experience I had with Emily.

We still have the weapon of statutory rape and the privilege of a closed court. O'Hara would face twenty-five years in prison and a dishonorable discharge. He must be made aware of these consequences.

ON THE OTHER HAND: Once their engines get running at full

steam, it might be impossible to stop them. Face what you know, Horace. There is no real protection from a grown man in heat.

ALL TOLD: The abortion option is dicey. I must contrive another scheme. Say that Amanda becomes pregnant. With the threat of prison over him, O'Hara would agree to an "elopement" marriage and then get it annulled. In such case, the baby would be legitimate and certainly awarded by the court to Amanda with total restrictions against O'Hara seeing the child.

STICKY WICKET: How do we keep Glen Constable in the game? Even if marriage/annulment/child happens, I say the odds are still in our favor of capturing GC. The point is, we have to keep GC in any picture if we are to obtain the Constable South Basin.

ETCETERA, ETCETERA, ETCETERA.

NOW THEN: The cream is rising to the top. It is basic, when we get to the bottom line, that Amanda burns ambitiously for everything Dutchman's Hook will bring her. In addition, Amanda wants to achieve something of high moral purpose.

IF I can link Dutchman's Hook with high moral purpose, it would be irresistible to Amanda.

THERE REMAINS: A simple, direct, bloodless way. The secretary of the navy owes me a few. He can arrange for O'Hara NOT TO COME TO NEWPORT but be shipped to . . . Nepal . . .

THANK YOU, GOD: Every man finds himself faced with dilemmas. YOU have shown me that it takes a great man to use evil devices in order to defeat a greater evil. Otherwise, greater evil would always triumph.

"Excuse me, Mr. Kerr," Allsop, his secretary, said, tiptoeing into the room. "Secretary Culpeper's assistant telephoned and asked if Secretary Culpeper could drop by and see you at half two."

"I'll be damned," Horace said under his breath. His own thought waves seemed to have been transmitted to another person of similar concerns. By God, that's more than a coincidence. It was celestial!

"Of course, delighted," Horace answered. "Is a butler at his station?"

"Yes, sir, Mr. Kendall's on duty."

"You have him order me up a little breakfast. Steak and eggs, home fries, and a rasher of bacon. And Mr. Allsop, gather up these notes and burn them in the fireplace."

The Kerrs' butler greeted Nathaniel Culpeper and took his top hat and cane. The secretary of the navy wove his way in, spotted the deepest and softest armchair, and flopped into it.

"Tea and pastries?" Kerr asked.

Culpeper scrunched up his face.

"How about a nip of the hair that killed the dog, Nathaniel?"

"No, thank you, Horace. I've an epic case of tummy wobbles. I ran into a table of high-capacity drinkers from Colorado."

"Colorado? Do we have a navy base in Colorado?" Then Kerr turned his attention to the butler. "Kendall, fix Secretary Culpeper a brandy and bitters. The same for myself, only leave out the bitters and make the brandy a double."

They clinked glasses.

"May the sides of our ships be as strong as your stomach, Horace . . . Awful stuff, this." He winced. "Well now, Mr. Kerr, may I bask in your glory?"

Horace smiled and nipped from his cognac snifter.

"I have survived two Constitution Balls with my three daughters," Culpeper went on, "all beautiful women, but combined, they could not match Miss Amanda Kerr."

"Will that be all, sir?" Kendall asked.

"Do this again," Horace said, pointing to his glass. "In fact, open the French stuff and do not disturb us for anyone."

"Unless it's the president," Culpeper corrected.

"Our daughters do give us ultimate joy. Sometimes"—he inched into the meat of the subject—"the female lineage can create a nightmare in matters of family continuity."

"Indeed," Horace opined.

"That was a brilliant move you made last night. No one at the Mansion House could have predicted Amanda and Glen Constable. And no one failed to get your meaning."

Horace did not want to give Amanda credit at this point.

"Too bad you couldn't have hung on to the moment longer," the secretary went on. "I was hoping you would not get wind of O'Hara being posted in Newport until I told you of it, but bad news travels fast."

"Yes, it came in on the wings of a raven."

"Beg your pardon?"

"Nothing," Horace said.

"Horace, you belong to the most vocal group wanting to stand down the Marine Corps. You and Commodore Chester Harkleroad were leading the charge not to design space for Marines on the Vermont class."

"Chrissake, I was only following the party line. It's been GOP policy for over a decade. Right now I wish there was enough room on the Vermont to hold the entire Marine Corps and whip them down to Antarctica and put them on an iceberg."

"They'd probably make paddles out of their rifles and seal fins and row the iceberg right back up to Hampton Roads."

Out came Horace's exclamatory finger. "Harkleroad smelled this. He knew that fucking Major Boone might try some three-card monte in shifting personnel around. Nathaniel, how long have you known about this dastardly plot?"

"A week. The paperwork was all tidied up in advance. Senator Davenport will push the O'Hara commission through unopposed, by voice vote."

"You should have told me right off."

"I wanted you to enjoy the Constitution affair."

"Oh, I enjoyed it, all right. I was about to have the biggest orgasm of my life when I got kicked in the balls with the news."

The brandy and bitters had gone to work, helping Culpeper's stomach find its sea legs. The secretary dropped his eyebrows in that stern manner to make Horace brace himself.

"The navy has been in a state of nirvana. Congress has appropriated almost everything we've asked for. By the time my tenure

in office is over, before the twentieth century, America will have a
fleet second only to Great Britain."

Culpeper held up his hand to stop Horace's response.

"No one stands to benefit more than yourself," the secretary
added. "That is an incredible monopoly you've created. You nailed
the Chesapeake."

"What happened last night at the Mansion House was merely to
stake our claim and keep any ambitious greedheads out of my territory. An actual Kerr and Constable merger will take some time.
Everything depends on how soon Amanda makes a decision about
Glen Constable. After that, there is always agony in working out
the details. Amanda is involved in a petty schoolgirl romance with
this O'Hara person. I was counting the minutes until his ship
sailed. O'Hara in Newport with Amanda could be dangerous."

Kendall was buzzed for refills from the Scotch bottle. Culpeper
opined that the addition of ice to a drink was a civilized advancement. Otherwise, they were quiet for some time, but Horace was
relaying that "we've been together for a long time, Nathaniel" and
"we both owe each other a few."

"I have a simple favor. I do not want that Marine in Newport."

"The Battle of Trafalgar was less complicated," Culpeper
retorted.

"That one-armed yeggman, Major Ben Boone, is behind this."

"Here's how I see things. The Marine Corps is attempting to
make the case for their continuation. Ben Boone is an important
player. That's why we keep him out of cabinet meetings, whenever
possible. I had a quick and extremely reliable portrait of this
O'Hara person drawn up. He's the real thing, an extremely fine
prospect. He has in brains what his father had in guts."

"God Almighty, the next thing we'll have is an Irish president,"
Horace growled.

"There is this mystique about the Corps," Nathaniel went on.
"They aren't going to phase out quietly. In the past month, Richard
X. Maple has joined them and he waves a big stick at the Academy.

Senator Davenport is now in their camp. You know what he means when it comes to military appropriations. I just received word that an army brigadier of note intends to testify next week that it is not, repeat not, the army's job to sail the high seas and take on penny-and-nickel expeditions."

"What general?"

"Brigadier Pete Wyatt."

"Jesus Q. Christ, Wyatt is so ancient they'll never get the fart stains out of his uniform."

"Precisely," Nathaniel answered. "We don't make Pete famous at this point by attacking him. Horace, we have reached a sea of smooth sailing. I am taking the majority position of the admirals, but at the same time I have advised them to proceed with caution on the Marines and I have told the Republican leadership to back off. We have a great navy in the dry docks ready to go down the ways. Your own problem is not with the Corps, now is it?"

"What the hell am I asking? This is not the war of the world, Nathaniel. This is merely a case of sending one little Marine out of sight. I am not without recourse in this matter."

"Horace, I've always enjoyed you at my side. You are a magnificent bully. I've watched you bully two presidents and tongue-tie a secretary of state. I know it must be very difficult for a bully of your stature to have to stand down over such a trifling matter. If Lieutenant Zachary O'Hara is suddenly transferred aboard ship, it could open a Pandora's box."

"Nonsense, Nathaniel. Outside of a tight circle of a few friends, no one has the slightest hint that O'Hara and Amanda are anything other than casual friends."

"Amanda is not your run-of-the-mill schoolgirl with a crush," Culpeper said. "She is this year's toast of Washington, as prominent as any young unmarried woman in the East. Unfortunately, O'Hara is not your run-of-the-mill soldier boy. He comes with a pedigree."

"Earned by his father's blood."

"Indeed, we all climb on our fathers' backs. Their romance is just too juicy for there to be any smell of foul play on the navy's part, like a transfer of assignments because Daddy Kerr has pull. Do you actually believe you can keep a lid on it in Newport, the gossip capital of the universe?"

"The risk comes with them rattling around together for an entire summer."

"I can see the headline in the *Baltimore Sun*: " 'Marine Sweetheart of Shipbuilding Heiress Shanghaied.' "

"I'll buy the goddamn *Sun* and shut down its goddamn presses."

"Alas, democracy breeds pamphleteers. Every poor working family in America will hate your bloody guts, Horace. Romeo and Juliet, Baltimore style. You'd be setting the two of them up for martyrdom. If there is the slightest hint of conspiracy in this boy's transfer, the navy will have too much to lose. Your request is declined."

"You can't know what I've been through. Your daughters are well married. As for Upton, I tried with him. If you had a son, you'd know."

"Don't ask me to shoot one across your bow."

"Say it."

"It seems to me one must stand by one's son, no matter what."

"It was Upton who fled to England."

"Beware, Amanda may be more Horace Kerr than Horace Kerr is," Culpeper pressed.

His words struck deep. Horace had played on his people like a master. At Dutchman's Hook, he'd press his managers into a corner, make his point by raw power, then reward them afterward to retain their loyalty.

Better to back off with Nathaniel Culpeper. "What am I to do?" Horace groaned.

"This summer you will practice restraint and compassion. Restraint, compassion."

"I wonder," Horace wondered.

"I have known of this affair from the day O'Hara stood guard at my door and Amanda came crashing into the office. The moment was lightning, their infatuation has lasted over three years. She cares for him, I daresay, because he is strong, as strong as she is. Neither of them will bend to threats. They got themselves into it, Horace. Stand aside and let them get out of it. Any pressure from you will only make them more adamant."

"And do you think all this is going to end?"

Nathaniel Culpeper mulled it over.

"Amanda Kerr is a woman outside of her generation, marked for greatness. She does not act in a haughty manner, yet everyone who comes into contact with her senses her keen mind and sees her regal bearing. She simply *is*. Having battled you to a tie score for nearly twenty years, she is also aware of her potency, her possible reach. Faced with a decision Amanda will surely conclude that as the wife of a Marine, she will end up personally unfulfilled, no matter how much she loves him."

"Suppose she wants O'Hara *and* Dutchman's Hook?"

"That's certain to be her battle plan, right now," Culpeper conceded, "but there is a flip side to the coin."

"I don't follow you."

"O'Hara's side. The core of the Corps is this insatiable drive. They are born different, beyond the lure of the spoils of commerce, industry, and governments."

"Come now, Nathaniel, military officers are ordinary human beings with personal ambition."

"Their ambition is to serve at the highest level. Strange breed, what? But, without an officer corps, no nation could be a viable nation."

"And you believe O'Hara is so smitten?"

"He and the colors are one and the same. As Amanda Kerr would not be fulfilled in life by their marriage, neither would Zachary O'Hara."

"Do you honestly think that he'd choose the Marines over her?"

"We'll find out, won't we?"

Later in the afternoon, Horace requested that his daughter visit him in the parlor before dinner. "You heard?"

"Yes," she said.

"Is this going to change things about?"

"No," she answered immediately and firmly.

A feeling of comfort swept over him and eased out the tension.

"Glen has invited me to visit the Constable farm outside Richmond for a week or so. His daughter, Dixie Jane, will be there. I ought to get to know her," Amanda said.

Horace drank that music in. There was nothing frivolous about it, no question of her resolve.

"Of course that pleases me right well," he said.

"Mother will be returning to Inverness to pack us up for Newport. I'd have to go to Richmond without a chaperon."

"Not to give it a second thought," Horace answered. "I'm heading for Dutchman's Hook tomorrow and I'll be staying at my apartment there. Your uncles Donald and Malcolm are coming down to run some trials with me on *Lochinvar*," he said in reference to the Kerr racing yacht.

Amanda smiled at her father's persistence. Horace had a professional crew, but she was the one woman allowed aboard for the match races and often relieved her father at the helm. His passion for the regatta was still on the rise.

"How did the old *Lochinvar* fare this winter?"

"Well, I hope. We've outfitted her with that system I told you about."

"The 'Butterfly'?"

"Good, you remembered."

"Will you be sailing her up to Newport?"

"No, that's Malcolm and Donald's job. I'll come back to join you and Daisy at Inverness to train up."

The Next Day—Dutchman's Hook

America's Cup had become bitter vetch for the British, who had pursued it futilely with a dozen challenges. For four decades, beginning in 1850, the Yankee upstarts had made something of a mockery of Britannia's mastery of the sea. Not that anyone was surprised when the Yankees put a fine boat on the water, but they were commercial people, not sportsmen. It was difficult to comprehend that the Americans could build, crew, and captain a yacht better than the English. Actually, it was the lack of sportsmanship that grated on the Brits. The Cup was on display at the New York Yacht Club and the true sportsmen were forced to race on American water under American rules.

If horse racing was the sport of kings, then yacht racing was the sport of gods and America's Cup became a search for the Holy Grail.

The United States entered the 1890s on a golden wave of unprecedented personal wealth. Suddenly the city of New York vied with London as the center of the universe.

For their playground, New Yorkers had the South Shore of Long Island, a hundred-mile stretch of magnificent beaches and sailing inlets. Tens of dozens of great and small summer mansions and magnificent resort hotels burgeoned and the villages linked by rail line. The overflow of wealth found pretentious outlets in places like Saratoga (for the horsey crowd) and Asbury Park.

Yet Long Island and the South Shore was the gold coast of gold coasts, and Islip, the world capital of yacht racing . . . out past Sandy Hook and into the winds!

America's Cup seemed permanently ensconced in the New York Yacht Club. There were lesser sailing venues—north of Long Island to Maine and south from the Chesapeake to the Gulf, dozens of new yacht clubs came into existence—but none was so grand as the NYYC and its territory.

In the beginning, racing yachts had been modified versions of commercial schooners, and the rules of racing were lax and sealed with a handshake. Over time the yachtsmen acquired the costly hobby of building pure racing boats. Hulls, masts, and rigs evolved from sloops and cutters to a fairly standardized yawl rig of under a hundred feet at waterline, carrying a sail capacity, give or take, of ten thousand square feet.

Then came the bottomless-rules committee, which demanded of the British that they give a full and accurate measurement of their boats, six months in advance of a challenge. And other rules, all stacked against them, in their eyes.

It was the competition between American syndicates to represent the United States that advanced into the development of the big racing yachts.

The Kerr family raced around the Chesapeake. Horace was a builder of warships. It took a long time for him to get the message that hale and hardy Yankee labor could handcraft a yacht, matching the jewels that came from Scotland and Scandinavia. The Kerrs' yachts had all sailed over from Scotland.

The family raced for years on the Chesapeake in match races for purses that often exceeded a thousand dollars. Alas, Horace yearned to get into the big action and entered in the challenge round of 1885 and was skunked by minor NYYC boats. So much for *Lochinvar II*.

With fewer people and better sailing waters, Newport became the new gathering place. Although New Yorkers and the NYYC dominated the Newport scene, there was room for tycoons of the Kerr ilk coming from all over the country.

Horace's brothers, minor players in the shipyard, set up permanent residence in Newport. They were damned good yachtsmen, Donald and Malcolm; Donald as navigator and Malcolm in the sail trimming. Back in Islip, New York, a crew and a professional racing captain were hired and *Lochinvar III* made a decent entry into the big time.

Horace was at the helm, of course, and after he won a few match races, his ambition grew.

Horace felt that the only way to get into Cup contention would be to invent and exploit something totally unique . . . not exactly circumventing the rules, but something that could slip in under the rules until it was discovered and the rules were changed.

For the season of 1891, *Lochinvar III* would be carrying a secret system, spoken of in whispers as the Butterfly.

The basic thesis was that there should be an underwater device that could respond to what was happening with the wind and sails.

The Butterfly was a pair of mobile vertical trim tabs attached to both sides of the bottom of the keel, operated from cables inside the keel.

The tabs were free-floating and as sensitive to currents as the feathered ends of birds' wings are to air currents.

Belowdecks, a system was installed to take instructions from the movements of the Butterfly tabs. A highly polished cannonball weighing a half ton, slotted into a rail, rolled instantly on command from side to side across the centerline, acting as a counterbalance when the wind tilted the boat.

. . . for the ultimate purpose of maximum rudder stability. A special crewman on deck read the Butterfly meter and moved the ball by a handle connected to cables below. One could liken it to dancing with a partner on ice without skates.

If the ball rolled too nervously, the operator could lock it into neutral and shut it down.

Thus, the theory went, they would always have a dead-on accurate register of currents in relationship to wind shifts.

Sails and masts would be operating to their maximum limits.

. . . and if calculations proved right, *Lochinvar III* could pick up a half-knot on upwind legs and in squirrelly currents and rough areas . . . perhaps.

If it worked, the apparatus could be stored so the fucking NYYC rules committee might take a couple of years to discover it.

And if it didn't work . . . what the hell . . .

· 22 ·

THE JERSEY SHORE LINE

Dearest Amanda,

I am sorry I was only able to get that short note to you, but a rapid fire of events overtook me.

I am settling in Newport at the Naval War College. It is a dream assignment and a great privilege to work under Major Boone.

The manner of our parting at Inverness has left me empty. I was able to bear it because I thought I would soon be aboard ship. Life does not seem to work at its fullest without you. Now that you will be in Newport soon and I will be within touch of the golden silk threads of your hair, I am overcome with joy.

I have never thought strongly about miracles, but surely some mysterious force is bringing us together for a resolution of our feelings.

My duty hours are quite flexible. Please let me hear from you. Tell me what your pleasure is.

> *With most affectionate regards,*
> *Zachary*

Two Weeks Later—Inverness to Tobermory

The special train was hitched up for its yearly run to Butcher's Hill, to the siding in Inverness, where it was loaded for the annual trip to the Kerr family compound of Tobermory in Newport, Rhode Island.

Horace made it back from Dutchman's Hook the evening before departure after seeing his brothers sailing off on the *Lochinvar*.

He didn't know if good news or bad news would be coming back with Amanda from her visit to Constable's horse farm near Richmond. At breakfast she gave her father a wink and thumbs-up. All smiles, Horace said he'd catch up with her.

The train was nearly loaded, preened for her departure.

The first car carried senior household staff for the "big house" at Tobermory and several executives and their families from Dutchman's Hook to activate the summer business office in Newport.

The second car was an armored number that hauled some of the valuables of Inverness with Pinkertons to guard it. A Rembrandt and a da Vinci led a collection of paintings to be rehung in the Tobermory salon. A safe held family jewelry, heirlooms, and several cases of contracts and business documents. There was a smattering of ancient vases, Greek statuary, Beauvais tapestries, and the like.

The third car was an opulent affair commissioned by Horace from the Pullman Company, containing his parlor, office, and bedroom. The next, a car of compartments for the family, including Emily's retinue. There were extra seats for whatever leftover cousins had been swept up.

Next in line, a freight car carried their favorite saddle and carriage horses, in comfy padded stalls, with space for the handlers and tack.

This yearly maneuver took place before the summer's heat smothered Inverness. The staff made the transition like flawless stagehands changing a set. The second butler and assistant housekeeper had already been dispatched to Newport to make certain that the big house at Tobermory was tuned to perfection.

The shift, this season, was particularly heavy for an extended stay of family. In a weak moment Horace agreed to a full clan gathering for Thanksgiving, with some coming from the old country.

Time dragged as Daisy inspected each car and gave an all clear to the engineer, then plopped in the parlor as Horace checked his pocket watch.

The whistle!

The train pulled out of Inverness, bang on time, cleared the industrial area, and was soon in the Maryland countryside. By late afternoon, it skirted Wilmington and transferred to the Jersey Shore Line Railroad, "the fruit and vegetable express."

Horace cleared his desk of papers, which were bundled up by his executive manager and lawyer. Hugging close to the seaside, the train traversed endless vegetable farms and fruit orchards.

It pulled to a siding to give right-of-way to a freight train filled with late spring crops to be rushed to market.

"How long will we be held up?" Horace inquired of the train master.

"Could be a half hour or more, sir."

Excellent, Horace thought. At last, the opportunity to see Amanda. He went to her car, knocked, and entered her compartment. Amanda's feet were tucked under her, her face close to the page of a book.

"Father," she said, smiling.

"At last," he said. "This move simply wears me out."

He took a seat as Amanda marked and closed her book. "How did old *Lochinvar* do?" she asked.

"Quite well, actually. We sailed her down to Hampton Roads. I wanted to run her through the rip at Cape Henry. The Butterfly shows signs of promise but is going to need a lot of fine tuning at Newport. To hell with *Lochinvar*. What about Richmond?"

"Everything went as well as I wished," she said.

Horace wondered if this beautiful girl of his was playing cagey with him. Amanda had obviously worked a lot of things out. What were they?

"And you and Glen?"

"We enhanced our friendship. I was there for almost two weeks, you know."

"Did you find Glen amusing?"

"He was good company. Glen is gentle, kind, and sophisticated."

"The family?"

"Manageable, bearable."

"The Constables are rather traditional. So one might conclude that things are going along warmly between you and Glen?"

Oh, put the man out of his misery, Amanda. "There is no raw, savage lust, Father. Everything is decently in bounds, but I was very, very taken by his daughter, Dixie Jane. She's ten years old and an exciting little girl."

Phew! That's a way to Amanda's heart.

"I have invited Dixie Jane to Tobermory for half of July and August. Her mother and Mom approve."

"And I approve as well."

"Thank you, Father. Glen will try to get up on weekends."

"Well then . . ."

"Please do not rush things," she warned.

Amanda untied her file and took out a number of letters and papers. "I'd like you to sign off on these," she said.

He flipped through them and frowned. "Four thousand eight hundred and forty dollars for five tutors during the month of August! Who in the hell did you hire—Socrates?"

"It's Dixie Jane. She is frightfully behind on her education. She can scarcely read and write, to say nothing of the fact that she has no idea who fought the Battle of Hastings, when and why it was fought, and less idea of how to find New Zealand on a map."

"Well, it seems there's no end to your generosity on my behalf."

"Some of those bills are advances on my own tutoring at Inverness this winter."

"What is this here? Greek?"

"Ancient Greek."

"You are a connoisseur of art and classical music. You know Shakespeare better than most actors. Why the hell do you have to know about the Battle of Hastings, much less ancient Greek?"

"I wish to learn what is taught at Harvard."

"I would be very happy to see you go to Wellesley if you so insist. There are women's institutions, colleges of sorts, popping up. Reasonable tuition, fine room and board."

"Boston is too far away, Father. Besides, those girls are so nasal. They look down on Baltimore as though we were a colony."

"I can't buy your argument, Amanda. What about Brown University? They are starting women's classes and it's only a stone's throw from Newport."

"The girls at Brown are quarantined in separate classrooms like rats with the plague."

"Then Goucher! It's right in Baltimore and it is a Methodist school."

The thin list died out.

Horace Kerr was about to cop a poverty plea when a strange sensation arrived. Tragic, but every so often a woman arises from the ashes like a phoenix, a woman of extraordinary intelligence and courage, beyond the scope of a normal woman. What was she to do?

He stared from the window to fields of beets and a beehive of black stoop labor attending them. Matthew Fancy had arisen from the ashes. To what avail?

The sensation would not leave him. Remembering Matthew got him thinking about the other time an epiphany had overcome him and he had freed his slaves nearly three decades earlier.

He took his daughter's hands and held them. She was surprised because they rarely touched.

"What if I underwrote an Amanda Blanton Kerr women's college?"

"Father," she whispered, trying to gain her equilibrium. "Oh, my dear God," she said. Don't get flooded with ideas, she told herself . . . but . . . girls learning medicine and science . . . girls learning whatever there was to learn!

"I can hardly speak," she said.

"Frankly, I don't like some of your strange friends and stranger ideas. You must carry it off with dignity for our family honor. I don't want a women's school in a constant state of anger. It is an advanced idea, but maybe its time has come."

Amanda studied Horace Kerr curiously. Now calm, she said, "It is a powerful offer. Are we speaking quid pro quo?"

Horace was struck by the lightning speed of her mind. "I honestly don't know," he answered.

"There is a missing member of our cast," she said.

"Lieutenant O'Hara?"

"Yes."

"I cannot tell you what great happiness you gave me the night of the Constitution. Yes, I was shocked to learn of his transfer to the War College. You tell me, Amanda."

"Things have been coming into focus," she said. What she didn't say was that an Amanda Kerr College could be her price. "It feels a bit like a conspiracy in the king's palace."

"Every house in Baltimore and every house beyond is a kingdom with a conspiracy. Put two human beings together and they'll conspire. Glen Constable?"

"He'll do," she snapped abruptly.

"If indeed this young daughter of his—"

"Dixie."

"If Dixie is at Tobermory, it would seem quite natural, and there is no hint of your past involvement with the Marine."

"Yes," she said crisply.

"Can we look forward to letting your mother know?" he asked.

"You mean, letting the world know."

"That's exactly what I mean," Horace answered.

"It will take some time, Father," Amanda said coldly. "I want to make certain he is properly housebroken."

"Mistresses?" Horace said right on.

"Doxies."

"Then you must be his doxie from the first night. You must quench—no, drench, his lust."

"I can do that," Amanda assured her father. "When we finally create our Kerr monopoly," she continued, using unmistakable pronouns, "I should like to be familiar with Maryland's banking laws, offshore shelters, the nuances of shipbuilding and boardrooms."

"You are nothing short of brilliant. How you do play your cards! Amazing."

"You must have been shattered when I wasn't born a boy."

"I was," he said. "Truth. I wanted another son desperately, but I soon knew I would not have traded you for ten sons."

They embraced, warmly, and, one could say, lovingly.

"You must hear me out," Horace began. "Women have been pissed off since the beginning of time and not without some justification. A new era will dawn only when enough women with brains can come up to your measure. Physically, men never had much to fear, but it will be frightening to know that females may be our equal in matters of intelligence. Men are not going to stand by idly and say, 'Come on in, girls, sorry for the past five thousand years.' You will bash your head in trying to change the way boys and girls work."

"We got rid of slavery, in a manner of speaking," she answered. "You had Matthew Fancy."

"He never argued a case in court."

"We will see a woman architect, or doctor."

"The Joan of Arcs and the Cleopatras and the Queen Elizabeths are aberrations and always seem to come to a tragic demise. Step into a boardroom, Amanda, and a wall of molten flame will rise up against you. The basic truth of man's nature is that men will manage the world, fight its wars, and invent its inventions. I can leave you all my power and riches, but you will have to come to your own peace with your woman's rage."

Amanda heard her father as she had never heard him before.

"The occasional Jew may slip into the room with the long polished table. They can be uncommonly clever as well as having incredible money connections. Catholics? Stone-age Christians. In time a small portion of them will elbow their way in. But it will be *no* to a Matthew Fancy and *no* to an Indian, and oh, my God, *no* to a member of the female gender."

Horace had never said these words aloud and it made him feel unburdened in many ways, with his daughter listening, mesmerized.

"I am not the enemy, Amanda, so don't point your finger at me. When I was an immigrant boy, I had a number of your liberal ideas. I looked over the lay of the land, knew I wasn't going to change things, so I got into step."

Horace went on. "Our most thrilling declarations for freedom and our most noble documents notwithstanding, America belongs to white Protestants. The Civil War did not change things, it merely altered them with scar tissue. The true battle cry of freedom has not come to pass."

He stood at the window and studied the fields outside. "Sugar beets on the Jersey Shore Line. The farmers in Europe are growing sugar beets as an answer to sugarcane just as they planted flax to try to replace cotton."

He turned to his daughter and felt comfortable, probably for the fist time, in putting his hand on her shoulders.

"Do you believe that if we had known about sugar beets a hundred years ago it would have prevented slavery? The Constitution Ball affirmed that, did it not? A room filled with white Protestants."

"Father, how can I make it?"

"Fulfill the plan we are hatching. You must have a husband of repute fronting you, carrying out your interests. Glen Constable is delicious, a pure white Virginian of the proper faith and a sharp businessman. Bear in mind, Amanda, you will always hold the purse strings."

The freight train blew past them noisy and rumbling, setting off a blast of air that shook their car. In a moment it passed and the engine of the private train belched into motion.

· 23 ·

THE BATTLE OF MARATHON

Early Summer 1891—Newport, Rhode Island

Ben Boone made a perfunctory knock, then entered the adjoining office. It was clogged with half-full sea chests, their contents being separated on a worktable twenty feet in length, set up on sawhorses.

Books, maps, retrospective reports, documents, artists' renderings, memoirs, studies, scholarly dissertations, monographs, and whatnot. This was Ben Boone's collection, gathered for over a generation. It was being sorted out chronologically and dated back to a time before Christ.

Second Lieutenant Zachary O'Hara was asleep atop the table, his jacket rolled up as a pillow.

"Hit the deck! The United States Navy has provided you with a bunk."

Zach popped one eye open, then the other, rolled off the table, and tried to arrange himself.

"It took me years to collect this crap. You're not going to get it sorted out in a week."

The major knew his man was working around the clock out of sheer exuberance . . . partly. And partly to keep his mind off Amanda Kerr, who was due to arrive in Newport soon. The annual "march of the moguls" to their summer "cottages" had begun its entry into the town like overloaded elephants hitched trunk to tail.

"Get your eyes drained or you'll bleed to death. What are you working on here?"

"The stuff Captain Storm sent you from China."

Ben picked up the thick notebook which had been opened and left lying alongside Zach.

"It's a jewel, this. It covers the years from the Sea of Japan to Borneo to the Indian Ocean." He flipped the pages. "'The Thirteenth-Century Mongol Invasion of Japan,'" he read, and set it back on the table. "Storm's monograph is the finest treatise on the subject. Unfortunately, most of the reading here is dull going. It will suck you dry. It shot me down so, I couldn't face opening another trunk."

Zach didn't seem to hear him. "How did you get all the foreign documents translated?"

"Maybe that's what wore me out. I had every professor of language in every university from Hopkins to Harvard translating, pro bono."

"Sir, it's not dull to me."

"It will be. Give it time."

"Whenever I get into a new paper, I feel like—what?—a spelunker entering a dark cave and inching my way in. Then *bang!* I come to this gigantic room illuminated with prehistoric drawings on the walls. I can't get over man's ingenuity to do battle four thousand years ago."

"Yeah, he got up off all fours with a club in his hand looking for a fight. And each century, man improved his capacity for slaughter. Anyhow, show up at my cottage for chow this evening."

"Aye, aye, sir, thank you, sir."

"And get your ass circulating around Newport. Take a little liberty. This shit will always be waiting for you when you get back. Newport is where good guys go to die."

During colonial times, Newport had been a major commercial center along with Boston and New York, its wharves filled with ships and its town hall buzzing with the new ideas of democracy.

Before the Revolution, British warships patrolled Narragansett Bay, collecting the king's royalties and impressing merchant crewmen.

Militia forts defended the coastal towns as best they could, but were scarcely able to stand up to the firepower of a flotilla of British barkentines.

Narragansett Bay was so choked that the Rhode Island Colony commissioned a "navy" of two vessels, which sailed forth to badger the British.

One of these vessels, the *Providence,* would later become the flagship of John Paul Jones and land marines to combat for the first time. It was the Rhode Island delegation to the Continental Congress that proposed the formation of a single navy to protect all the colonies.

Newport paid the price during the War of Independence. Her docks, dry docks, and warehouses were completely wasted and she ceased to be a commercial destination.

After the war, after a time, Newport returned to life, but the basic character of the place had been changed forever. Wealthy Southerners deserted their scorching plantations in the summer and made an exodus to the town. Then they came from everywhere in the country—the grand new entrepreneurial tycoons, the captains of industry, and the wealthy of all stripes flocked to Newport, established palatial summer homes, and converted the town to a center of culture and a showplace of rank, flying the colors of privilege from their yacht clubs.

The influx of wealth required a large pool of servants and a middle class of merchants and craftsmen as a support system.

An enclave of former slaves found the atmosphere less threatening than the South.

After the Civil War, recreation and vacations for ordinary people became part of a better way of life.

Advancements in electricity led to amusement parks and fun palaces.

Newport arrived, somewhat decently balanced between Vivaldi from the mansions and rinky-dink jazz on Moonlight Bay.

The United States Navy never grew tired of its love affair with Narragansett Bay. During the Civil War, when the Naval Academy was forced to relocate from Annapolis, it settled in Newport for the duration. There was always a sprightly naval presence in the town, from sailor boys to high-ranking staff officers.

Coaster's Island, a hundred-acre affair, was connected to the town by a pair of short causeways. It held a drab, massive Victorian public building that had housed the Rhode Island poorhouse and insane asylum.

In the early 1880s, the navy took over Coaster's and remodeled the main structures, converting it into the world's first naval war college.

Major Benjamin Malachi Boone had been the lone Marine on permanent assignment. Despite his humbled branch of the services, Major Boone was accorded the special respect due an eccentric one-armed maverick genius who had led the charge at Chapultepec.

Ben carved out his space in the attic, which no one else wanted, then seriously pursued his collection of documents on amphibious warfare. He badgered ship's captains, seagoing Marines, U.S. consulates, and whomever to send him material, which he got translated by twisting the arms of college language professors.

Ben was a brilliant curiosity, constantly in demand to give lectures, back and forth to Washington for consultations, able to afford less and less time for mining his amphibious pile.

The Corps, always squeezed in its budget, was unable to assign him personnel. His collection got musty and he grew cranky.

The size of the Marine Corps contingent at the Naval War College doubled with the arrival of Second Lieutenant Zachary

O'Hara. Ben believed that he had found a new right arm to replace the one he had lost on maneuvers.

Because of the major's longevity, modest needs, and respect, he was assigned to a small but lovely cottage on one of Coaster's bluffs, with a view to the bay. Boone had an orderly and with his per diem and poker winnings, he was able to afford a maid and a cook. Many were the flag officers who wore a path to Ben's door for a drink, a fine meal, and most of all, an evening of wisdom.

The "whiskey" hero had a sharp tongue to match his sharp mind. He could be intimidating. Ben's kind of power intrigued the power cult of Newport. He was on everyone's elite list. When the beast in him arose, in quarterly cycles mostly, he had no trouble linking up with a fine lady.

After a dinner beyond Zach's normal fare, he took up a rocking chair next to Ben's on the porch overlooking the Narragansett.

"I'd like to run something past you, Major," Zach said.

"As long as it's within budget."

"The empty space down from our office. I have a use for it."

"You'd suffocate. Can't get cross-ventilation in there."

"Suppose I use it only at night or on cool days."

"What for?"

"Building scale models like the ones they have here for naval battles in the lecture halls."

"Those admirals look like croupiers in Monte Carlo shoving battleships instead of gambler's chips around."

"Well, this is a war college."

"You're not here to play board games. A good general keeps a battlefield in his head."

"I'm just a lieutenant, sir."

"You studied the Battle of Marathon at AMP?"

"Yes, sir. Captain Storm taught that one personally."

"Refresh me, Zach."

"Four ninety B.C. comes to mind."

"Close enough."

Ben stopped his rocker and swept his arm in a semicircle. "If you look closely, you'll see the Persian fleet."

Zach squinted and studied the nothingness before him.

"Yes, sir, I see it."

"Well, what's going on?"

"The way the squadrons are moving, there must be six hundred boats, trières. Maybe between fifty and a hundred oarsmen on each of three levels. Another thirty or forty crew and infantry—that is, heavy and light bowmen and enough arrows to run a three-day battle. Supply boats with food and water, maintenance and ordnance crews, engineers."

"Miss anything?"

"There are a hundred boats pulled with a hundred oarsmen, each, and each carrying five horses, cavalrymen, and handlers."

"To what end?"

"Darius, the Persian emperor, has won the largest empire in the world. He had to use great resources to hold a line against the Russian tribes to his north. Crossing the Libyan desert is a bone in his throat. It was time for him to take the Greek option."

"Which was?"

"He had installed governors and garrisons in the Greek provinces, but they were loosely held and in a constant state of rebellion. A few years earlier, Darius had sent a fleet to punish the city of Eritrea for failing to pay its taxes. Athens came to the aid of Eritrea and the Persian fleet was badly mauled by the sea. Darius was a sore loser. The Greek provinces, anchored by Athens and Sparta, had to be punished and brought under control. In truth, Darius was coming on to move the boundaries of his empire. Beyond the Hellenic region lay Rome and Gaul and all of Western Europe."

Ben Boone was somewhat impressed. He threw an attack of questions. Many of the answers had to be a matter of personal analysis. Zachary O'Hara was intensely joined.

"This was a cumbersome fleet with primitive vessels and spit-to-the-wind navigation. It crossed the Aegean and rolled up the Cyclades Islands, constantly needing more supplies and conscripts.

It takes a lot of water to keep six thousand galleymen rowing and a lot of shovels to get rid of the shit from five hundred horses. They moved up on the Macedonian coast, north of Athens."

Zach was on his feet scanning that ancient horizon, pressing his recollections. He described the Persian landing sites, a long sandy beach buffered and protected by a swampy marsh.

"Darius debarked and set up a perimeter, then uploaded and assembled his forces, pitched tents. He planned a march to open ground, where he would engage the enemy with his cavalry of long-bowmen and make mud of the Greeks. Fact was, no one could stand against his horsemen on open ground.

"It was a mistake from the beginning," Zach concluded.

"How so?"

"Darius's leisurely unloading of his army gave the Greeks under Miltiades time to organize a defense, round up allied militia, set up ambushes in the passes, lay trees down across the mountain roads, and get a runner down to Sparta for help."

"Would the Spartan forces arrive in time?" Ben asked.

"No. The Spartans were involved in a pagan ceremony and would not move their troops until after a full moon passed. However, the Athenians maneuvered the oncoming Persian army away from open ground, so that Darius was flanked on one side by the sea, had a swamp at his back, and was stuck with one of his flanks in the foothills of Mount Ethos. It was not the maneuvering ground Persia wanted."

"Having dictated the battle site, Miltiades used his smaller numbers to outfox the enemy."

"Normally," Zach went on, "the center of an Athenian line was held by a phalanx of long spearmen, ten deep. Miltiades thinned the center out to four deep and gave it fallback positions and put his best forces on the flanks.

"Conversely, Darius put his best troops, the 'Immortals' and other elites, in the center, and the Persian flanks were turned over to conscripts from around the empire.

". . . the Persians caused the Greek phalanx in the center to retreat to secondary defensive positions, as the Greeks had planned.

". . . Athens stood off a weak attack on her flanks, wheeled and executed a double envelopment of the Persians, an absolutely perfect pincer movement, for the first time in history.

". . . the Persians were squeezed inside of a circle with no maneuvering room and effectively unable to use their longbowmen. The Greeks were winging spears, taking target practice. Their archers' strength nullified and in jammed disarray, the Persians fled into the swamp and back to their boats. Darius lost seven to nine thousand men, and Miltiades fewer than two hundred."

Ben Boone was very impressed. "If Persia had won, we would be looking over Xerxes Bay right now instead of Narragansett, speaking Farsi instead of English, and going to church in a Zoroaster temple. What happened, Zach? The Persian bowman was the finest in the world. He was well supplied. The Spartans were out of the action. Why did he fail? What have we learned from Marathon? After all, it was the might of an empire thrown at a weaker force."

Zach needed time to consult with himself.

"The makeup of the Persian force and their battle mentality were unsuited for the occasion. They'd usually burst in with the best cavalry archers in the world, then set siege to their goal. It had worked everywhere else. The Persians were hill and mountain men who never developed chariot forces, but there are two main reasons I can see."

"That's interesting."

"This may be conjecture, but Darius had to conquer Athens because the place was a hotbed of ideas that went against the very nature of royalty. Athens had the idea that kings or royal personages were not demigods on earth with divine rights but mere mortals. Athens, as a democracy, had made man flourish in thought, art, literature, in a manner not believed possible. It proved the idea that an imperial force could not defeat free men."

Ben wondered why he had never come to that conclusion, even

though his own life was an amalgamation of free thought. Lord, he'd have to give that one some scrutiny.

"That's very esoteric, Zachary. How about a bread-and-butter military conclusion?"

"The nature of amphibious warfare is to attack, take your objective, and hold it till reinforced. Darius was not offensive-minded enough. He chose to make a soft landing, picking a place away from the battle site, and unload his army in a leisurely manner. He lost the element of surprise. He allowed the Greeks to select the battle site."

Zach had come down to the key element of amphibious warfare that had to be instilled in the Marine Corps.

"What should Darius have done?" Ben asked.

"He should have made a hard landing. The Persians should have come in with fifty boats filled with Immortals and elite troops, hit the beach running, moved inland, and staked out their battle site."

Ben was near dazed with the clarity of Zach's analysis. In truth, he had hit on the key to the way that amphibious warfare had to develop.

"There is a big problem with this, Zach. As of today, there isn't a commanding admiral or general who wouldn't select a soft landing over a hard landing."

"Yes, sir, casualties."

"Casualties. What military staff of a democracy would order a landing and knowingly take heavy casualties?"

"There is no other way except to hit the beach running and break the enemy's back on the initial assault."

Ben closed his eyes and squealed his rocker into motion. "I'm going to have this study classified as secret . . . let it out piecemeal . . . until there can be a realization that a hard-landing alternative must be the centerpiece of the doctrine."

✦ 24 ✦

GEORGE WASHINGTON
BARJAC

The Eastern Shore—a Retrospective

Major Pierre Barjac was at the side of George Washington when Cornwallis surrendered at Yorktown. Barjac, an aide of the Marquis de Lafayette, had served the American cause well.

The Calvert dynasty that founded and governed Maryland, as the Barons of Baltimore, awarded Barjac a land patent of three thousand acres on the Eastern Shore.

The Calverts were of Irish Catholic descent in a sea of Protestants. Maryland became the most tolerant of the colonies. It did not go unnoticed that Pierre Barjac was also of the R.C. persuasion.

Pierre Barjac began his plantation with little agricultural background, but slaves, overseers, and some of the richest land on earth provided a fortune and a lordly way of life.

Tobacco, a ceremonial drug of the Indians, found its way to

Europe and addicted the continent. Tobacco was the golden crop and the Eastern Shore yielded the gold of gold in bonanza fields!

Greed-driven plantation owners oversaturated the market, as greed is apt to do, and there were wild swings in prices, causing that blessed land to go into an economic skid.

By the time Major Pierre passed on, slash-and-burn farming tactics had taken their toll. Jacques Barjac inherited a plantation on the fringe of failure.

Jacques Barjac was the basic high-living rotter who pushed his slaves to the brink in order to keep his privileged life and stay ahead of his gambling debts.

Jacques's three sons bailed out. The youngest, George Washington Barjac, obviously named, bought a commission into the Marine Corps and fought in the Mexican War of the late 1840s. He commanded a company that took the fearsome, disease-ridden overland march from Vera Cruz to Mexico City.

Barjac's company was on the flank of a company commanded by Ben Boone during the storming of Chapultepec. The two men were bound for life by the experience.

When Father Jacques sent out a desperation call, it was ignored by his older sons, but six years' service in the Marines had satisfied George Washington's wanderlust, and he returned to a decrepit plantation.

The father, on his deathbed, was filled with remorse and the need for salvation. George was faced with selling the place off or making it go.

Overbreeding of hogs had all but ruined the marshes and creeks along the boundary. They were sludgy and contaminated by slimy oxygen-sucking algae blooms . . . and the fields were not much better.

The Eastern Shore survived despite gluttonous landowners because of its unmatched abundance. There was timber and ship-building, blizzards of water fowl and wild hogs and wild horses. The soil was fertile for near any crop, grain and fruit orchards and vegetables. There was fur trapping of beaver and muskrat and raccoon, and bursting oyster and clam beds, and multitudes of fish in the bay, and a growing taste for the fascinating crab.

And, there was tobacco, a tarnished but still-golden leaf whose producers were getting in step with the world demand. Many tobacco plantations and small holders converted to general farming. A good farmer who used his acres wisely could make a go of it, given the hunting and fishing at hand.

Despite the dilapidation, Barjac Plantation was too promising to cash out.

The bedrock problem of the Eastern Shore was the constant migration of labor, always causing a shortage of fieldhands.

George Barjac calculated as deeply as he could in an effort to match the type of crop he would grow with the type of labor that was available.

Slaves sold for a few hundred dollars for a young girl to as much as twelve hundred for a top field buck. The negatives were providing subsistence and the never-ending problem of runaways.

. . . and thousands of free blacks wanted out and they fled to the cities and the frontier. The most skilled made it to a shipyard, but almost all other work was menial and conditions for free men of color were often as brutal as slavery. Free blacks lived off fish heads, and filled the jails, burdened with long sentences for trivial or imagined offenses. When farming slackened in the winter, the free blacks had to undercut the plantation owners who hired their slaves out to the canneries or as domestics.

There were times when a free black who could not get off the Shore sold himself to a white master.

. . . and the indentured came from Britain, working off their passage in the fields for five to seven years. It was a means for the English to unload their prisons and dump their convicts on the Eastern Shore.

. . . there was contracted prison labor working shackled and collared, a desperate and violent crowd whose only escape was into the arms of sweet death.

This was a place of whippings and mutilations and brandings and yelping bloodhounds.

Some slivers of decency in this black hell were provided by the Quakers, Methodists, and liberal Catholics who formed a kind of barrier against the hard-nosed Anglicans and Presbyterians.

It remained a torturous place, sucking the life out of cheap labor, but never enough labor, to keep up with greed-driven crops.

In the Corps, George Barjac had dealt with Indians and Mexican peasants. Even during his hard military contact, he retained a moral code that kept him on the side of civility.

If, indeed, he was to take over the plantation, he knew he had to make a decision about labor that included a measure of human decency. He had a number of ideas. He would not promise anyone an easy life, but in terms of the day, a relatively fair life.

Barjac came to a gambler's decision.

Although tobacco was not as golden as it had been, the Maryland leaf had a great number of things going for it, mainly its addictive qualities. Every generation, his own included, had a love-hate affair with the smoking of tobacco, but each new generation would fall under its spell. There would always be a demand for tobacco and it would be a lifelong proposition to rid oneself of the habit.

The question was how to match up the demanding handwork of tobacco with available labor.

Using the sainted Lafayette, Washington, and Barjac names, he charmed his way to heavy financing from France and put his plan into motion.

Barjac added another fifteen hundred acres of land, purchased a sturdy oceangoing schooner, and built a support system of a deep inlet, pier, and warehouse.

In the 1850s, he offered his most productive slaves and some free blacks a lease of up to a hundred acres, a cabin, animals, equipment, seed, vegetable plot, and he guaranteed the purchase of their tobacco crop.

. . . in exchange for half of the harvest.

Those who took the proposition came to realize that sharecropping and credit at the company store meant debt that could never be overcome, but which was passed down from father to son.

To make feudalism work in the nineteenth century, George Barjac played good owner/bad owner with astonishing skill.

As a one-man dispenser of justice, Barjac was wise enough to let his *people* dip one toe in paradise. There were meaningful perquisites, trapping and fishing rights, the opportunity to open new acres, and protection from the whites.

There would be no corporal punishment. However, any breaking of rules meant instant eviction.

Tobacco wore out one's body and tested one's soul, what with the backbending labor in preparing the ground, the hand planting, hand nourishing, handpicking, hand curing by the Indian method, and hand packing into thousand-pound hogshead barrels, which then had to be rolled from warehouse onto pier and aboard his schooner *Maria-Belle,* named for his beloved, pleasantly plump wife.

The bane of the Eastern Shore was that it was one of the Lord's chosen breeding grounds for mosquitoes. The mosquitoes were fed upon by the masses of fish and fowl and larger insects, but not even a planter's wife could escape the infestation. Maria-Belle Barjac blessed George with three sons and four daughters, then died young from the summer fever.

George Barjac lamented her death for a proper period, then set out on a lifelong dream, to obtain French culture and plant it in Maryland.

He took his eldest son and daughter, Max and Lilly, to Paris for serious refinement as the start of a plan to "rotate" all seven children.

Paris had a permanent collection of aristocracy from all over the continent. When Barjac entered the scene, he was a bit of a legend himself, and was whisked right into the salons of the top echelon.

Max entered a university, studied economics and banking, and kept his Left Bank life and debts under reasonable control. He respected his father and was ambitious to secure a future in the dynasty.

For Lilly, not yet sixteen, it meant convent training and finishing school. One could liken the Paris aristocracy to a swarm of Eastern Shore mosquitoes trying to get at this pretty, rich American thing.

There was no shortage of needy aristocracy to keep the old dreams alive. Countess Josephine Bayard, known affectionately as Fifi, was a widowed, childless, clever guardian, a little past her prime. Her forte had become to house a few young ladies of proper foreign families, teach them how to negotiate the risky cultural currents, supervise their education, dress them to snuff, school them on flirtation and seduction and the right places to be seen. When Fifi had a freshly schooled American heiress to offer, aristocracy knocked on her doors.

Countess Josephine Bayard took Lilly as her ward. Although frayed, Fifi was yet desirable, not quite forty, and playful and wise.

In addition to having her to "finish" his daughter, George Barjac took fond notice of her and made the ocean crossing to France as often as possible . . .

Then things went awry and George was summoned to France, unexpectedly. Lilly had lost her head over Baron Felix Villiard, a vain bachelor twice her age from a family of vineyard wealth in Burgundy. Count Felix was "it" in Parisian society, a critic of taste and fashion.

Villiard's fame had come from his work as an Egyptologist, that is, opening the tombs of pharaohs. In this pursuit, he had spent half his life. His heart was not in the wine business, and several seasons with moderate vintages had made his finances shaky.

Lilly was a tender thing with an ambitious father who owned an enormous plantation in the New World, and she was ripe for the plucking.

Countess Josephine liked neither the peacockery of Felix Villiard nor his "holier than thou" tomb sacking and was suspicious of his finances.

Despite her advice, George Barjac could smell his goal. With his daughter Lilly ensconced in Paris, she and Felix could establish him as a lion of society. For the moment George Barjac was blind to the rest.

He was euphoric when his daughter was married at the Cathedral of Notre Dame in a show of raw plenty, a throwback that made the old aristocracy nostalgic. Barjac was a full member, albeit a Yankee member, of the cream of the fantasy players.

After Lilly and Felix wed and drifted off on a royal barge down the Loire River, George turned his attention to Countess Josephine Bayard. Fact is, Fifi had taken George's just measure from the first moment he had arrived in Paris.

Fifi became the wife of a Maryland planter of renown, calved two children of her own with him, and established a small bastion of art, music, and literature on the lowly and removed Eastern Shore.

They were a splendid couple, and she kept splendid control of a menagerie without having recourse to internecine warfare.

And what of Lilly?

Lilly and Felix journeyed on a well-known road of marriage that settled somewhere between the tepid and the occasionally simmering.

Lilly lived in the magnificent Château Villiard in the country, and in a breathtaking Paris residence near the Bois de Boulogne.

She traveled with Felix to Egypt on her first and only archaeological dig, discovering that a barge on the Nile was not a barge on the Loire. Egyptology was not her game, but despite prior warnings, she had chosen a man afflicted with it and she dared not protest his long absences.

By the time she reached nineteen, Lilly was the mother of twins, Chantel and Maurice. The molding of Baroness Lilly was right on course.

For several years she summered in Newport with the twins while her *mari* plundered tombs and vanished into the seedy mysteries of Cairo.

George Barjac grew remorseful about having fed his daughter

to a dilettante. His own marriage to Fifi had set off chimes of happiness. The blandness and lack of fire of his daughter's marriage and the questionable motives of his son-in-law in entering into it soon tinged him with guilt.

George built Lilly a lovely private summer villa a bit removed on the Onde la Mer estate, as a second home.

There was a saving grace. The flaws in the Villiard marriage were numerous, but it developed a central theme, vital to both husband and wife. Together Felix and Lilly had power.

Power as a couple was understood by them, and a well-worked-out series of compromises ensued. In Paris, they moved well together, and from time to time pleasured each other. In Paris, they did not tempt scandal.

. . . but Cairo was another thing.

. . . and so was Newport. The twins were immersed in activities with their cousins, and with impeccable cleverness, Lilly was able to have summer dalliances. She chose men who were visiting Newport as artists or writers, and she crafted short affairs beyond the reach of scandal.

Lilly's sisters and brothers and sisters-in-law and brothers-in-law were strongly in sympathy and put up a "blue" wall of silence.

And Lilly always went home to Paris at season's end.

✎ 25 ✎

YOLANDA

Early Summer—1891—Coaster's Island

Every day at dawn, the major and the lieutenant did a drill of stretches and pull-ups and ran several laps around Coaster's. Soon the water would be warm enough for Zach to add in a half-mile swim. Fortunately, Ben could skip that exercise, having learned that swimming with one arm was a losing proposition.

Zach reached the giant eucalyptus tree first and jogged in place until Ben caught up.

"Enough for me," Ben panted.

"I want to do another round," Zach said, and sprinted off.

Ben plopped, took a swig from his canteen, and viewed the small-boat marina bobbing about as he lit up.

Ben was worried, for sure. His command consisted of but one man, but that one man, Zach, was tidying up his dreams and visions.

An envelope was on Ben's desk. Amanda Kerr had reached Tobermory. The contents of that envelope could blow everything up in his face.

Three days earlier, he had given Zach permission to construct a scale model. Zach worked the clock out and set up the Battle of Trafalgar, after which Ben gave a discourse. How quickly O'Hara absorbed Horatio Nelson's crossing the T and smashing the enemy fleets.

"Sort of like a naval version of hit the beach running," Zach commented.

Zach was so filled with energy that Ben wondered if he would go into orbit. Was that girl going to derail him? If the news was good or bad, should he let Zach free-float into a mess in Newport or should he cook a little *Semper Fidelis* pressure under him?

Another swig and a three-minute sitting nap.

"You here already?"

Zach came alongside and cooled down.

"What are you doing tomorrow?"

"Thought I'd work," Zach answered.

"It's Sunday. George Barjac has twice invited me to bring you. You come with me."

The request had the ping of a command.

"Sure, what's the dress code?"

"Informal, mess jacket."

"Are you sure you need me, Ben?"

"I do not want George Washington Barjac to be insulted. He's my buddy-buddy from before you were born. You know how important the man is to the Corps."

"I guess I have become a little antisocial," Zach said. "What's the event?"

"Sunday picnic, lawn games, three-hour lunch, mobs of kids and grandchildren, first family, second family. You'll like them. And, by God, they're Catholics."

"Why didn't you tell me that in the first place?"

Zach helped the major to his feet. They double-timed it back, but Ben did not turn off to his cottage.

"Come up to the office for a few minutes."

They headed into the building and up the stairs in silence. No need to ask what this was about.

The envelope lay on Ben's desk.
"This came this morning. I'll wait downstairs."
"Why don't you stay."
"Sure."

Dear Zachary,

 I have been remiss in failing to contact you sooner. Immediately after the Constitution Ball, I went away to Virginia on a personal matter, and by the time I returned to Inverness, you were gone.

 Let me congratulate you on your commission and your new assignment.

 A few nights before the Constitution, at the wedding of Beth and Casper, I was swept up in the sentiment of the moment and told you I still loved you.

 This passage of time has allowed me to clear my mind and gain a fuller understanding of what my future course need be.

 I do not believe you were sent to Newport as an act of a merciful God, but because of keen judgment on Major Boone's part. If anything, it will test our resolve to go our proper ways.

 That day at the glen, I epitomized the selfish side of my character and tried to lure you into a battle in which we both would have been slain. You had an honest grasp of what was, and is, a hopeless situation. I totally agree with you now, that to carry our friendship further would be to court disaster.

 Falling out of love has not been my easiest task, but it has given me the maturity to be able to transform my thinking. I know what must be done.

 Glen Constable and I have set out with the idea of a future permanent relationship. He can afford me a steady life and companionship. I must tend to my roots and the meaning of my family.

 I have undertaken to play big sister this summer to his young daughter, Dixie Jane, who is a lovely child but sorely undereducated and unprepared to live a life of important intent. Dixie Jane and I were together at the Constable farm near Richmond and have developed a deep affection for each other.

I do not foresee a formal announcement concerning Glen and myself until after the coming winter season. The courtship came on quite suddenly and we should allow for a proper time to pass. Yet it seems a natural conclusion.

I won't pretend this is any easier for you to read than it is for me to write, but what was between us is being tucked away, forever.

I know that Newport has greeted you with open arms and hope you are already back in the chase. I will not see you formally or entertain any pleadings, and I know you will respect these wishes.

For certain we will run into each other by chance during the season and I trust we will greet each other, at such times, in a civilized manner.

Good luck, dear Zachary.

> *With kindest regards,*
> *Amanda*

Zach handed the letter to Ben.

"I don't have to read it," Ben said.

"Yes, please," Zach answered.

Ben read it sadly, and was sad for the young lieutenant.

"I don't want to lose you, Zach."

"I dug my own hole. I'll cause you no grief. I want to stay."

"You going to be able to make it?"

Zach nodded.

"And you feel alone, hung out to dry, and wish to hell that someone understood how much it hurts, don't you?"

"It hurts in a way I can't even start to explain."

"I'm sure it does."

"How can you know how I feel?"

"I suppose I can't. You must be the first Marine in a hundred and twenty-two years who has felt the pain of a love lost."

Zach was jolted.

"You join the Corps because you're lonely and you've made yourself believe you can live without a woman's love. Then you try love and get divided in half and . . . she's gone," Ben said.

"I'm sorry, Ben, I didn't know."

"Sure. So, go drink your pain under, then go into Newport and get yourself into a little trouble."

"What happened, Ben?"

"None of your fucking business."

"What happened?" Zach repeated.

Ben rocked his chair. Its familiar squeal helped his thoughts.

"I'm going to give it to you in one long sentence. Don't mention it again, ever. It's off-limits."

The major opened his vault.

"After the Civil War, I commanded the Marine detail at the Boston Naval Yard."

On first try, her name did not come out. "Yolanda," he said at last. "Yolanda came from a Portogee fishing family out of Gloucester. We had a contract with one of their fishing co-ops. We bought large quantities for ships heading out on long cruises. She ran that show as our buyer . . ."

Ben looked out the window to the sea, as he always did, for solace.

"If she stood alongside Amanda Kerr, you couldn't tell who would be the more beautiful. A Portogee and a one-armed hillbilly, but could we make music. I was a first luey and the Corps didn't know quite what to do with me when that horse ate my arm. Anyhow, I was well respected for my service to Winfield Scott. The Corps was so small they couldn't afford to lose me, so I was pegged and branded to remain a staff officer."

Ben silenced his chair.

"The commandant, the one long before Ballard, refused us permission to marry. She had Negro blood in her and her skin was too dark. Some of the boys were permitted to marry Asian women; there was no way I could be stationed between Quantico and the capital. Officers' wives, particularly navy wives, would make life unbearable."

"What the hell are we?" Zach said. "The French Foreign Legion?"

"Corps was only half of the problem. She was a Portuguese Catholic. Fucking Portogees are like super-Spaniards, super-Sicilians with their blood feuds and blood libels and lust for vengeance. She fled to me and that had to be avenged. We were able to set up a cottage away from the base. The Corps looked the other way."

And now, quiet.

"We had over two years together before her father and brothers found her and waited till I was gone . . . then took her life."

❦ 26 ❧

ONDE LA MER

There was great consternation in Newport when it was learned that George Washington Barjac, a Catholic, had purchased five wooded and prized acres of cliffside land.

The mansions of Newport had been solid affirmations of the success of the Reformation. How to handle the invasion? It would do no good to ostracize Barjac, but he was building a family hamlet up there. The architecture was vulgar, low, and hugging the bluff lines. No grandeur. However, it was in keeping with the shore below it . . . rather graceful, actually.

Attitudes mellowed in time.

Hell, Newport was a tolerant place. Didn't it have the first Hebrew synagogue in America? What of that?

On second thought, having George Washington Barjac as the Newport house Catholic had a certain enticement to it. The man was an entrepreneur, a tobacco king, and his wife, Josephine, could charm a lion out of a meat bone.

Fifi Barjac had a head start over Rhode Islanders in playing the arch game of court. Court had been in her blood for generations, centuries. The influx of their Parisian utterness soon had curious noses sniffing. From her accent to her scent to her opinions and tastes, she set an impeccable standard that made her the pied piper of Newport.

Their salon showed the shadowy, fuzzy art that was now gaining notice in Paris, and words were spoken at readings by the authors of the day, and music was performed by the composers and singers and players that no one but Madame Josephine could obtain.

Even the highest lords of industry looked for the chance to rub elbows in that certain Fifi French aura.

"Benjamin Malachi Boone!" George roared as Ben's shay passed through the carriage gate. George was grayed and thinning atop with a potbelly amidships, but as neatly pruned as a Faustian character, and he greeted Ben with a bear hug.

The lady alongside George made a full statement of her command, with no words needed. Josephine was a stunning matter, in full bloom and of easy manner.

"And you are the son of Sergeant Major O'Hara!"

"Yes, sir."

George took a step back, examined Zachary, and nearly broke into tears as he pinched Zach's cheeks and unloaded a juicy kiss that landed somewhere on the bridge of Zach's nose.

"I, of course, was long out of the Corps when your sainted father served, but I had the honor to meet him on a number of occasions and I even saw you a few times as a boy, but you wouldn't remember."

"He spoke of you with great reverence," Zach said.

"My wife, Madame Josephine Barjac."

She kissed Zach on both cheeks, her eyes twinkling. The host and hostess each took an arm and led him up a long path toward a knoll.

Halfway up the path, Lilly Villiard came to meet them with a big embrace and kisses on the cheeks of Ben Boone.

Zach became instantly aware of her. She was a petite lady with eye-catching roundness and of elegant carriage. Her milliner's creation was a broad-brimmed hat that curved to form a classic silhouette of her face. Her white skin was framed by black curls that lay across bared shoulders.

Lilly's nose was definitely Barjac, but she wore hers as an attraction.

"My daughter, Baroness Lilly Villiard, and this, dear Lilly, is the son of Paddy O'Hara, one of the great men of the Corps."

Zach shook her hand and nodded, taken by the way she bore her four decades with little flaw, like a nicely turned out Limoges statuette.

"Nice to meet you, ma'am," he said.

"Call me Lilly," she said.

"And I am George and this is Fifi and this is your home. Lilly will introduce you around and we will catch up with you."

Lilly took Zach's arm pleasantly and they ambled up ahead, exchanging getting-acquainted banter.

At the top of the lane, they passed through an arabesque archway that led to an immense lawn and garden. It was as though a book had been opened in its center and a lace valentine had popped up; a tree bearing a swing bearing a little girl, a row of pansies with their faces all bent in the same direction, a dog leaping for a ball, two boys rolling down a slope, a girl running a hoop, ladies in little boxy straw bonnets, and two gentlemen in conference with their heads close and hands clasped. Behind the tree, lovers sneaking a kiss.

If one jiggled the tabs, the valentine went into motion, the tree swung, the pansies swayed in unison, the doggy went up and down on his hind legs.

Zach had never seen a scene like it, except in an illustration in a book. The whole place seemed to be floating.

. . . until a scream as a child fell into the frog pond, was fetched by his nanny, and the mud scraped off.

It was easy to tell the Barjac sisters from their sisters-in-law, not only by their fine noses, but a universal twinkle of mischief and matching scents.

"*Oh, hi* hi," followed every introduction.

Zachary acquainted himself at each level. He fungoed fly balls treetop-high to the boys and was a one-man demon on the soccer field, but it was his skipping rope double Dutch that won him all the maidens. Zach knew his double Dutch. Gunny Kunkle at AMP used it as a torture device.

He moved among them well; no stuffy yachting type or golden-armed admiral, but a Marine like Uncle Ben and George Washington Barjac himself. Winks, smiles, nice little touching.

Onde la Mer was a mood piece, a low rippling spread along the cliff, a departure from the massive Protestant manor houses, a cloud misting in and out of the levels with a central Moorish fountain and graceful archways. But France was also represented in a tiled roof overhang on the big patio and a square like that of a Mediterranean farming village.

Walkways went out like spokes to a number of petite villas set on the bluffs.

A long table had been set for the children and their nannies. The adults' tables were at a remove, with smaller and more intimate seating.

Seeing that Lilly and Zach were pleasantly fine, Fifi seated them at a table for two, where they could be properly viewed and gossiped over.

Zach had doffed his jacket for the games on the lawn and could not help but note that Lilly seemed to enjoy a quick feel of the steel in his arm, and for a flash or two, their eyes said it was very pleasant.

The big serving table was filled with creatures he had never seen before and other foods foreign to the enlisted men's and officers' messes. Lilly had a cart with samples of everything rolled up to their table, and she filled their wineglasses. They clinked and everyone looked toward them and clinked.

Then Zach won the day. There was an outbreak of hugs and

kisses and English and French babble as the children were paraded through with their nannies.

Zach took the hand of one of the granddaughters and kissed it gallantly.

"But you don't know my name," she said.

"You are Alice with the blue ribbons to match your blue eyes. And this is Madeleine and Paul and you are André and Nicole."

George and Fifi were impressed.

"You have made yourself very popular, Lieutenant," Lilly said.

"This whole thing doesn't seem quite real," he said.

"We are all on our good behavior today. Everyone is talking to everyone, but it's still early." She smiled toward Fifi and her father and raised her glass once more.

More dishes arrived as works of art.

An hour into the meal and the music of flute and harp made the wine go down like magic nectar.

Zach became light-headed. Impromptu singing broke out and storytelling on a borderline of salty humor, and a good Gallic argument erupted with much flurry and no blows.

Then more stories.

Then toasts.

And the patio filled up with children.

Now dancing.

And a slow balloon descent back to earth.

They eased off, two by two, leaving the table as though limping from a battlefield.

Lilly found an empty hammock. Zach insisted, weakly, that she take it.

"No, no, Lieutenant. You must be exhausted from working your way through lunch. Let me spoil you."

He lay on his back, swinging in a kind of levitation. Zach stared at a starling nest in the tiles. As the birds came out for their own cleanup feast, he was taken by the number that had been able to fit into the nest, and a scent of tobacco soon held the courtyard and he blinked curiously. Lilly was smoking a cigarette in a long holder.

"Hello," she said as she rocked the hammock.

"This is nice."

"Good. You're looking at me strangely."

"I've never seen a woman smoke a cigarette."

"Do you mind?"

"No."

"That might only be the first of our naughty habits."

Major Ben and George Barjac came up behind Lilly. Zach gave them a wave, a grin, and he konked off to sleep.

Ten Days Later—the Naval War College

Zach laid the monograph on his desk and made an ugly face at it. There was nothing so puzzling as the memoir of an admiral or general who was defeated in a battle explaining how he had really won.

Ben's footsteps on the stairs gave him a reprieve. He came to his feet, smiling.

"Welcome back from Washington, Major."

They gave each other light jabs on the left shoulder, a way of personal greeting. Ben nodded at the workload on Zach's desk.

"Doesn't look like you've missed me," Ben said.

"I feel like we're really up and running," Zach answered.

Ben took a document from his briefcase and handed it to Zach.

Naval War College Project Random Study Sixteen is hereby reclassified as Top Secret. Second Lieutenant Zachary O'Hara, USMC, is accorded Top Secret clearance in matters relevant to this study.

The meaning of it thrilled him. Zach had entered the ranks of a small circle of men, keepers of national secrets. Ben let him think about it.

"How did this all come about?"

"The way you've attacked this project means we are going to have a comprehensive look at the hits, runs, and errors of over five thousand years of amphibious warfare. Your line of logic says we need to lay a foundation for modern thinking to be examined and tested."

"Hell, I'm not that smart," Zach said.

"Could be. Could be that the subject has been badly over-looked. If you keep going the way you are going, 'Random Study Sixteen' can become an important work. Here's where we start having some fun. You remember Richard X. Maple?"

"Yep."

"Maple is leading an American team to draw up a naval proto-col with the British Admiralty defining areas of vital national inter-est, joint use of facilities, intelligence sharing, joint training. You yourself predicted this at AMP."

"I didn't realize anyone was listening."

"What do you know about the Amnesty Islands?"

Zach shrugged.

"It is a small archipelago of both volcanic and coral origin south of Jamaica, in the middle of nowhere, between the Mona and Windward Passages.

"Back in the 1700s, the British were unable to stop a brigand, Sebastian Lyme, from becoming the scourge of shipping on the Spanish Main. So they made a deal. Lyme was declared an earl and awarded the Amnesties as his earldom in exchange for protecting the British shipping lanes. Lyme only partly behaved. Entrance to the Amnesties is treacherous, with squalls, reefs, shifting channels, rock bottoms, and a convergence of rough weather.

"So long as British cargo was protected, the Brits turned a blind eye to the islands' use as a pirates' haven bulging with contraband."

Zach got the flow. "Are the British turning the Amnesties over to us as part of the protocol?"

"That's it. Paragraph ten. The Amnesties didn't mean doodly shit to America until our recent ambition to build a canal. The islands will become very important, afford us an advance base, not a great one but a place from which we can monitor the seas to and from the isthmus."

"What's doing there now?"

"Still an earldom with the worst kind of sugar plantation oper-ation. Dirty history, slave breeding in cribs, penal colony, black magic, orchids, mosquitoes, smugglers' paradise, Chinese colony runs the port . . . There are a few thousand blacks working the cane fields and refinery. They die off young."

"Trouble?"

"No, but I've never seen a black man from the Caribbean who wasn't rightfully pissed off. There were a few surviving Carib Indians on one of the islands and they staged an insurrection about ten years ago and joined the other two million murdered by the Spanish, who were replaced with slaves. We're not getting involved in local politics. We have other fish to fry."

Ben spread a map. "Each island has several names. They've never been fully surveyed. For our purposes, we have identified them as Sinkhole, Mudhole, Blackhole, Asshole Major, Petite Asshole, Rat Hole, Bunghole, and the large island here, Shithole."

Zachary toured them with a magnifying glass, smelling out Ben Boone's prints. "Looks like the Amnesties are off the trail, isolated, away from prying eyes, and filled with beaches and jungle, a perfect training ground to practice landings and jungle warfare."

"I've wanted these islands for a long time," Ben said. "'Random Sixteen' ties in perfectly. The Corps can work up dozens of exercises. The navy can have itself a firing range. Future joint Marine-Navy maneuvers will home us in on the full possibilities of naval gunfire. All the things that 'Random Sixteen' will call for, future weaponry, wireless ship-to-shore communications, crafting the perfect landing boat, can be proven there. The navy has to give the Corps these islands to garrison. *Capisce?*"

"What are our chances?"

"'Random Sixteen' now becomes essential to shaking the Civil War dust off them hound-dog admirals."

"Nothing," Zach said, "nothing is going to get in the way of me getting this project done, and a hell of a lot faster than you think."

They went over it again. It was heady stuff, a sweet coming together, and by Christ, Ben the old master could pull it off. They were glowing from the challenge.

"Anything exciting happen in Newport?" Ben said, slyly shifting the subject.

"I've been to Onde la Mer a couple of times," Zach said. "Three nights back, there was a reading in the salon by Mark Twain, just the family and a few close friends. It bends a man's mind."

"Sorry I had to miss Twain," Ben mused. "He's not an imitation English writer, but the first pure American author."

"It was some scene. The Barjac family sitting in a semicircle around Mark Twain and the kids listening like he was a holy man. George Barjac amazes me, how he controls that platoon of his."

"Mark Twain and George Washington Barjac and Madame Fifi. You should see Barjac's organizational chart. The empire is broken into interdependent regiments commanded by sons and sons-in-law. Max, the oldest, runs the eight-thousand-acre plantation. George has two magnificent clipper ships, the *Bunker Hill* and the *Yorktown*. No raiders get in their way. They carry heavy artillery and a crew of sharpshooters. The *Bunker Hill* takes the Maryland tobacco directly to Marseilles to their cigarette factory. The *Yorktown* cruises the Mediterranean markets in Morocco, Syria, and Turkey for blending tobacco.

"Barjac has taken over a plantation in the Vuelta Abajo Valley of Cuba. World's prime cigar leaf. They've a slew of Chinese coolies, the best cigar hand wrappers anywhere. A son-in-law, the tall guy . . ."

"Laroque, Collette's husband."

"Yeah, Laroque, he's important. So inside the family, we have the banker, the lawyer, the distribution, etcetera, etcetera. George runs a tight regiment. But, Zachary my man, let us not bullshit. You're not really interested in them. You want to know about Lilly Villiard."

"Did you not set me up, Ben?"

"Maybe I did. I thought you'd need some diversion after you heard from Amanda. I was worried about how it might affect your work."

"Amanda Kerr is out of my life."

Ben wasn't so sure but didn't press the matter. "What do you want to know about Lilly?"

"The usual."

"The Barjac women would rather flirt than breathe, but I think they stay close to home."

"Lilly is the one who comes to Newport alone," Zach said.

"Lilly is the only one not involved in the Barjac family business. She and her husband run a big show in Paris part of the year, and that's her life. Her social power is the flame. Otherwise her marriage is flat. Her father, George, has always had remorse about pushing his way into the Paris scene at her expense.

"For years," Ben went on, "she brought her twins to Newport. Her daughter, Chantel, is married into a gruesome Swiss banking family and has a couple of kids of her own. The boy, Maurice, has taken up grave robbing with his father. So Lilly comes alone. I've known her since birth. She's exquisite and very sad. George and Fifi give her a lot of slack. Anything else, Zach?"

"Did you ever fancy her?" Zach asked bluntly.

"It might have passed through my mind, but a Marine does not fuck the married daughter of his best buddy."

"I'd better drop out of the Onde la Mer scene. I'll end up screwing up your friendship with the Barjacs."

"If the lady invites you to her villa, maybe you should go."

❦ 27 ❧

DIXIE JANE

A Few Days Later—Tobermory

Glen's former wife, Nini Constable, was able to hold a small fixed smile when she turned her daughter, Dixie Jane, over to Amanda for the balance of the summer. Nini's emotions were always well contained, but she did pale at the sight of Amanda Kerr's stunning beauty.

The ex and the possibly future Mrs. Constable greeted each other with civility as Amanda showed Nini where the daughter would be "camped out."

Nini Porter Constable could be graded among her cast as "Elite Standard." She was a well-trained lady who functioned smartly but by rote. Neither passionate rage nor uproarious high spirits could penetrate her bland wall.

Amanda and Nini exchanged an afternoon of dull pleasantries about Dixie Jane's care. The girl managed to look pious and promised her mother to be a model houseguest.

And by the by, if you need to get in touch during the last few weeks of August, here is the address of Mr. Rudolph Dorfman in Asbury Park, just in case, you know.

When Nini left, Amanda and Dixie Jane went into hugs of unrestrained exuberance and ordered up banana splits to be served on the veranda. They went over a few ideas for the summer and the incoming tutors. Amanda was so damned glad she was here.

They had parted happy with each other at the Constable farm, and Amanda realized Dixie Jane had made a mark on her.

Amanda got to thinking about Amanda. She really had missed Dixie Jane and wondered about the new role . . . big sister . . . extra mother . . . perhaps an announcement during the upcoming winter season. Dixie Jane made it comfortable.

Actually, her name was Virginia Jane. She had a dog named Dixie who had gone to dog heaven when Virginia was only five. So great was her grief, she changed her name to Dixie in remembrance of her first great friend.

The Constable family, Virginians all, felt the name suited, so Dixie it was, sort of a last hurrah for the Old South.

"But I don't want to go horseback riding," Dixie Jane emoted. "That's all I ever do at Grandpa's farm."

"You've never ridden on a beach," Amanda said.

"I prefer to sail, or rock-climb, or simply meditate. I don't want to go riding."

"I guess I'll have to find some other little girl to give these to," Amanda said, holding up boy's riding britches.

"Oh . . . oh . . . oh . . . let's go riding!"

Once Amanda hefted Dixie up into the saddle, the girl never wanted to come down again. And when they sailed, Dixie wanted to sail over the horizon. And when they played a duet at the piano, she dreamed she was giving a concert.

They raced the beaches at sunset, wild rides to Valhalla, and they found the coves of the Hebrides. They skinny-dipped at night and read Mark Twain on their bellies before the fire.

Glen Constable had feared that his daughter might become a lifelong victim of the divorce. She had gone from a chattery little butterfly to a doll-clutching, whiny, very lonely person.

Particularly after Rudolph Dorfman became a caller. He tried to be nice to Dixie, but she knew the only reason he was doing so was so that he could get close to her mother.

His beard was black and scratchy. All his family in Richmond had scratchy beards; even the women scratched.

Mr. Dorfman tried to make jokes that were so bad even he didn't think they were funny. Rudolph Dorfman and his scratchy brothers had a big department store in Richmond. He offered to let Dixie Jane take anything she wanted. She only took a few hair ribbons so as not to make him feel bad, but she hoped her mother got the message.

Nini didn't. Oh, Mother will be in Asbury Park during the last half of August! How charming!

When Glen Constable came to Newport on his weekends and otherwise, he could scarcely believe the change in his daughter and he was grateful for the deepening relationship between Dixie and Amanda.

When Daddy left, did those two have fun!

Newport was like a seven-layer Viennese cake, from the grandeur of the family names to the beaches on which every sailor wanted to be washed up.

Yachts of the New Yorkers took over. In due course, the New Yorkers would probably own the yacht club as well.

. . . came their great moment every day when the sun went under the yardarm at the yacht club and the cannon boomed, nary a moment late, the gentlemen's bar was open for business. *Boom!* crackled the cannon, and in came the skippers, and conversation grew giddy after one drink . . . and a number of toppers.

At the bottom layer of the cake there was a pleasure park all lit up and a plunking banjo at a black nightclub on the wharf. By day the water was filled with tiny one-sail dinghies fit for two persons and beaches where some of the women paddled in the waves and oodles of sweet shops and saloons filled up with horny sailors.

Dixie Jane and Amanda spent a great deal of their days away from Tobermory.

Their favorite fun was to take a sunset ferry cruise around the bay, fill up on hot dogs, lick off mustard, and slurp a bottomless sundae. The dance floor would fill up with couples tripping the light fantastic.

Dixie Jane gasped the first time a sailor asked Amanda to dance. Amanda could dance wildly. She was nice but never too friendly. Came the incredible moment a young man of ten or eleven asked Dixie to dance. Most of all, Amanda and Dixie liked dancing with each other, as a number of women without beaux did.

. . . when it became dark the shore line lit up like a foreign port one was just entering. They skimmed past an exhilaration of whirling lights of the pleasure park. As the sound of the calliope drifted out to the revelers on the ferry, Amanda would suddenly become sad and hold Dixie Jane's hand, tightly.

They paddled into darkness, mansions in the distance, mystical inlets.

And sentimental singing and lovers spooning on the darker sides of the decks.

And happy trippers came down the gangplank weary, with "Moonlight Bay" growing more and more distant.

Glen Constable lowered his eyes when Amanda emerged from the cabana onto the beach, as though Lady Godiva of Coventry were passing. Her swimming costume wasn't exactly vulgar and they *were* on Tobermory's private beach, but her arms were completely bare and her legs were bare well above the knee and the neck and back were daringly scooped and the material rather clingy.

Even Dixie Jane's suit was more modest, but Amanda had her own ideas of sporting wear . . . those boys' riding britches . . . well . . .

Amanda gave Dixie and her playmates stern instructions. They decided to go crabbing on the nearby pier.

Amanda ran and dived into the water without a swimming cap and stroked a good hundred yards. One didn't see too many women actually swimming. Their suits would balloon up with water. Women waded. Amanda swam.

She ran back, checked Dixie Jane, passed on a wicker strand chair, and spread a big Indian blanket on the sand. What with her wetness and the thin stuff of her suit, Glen could distinguish both cheeks of her backside and her nipples.

She toweled off, lay on her tummy, stretched and groaned and let the sun kiss her. Glen sat alongside in position to be able to watch the kids at the pier.

"Horace seems in good form," Glen said.

"He's really enjoying the sailing this year. Maybe we'll take a run with him next week."

"That would be dandy. Over cigars last night, he conveyed both of your passions to build the Amanda Kerr College."

"For women," Amanda added. "I hope we can find the right piece of land and break ground by next year at this time. How proud and puzzled parents will be looking up to the stage with their daughters holding diplomas. A premedical graduate on her way to Johns Hopkins. It makes my heart beat so fast thinking about it. Every day seems to tell me I'm heading into the best of life."

"I think you will become one of the most looked-up-to—no, adored women in the country."

"Poo," she answered.

Glen now wore his uncertain look. "I wake up some mornings and my heart clutches. No Amanda. Is she real?" He stopped.

"We're fine, Glen," she consoled.

"I don't wish to complicate matters, but you are so enchanting and I'm over the hill."

"Not so. You are handsome, clever, kind, and a wonderful father."

"Amanda . . ."

"I don't want to discourage you, nor am I putting you off. It would not be fair to either of us until a number of things are resolved."

"Is O'Hara one of them?"

"He's certainly a part of it. I was shocked when I learned he would be stationed in Newport, but I am also surprised at how little it has annoyed me."

That cheered him up, some.

"Everything I see about you assures me, Glen. I know I love Dixie Jane. I know I want my college, but you and I haven't been together that long. Perhaps by the time summer is done, I'll know for sure."

Amanda eased her shoulder straps down in order to leave no marks. Her back glistened. Glen dropped a few grains of sand on her and she cooed.

"Sometimes, I'm afraid to touch you."

Amanda rolled over to him, sloe-eyed. "Give us a kiss, Glen, we won't melt."

"Dixie might see us."

"Wouldn't that be lovely," she said.

Glen had nice experienced touches. Her arms went about his neck and she drew him down on the blanket. They kissed and kissed again. Amanda turned again to her tummy and uttered a contented "ummm."

Glen traced her open back with his lips. Amanda gasped and grasped the blanket, not out of passion, but to conceal the fact that she felt nothing. She had never felt anything for him, from him. Could this ever change?

"Happy?" Glen asked.

"Ummm."

Dixie Jane gave a shriek of joy and horror as she pulled a huge crab up to the pier on her line.

The two girls lay on Dixie's bed cattycorner so their feet met in the middle of the mattress and pumped as though they were pedaling a bike. Dixie Jane rendered a nasal imitation of her math tutor. They pumped feet some more. "We are going sailing on the *Lochinvar* tomorrow with my father and uncles."

"Oh dear."

"What?"

"I promised Emily I'd have tea with her," Dixie Jane said.

"She'll understand," Amanda said. "You are very kind to her."

"We have some nice talks, mostly pretending. Amanda, how did she get that way?"

"Fell out of a swing when she was a little girl. At least that's what's been passed down. I'm not certain. She's just disturbed."

They pumped their legs clockwise then counterclockwise then clockwise again while they covered a number of subjects.

"Amanda."

"Yes."

"Am I going to start having a period soon?"

"Not yet. You're going to have to show some boobies first."

"I hope they're beautiful like yours. My mom's boobies are beautiful, too, but she ties them all up. I hope Scratchy-beard leaves marks on her."

"You want to get whacked?"

"And Mother would never talk to me about periods."

"Your mom's got to live, Dixie. She's been hurting for a long time. If you're not happy about Mr. Dorfman, then your mother can't be happy, either."

They stopped pedaling, and as great girlfriends are wont to do, lay on their backs, side by side, staring at the ceiling.

"I would have never learned about periods until it was too late if you hadn't explained to me why you couldn't go horseback riding that day at Grandpa's. Is it a secret you try to keep from your husband?"

"No, but men don't usually like it and they can make a woman feel guilty."

"That's disgusting. When you open your college, are you going to teach girls about periods?"

"They'll already have them, but perhaps we can teach them why."

"Excellent," Dixie said.

In the long silence that followed, Amanda had come to learn that her pal was steaming up to ask a heady question and would probably approach it diagonally.

"If you could make one wish, what would it be?" Dixie asked.

"Well, I have another good girlfriend, Willow, who you haven't met. We used to lie like this. I would make Willow the first American Negro woman to become a professor."

"What would she teach?"

"She could teach white girls how to beat their daddies at checkers."

"I can already do that."

"She'd teach law. Willow Fancy, doctor of law."

"Do black women have periods?"

"Yep, but Willow won't be having one for a while, she's expecting a baby anytime."

"Do you miss Willow?"

"Yes."

"She can't come up to Newport, can she?"

Amanda propped up on an elbow and gave Dixie a tickle. "Miss Dixie, you started all this because if I told you my wish, then I would have to ask you what your wish would be."

Caught. Amanda always knows what I'm thinking.

"So, what is your wish?"

"I wish you loved my daddy more."

"We have not been seeing each other for all that long. It can take two people time to feel strongly enough to make a lifetime decision," Amanda answered, knowing that the girl's keen mind was interpreting her tone of voice. "I care for your father very much and I want it to grow. What makes you think I don't love him?"

"It's easy to see when you come into a room."

"I don't understand you."

"If you see me in a room, you always break into a big smile and we always hug. You never smile more than a blink when you see Daddy and you scarcely touch him, maybe let him peck your cheek while you sort of turn your face away and say 'ummm.'"

Amanda floundered for an answer. "Well, Miss Dixie, your father and I were necking on the beach today."

"Yes, like I neck with my new puppy."

Dixie yawned and stretched. Amanda doused the light and adjusted the overhead fan, then lay with her arm about the girl. Amanda wanted to cry out, "I don't feel anything!"

Dixie finally slept. Amanda got up quickly, not wanting to leave tears on the pillow. She went to an adjoining bedroom and crumpled up on the bed, gritted and gritted until she stopped her tears.

She'd never stop scanning every room she entered for sight of Zach. All summer, everywhere. What if she saw him with a girl on his arm? Was not seeing him better than seeing him with someone else?

There was a stirring and Amanda looked over to the connecting door to see Dixie standing.

"Do you love me?" the girl asked shakily.

"I love you very much, Dixie Jane."

- 28 -

THE YANKEE

A Fortnight Later—Onde la Mer

The gentlemen's smoking parlor would have made any prince of the desert proud with its Arabic-Ottoman furnishings and hangings and hand-beaten gold and jeweled objects of art and a flow of incense of biblical origin. The floor was covered by a silk carpet, the largest Hede ever imported, with nearly three million knots for every square meter. It was light sand-colored, like the desert, and one could only surmise its value.

This den was a fiercely held male domain that even Josephine respected. On special gatherings, such as Bastille Day or someone's sixteenth birthday, children, the ladies, and other impostors gained entry. Otherwise nothing ludicrous took place, depending on one's definition of *ludicrous*. Purple jokes and bawdy boys' talk for the main but it could get rowdy, George Washington Barjac type of rowdy, and every Protestant kingpin millionaire hungered for an invitation.

Lieutenant O'Hara had not visited Onde la Mer for some time and came this night with Major Boone, almost on orders.

Zachary found himself with a disgusting cigar in his teeth delicately fencing and gracefully losing to Papa George, who, considering his age, was still a fairly decent swordsman.

. . . when Lilly opened the door wide and entered like a waif among the ogres, went directly to Zach, and signaled him to drop his weapon and follow her.

"I am requisitioning the lieutenant," she said.

"But, Lilly, I am winning," Papa cried, "and we are about to enjoy some cultural entertainment."

Lilly stood on tiptoes, kissed her father's cheek, and said, "Ta-ta, Papa," and left with her prisoner, passing four turbaned musicians and a lady dancer of note entering.

At the center fountain, Lilly took the cigar from Zach and hissed it out in the water.

"Thanks for that," Zach said. "I never did get the hang of these things. I must say that these smell better than the ones in my da's saloon."

Lilly started to load her cigarette holder, then retreated. "You don't care for any kind of tobacco, do you?"

"My aunt Brigid smoked a clay pipe. She and my ma both died of consumption. I think Da felt that tobacco had something to do with it. Might have been the only bad habit he didn't have."

Zach took her holder, snuffed out her cigarette, and took a deep breath of pure, unfouled air.

"I missed you at our gallery showing. We hung a Turner," she said.

"I've been burning the candle at all four ends," Zach answered.

"Ben told me how obsessed you are with your work. No matter, I'll be happy to give you a personal tour."

Music whined Oriental from the parlor along with the crisp crackles of finger clappers.

"Fatima," Lilly said. "I've seen her dance. A dozen years ago I

was a fairly decent belly dancer, for special occasions. Would you
see me to my villa gate?"

"Love to."

All spokes led out to the bluff walk, where the sounds of the
sea, Onde la Mer, took over. They walked until they were out of
the light to a place of dancing flames between two torchlights.

"Are you playing some kind of bourgeois game with me? By
bourgeois I mean—"

"I know what *bourgeois* means," Zach said.

"You do? I'm intrigued. How?"

"Victor Hugo," he said, and kissed her well, pulling her toward
him very slightly to see if her body was part of her kiss. She came to
him liltingly. Lilly handled it easily and Zach felt some of his own
sorrows leaving him. He tugged her toward him again, but she put
her hand on his chest.

"We'd better have a chat," she said, leading him to a bench.
"That was very pleasant, but I have a feeling you have absented
yourself because you have a feeling I was leading you on."

"That's what I think. You were leading me on," he said.

Watch this young man, Lilly, she told herself. He doesn't min-
uet. He polkas.

"Paris invented flirtation, I think. It comes naturally, rather
expected. The problem with flirting is that it always has a tinge of
naughtiness to it. If I overstepped, I'm sorry. It is just the vanity of
an old girl in need of a little flirt."

"You're not an old girl and you're very beautiful."

"I should be," she answered. "I spend enough time before the
mirror every day troweling my beauty on."

Zach took her hand, kissed it, and gave it back to her.

"Come on, Lieutenant, you know you can have any girl in Newport."

"Their fathers are all lay preachers with shotguns. Washington
and Newport are both fine places, but that's not why I joined the
Corps. I'm almost embarrassed to be here living like a duke."

"But wouldn't Paddy O'Hara be proud? You saw how my papa greeted you. Are you ill at ease when people come on so strong?"

"It's a fact of life." Zach stopped.

"Well, there are a number of women, older, and single, in Newport. It has always been a courtesy of the navy to dispatch a handsome young officer to escort them. To get them home safely when they're too stiff. However, you're quite a number, Zach, all on your own."

"So are you," he answered.

"But I am not a surrogate mother nor the summer replacement for a twenty-year-old sweetheart with whom you are very angry."

"Ben talks too much . . ."

"Ben, indeed. Newport bleeds gossip no less than Paris. It's the glue that holds the bourgeois drawing rooms together." She rallied herself.

"I am a grandmother," she went on, "certainly old enough to be your mother, and I am married. I despise an aging woman clutching at some young cadet. How do I feel for you? Let's have a pleasant friendship."

She arose and he arose and they lulled their way toward the little bridge to her villa. There was a gate. The bridge crossing over was but a few feet long over a small ravine.

"I suspect," Zach said, "you are trying to spare my pride. You think I am too clumsily inexperienced."

"All men are clumsily inexperienced," she said, "but none quite so clever as you, Zach."

"And I make you pleasantly nervous."

"Pleasantly."

Zach took her beneath her arms and lifted her so their eyes were level and his lips found hers and they maneuvered them until they discovered a softly sealed position and worked them back and forth, together now, half of forever, then he let her down to her feet.

Lilly leaned on him, dazed, and tapped his chest. Her defenses had been shredded. She whirled out of his grasp.

"You are so——!"

"What?"

"So damned American. You are a Yankee bastard!"

"The summer is half done, Lilly. You are beautiful and I want you."

"I'm shaking all over, Zach," she gasped between kisses. "You saw right through me, you beautiful Yankee bastard!"

"Yes?"

"Yes."

"Yes?"

"Yes."

"Christ," Zach said, "we have a logistical problem. I have to go back to retrieve my hat and sword and Major Ben and say good-bye."

"You're right. It has gotten late. Do you know the private road alongside the Burton estate?"

"I can find it."

"It's an access road to the houses farther down the bluff and it bypasses Onde la Mer. I have a private entry off it. Tomorrow, say two hours after the cannon sounds at the yacht club."

"I'll be there."

Their departing kiss and the sudden freedom of her hand to wander left no doubt.

It was a long day for Zach. He imagined that she was going to have a change of heart and cancel their rendezvous. The Barjac family seemed to know what one another was thinking. *Lilly won't be joining us for dinner.* Would a raised eyebrow from Papa George or Fifi be enough to tell her not to make a fool of herself?

Easy, Zach, he cautioned himself, and stop thinking bad thoughts. Surely Lilly knows the rules of conduct of Onde la Mer, but would she be overreaching with a lad so young? His yearning for something tugged at him.

When the cannon boomed from the yacht club, the shell seemed to land at Zach's feet.

He opened her garden gate. Lilly was framed in a scarcely lit doorway in a lush emerald gown that set off her black hair, brushed down straight on white shoulders.

They came together softly into a room of candlelight flitting under a breeze that sent shadows bounding to and from the white walls.

She held a finger to her lips—say nothing—she let him see her all. Zach was stunned. Lilly was white ivory and rounded like a Grecian statue. He'd never looked upon her likes.

She gracefully slipped his jacket off and shirt buttons open and she saw the likes of arms and chest she had only seen on powerful men working in the fields. Oh, rock of Zachary.

He could be rightfully vain of his body but was not so. This was Lilly's place and Lilly's sporting ground.

Lilly was nearly unable to fathom the tenderness of how his eyes watched her breathe and move her cheeks under his touch like a dancing feather. He kissed her eyelashes. His patience and wise fingertips were not what she had expected.

"You are very strong," she said.

"You're the boss."

Who was this lad? How much of his cool demeanor was a ploy? He was waiting so calmly for her to set the tone and the cadence, but he was going clear through her by touching her shoulders.

All right, she accepted his silent dare. Let's see what you're made of, Lieutenant.

No explosions, now, but a lover's test . . .

The lovers' room took him in and the lovers' place laid him down on silk. Lilly sat above him and glided him in a fraction. Her hands pinned his shoulders still, her face came close to his so they stared in each other's eyes. She lowered herself every several seconds a fraction of a fraction, lower, and their eyes daring each other to retain sanity.

. . . each tick now whirling their heads, the room. Their eyes never unlocked. And farther and farther until they both looked half mad and beaded into sweat.

. . . and she finally could come down no farther . . . and they locked and played each other with tiny pulsations.

"My God," Lilly managed as the sweat now burst. They remained locked. "Where did you learn this?"

"From a very wise woman, tonight," he answered.

It was clear to Zachary that Lilly Villiard came from a tribe of Parisians for whom pleasuring a man was a way of life.

The main path offered little detour after little detour. In another time, Lilly could have been a ranking member of the sisterhood of courtesans. There were so many new delights; an enchanted seascape of diversions.

They spoke to each other, offering wise entreaties, and found a level of humor and fun, glad to see each other and to handle a clumsy moment with laughter.

Zach discovered what he already knew by instinct. He enjoyed giving pleasure often more than he enjoyed receiving it. A lover such as that was rarely come upon by her. Lilly Villiard became ambivalent about how much pleasure she was supposed to take. She began to regard each new set of sensations as dangerous and she grew afraid of where wild abandon would lead.

They came to a level of very happy lovemaking but avoided the thunder and lightning on the horizon.

Lilly and Zach spent their time together judiciously, inconspicuously joining the family's social life. Zachary was popular but hardly invasive, and came and went from her villa so no one really knew or seemed to care.

From time to time he acted as her escort away from Onde la Mer. There didn't seem to be a hell of a lot of gossip. Barjac was the Catholic and the Marine family of Newport.

Although there was diminishing return as lovers, they greeted each other smiling, never found the other boring, and lost any awkwardness over the difference in their ages.

There were times, wonderful for them both, when he just wanted to rest his head on her bosom and be held, even till dawn.

This was the first and only moment of Zach's life that included serenity.

. . . close your eyes and rest, Lieutenant, but let us stay clear of dangerous places.

They had gone full circle. The wall he had built against Amanda Kerr was eroding even as he made love to Lilly Villiard.

Alone at night in his quarters, the ache for Amanda returned, punctuated by every sounding of the ship's bell and the mournful foghorn.

✎· 29 ·✎

FOLLOW ME!

Ten Days Later—under the Eucalyptus Tree

The day of reckoning had come upon Ben Boone sooner than he expected. A draft of the protocol with the British was initialed by Rear Admiral Richard X. Maple.

Ben had hoped for more time so "Random Study Sixteen" would be further advanced. It held the core reasons for a Marine takeover of the Amnesty Islands' garrison.

Maple was the key man to sell the idea to the commanding officer of the navy, Admiral Langenfeld. If Maple could get the boss aboard, the secretary of the navy and the president would certainly agree.

Zach was ordered to quickly draw up a list of preliminary conclusions from "Random Sixteen." Telling the flat-out truth as they saw it at this early stage was apt to ruffle the dander of many of the top brass.

The major had hoped the Corps would get the islands first, then come along with "Random Sixteen."

The opposite was happening. And there were still those, led by Commodore Harkleroad, who wanted to put the Corps out of business.

Ben stopped under the eucalyptus tree, midway on the daily exercise run, dug into his kit, and reread Zach's initial thoughts. He shuddered.

Zach ran up the path to him, took a towel he'd left in a crook of the tree trunk, and wiped the sweat off.

"I didn't realize when you came out of AMP I was getting the new von Clausewitz."

Zach was exhausted. He had worked most of the night through and started the day on three hours' sleep.

"I knew it," Zach muttered.

"'Conclusion,'" Ben read:

'Naval gunfire used as artillery in advance of a Marine assault has severe limitations. Guns of warships are designed to fire flat projectiles against enemy naval vessels. A missile running parallel to the water cannot give the offensive artillery support required to move troops inland (as can a land-based howitzer cannon, which arches its shots) . . .

'Naval gunfire can force an enemy on the beach to retreat temporarily, but fire must cease once the Marines reach the waterline, otherwise ship guns could be firing too close to landing troops.'

"'Conclusion,'" Ben said:

'The navy must turn over command and control of the landing force to the landing force . . .

'A beachhead is a place of tremendous activity, landing troops and supplies, beaching landing boats, gathering the wounded, etc. . . .

'At the present time, communications—blinkers, semaphore, flags, flares, message boats—are too slow and cumbersome to allow prompt reaction to conditions on the beach.'

"'Therefore,' says von Clausewitz, 'until a system of hard-wiring from ship to shore or a system of voice projection over space is developed, closer integration of the sea force and the land force is not possible.'

"'Conclusion,' and it's a honey: 'The navy must turn over command and control to the Marines, at the waterline.'

"Shit," Ben said. "Those people would use tom-toms and carrier pigeons for communications before they'd turn over command and control to us."

"You forgot smoke signals," Zach said.

"Let's see. 'Conclusion,' here we go:

'From the waterline, the Marine force will seize territory inland and hold it till relieved. This could be the second or even the third day.

'Therefore: A Marine must carry sufficient ammo to fight with for three days. The present single-shot, heavy-caliber 45-millimeter ammunition is not suitable for an assault . . .

'Assault Marines should be armed with a five-round bolt-action thirty-caliber rifle of the highest accuracy; namely, the Krag Jorgensen already issued to the army . . .

'Moreover, every Marine should be qualified as a sharpshooter or expert, so he will expend his ammunition wisely and accurately from distances up to five hundred yards.'

"What are we going to do with those smoothbore, single-shot forty-five-caliber elephant guns?"

"Shove them up a museum's ass," Zach said, coming to his feet.

"Don't get your shit hot, I haven't finished, yet. 'Conclusion: calls for the development of automatic weapons as an urgent priority.'"

"Ben, where did I hear it said that the invention of a fully automatic weapon will be the greatest killing machine in all warfare? Which of your lectures did I pick that up at? A couple of sets of machine guns on either flank of our beachhead in an elevated place will go a long way to assure the success of that beachhead."

"'Conclusion,'" Ben read on:

'Nothing is more imperative to the future of amphibious warfare than a proper, self-propelled landing boat with a crew of three capable of holding twenty or more assault troops . . .

'Such a landing boat, of shallow draft, with flat bottom, and armor-plated, must be able to handle breaking surf and deposit the marines at the waterline . . .

'The boat will not be beached. It will take on wounded, have reverse capability, turn around, and go back to the mother ship for more men and weapons. *A continuing line of boats from ship to beach and back is the heartbeat of expeditionary landings.*'

Zach folded his fingers together like a sinner at prayer. "It all depends on how far away from home the eagle wants to shit. Islands are going to be fortified, Ben, as outer defenses. We're not always going to be able to make soft landings. And we're not going to dump men halfway around the world without the support of the nation, advance bases, naval protection, and the basic weaponry . . . and men."

"We are at peace, Zach. We are a democracy. Military planners will be very cautious, that's human history. They learn too late that these theories should have been developed before we're standing ass deep in wet cement waiting for it to dry. 'Random Study Sixteen' has too much truth in it. It shakes up too many stagnant doctrines."

At that moment Ben Boone felt an anxiety of the kind he'd felt before only when being shot at. It all came to a head so damned fast. It wasn't the end of the career that half paralyzed him now. It was the realization that these basic ideas were going to be rejected and the price might be a lot of dead American fighters.

He wanted to plead with Zachary O'Hara to modify things, slip around with the usual dodgy language of a military study. He saw Zach and he saw right. He could not ask this young officer to change his conclusions without losing his own beliefs.

Well, now, not much left to do but continue to turn it in and pray for Richard X. Maple.

✎ 30 ✎

THE CASINO

Late Summer—1891

Despite the unwelcome appearance of Lieutenant Zachary O'Hara in Newport, the summer of Horace and Daisy Kerr had gone well. After a few indigestions, Horace felt that the compact he'd made on the train with Amanda had gained roots. Amanda had proven she intended to purge herself of that Marine. His name was not mentioned and there was not so much as a hint that they had seen each other.

If there was a void in Amanda's life, the Kerrs felt that Dixie Jane Constable filled it. Amanda had many friends, particularly in the arty circles, but she rarely made an intimate friend. An exception had been Willow Fancy. Willow was married now, having a child, and they had drifted out of the center stream of each other's life.

With Dixie Jane, it was like true love. Amanda could have this child as her own as sister, teacher, and the wife of Dixie Jane's father.

Amanda moved about Tobermory with a lightness, got to know her cousins and uncles better, and was a most charming co-hostess with her mother.

How magnificently Amanda eased into the woman's role. Well done, Horace! Horace had passed the summer with waning suspicion and scarcely uttered a harsh word.

For Daisy Kerr, nirvana! The slightest hint that Amanda and Glen might announce during the coming season filled her head with sugarplum parties. Daisy and Horace watched their daughter create the perfect Newport portrait of herself and Glen with Dixie Jane between them and a candy-striped party tent behind them. By Jesus, what a picture. Queen Amanda taking on the empire with Glen Constable as consort. That's the way they had entered the Constitution Ball and Amanda's moment of realization.

Horace Kerr knew that when one is on the right course, one picks up allies. The strongest notion that had ever gripped his daughter was to found a women's college. It would be her giant step into becoming one of the great women of the century.

The second ally was Dixie Jane. Horace and Daisy loved the child no less than if they had been her own grandparents. There were genuine virtues in the child, her fine manners and response to affection and, mostly, how kind and gentle she was with Emily.

The third ally was Baroness Lilly Villiard, who had appeared in Newport socially with O'Hara. Seemed proper enough—old girl, young military escort.

George Barjac and Horace were fellow Marylanders, both Republicans who'd freed their slaves early. They were occasionally at odds about who was dumping the most waste into the Chesapeake, Dutchman's Hook or Barjac's tobacco plantation.

Horace prayed regularly that Lilly Villiard was atop O'Hara . . . or under him . . . five nights a week. There could be no doubt that if and when Amanda got a wisp of Lilly, she'd wish O'Hara dead.

The trees began to doff their summer's wear as the sun rose lower and cast longer shadows. Dixie Jane saw them from her win-

dow as icy fingers crawling toward her. Nini Constable would be
fetching her daughter soon.

Amanda instructed Dixie Jane to muster maturity and to open
her heart to create a special attitude for the situation.

"We have to make do with the mother and father given us. Nini
needs her girl and Dixie Jane will need her mother. Your mom and
Mr. Dorfman want to make you happy and you have to do your
part."

Dixie Jane had been thoroughly lectured on the sadness of
divorce and of her duty not to make things more difficult. Nothing,
she was told, can take the place of blood.

Dixie Jane wanted to know only one thing from Amanda.

"Are you and my daddy going to get married?"

"We certainly seem to be heading that way," Amanda said in a
non-Amanda answer.

"Can you promise?"

"I promise I love you and I'll always love you."

Nini arrived with lovely news, or so she thought. Dixie Jane
was invited to join her and Mr. Dorfman on a buying trip to New
York. Afterward, they would take a "get acquainted" vacation at
Saratoga Springs and the girl could bring a cousin or companion.

Dixie Jane imitated Amanda's great composure at a farewell
picnic and went off with her mother, quietly hiding her despair.

Amanda knew Dixie Jane was treating her mother with the same
indifference she herself had shown Horace and Daisy. The breach
could take years to mend, and oh, the vengeance of a ten-year-old
girl certain she had been rejected and was about to be abandoned.

When Nini and Dixie Jane left Tobermory, Amanda could hear
dizzying cycles of Daisy's voice, uncommonly shrill . . . "Well, I
hear that the Dorfmans own half of Richmond, but isn't it cheeky of
him to go off with Nini Constable and Dixie Jane to Saratoga
Springs . . . Nini said nothing about a chaperon . . . but they are
probably not going to have a proper announcement . . . There is a
strong rumor that Dorfman is half Jewish or his late wife was Jew-

ish or half Jewish or some such, never mind, Dixie Jane will come flying back to your arms, Amanda. Amanda. Amanda? Are you all right, dear?"

"I'll miss her so."

The elephant train, that march of the moguls, went into reverse as the seasonal visitors to Newport closed down their summer cottages and headed home for the winter.

Horace Kerr stuck to his promise to hold a family reunion at Tobermory over Thanksgiving, though he made that promise before he learned Zachary O'Hara had been stationed in Newport.

The summer had given Horace no cause for alarm. Daisy was already in motion for the Thanksgiving event. In addition to Horace's immediate family in Newport, there was a Scottish branch of the clan, some of Daisy's relatives and leftovers strewn about America.

Daisy would have to find accommodations for those they could not fit at Tobermory. There would be a hundred people in all.

The logistics of number of servants and tons of food were staggering, but when Daisy had a gala to oversee, she was renewed.

Horace had a telephone line and switchboard direct to Dutchman's Hook so he could keep an hourly control of the yard, and he sure as hell enjoyed being able to holler from Rhode Island all the way down to Maryland.

Narragansett Bay was emptying of those pissy little day sailboats. Wind and weather gave bite to his sails on *Lochinvar* and a real chance to test out the Butterfly. So far, the results were tepid.

As it headed into a stiff wind and through riptides, races, and fluky currents, the weight shifts had enabled *Lochinvar* to pick up a quarter-knot speed. If one were running a fifty-mile course, that would be enough to whip anyone. However, the Butterfly kicked in and out and often mysteriously, with no rationale.

Horace decided that at the right moment, he'd sail *Lochinvar* on the cruel course to Immigrant Reef, a three- to four-day test of seamanship.

When he was at the helm, his mind drifted to making the ultimate gesture of inviting Upton over from London for Thanksgiving.

Horace had a growing begrudging pride in his strange boy who now headed one of the top syndicates at Lloyd's and was a member of the governing board.

These times saw an astonishing development of direct communications between America and London by telegraph and telephone cable. Horace gleaned enough information to know that Upton had his finger in the pie and made and covered his bets beautifully.

Of equal interest was that Upton was accepted in "normal" social circles in London. In fact, he had an impressive standing with some royalty. Horace assumed Upton did his queer thing away from observation.

It was difficult for Horace to feel *he* should be the one to break the ice. One touchy problem about Thanksgiving was that Upton might feel free to bring one of his pansy friends over with him.

Would an invitation to Upton show that I have the magnanimity of a great patriarch or would it cause me unbearable embarrassment?

He wouldn't go near Daisy on that matter. Better not push it. Things were going too well. With the Constable merger just on the horizon, the Kerr name would have the strike of a rattler in that rarefied air that Vanderbilt and Harriman breathed.

Emily had done nicely during the summer. Thanks to the tenderness of her mother, sister, and Dixie Jane, she had moments of smiling and lucidity.

Upton? Don't have to make a decision this instant. By God, with direct communication to London he could do it in a day.

Folks came to Newport to play. Two centuries after the Pilgrims landed on Plymouth Rock, lawn tennis landed in Newport, which became its American capital. The medieval game of court tennis had been modernized and formalized by the All England Lawn and Cricket Club in Wimbledon.

For centuries it had been played in the interior courtyards of palatial mansions and châteaus of England and France.

If the paintings were correct, one could make out Henry VIII prancing about a court, racket in hand, though that might be stretching it, given His Majesty's obesity and gout.

When the game was moved outdoors, it remained an elitist sport played on lawns clipped to near velvet. Wealthy vacationers took to the new sport and formed clubs near their own winter mansions in Brookline and Forest Hills.

As with golf and yachting, tennis socialized into private venues which protected its exclusivity. The American palace of lawn tennis, indeed, was the Newport Casino.

The massive clubhouse was proclaimed a Victorian marvel, shingled, gabled and clock-towered, bulky, asymmetrical, and rambling, enclosing a center court as though inside a horseshoe. Covered stands of boxes and preferred seating were on the shady side; open stands, opposite, where ordinary folks could be spectators.

Horace Kerr was a founding member, and, in his more youthful years, played fairly well.

Though Horace believed that Amanda, with her grace and speed, would be a natural player, she refused, for women had to play in full-length skirts, cinched waists, and heeled shoes, an absolute regulation costume of the club. Moreover, the men smiled on the ladies condescendingly.

Bellevue Avenue was a chatty street during the summer where the new and expanding middle class could rub elbows with the elite. There were archery ranges, some theaters and eateries, and an open-to-the-public lawn-bowling pitch. The horse rink and shows were close by; the entire scene very American in texture.

One could shop in the casino store on Bellevue Avenue, but the club itself belonged to the mighty. The clubhouse was an extravaganza of high taste and on this day boasted a finery of ladies wearing boxy, bindy millinery creations, bustled and laced, with gentlemen in white ducks and boaters.

After Dixie Jane departed with her mother, Glen Constable came up to spend ten days, just the two together, to let natural impulses take over.

Yes, there was a buzz as Amanda Kerr entered the casino on the arm of Glen Constable. She nodded and blew a kiss and waved and winked as they were ushered to Kerr's courtside box. Glen floated. Who could blame him if he was so smashingly pleased with himself?

First, a well-played match between the Newport men's singles champion and the champion of the Marion Cricket Club of Philadelphia.

Glen had played doubles with them both and displayed nonchalant modesty as he leaned over and coached Amanda on some of the nuances of the match.

Great stuff, what!

They were served and sipped lemonade as attendants drew new white lines on the court after the first match. There was a rising air of anticipation when the next match was announced. The Newport mixed doubles team would play an exhibition with Lotte Dodd and Wilfred Baddley, the Wimbledon champions.

The covered stands were packed with over three hundred gaily festooned ladies and gentlemen wearing jackets bearing their club emblems. CAVALIER LAWN TENNIS CLUB, RICHMOND, VIRGINIA, Glen's insignia read.

Over the way another three hundred spectators sat in open stands. Many of the women held annoying parasols.

First game.

Lotte Dodd zipped her underhanded service with a spin that gave notice. Miss Dodd and Mr. Baddley won on four straight spinning serves that hopped wickedly off the grass.

As they changed sides, a massive groan erupted. The first sprinkling of rain was soon followed by a sudden swift shower. The open stands evacuated. A nasty wind slanted the rain and it pounced in under the covered stands.

Glen and Amanda jostled themselves into the foyer, laughing as
everyone shook the water off themselves like spaniels coming out
of the surf.

. . . and came face-to-face with Baroness Lilly Villiard and
Lieutenant Zachary O'Hara, directly in their path. The foyer grew
tight for space. They fought for their bearings.

"I'll see you now." Zach spoke first in a command to Amanda.

"I am Miss Kerr's escort, sir, and that was rather rude."

"I'll see you now," Zach repeated, raising his voice. All around,
eyes went to them.

Amanda held Glen at bay.

"Kindly let us pass," Glen said.

Zach was planted and radiated a sense of menace. Glen stepped
in front of Amanda and Zach clutched his Cavalier Tennis Club
jacket and froze him.

"I'll see you now," Zach repeated again, opening his hands and
pushing Glen off balance.

The four were center stage in a room suddenly chilled.

"Glen Constable," Lilly said. "I haven't seen you in years. I was
off to France and I believe you had entered Harvard."

"Yale," Glen corrected. "Let's take this outside, sir."

Seething, Amanda stepped between them.

"Glen, he's making an ugly scene. I'll speak with him." She
lashed at Zach. "All right. I've a booth reserved in the restaurant."

Lilly swooped in and took Glen Constable's arm. "See me to
my carriage," she said quickly.

"Please go, Glen," Amanda said, "and wait for me at the yacht
club. This won't take long."

He grunted, but Lilly had them moving toward the door.

Amanda's cobalt-blue fire blazed into Zachary's green fire. She
nodded in the direction of the restaurant and Zach took her wrist
hard enough to convey his determination, led her to the restaurant
archway, and pushed his way through a waiting line. Miffed grum-
bles followed them.

"The nerve!"

"Who does he think he is!"

"I'll see that he is reported."

Tonyo, an archduke of a maître d', whisked them in like a magician who had snapped a tablecloth off a fully set table without spilling a drop of water.

He showed them to a booth, quickly curtained them in, and returned to the waiting line and held up his hands. "Poor girl was about to pass out. She'll be fine. So sorry. Let me send a round of drinks to your table."

Zach and Amanda snorted in anger.

"Let me go. You're hurting my wrist," she demanded.

"Promise that you'll stay put."

"You are hurting me."

"I'll see you now," he threatened and pleaded.

"All right, then. I'll see you."

Zachary released her. They stared empty-eyed and panting at a magnificently intricate tablecloth holding a king's array of crystal and silver.

Tonyo buzzed and entered with a bottle of port, poured the glasses uncomfortably, and cleared his throat.

"See to our privacy," Amanda commanded, "and leave the bottle. I'll ring when I need you."

"Yes, Miss Kerr," he said, and snapped the curtains shut behind him so the brass rings clinked with authority.

Zach bumbled at his glass, starting to realize the import of his behavior. He felt Amanda's fingertips touching his lips.

"Oh God," she said softly, "I love you so. What are we going to do?"

He dared look and tears were there. He opened his handkerchief. "Here, now."

"It's all right," she said. "I've earned these tears."

Amanda blew her nose, which ran like a little girl's who had fallen and scraped her knee hard, and as quickly as she had foundered, she returned.

"I've never seen you in officer's dress blues. You're beautiful."

"Those are sad lines under your eyes, Amanda."

"Yes," she said, and quickly changed the subject with a reflexive reaction to the stab of a few minutes back. "She is very lovely," Amanda said unevenly.

"And very kind," he answered in a whisper. "Her family took me in."

"I'm certain you prospered from the experience," Amanda said, to boost her sagging pride.

"She's only a friend."

"A little more, I'd say. I suppose you'll want a complete report on Glen Constable and myself."

"I don't care to know anything, ever," he said.

"Are you that certain?"

"I am certain of how we love each other," he replied.

"After my letter, taking up with Madame Villiard was not wrong of you. But, almighty God, this summer has hurt."

Amanda sipped her wine, then he covered her hands with his, and she shivered. "In the garden on that first night when you took my hand, I'd never felt anything like it, till now."

He brushed her cheeks with kisses, and she rubbed his gold bars. "My Marine. Take me somewhere now, please. I have to be with you, Zach."

"It won't take long before the world crashes into this booth. That stupid scene I made was like some dumb Samson pulling the temple down on our heads."

"The beach tonight or I'll find a place nearby," she said.

"Listen up, darling. We can't do anything around Newport."

"I don't care about gossip."

"Listen up," he repeated. "I just did a terrible thing out there."

"But you did it and we are both here together now because you did."

"I could have ruined my work," he said. "I could have let Major Ben down, the Corps, and both of us as well. Look at me, Amanda."

"What's going on?" she said.

"Amanda, my assignment here will probably be the most important thing ever asked of me, in my life. Do you understand me?"

She sighed heavily, let it set in, then nodded.

"It can't be interrupted, even by you and me."

"How long will it take?"

"If I bear down, burn the midnight oil, I can finish it by the end of the year."

"God, that's a lifetime," she said under her breath.

"Three months, maybe four. I'd better see your father and Mr. Constable now and tell them."

"No, Zach, my father will derail your work. Hold on now. Be quiet. Let me think. I'll hang on. I won't disturb you. All right, here's what we do now. I was livid when we ran into each other and I was very angry when we were seated in the booth here. I will leave after you go, and as far as Father and the world . . . and Newport . . . are concerned, I dismissed you in a rage."

"I don't like a lie," he protested.

"We're going to have to resort to a few. If there is suspicion by Father or Glen about us, I won't be able to hold the fort till the end of the year."

"Christ," he said.

"Now, you hear me," she said. "You and I are out of business until your report is turned in. Then we will make our time and place."

Zach's fist rapped the table over and again in frustration.

"I want to marry you, Amanda."

"Me, too," she said. "If my father refuses permission, I'll be twenty-one next summer and can do as I wish."

He flushed.

"What?" she asked.

"By next summer I'll be long gone on sea duty or to a foreign post. I may be gone for a year, even more."

"I'll wait. We'll marry."

"Yes."

And then the terms of the plan crushed them! Zach's mouth went dry. The last time he'd shaken with fear was halfway up a ship's main mast his father had dared him to climb.

"We may be talking about two years apart."

Amanda's face fell.

"When I finish my assignment in Newport, I have thirty days' leave before I have to report to my new post. Let's work something out for that time, early January into February."

"Thirty days! That will keep me alive, Zach!"

"Let's plan it carefully."

Now she held his wrists tightly. "Zach, stop, Zach, stop, stop," she cried. "I tried to talk you into taking me to the Constitution Ball because I was plain selfish. I could have hurt you then, badly. If we run off now, I'll come through it, but this could ruin your career."

"If we can't have each other, even for just a thirty-day furlough, my life is ruined, anyhow."

"It's very dangerous for you."

"Don't let me go off without loving you."

"Zach . . . Zach . . ."

"Will you go away with me?"

"Yes, I'll go away with you. You leave now and then I'll leave, 'in anger,' as I said. I'll work out a plan for us. Willow Fancy will contact you."

"Good," he said, "and if you have to reach me, it would be best to contact me through Major Ben."

"Are you going to tell him what we're doing?"

"I'll tell him exactly what you tell your father. I was dismissed by you in anger."

"But he's your commanding officer. It will be hard for you to lie to him."

"One way or the other, I have to be with you."

"I'll find us our plan. I love you. I'll close my eyes, and when I wake up it will be January."

Zach stood shakily. Amanda pressed the service buzzer and a waiter opened the curtains.

"Miss Kerr?"

"Leave the curtain open and get Tonyo here this instant."

"Yes, ma'am."

In a blink, Tonyo arrived.

"Miss Kerr?"

"Tonyo, see the lieutenant out," she said in an angry voice, "and when he is off the premises, have my carriage brought to the members' entrance."

"May you rot in hell," Zach said, and followed Tonyo out.

❦· 31 ·❧

THE BARONESS

That Evening—Lilly's Villa

Lilly got out of her wet clothing, bathed, yanked a dressing robe off the rod, ordered up a plate from the main house, had a magnum of champagne uncorked, dismissed her maid, and drank heartily between nibbles.

The knock on her door was timid. Lilly arched her back. "Yes?"

"Can I come in?"

"You can go to hell."

Zach tried the door. It gave. He stepped in like a brave patriot standing before the chopping block.

"I lost it, Lilly. You've been kinder to me than anyone in my life. I feel rotten hurting you."

"Well, Mister I'll-see-you-now, welcome to the endgame. All trysts end in hell."

He asked if he could be seated. Lilly was starting to feel tipsy.

He inched down opposite her. She held up her champagne flute and was about to toss the contents in his face.

"I'd feel better if you threw it at me."

She obliged, along with a slap. "Pour me another glass," she commanded, and this time drank it.

"I put myself on report for my disgusting behavior."

"Grand! Will Uncle Ben have you flogged?"

"No."

"Oh, too bad. So?"

"I guess the superintendent will hold a captain's mast for me. I'll probably be confined to quarters and docked some pay."

"Don't worry, Lieutenant. You have all those rich ladies who will take care of your odds and ends."

Zach held up his hands, helplessly.

"So, throw something at me," he said.

"Lilly does not get *that* angry or *that* sad."

"I take that as a well-earned insult," he said.

No, she didn't crack a smile. She was hurt.

"One cannot take a summer's pleasuring that seriously," she said.

"I want your forgiveness."

"It is not forthcoming."

"Shall I go?"

"No, kindly torture yourself for a while."

"I lost it," he bumbled again.

"I lost it once. I was thirteen, before I went to France. I held a large Ming vase over my head and smashed it on the floor. Papa made me glue it back together. It took nearly a year, but it established my boundaries for future tantrums."

He pointed to the champagne, filled a flute for himself, and gulped it down.

"I believe the playwright has a direction in his script that says 'a pregnant silence followed,'" she said.

"That wasn't me at the casino," Zach said.

"Oh yes, it was the real you exorcising a demon. And now I'll

show you the real Lilly. Notice, I speak calmly. I do not rant, nor
do I double over with laughter. Have you not realized how perfect
I am in everything, my walk, my dress, my ha-ha-ha quips, my
kisses? I am studied perfection and always under control, unless
suddenly hit by a wet fish."

She wobbled from her chair, went to the French doors, flung
them open, and let a sharp breeze find its way in. Her gown fluffed.
She breathed in the sharp air. Zachary tried not to look at her
bosom.

"The moment I saw you, Lilly, I knew I was going to need you
to heal my wounds."

"You wanted Mama!"

"Yes," he croaked.

"Mama wanted sonny boy just as badly, Lieutenant. It's a nasty
sport, but you are one handy player."

Lilly pushed the doors together and turned to him, opened and
disheveled.

"Stop kicking yourself," she said, tying her gown together.
"The baroness chose to play with the soldier boy."

"I wanted the summer to end with you returning to Paris holding a deep affection for me. I prayed for that," he said.

"Ah, that must be the reason for all the candles lit in the family
chapel," she said.

"I think I'd better go."

"I haven't dismissed you," she retorted.

Zachary helped himself to the Maison Villiard cognac, feeling it
all the way down and up again.

Lilly fitted a cigarette into its holder and he held a flame beneath
it. His hands were steady as she blew a long thin stream into his
face. The smoke had a strange sweetness Zach had come to recognize. She relaxed, drifted, and rambled.

"I wasn't exactly an innocent bystander," she said, "but the rule
of the game is never to go to the guillotine for a summer lover."

"My behavior was shocking," he said.

"Hmm," Lilly mused, "have you ever been on a plantation filled with slaves?"

"No."

"I was born on one," Lilly said. "Thank God, on the right side. I've been on the other side of the field where the shacks are and people lived with death before death. And I said to myself, what a lucky girl am I. In payment for my good fortune I must master the art of being a woman. We all make some gesture of rebellion. I did mine with a Ming vase. Later, I adored being the Baroness Villiard. The one lesson I learned early as a woman is that you don't go into the billiard room and whip the boys at the pool table."

In the sad and wistful calm of the moment, she had another glass of the stuff and liberated her tongue for fair.

What came about in life were the compromises and understandings of the grand salon at work.

"Felix and I decided to remain a bombastic couple and once in a while he even gives me a decent performance. We are the epitome of discretion. No scandal with the Villiards. So I was twenty-five and beautiful and kept my indulgences to a short, sweet duration."

Lily lifted her feet and lay back on the couch.

"Once upon a time," she said, "I fell madly, madly in love with a Russian concert pianist. He took me places that shattered my fantasy of my own perfection. He turned me into a bitch in heat . . . a dribbling, streaky-faced, jealous clinger . . ."

"Go on," Zach said.

"I never understood the agony you can put yourself through when you lose control. I was so crushed that my doctor and I concocted a story that I had respiratory problems and needed to go to a sanitarium in Switzerland to recover. It was the beginning and end of love affairs I could not walk away from. Life as Baroness Lilly Villiard is plenty good enough for me.

"From the start, even with your American naïveté, I knew you would be trouble. So? I am court-trained to give a man pleasure, but once in a while I get fringe benefits from that rare lover, the equal-pleasure partner. You were daring me into strange places and I came close to letting go a few times. What a mess that would have been."

She sat up. "Are you hungry, Zach?"

"I'm fine."

"What did Amanda Kerr make of your performance at the casino?"

"She chewed me out and dismissed me."

"I don't believe you," Lilly said.

"Makes no difference," he answered. "I'm going to be confined to quarters. I have to finish my job. I can't bungle it."

"And she loves you very much."

"It has to pass. I'm going to be shipped out after I turn in my report. Probably sea duty."

"You don't mean to see her again?"

"No, I don't."

"I don't believe you."

"I have a thirty-day furlough coming," he spurted unintentionally.

"And the two of you are going to do something desperate, aren't you?"

Zach need not have given an answer. He was wearing it.

"Do you wish to marry?"

"We can't. She is underage and her father will never give permission, so neither will the Corps."

"Running off is even crazier."

"We can't help ourselves. She is strong and capable. She'll get through and carry on."

"And Lieutenant O'Hara?"

"We will have our time together."

"To what avail? A court-martial?"

"If need be."

"Sergei Zolofskovitch loved me in the same way. He was willing to leave his wife for me, and take my children. We'd have a villa in Spain or Italy and be a gossip piece for the rest of our lives.

Had I your courage, I would have become the mistress of a crazy
Russian. When he played a concert he'd transform his audience
and bring them to tears of exaltation. That was the way he made
love as well."

"Ever sorry?"

"No, I would have ended up a drunk or a dope fiend."

She lay back on the sofa and Zach stretched near her on the
floor. She gave him a cushion and her hand dangled down, able to
stroke his hair.

"Papa George does not want to lose your friendship."

"I'm glad for that."

"Zach?"

"Aye?"

"Have you made love to Amanda yet?"

"No."

"It is really a dangerous game you are playing."

"We realize that."

"God, the places you will take each other."

❧· 32 ·❧

COME YE THANKFUL

Autumn 1891

Everyone close to the boating scene speculated that the Kerr brothers and their mongrel yawl, *Lochinvar III*, were up to some mischief.

Yachtsmen, when not racing, were the friendliest of old-boys'-club sorts. Donald and Malcolm Kerr were as friendly as any chaps whose crooked fingers ever held a gin glass.

This year at anchor, *Lochinvar III* had an armed crew aboard. At dockside there was a constant flow of new sails, masts, lines, rigging being delivered, and they were taking the boat out twice the number of times usual.

Horace was the motivator. Poor old dear was looking for speed, but a Scottish schooner could fart only so fast.

The Kerrs did draw raised eyebrows as the Newport fleet sailed south or up into dry dock. Horace Kerr was remaining at Tobermory for Thanksgiving and brazenly announced he was going to make a run to Immigrant Reef.

The damned fool was going into rough seas and flirting with a nor'easter. It was a reckless side of Horace that had won him an appreciation as an entrepreneur, but this was going to get him into serious trouble.

At Tobermory, every pumpkin in Rhode Island that survived Halloween was purchased and its innards had been gutted for one of a thousand pies.

A concrete pond that was dug by engineers from Dutchman's Hook held a slim two inches of water, enough to freeze over for curling matches and ice skating.

Rooms were assigned at the three homes and a beachside resort hotel and its staff hired for the overflow, second cousins and such.

Daisy got it all ready. No banister rail went undecorated and sleighs were on standby in case they got a decent snow.

On the third day before Thanksgiving, Kerrs arrived from everywhere. Welcome parties were held at the homes of Malcolm and Donald in order to save the grand climax banquet for the main house.

Matching faces with places and times flown by led to jolly stuffy kisses, backslaps, and pinched cheeks. Horace commended himself for his largesse and was in high spirits.

He had not exactly spoken or written to Upton, but had had a representative in London extend an invitation. Upton returned a kind note by cable that he was otherwise engaged but appreciated the thought.

Thank God.

There was a treasure hunt for the children with a grand prize of a hundred-dollar gold piece from great-uncle-uncle-cousin and second cousin of all of them, Horace, and an ice hockey exhibition between the Providence Pilgrims and the Springfield Manufacturers, and music up from Baltimore consisting of teachers and students from the Peabody Institute, with top-quality soloists.

. . . and nonstop activity for the kids.

Why didn't I do this a century ago? Horace wondered.

The children were fed at their own afternoon affair, served by a black staff dressed as Pilgrims and Indians. Those who were still awake into the evening were skillfully attended to by nannies and governesses.

Daisy had arranged the tables in the grand salon in a circular manner so that rank was not an issue.

For favors, there were golden cuff links of ships, golden brooches of ships, and models of the greatest of the Kerr ships.

Malcolm and Donald arrived in handsomely tailored jackets as former vice-commodore and commodore of their Chesapeake Yacht Club.

They glutted themselves into a state of slow motion as the glee club from the naval training school sang hymns of thanks and humility.

With toast upon toast the gentlemen enjoyed their cigars.

. . . until all that one craved now was a snooze. Horace zeroed in on the moment. Before he lost his captives, he clinked his glass with a spoon and held his arms wide like a preacher.

The room quieted. Don't drag it out, Horace, nail it now.

". . . I am so filled, as though I have launched the ship of my life. For our final toast I am going to let you in on a deep secret that I planned to hold until Christmas. The moment is so soaring it demands I share it with you."

Well, that sobered them up.

"You are, of course, all aware of the great work of the Kerr Foundation, begun by our beloved patriarch, Angus—"

"Hear! Hear!"

"—who passed on to me his great bent, and charitable institution over which I have presided, with the assistance of my brothers, Malcolm and Donald"—who stood and were cheered.

Horace listed the foundation's generosity, orphan home, the church, a school for Negro children of exceptional promise, support for the arts including the purchase of a permanent box at the Metropolitan Opera, a stud farm to perfect quarter horses, grants to over twenty-three charities, "which I shall not list . . ."

Backdraft of laughter.

"... and now, our crowning achievement."

Silence raged.

"My daughter Amanda has been inspired to establish a college in her name for the advancement of women's education ...

"Therefore ... to that end ...

"I am proud to announce that the Kerr Family Foundation has purchased eight hundred and thirty-seven acres of pristine land midway between Baltimore and Washington along the Patuxent River near Severn."

The room arose, profoundly.

"I grant Amanda this deed for the campus of the Amanda Kerr College for Women."

The rest need not be recorded, nor could be, over the din and shouts of "hurrah" and orchestra playing "A Mighty Fortress" and the black Pilgrims and Indians whooping.

Amanda was shocked, barely able to come to her feet to receive a clout of an embrace she'd never known from her father, and Daisy was up and the rafters rang ...

> For they are jolly good fellows,
> For they are jolly good fellows ...

Maybe Amanda would pull Glen Constable to his feet! Maybe! Come on, dammit!

With a last gasp of rationality, Amanda realized that this was pinnacle Horace Kerr stuff, boxing her in, and it was Horace who jerked Glen to his feet.

> Hip-Hip Hooray
> Hip-Hip Hooray
> Hip-Hip Hooray

The commodores and commoners of the Kerr clan returned to their lesser domains in the next few days. But what gaiety it had been!

"Great fun!"

"Really great fun!"

They caught their trains and boats with bubbling hints of major occasions to come . . . a cornerstone for the college . . . a merger with Constable . . . maybe a royal wedding . . . heady stuff.

Daisy had watched Emily's every blink and she had held up rather well, particularly at her teas, but when departure after departure took place, she began to show signs of weird behavior, warning of a coming attack.

Since Horace was preparing to sail to Immigrant Reef, Daisy decided to accompany Emily back to Baltimore, settle her in, and return to Newport.

House empty except for Amanda? Glen Constable needed very little convincing to remain at Tobermory and keep Amanda company while Horace made his sail.

Having drained all his milk of human kindness, Horace set out on a rough-water run with himself at the helm.

❧· 33 ·❧

UNCLE BEN

The Next Day—Ben Boone's Cottage

Ben wondered whose uninvited horse was hitched to his post. He stepped up on his porch and ran directly into Amanda Kerr, fuming with tenacity.

"I would have called you by phone, but our switchboard has an operator on it and I wish to speak privately."

"I see. It's chilly out here. You should have waited inside. It's open."

"I'd rather not take that liberty."

"Come in."

A fire had been laid. Ben set a match to it and rustled up tea. The tea took the chill off.

"I hear your father is sailing to Immigrant Reef."

"Yes."

"Nasty business this time of year."

"I must see Zach," she said abruptly.

"I thought you two split up?"

"We have, but something unforeseen has come up."

"Well, you can't see him. He is confined to quarters. He's persona non grata."

Amanda closed her eyes and hit each word, hard. "I . . . must . . . see . . . him."

"About what?"

"It's a personal problem about that day at the casino."

"Oh, that problem. Sorry."

She insisted, yet again, switching, trying to change her tone. Ben wore no mischievous twinkle this day. He was a sudden, abrupt character she did not know.

"Zach said if I ever got into trouble, I could come to you. You could be trusted."

"I am his commanding officer, not his uncle Ben."

"Will you hear me out?"

"Lady, that boy was one punch away from a summary court-martial. Just count his luck, this time."

Amanda set the beggar in her aside and spoke up with clarity. "I love him!" she said.

"You don't get it, Miss Kerr. Lieutenant O'Hara is a very gifted young officer. Do you have any idea what he is doing?"

"No, none."

"The man is working on sensitive material, highly confidential matters. If you really loved him, then you'd leave him alone. He has a big career ahead."

She stared at the fire, which was popping now. "Sometimes," she said wistfully, "I wish he was dealing in something other than blood and death."

"That is right amiable of you. I am from a hillbilly family who ran a station on the underground railroad to help slaves escape. My kin were strung up for it. I know you want to create that perfect world of love and peace for one and all, but it doesn't work that way. It never has. Thank God we have men like Zach to defend us. Now please leave."

Amanda stuffed it and stood to go, but was not quite able.

"Zach and I have not been forthcoming," she blurted.

"What do you mean?"

"I did not send him packing."

"Zach lied to me?"

"Yes . . ."

"And you lied to your father."

"Yes . . ."

"He lied to me?"

"Yes."

"And you're planning to do something crazy?"

Amanda froze at the door and chewed at her finger . . .

"Come back and sit down," Ben said.

She did, and looked up at him with Amanda eyes; few had ever seen such a set. She spoke with calm. "Who am I talking to?" she asked.

"Uncle Ben," he said after a time.

"Sorry, I did not hear you. Who am I talking to, his commander or his uncle Ben?"

"Uncle Ben," he repeated.

"All right now. At Thanksgiving, my father announced to a huge family gathering that he was turning over the deed for eight hundred acres of land for me to start up a college. And then he pulled Glen Constable to his feet and held our hands up to the crowd, not quite subtle, to say there is going to be a future announcement. I don't know exactly what he is doing making this sail on the *Lochinvar*, but the way his mind works, it is all part of the same plan."

Ben's left hand shook her shoulder.

"What gave Kerr these notions?"

"I promised my father I'd get Zach out of my system."

"And ascend the bloody throne?"

"Yes."

"It's panning out real well. Lies, deceit, conspiracies, the way you people do it."

"I really tried to stay away from Zach . . . I really tried, Ben."

"And you want him to go over the hill with you."

"No, I want him to do his work, and at the end of the year he says he has thirty days' leave coming."

"Jesus Christ! How old are you, Amanda?"

"God's sake, Ben, it's been three months since the casino. I haven't seen him or spoken to him or written to him."

"Get out of his life!"

"No! We are going to have our time togther."

"Jesus Christ, woman! Where are you going with him?"

No answer.

"Out of state?"

Again, her silence.

"'How do I love thee, let me count the ways.' Statutory rape, crossing a state line for immoral purposes, kidnapping. Your pictures posted in every post office and railroad station and every bloodhound in the East hunting you down. Jesus Christ, woman! Are you willing to die for this, the two of you?"

"Aye, we are."

Ben walked to the fire, dazed, poked at it, flopped into his easy chair, and stared at nothing for minute after minute. He found his water pitcher in the icebox and uncaked his throat.

He finally groaned. "I sensed something like this. I've spent a lot of nights thinking about you two."

"Help us!"

Ben knew what would be and his house of cards collapsed.

"There is only one way you can go off together and possibly . . . I mean just possibly, make it stand. Afterward, you may not be able to carry on, together."

"Just our time, that's all I beg for."

"With the way Horace Kerr is tightening the screws, you can't hold out for another three or four months, either of you. How's your guts, Amanda?"

"Try me."

"Here's what we'll do. I will keep Zach under house arrest so no one can get near him. You will go to your father now and tell him the truth, then leave Tobermory and wait for Zach, somewhere. But before you go, tell your father where and when you are going and write a dozen friends and tell them you will be vacationing with Zach, where and when. In that manner, he will not be able to brand you as runaways."

"I'll do it."

"And let your mother know as well."

"Aye, but I'm not certain of how she'll respond to this."

"She must know as well."

"All right."

"And you must let Zach go at the end of his furlough. Maybe you can come with him afterward. Maybe you'll have to wait a long time. Maybe your month will be the end of it."

"Yes," she said.

"Swear it on Zach's life," Ben said.

"I'll swear it on my life, not his."

✤· 34 ·✤

AN IRISH HUNTER

The Following Evening—Tobermory

If one looked up to Tobermory, he could see that the pumpkins in the windows had been replaced by Christmas wreaths.

If one could look inside the corner apartment on the second story, he'd see an elegant gentleman leaning on the mantel and swirling a snifter of cognac. Across the room, a gorgeous woman in silk taffeta was seated on a large ottoman. Together they made a cameo of beauty, peace, success, and comfort.

Dixie Jane's absence over Thanksgiving weighed heavily on Glen.

"I had a talk with Nini. The child put on a tantrum. I can't believe Dixie Jane preferred to stay in Richmond."

"She is trying to tell anyone who will listen that she does not like being bounced about."

"I hoped the effects of the divorce would disappear over time."

"Sometimes they never do. Dixie Jane is in a position not of her own making, so when she hears anything slightly unpleasant, she takes it as personal rejection."

"We've a beautiful Irish hunter on the farm, as perfect as I've ever seen, ready to be saddle-trained. I'm going to pressure Father to let me give the horse to Dixie."

Pleased with his largesse, Glen rolled a cigar between his palms to soften it. At this time in the procedure, the lady generally took the cigar, nipped the ends, and lit it for him. Lord, even Nini did that! After a moment Glen took the cutter from his vest pocket and did his own decapitating.

"Well, don't you think this will settle her account? I mean, an Irish hunter of her class."

"Glen, your family has a very large horse farm. Dixie Jane has been up to the top of her boots in horse caca all her life."

"Then surely she knows the value of such an animal."

"She is not looking for something gift-wrapped. She is protesting being abandoned."

"How the devil can you say that, Amanda? Despite her obvious faults, Nini is a devoted mother. That Dorfman fellow will take some getting used to, but he has a very kindly attitude toward the child. As for me, I intend to spend every living moment making certain she will be with us at Inverness for Christmas."

Sip, puff, sip, puff. If only Amanda were not so beautiful!

"I am the one Dixie is protesting to," she said.

"Yes, to hell, I'll say it. She wants you, almost as much as I want you."

Amanda heard and watched his discomfort.

"When I saw you and Dixie wrestle, how I wanted to jump in, and how I prayed I could slow the moments watching you sleep on the beach, and how I loved to watch your eyes stop a man in his tracks. What must I do, Amanda? If we make our engagement announcement over the New Year's, all the gods will shower the earth with passing comets."

Amanda went to him and lifted his fallen chin.

"I do not love you, Glen."

He reached about, light-headed, and backed into the sofa, half his life suddenly sucked from him.

"I know that. I've always known, but I know that you will grow to love me. At Christmas . . ."

"We are not going to share Christmas or anything further," she said.

"O'Hara?"

"Yes."

"What in the name of God is it that you want!" he cried.

"I need to know that I'll not have to spend my life turning into every corridor looking for him."

"I feel totally crushed!"

"I cannot imagine anyone being more cruel to you than I am now. And I've badly hurt Dixie Jane."

"Amanda, I beg you . . ."

"No, Glen. I despise myself. I have used you deliberately, from the beginning."

"And I've used you, Amanda. I used Dixie Jane, praying you'd grow inseparable."

"I love her and I hurt her," Amanda said, "but Dixie Jane is not enough. Zach and I tried to purge each other from our souls. We have lost the strength to fight it any longer."

Glen's worst fears were here. He floundered about and lost the dignity to stave off a flood of self-pity.

"What a peacock I was to have this magnificent creature on my arm. How I long for your body. See here, gentlemen, I'll not have you baboons slobbering at the sight of her. Amanda Kerr will be mine, belly, breasts, and ass."

He grunted, emptied his cognac snifter in a gulp, and nearly gagged over it. "Your father know?"

"He will when he returns from his run to Immigrant Reef."

The terribleness of the moment hung.

"You are going away with him?"

"I plan to leave my father's home, forever."

Glen pressed his hands together in a gesture of prayer. "When the madness ends, and it will end—when O'Hara is shipped out for months and years and when you've spent your passion, I'll be waiting."

"I'll not have you wait. You are too fine a man to take this. In due course, you will come to hate me, and my reputation will be skewered."

When he realized the full impact of her rejection, his hurt turned to anger.

He suddenly poked out his chin and balled up his fists. "Well, Amanda, it appears you're well on your way to becoming a Marine's whore."

·· 35 ··

NOR'EASTER

Early December—1891

The decision to make a December run to Immigrant Reef smoked with challenge. At best, it was audacious. In the end, Horace Kerr won begrudging admiration for sheer bravado.

Halfway through the 390-mile course, *Lochinvar III* was side-swiped by a nor'easter and thereafter assumed a hero's role in getting home.

Malcolm navigated brilliantly, sensing the heavy air and direction of the roiling seas, and darted the boat away from the monster's anger.

The Chesapeake crew, used to finer weather, worked the pressure off the mainmast to keep it from snapping, managed to switch mainsails, and kept a split rudder intact.

It was Horace Kerr at the helm, bullying the bully storm, growling at enemy whitecaps. The man and the moment converged, and *Lochinvar III* limped home to whatever bells, whistles, cannons, and foghorns remained in Newport.

The deck was a tangle of snapped stays, ripped sails, and rigging lines, yet not a man had been lost or badly injured. They got down the gangplank on their own two feet. Was it brilliant seamanship, hand of the gods, or shithouse luck that had brought them through? Some of each. Horace Kerr would certainly convert the incident into a fate that served notice at the New York Yacht Club.

An upscale bed, board, and brothel had been rented for the crew to go cattin' in the satin and drink from a bottomless well of booze. Damages would be paid, immediately.

Horace had a handsome bonus that he kept in the company safe for his lads until after their party. No one was quite sure what they were celebrating.

The Butterfly? Didn't work. In simple terms, the movement of the undercurrents flowed through the tabs, relaying information to the sails faster than the balance ball could react. When the storm blew full fury, the balance ball tilted the hull in stuttering misdirection until the system was locked down. The goddamn engineers at Dutchman's Hook were in for a long winter.

On the other hand, some of the responses from the keel gave encouragement for further experimentation.

Daisy was on the dock, having returned from Baltimore. Horace looked his wife over with a yummy grin that had been missing for some time. A small reward.

Horace, Donald, and Malcolm returned to Tobermory reinvented as brothers.

The Turk was on hand to steam them on hot rocks, lay them out like three slabs of beef, and knead them into a state of stupor. Horace's early lust was spent by the hot rocks. As soon as his head hit the pillow, he was snoring.

When he came awake, Dr. Quincy was holding his hand and taking his pulse. "Have you seen my brothers?"

"Yes, my partner is attending to them."

"How are they?"

"Lumps. Up we sit. Take off the nightshirt. Let's have a listen."

"My old gal *Lochinvar* was a real warrior. What do we call them, Amazons, Brunhilds . . . ?"

"Damned fools. She'll run no more match races."

"Then we shall send her to Valhalla properly. Chrissake, Quincy, don't poke my ribs."

The lacerations, knots, and bruises were acceptable, given the fierceness of the ride. His right eye was encased in purple.

"Little beefsteak on that eye. Might want to tape you up later—"

"The devil!"

Daisy tiptoed in and expressed relief with the results of the examination. Nothing broken, nothing badly torn, the usual medications.

"I'll look in on you again in a few hours," Dr. Quincy said in departing. "You are very lucky."

"It's called seamanship," Horace shouted after him. "Daisy, get me out of this goddamned deathbed."

She helped him to his office and to a comfortable easy chair. He uncapped a decanter and babbled about his foolish courage. Not that Horace asked, but Emily was settled in fine down at Inverness.

Horace sat upright suddenly and grimaced.

"Where the hell is Amanda?"

"She went to the theater in Providence and called late last night. She missed her train and stayed over with the Burtons. I expect her momentarily."

Horace wished to protest further, but loud voice and movement were accompanied by sharp pain.

"I have a surprise for you, meanwhile," Daisy said, and pulled the service cord.

In a moment two servants entered. One carried a small covered painting, the other an easel, and set them up before Horace.

Daisy drew the cover off. It was a rendering for the portrait Amanda had sat for in her Constitution Ball gown. The artist, John Singer Sargent, had sent it to Inverness for comment, and Daisy brought it back with her.

Horace studied and studied. "Splendid, well done," he said

softly. "But no one could ever truly capture her radiance that night. She was ethereal."

Daisy understood she would be demoted to the old dowager mother. She'd known that for a long time, but loved Amanda no less than she loved Upton and Emily; in fact, she rather gloried in her daughter's independence.

A finished portrait of this rendering would be a powerful statement of Amanda's ascension. Daisy would handle it gracefully.

Horace leaned back and took a critic's view of the canvas. He nitpicked here and there. Damned Sargent charged an arm and leg for the commission but was obviously worth it. Horace looked quickly to his wife, then turned his eyes away. Where will we hang the portrait? He dared not say; she dared not ask.

"Father," Amanda said, breezing in and over to embrace him.

"No, no," he said, "I'm a little banged up."

"The news of *Lochinvar* is already up to Providence. You've set a few fellows on their ears."

"Really? What are they saying?"

"Mr. Burton said that you're something out of Viking mythology."

Horace rumbled for joy in the back of his throat.

"Dear, I brought up a rendering of your portrait from Baltimore," Daisy said.

Amanda studied it approvingly. She had instructed Sargent to cover the sadness he had detected. He'd done so, quite well. Amanda smiled to her mother to convey that she would not let Horace take Daisy's portrait down from the grand entry.

"The Butterfly?"

"I'll tell you about that later," he said. "I was hoping you'd be at dockside to see me in."

"I missed the ten o'clock train last night out of Providence. The Burtons put me up."

"Oh, yes. Did Daisy say something about the theater? In Providence? In December?"

"It was Brown University and it was a lecture. Dr. Hoftsaddler gave the most extraordinary talk about the possibility of human life on planets beyond our solar system."

"Nonsense," Horace said. "I've heard those old wives' tales from every seaman who works at the Hook. Hoftsaddler? Well, you know those Germans, always seeing elves in their woods."

There seemed an awkward moment as Horace adjusted himself in his great chair. Daisy could usually feel an Amanda strike coming on before Horace caught it, and she'd rather be elsewhere.

"Why don't I see to a little tea or something. Soup?"

"Now that we three are together; so many things have gone past us recently, I am filled with a great sense of—what?" Horace said. "A great sense of comfort after an arduous journey. I don't mean *Lochinvar*. I mean all of us. If I were a Catholic I'd say I'd passed through purgatory, though God knows what my sins might have been."

Daisy touched his shoulder and he made a kissing gesture to her.

"This sail to Immigrant Reef was the climax of a summer that has restored my faith, revived my spirit as only could happen at the helm during a storm.

"It told me," he went on, "that indeed the Kerrs are made of sterner stuff. I must say Donald and Malcolm acquitted themselves well. But it is Amanda I speak of now. You, my darling, have shown great resources in turning back raw savage lust. I know you must have called upon every fiber of your being. The road to Jerusalem, to Rome, is always paved in broken glass."

Damned ribs were really sore! "The beautiful ingathering of Kerrs for Thanksgiving, Amanda's steadfastness, and my cleansing sail to Immigrant Reef have carried us, one and all, past a new threshold. No . . . no, please let me finish. After the incredible downwind run, I had the chance to talk something over with my brothers."

"It is so nice that you're talking things over with them," Daisy said.

"*Lochinvar*! What did the poet write? 'Set every threadbare sail, give her to the god of storms, the lightning and the gale, etc.' We learned that although the Butterfly came up short, it did tell us that some kind of split-winged keel will work. I mean to challenge for the right to defend America's Cup!"

"Dear God!" Daisy cried.

"Challenge every goddamned yachtsman in the goddamned New York Yacht Club—"

"But Horace," Daisy interrupted, "all the *Lochinvar*s were built in Scotland, and the rules committee disallows foreign-built boats for the trials."

Amanda had reached the end of her father's speech long before he delivered it. He thumped out his words as though he were Patrick Henry in the Virginia House of Burgesses.

"We shall launch a new series of racing yachts, built in America and carrying the name *Amanda K*. And let me tell you, the Constable yard is as good as any with this type hull."

Daisy grasped at whatever there was to grasp at. Amanda walked to the French doors, closed them, and locked them.

"The Kerr family over Thanksgiving," she said, "were very nice people, members of an astonishingly successful family, here and in Scotland."

"And our name will be carved on the cup!"

"Father, you are babbling."

"Don't you speak to your father that way."

"Hardly babbling. Daisy, I think our daughter is overcome by the moment."

"I am not worthy of the honor," Amanda said.

Horace laughed. "Hell, daughter! You were *the* Kerr from the moment you were born."

"Father, there is no kingdom of Kerr except in your frightening mind."

"Do not dare to speak to your father in this manner, particularly in his present condition," Daisy declared.

"You've been pounding me all my life, and all my life I've known the reason. The truth, Father?"

"This is no time for truth," Daisy said, throwing her hands in the air.

"The truth is that you have blown me up out of all human dimension for the simple reason that I'm your lone surviving child, the only one left you feel is worthy to ensure your immortality!"

Horace Kerr gasped and flung his head back as wave after wave of shock ripped through him. The room seemed now a shallow empty box with high white walls and white ceiling and white floor and two fuzzy white fixtures before him.

Then.

Amazing how rapidly Horace Kerr recovered! No one caught him in a tactical surprise, no admiral, no labor union, no president. He mulled until the shock went along its way, then pointed to his humidor and wordlessly ordered Daisy to prepare him a cigar. He sucked in, grunted, and blew the smoke directly into Amanda's face.

Daisy watched her daughter, unflinching. As for Horace, she had witnessed him at one time or another operate on every level of rage and intimidation. Dear Lord, she thought, he is entirely too calm.

Horace groaned as he stretched his hurting limbs and reorganized his mind into an art form of cold taunting cynicism.

"A little port, I think," he said to Daisy. "Mmm, good stuff. Is there something you wish to tell me, Amanda? An abdication speech?"

"I haven't sent Zachary off. He has a one-month furlough at the beginning of the new year. I am leaving Tobermory today to wait for him."

"That's marvelous!" Daisy cried.

"Go to your room, Daisy," he commanded softly.

"No!" she answered.

Horace thought it out deliberately, poured another large jigger of port, and whacked it down. "I am hearing screechy sirens from hell, screaming Valkyries. So, we have a full-scale rebellion." He laid down his next words, detached, with precision. "Glen know about this?"

"Yes."

"No matter. You'll be far too soiled for him or anyone of a proper family. Dirty pants. Do you think you can survive a fishwife's life after the gates of Tobermory and Inverness are locked to you? You shall suffer every minute of your life. You will never come back."

"I have no intention of coming back."

"Amanda will not be in need," Daisy cried.

"Oh, yes, the Blantons, that blight on humanity. God bless the Blantons, who traded you off in order to indebt me."

"I have remained loyal to you through the disasters of our other children . . ." Daisy fought back as she had never fought before.

"Loyalty is hardly your long suit, Daisy. All your years of trotting back and forth to England. For what? To see Upton?"

Daisy sank into a chair, shaking, but was aware of her daughter's strong hand on her shoulder.

"Amusing," Horace said, "but the Hook was on the brink of a four-ship contract when your little dillydally in London first reached my ears. I wasn't going to lose that contract. Later? I could have made a public fool out of you but I needed you as a head housekeeper to run my mansions. What did that lover ever want with that beggar's snatch of yours? So I remained decent, publicly decent. Actually, I was midway through treatment for a social medical embarrassment. Aren't you pleased that I spared you? Lord, can a man have no protection from female vileness?"

"Keep talking," Amanda said. "It makes me love you."

"Loyalty. You knew about your mother and her limp-wristed English faggot?"

"The closets of Inverness are full," Amanda said. "We'll have to start storing skeletons up here in Tobermory."

"You are glacial, Amanda, but what a fool. Where will you and your shanty-Irish taig boy be able to hide?"

"We do not intend to hide."

"Be careful, Amanda!" Daisy screamed to her. "Emily did not become the way she is from falling from a swing. Norbert Jolly took advantage of her innocence and made her pregnant before the cotillion. We had it aborted."

"I demand you say nothing further," Horace roared, crimson-faced.

"To hell," Daisy said, and turned to Amanda. "To my everlasting disgrace, I took part in the ritual! I took her to New Orleans, to the bayou, where some witch butchered her.

"Horace gave no hint of deep sorrow, only the cruel ice of a blunt predator cornering his quarry."

"Where do you think you'll go where I will not find you?"

"We are not going to hide. You know where Zach and I will be."

The long ash, which rarely left the end of his cigar, collapsed and dribbled down his vest.

"You're going down to the swamp with the niggers!"

"I am going to Nebo to be with loving friends."

"And you think I can't overrun a bunch of jigaboo shacks. I'll burn Nebo to the ground."

And then, in a second, Horace switched gears.

"Let us be calm," he said.

The two women tried to let the rancor from his tirade pass on through.

"May I speak?" he asked rhetorically. "I did my best to spare you, Amanda. I stuffed it all inside me, knowing what I know. Now, let me share some truth with you. I have known from the very beginning this Zachary O'Hara was a smooth operator, and smelled the whiffs of his scandals rising in Washington even as he courted you. I thought you and I had come to understand, when we made our bargain on the train, that you had also caught on to him.

"What is clear," he went on, "you wanted him for one reason alone. You couldn't have him and you had to win. You caved in the minute he confronted you at the casino. He didn't really want you or he could have had you all summer.

"Major Boone served up that French whore, Lilly Villiard, and O'Hara tired of her and thought he'd look you up again.

"I suggest O'Hara picked over the virgins in heat in Newport and realized you were the best of the lot. He will piss away whatever inheritance Daisy gives you so he can have a high life. But, Amanda! You haven't a shred of sacrifice in your soul. You want the empire but will have thrown it away for this Irish garbage."

"Thank you for trying to save me, Father, but you are a perverse liar."

Horace roared up from his seat like a sea monster erupting from its lake-bottom lair. He limped to her portrait, jerked it off the easel, lifted it over his head, and smashed it on the corner of the desk, then fell into the chair and lifted the phone.

Amanda reached into her bosom and took out a teardrop-shaped vial on the end of the thin chain she wore.

"If you phone for your Pinkertons, they will find me dead on the floor."

"Bullshit!" Horace roared.

Daisy was on her feet, in front of her daughter. Horace Kerr smirked, and clicked for the switchboard.

"If Amanda didn't have poison, I'd find her some."

He clicked again.

"Service," the operator said.

"You don't bluff Horace Kerr!"

"Service," the operator repeated. "May I help you, Mr. Kerr?"

He hung up.

Daisy now held her daughter together.

"I will see Amanda safely away from here and I will brook no effort from you to lay a finger on her." And Daisy voiced her first words of liberation: "Or *they* will know about it."

"Who are *they?*" he asked.

"*They* are the *they* we spend every living hour of our existence trying to impress. *They* are your Republican cronies in the cabinet and your stout sailing pals and the bankers snickering over your headlines in their cozy clubs. *They* are your executives and your workmen at Dutchman's Hook and *they* are your church. For a man who fears disgrace and scandal more than death, it would be a fitting end when *they* all learn about how Sir Henry Pearson adored my 'beggar's snatch.' The diary of a life is already written and in safe hands. Are we free to leave?"

His eyes bulged. He gasped pathetically.

"That's blackmail."

"Indeed. Are we free to leave?" Daisy said.

"Go. Get out!"

Daisy trailed Amanda to the doors.

"Daisy," he gasped.

"Yes?"

"Will you return?"

"Of course, Horace. Emily needs me and I am your wife, but the moment you try to send your goons into Nebo, I shall orchestrate the utter destruction of kingdom Kerr."

⟬ 36 ⟭

LINE IN THE WATER

Three Days Later—Early December 1891

The guard unlocked the main door of the administration building. Ben entered quickly and glanced at the wall clock. It was two-thirty in the morning. Down the corridor his heel clicks resounded, cutting the silence. Ben turned into the secure area. The iron-barred gate of the code room opened.

"Coded communiqué by telegram, Major. I'll have it decoded in a moment."

As the machine spit out tape, the chief petty officer cut and pasted it on a message blank. Ben signed the log, took the message to a desk, and adjusted the lamp.

URGENT—SECRET—EYES ONLY BBOONE, USMC
FROM—RX MAPLE
DESTROY AFTER READING
SUBJECT—USMC GARRISON FOR AMNESTY ISLANDS

MEETINGS WITH ADMIRAL IN CHIEF US NAVY
PORTER LANGENFELD AND STAFF HAVE NOT GONE
FAVORABLY.

NECESSITY OF QUOTE LIMITED EXPEDITIONS AND
CAMPAIGNS UNQUOTE IN THE FUTURE IS BUILT ON
CONJECTURE AND UNPROVABLE THEORY.

FINAL CONFERENCE TO TAKE PLACE DEC 7 AT 0900
NAVY HDQS BEFORE RECOMMENDATION TO SECRE-
TARY OF NAVY.

B BOONE REPORT NAVY HDQS WASH IMMEDIATELY
FOR DEC 7 MEETING. BEN YOU MUST PRESENT NEW
COMPELLING BULLETPROOF ARGUMENT OR CORPS
WILL NOT GET AMNESTY IS

RX MAPLE

Ben made over the parade ground for the bachelor officers'
quarters. The light was burning in O'Hara's room.

Zach's behavior at the casino, three months earlier, could have
turned into a major brouhaha. The navy wasn't going to have its
sainted reputation in Newport besmirched by a Marine.

Major Boone got to the superintendent, Rear Admiral St. Clair,
first, and pleaded not to take Lieutenant O'Hara off "Random Sixteen." Since the rear admiral knew the potential value of the study,
Zach was slipped through with a rap on the knuckles.

Zach was determined to regain Ben's trust and no manner of
man put in the hours of work he did. His days consisted of three
meals, often brought to his room, an hour's exercise, and the rest of
the time working, mostly in his room. He pushed himself into sitting sleep every night.

The sudden, unexpected message from Maple filled Ben with
horror. There was only one way to read it. The anti-Marine people
on Admiral-in-Chief Langenfeld's staff were making a deliberate
move to see that the Corps was phased out.

On this night, Zach lay on his cot and arced darts at a target on
the billboard. Blue darts and red darts. The reds were winning.

Every so often Zach stopped, scribbled out a thought, a paragraph, a correction, then returned to the darts.

Came the knock.

Zach tumbled off his bed, covered his papers, and unlocked the door. As Ben entered, Zach took his jacket off the good chair and offered it. Considering the hour, Zach understood that a storm flag had been hoisted.

"On the conclusions and recommendations number ninety-two you turned in yesterday," Ben said angrily.

"Number nine-two, yes, sir."

"You cannot tell the navy they must issue the Marines Krag-Jorgensen rifles. You know, fucking A, that the navy and the army develop their own weaponry through separate ordnance programs, at great cost to the taxpayer."

"A Krag-Jorgensen fired accurately from five to six hundred yards is the only viable weapon to stop a machine-gun squad," Zach argued.

Ben, one of the legendary riflemen in the Corps' history, knew damned well that Zachary O'Hara was right.

"Sir, Gunny Kunkle 'borrowed' Krag-Jorgensens from the army when we were at AMP. Every man in our class qualified as a sharpshooter or expert."

Although the lieutenant was under discipline, he was not being cowed.

"We are all fighting for the same country, sir."

"Enough!"

After a scaly silence, Zach asked for permission to speak.

"It's two-thirty in the morning, Major. You didn't storm in here to talk about rifles."

A pained smile emerged from Ben. "You got something to drink here?"

"No, sir. Part of my punishment is to refrain from alcohol. I can fix some tea."

"Fix it."

Ben scribbled a note and buzzed the mess hall. In a moment a red-eyed pot-walloper appeared.

"Go to the officers' honor bar, fetch me a bottle of rum, and leave this IOU note."

Zach made a pot of tea. Ben contemplated until the rum arrived, then enhanced his mug and offered some to Zach.

"Punishment's over," Ben said, pouring. "You know why I beached you, Zach."

"Yes, sir. To save my ass from my temper."

"Suppose you disconnected on a battlefield like you did at the casino. Ever think of that?"

"Every day," Zach said.

"Well, the beef was over a woman. Usually is. What attempt have you made to contact her in the past three months?"

"None, sir."

"Telephone, letter, messenger? Have you jumped ship to see her?"

"No, sir."

"You'll get no praise for a job you should have done in the first place without creating this nightmare."

"I don't want praise, sir."

"Zach, 'Random Sixteen' is one of the most uncluttered, logical briefs I've ever laid eyes on. It has been repudiated."

"I haven't finished it!"

"The central theme of future small campaigns and incursions is being rejected by the navy. They are not assigning the Amnesty Islands to us. By cutting off our training ground to work out our theories, they are intending to stand us down. We're getting the shaft."

"Are they crazy?"

"Crazy or not, they're the guys with the fuzzy balls. Admiral Langenfeld rules by committee. Commodore Chester Harkleroad is the monster at the gate. The Corps is not even on the committee."

Ben needed rum. Ben drank.

The two men had worked so closely, they could pick up on each other's intentions. Ben was brewing something wild and Zach read it perfectly.

"Ben, one of the first things you ever got across to me was that military planners in a democracy in times of peace will steer clear of a distant threat or be accused of warmongering. America is napping in bliss. It doesn't want to be awakened. What we were talking about that night is not going to be apparent for at least another generation."

"But it is going to happen," Ben retorted.

"America has time on its side," Zach answered, "but eventually the threat will become clear."

"Can't wait that long. If they deny us the Amnesties as a training ground, it may be the bell tolling for our demise. The Corps has to present a logical purpose, or good-bye, Mama."

"It will show we're too desperate," Zach said.

"I remember clearly when we had the conversation. We were sitting on my porch exactly a week before you fucked up at the casino. We had corned beef and cabbage. We started playing war games."

Zach had picked up the correct vibration.

"You stood, Zach, and pointed to Narrangansett Bay and you said, 'What do you see, Ben?' and I said, 'It looks like Narragansett Bay,' and you said, 'Hell, no, it's the Pacific Ocean and right down the middle at the international date line is the place of our future troubles.'"

"Are you really going to try to sell this?"

"Yep."

The bell tolled 0300.

"What do you need me to do?"

"Write up some notes regarding that conversation. Two, three, four clean, terse pages. Have it ready by reveille. I'm on the nine o'clock train for Providence."

Well, there it was, a battlefield decision, *now*. It could be a career buster for the major. But damned, the prophecy was going to be true!

"They'll be ready," Zach said.

"Thank you, Zach."

"Thank you for the opportunity," Zach said strangely. "I feel privileged. At least we'll go down fighting."

Ben got to his feet, wobbly.

"Major, I lied to you."

"Really? Concerning what?"

"Amanda did not send me packing. We love each other. After my tantrum at the casino, I was afraid you wouldn't trust me to see 'Random Sixteen' through. Moreover, I knew I'd be restricted to quarters, and if her father knew too early, I wouldn't be able to protect her, so we made up the story that we broke up in anger."

"Amanda came to see me three days ago and told me."

"What can I say?"

"You've said it, Zachary. You've stuck to your guns here and 'Random Sixteen' will be completed. Now don't get excited, but Daisy Kerr called me earlier today. Amanda confronted her father and has left Tobermory. She will let you know where she is waiting for you through Willow Fancy. As for Horace Kerr, Daisy believes he will make no move against her."

Zach shook out loud and gasped and sank down on his cot trembling.

"Now get your ass in gear, son, and do this little job. We've only got a few hours."

37

J

December 7, 1891—Headquarters—the United States Navy

Admiral-in-Chief Porter Langenfeld's conference room held a half-moon-shaped table with nine seats, himself in the center.

Facing the conference table, a straight table where advisers came and went. The wall behind them held a huge world map.

The staff table was a step higher, giving the effect of a star chamber during the Inquisition. Fanning out were the mighty: two vice-admirals, Rear Admiral Richard X. Maple, Commodore Chester Harkleroad in command of the building program, and four captains of the highest standing.

It was a shipshape room of a shipshape boss who was adept in negotiating the political jungle. Captain Fitz Donovan, his personal aide of eight years, sat alongside and somewhat chaired the meeting, shuffling papers and whispering into the admiral's ear.

Before them sat Lieutenant Colonel Commandant Tom Ballard and Major Benjamin Boone of the Marine Corps.

"Ben," Porter Langenfeld said in a notably cavalier manner, "who the hell let you in the room?"

"It was raining outside. I wanted to come in out of the rain."

"We can all do your routines by heart," the admiral continued. "I am up to snuff on your random study. I've read the first of the paper's conclusions. It is a fairly commendable work. I will put together a committee to take up a number of your ideas for further study."

"That's what I'm afraid of, Admiral."

The table snapped out of its daze.

Fitz Donovan leaned over to Langenfeld. "There's nothing on our agenda concerning 'Random Sixteen.'"

"What have you got there, Ben?" the admiral said pointedly.

"Nothing of an official nature."

"Then what?"

"Thoughts that have been deliberately kept silent. They need to be heard and said aloud because the words carry great clarity."

Porter Langenfeld scratched on his muttonchop and considered that he was being baited by a master.

"What the hell is it?" the admiral demanded.

"A discourse between myself and the lieutenant who worked on 'Random Sixteen.' I decided to leave it off as an addendum to 'Random Sixteen,' as not timely. However, I asked him to take notes of our conversations for possible future briefings. Though ahead of its time, it presents a powerful and, I believe, irrefutable case for the Marine Corps to garrison the Amnesty Islands."

"An opinion by a junior officer playing soothsayer?"

Ben held his breath for several beats. "Yes, sir," he said firmly.

"Christ sake, Ben," Fitz Donovan said, "this isn't the Roman forum or a Shakespeare festival."

"But it is the Naval War College and that's what we do there," Ben retorted.

"I take it this paper is loaded?" Porter asked.

"Very."

Langenfeld leaned back in his leather chair, curious but wary.

He leaned forward in a manner that showed why he commanded
the navy, and pointed to the commandant.

"You in on this, Tom?"

"Yes, sir."

"You've read it?"

"Today."

The fucking Marines were putting on a squeeze play. If the
report accurately foretold a future dilemma and he refused to listen, the onus would be on him. On the other hand, he was going to
hear something he didn't want to hear.

"You know about this, Dick?" he asked Maple.

"No."

"Very well. Tom, Ben, come around to my office and we'll dis-
cuss it."

"No, sir," Ben said.

"No, sir," the commandant said.

"Tom, you are about to be retired with the rank of full colonel.
Are you sure you want this read to us?"

"I'd prefer to retire as a sergeant knowing this paper will be
heard than be retired as a colonel and have it silenced."

Porter Langenfeld's eyes went right and he received dry nods.
His eyes went left. Nods there as well, save Chester Harkleroad,
who had a sour set to his mouth.

"As far as I'm concerned this meeting was adjourned ten minutes ago. We are off-the-record. Ben, you may proceed."

Ben could all but feel heat come off Zach's papers as he
unfolded them and studied the arrangement of gold-banded
sleeves before him. Funny, he wasn't even nervous. He cleared his
throat.

"Is there any staff officer in this meeting who does not believe
that Japan is programmed for and launched on the creation of an
empire?"

The room went silent. A taboo word had been spoken in the
highest council in plain English. Porter Langenfeld's decision time

was at hand, to pass and slap the lid on a Pandora's box quickly, or
let these Marines say their piece. They wouldn't pull this rabbit out
of the hat without a strong basis in fact.

"I'm going to hear this," the admiral said. "Go on, Ben."

Lieutenant Zachary O'Hara had burst open a vault where they
had hidden their darkest thoughts and built an organized, penetrat-
ing, and chillingly accurate line of reasoning.

Japan has a unique history among all major nations. She has
never been conquered or ruled by an outside power. Over the centuries she has built a secretive, feudal warlord-oriented society
devoted to a god figure . . .

As the only Asian nation to remain free of European control, she
moved into the modern world with a mind-set, a patient and sub-
servient culture, hidden anger, and deviousness, to plan and execute
what the Japanese feel is their destiny, if it takes decades or even generations . . .

When the isolation ended in the mid-1800s, Japan elbowed her
way into the old-boys' club of European powers, making herself a
partner and setting down troops in the Chinese treaty ports. With
that foothold, Japan has demanded that China cede them Formosa
and the Pescadores Islands . . .

Russian-owned Siberia has ambitions to move into and take over
Manchuria and this is apt to incite the first conflict. The Japanese
homeland is limited in natural resources and must have Manchurian
coal, oil, iron, and whatever is needed to create a modern fleet. It is
predictable that before the end of this century, Japan will move to
conquer Manchuria and have a war with Russia . . .

The population of Korea will be Japan's forced-labor pool to
work the Manchurian mines, build railroads, and otherwise set up a
structure to conquer China . . .

Two gigantic new world powers are emerging in the twentieth
century, Japan and the United States . . .

America has already made its major expansion by extending her
own borders west to the Pacific. America's future is based on commerce without invasion and outside rule. She will need, as would any
naval power, advance bases to protect her shipping lanes . . .

The United States has made it known she will annex the Hawaiian Islands. Does this not say that the United States has already drawn a line in the water at the international date line where Japan is to be stopped? . . .

The Japanese are already engaged in "peaceful" emigration to and setting up of colonies all over the Pacific, including Hawaii . . .

When one studies Japanese military potential, one must come to the conclusion that when Japan breaks out, she will encounter very feeble opposition in conquering everything from the international date line to 10° South latitude. Within that bag are Manchuria, Korea, the Chinese mainland, the Philippine Islands, the Dutch East Indies, French Indochina, Singapore, Burma, Thailand, and Cambodia . . .

No European power can match the Japanese in a land war in Asia. Japan will conquer without major losses. No combination of European sea powers will be able to go halfway around the world and defeat the growing Japanese naval power; not Germany, Holland, France, Portugal, Spain, or Russia . . .

Only Britain can stop a Japanese challenge to conquer Australia, India, and New Zealand.

That brings us to the evolution of a historical partnership unique in human history—that between England and the United States . . .

These two nations, without contentious borders, speak the same language, are driven by democratic ideologies, have a similar religious base, and share an integrated history and heritage. The United States and England have fought their last war against each other . . .

The recent naval protocol between America and England is a precursor to a power alignment that will dominate the world in the next century by recognition of each other's spheres of vital national interest (particularly the isthmus) . . .

The Anglo-American alliance will be the only force that can defeat Japan in Asia and the Pacific . . .

Japan is aware of this condition. Therefore, watch Japan seize, without opposition, an array of Pacific Islands. The Solomons, the Gilberts, the Marshalls, the Marianas, by stealthy immigration and colonization, will be garrisoned and fortified, creating a Pacific ring of steel . . .

The United States and Japan will inevitably go to war over domination of the Pacific Ocean. It will be the greatest naval war ever engaged . . .

In order for the United States to defeat the Japanese empire, she must conquer this belt of fortified islands spread over thousands and thousands of square miles . . .

The basic Japanese doctrine will be a theory that the United States will not spend the blood and years needed to conquer these islands. Thus, the war will end in a stalemate with a Japanese empire intact . . .

During the intervening years of peace, the American military must be aware of these island fortresses and develop tactics to invade them from the sea in the future . . .

These tactics can be developed only by a Marine Corps working quietly on suitable islands away from prying eyes in the Caribbean, namely the Amnesty Islands . . .

What can be developed is an intimate coordination between the naval force and the landing force; meaningful joint maneuvers . . .

Unless the United States is willing to cede mainland Asia and the Pacific up to the international date line, we must enhance our understanding of amphibious warfare through a Marine Corps . . .

A lone fly broke the silence as it buzzed around near Fitz Donovan's papers and suddenly the wall clock went *boom, boom, boom.* A worry they had all kept hidden was suddenly exposed. Whatever time in the future something like this could happen would be well beyond their watch and probably beyond their lifetime.

Yet the warning had been issued in the highest place, and peace in heaven would be ruined if the Americans were caught unawares.

Yet . . . how could this seem so predictable?

"Now, then," Porter Langenfeld said after two moments of silence, "we have been deftly maneuvered into hearing the word *Japan* used in a perfidious manner. This was a schoolboy's rambling without merit. The United States and Japan are at peace and could conceivably become allies at large. America has always had a special regard for the Japanese since Admiral Dewey brought them out of isolation. Sort of big brothers. So whatever was stated in this message is preferably not to be mentioned in polite society. Do you have any more copies of this . . . thing?"

"No, sir," Ben answered.

"Fitz, destroy it."

Captain Donovan came around and took the papers from the major.

"Gentlemen, if there is too much gossip about this, it could cause the navy some embarrassing moments. We heard it, we dismissed it, now keep the lid on it."

An unintelligible grumbling of neither yes nor no. Ben watched closely. The J word had stuck.

"Admiral Marple?"

"Yes, Porter?"

"I want the War College curriculum inspected. I won't have that place turned into a den of jingoism."

Nothing left to do but stretch Ben Boone and Tom Ballard's necks.

Porter leaned forward in stern manner.

"Major Boone, Tom, I think we may have passed too quickly on your request to garrison the Amnesty Islands. When will this 'Random Sixteen' be completed?"

"In a few weeks, Admiral."

"I'm going to give it all a thorough review. Get the balance of the paper down here as quickly as it is finished.

"And Ben, you'd better stick around Washington. If we decide to change our position, we're going to need you pacing the halls. Understand?"

"Aye, aye, sir," Ben said.

"We will continue with this tomorrow at . . ."

"Fourteen hundred," Donovan said.

"Adjourned."

The admirals and the captains departed, passing Porter Langenfeld one by one with a very unusual wordlessness and without handshakes, yet each man tapped the boss on the shoulder.

Then came Chester Harkleroad.

"That took balls, Porter. I'll give you no problem."

Richard X. Maple was the last to leave. Langenfeld tugged X's sleeve and beckoned him to come close.

"Any chance we can get this young fellow . . ."

"O'Hara," Maple said.

"Any chance we can get O'Hara transferred to the navy?"

❦·· 38 ··❧

NEBO

December 10, 1891—Wyman Creek Landing—the Eastern Shore

Willow Fancy paced the dock anxiously, then heard the whistle of the ferry coming into view around the bend.

She spotted Jefferson's shiny, hand-painted livery van on deck. TEMPLETON BROTHERS SADDLERS, it read, and in smaller script, the address, and it even had its own phone number, Skerrytown 18.

Mr. Templeton, a Negro, was a frequent purveyor from the mainland. The ferryman unchocked his wheels and signaled him to roll off.

At the end of the pier he stopped, set his brakes, and jumped down into his wife's embrace.

"She here?" Willow asked.

"Yep."

He helped Willow up to the driver's bench and set into motion.

"How's the baby?"

"Matt's doing fine. Granny Laveda feeding him nothing but cotton candy and taffy.

"Amanda all right back there? You didn't have to hide her."

"I know, but me and Miss Daisy and Amanda all agreed she draw too much attention. Besides, woman, it's cold out here."

In a few moments they were able to turn off the road behind some high marsh grass.

Jefferson drew the curtain, leaned back, uncovered Amanda, and helped her up. Willow jumped down, followed by Amanda, and they hung on to each other, breaths darting, trembling, Willow tearing.

"Oh God, Willow."

"You're okay, Amanda, you're all right now."

They hugged and gasped, then Amanda stretched out her stiffness.

"How bad did it go with Mr. Horace?"

"Bad. I'll tell you later."

"Where's Miss Daisy?"

"Mother turned me over to Jeff in Annapolis. She was very brave for me."

"About time Daisy was brave."

"Ladies," Jefferson said, "we should get going."

Amanda squeezed in between them, the girls covered with a lap robe.

"How long before Zachary comes?"

"Maybe a month."

"You're going to be ready enough. I'm glad we've got you here."

The van chimed as they made on down the mucky road. Jefferson Templeton did not like coming over to the shore in winter. It made both horse and wagon really filthy.

Matthew Fancy died before his daughter, Willow, was born. One of Horace's accountants went over Fancy's books. He'd earned a good living and lived pleasantly but had given it all back, and more, to his never-ending petitioners. Horace awarded Laveda a generous share of stocks, which allowed her and her daughter to lead a gracious life.

Laveda's only surviving brother, Ned Green, ended up share-cropping on a defunct plantation on the Eastern Shore. The land was eventually taken over by forty black families, who created the crossroads village of Nebo.

Veda, as Laveda was called by her kin, purchased a 160-acre farm for Ned and his wife, Pearly.

It was hard-luck soil, variable loam and a marshy mix of sand and clay. The villagers of Nebo were all survivors of slavery, mostly tobacco workers.

Ned was one of the leaders. He and his people reckoned that if they could dam and trap the spring runoff waters, they could build up a decent topsoil.

After slavery, no one wanted anything to do with tobacco or cotton. The Nebo settlement, in communal agreement, rotated general crops. After trial and despair, they were able to get decent yields of corn per acre, crops from a fruit orchard, vegetables, peanuts, and some grain. This would have provided a marginal existence, but it was augmented by the men's doubling as hunters, trappers, and baymen.

The community owned four Chesapeake Bay skipjacks and was allotted a Negro fishing ground the boundaries of which were marked by buoys, a bridge, and a lighthouse. It was not a prime area, but the black baymen had a sense of sea harvest in their fin-gertips.

They tonged and raked oysters and clams and trapped the melding crabs and terrapin of growing popularity. There were fish aplenty, from catfish to drum, if the creeks and marshes were played right.

Very special permits for guns and ammunition were issued and the men became dead shots at the blizzards of waterfowl, sea ducks, honkers and geese and deer and muskrat.

Wild horses were captured and broken.

Wild horses, you say? In the beginning, they were transferred from the mainland to dodge the tax collector and gained their free-dom, like some of the slaves.

In the crabbing season, women picked and packed in a nearby canning factory, and some winter jobs were to be had in the boat-yards.

By order of a council of elders, which included the preacher and women, only the pick of the harvest went to market, and Nebo got a reputation as sweet as their onions.

Mind you, a black man was a black man on the Eastern Shore, where he trod with caution, fear his constant companion. Yet there was an arm's length of accommodation and civility, so long as the black man kept his place. Most of the night riding and lynchings took place at the southern end of the shore, which was in Virginia.

Nebo found itself a niche and was mostly let alone. Much of the slave labor had come from Barbados and other Caribbean Islands but had always been in transit. Those who stayed in Nebo were sec-ond generation, from the tobacco fields, and kept fine Christian tra-ditions.

One must remember that the Eastern Shore was the birthplace of Harriet Tubman and Frederick A. Douglass. She, of Dorchester County, had operated a brilliant underground railway, and he, of Talbot County, was the greatest and most powerful black voice the nation had ever known.

Since pre–Revolutionary War days, a community of Quakers farmed around Wyman Creek Landing and built a small town and a Friends meetinghouse. In the beginning, the Quakers were ardent abolitionists. Over time, many broke away from Wyman Creek in order to own slaves. The core that remained were antislavery, so their community and fields had served as a friendly buffer for Nebo.

Out of the mainstream, Nebo fared well. Many of the cottages were brick and painted and had charming flower gardens and nib-blings of finery. They kept the skipjacks and nets in prime condi-tion. The hunters and trappers in the village were skilled and the fields responded to the attentive care they received.

As masters of survival, the Nebo families knew their reality. The "Big Mosquito," Sheriff Charlie Bugg, was reality, and the tithe he received from Nebo kept his larder full. Most troubles

never got to court and no prisoner from Nebo had ever been sold
into contract labor. It was a livable arrangement.

The ghost of Matthew Fancy never entirely left Horace Kerr alone.
After his death, Laveda and Willow continued a somewhat mystical relationship at Inverness. Now and again, during slavery, a
slave-master relationship grew close and continued after emancipation. Matthew Fancy had been Horace's most trusted assistant and
one of the brightest men he had ever known. Laveda oversaw
Inverness with great skill and had a strong bond with Daisy, her
former owner.

Amanda and Willow were like sisters.

Laveda was drawn to the consuming beauty of the tans and
coppers and browns and rusts and flares of orange of the Eastern
Shore.

As a respite from Baltimore, she built Veda's Cottage, as it was
called, on Ned Green's land and sponsored a one-room school-
house, the only black school in the county, and named it for
Matthew, and kept its shelves filled with books.

After a bit of grumbling and hemming and hawing, and after
close personal inspection, Horace allowed Amanda to spend some
of the springtime and autumn in Nebo with Willow. Amanda's visits were golden times for the girls from the ages of ten until their
cotillion.

They were maudlin that last year in Nebo over the inevitable
drift into separate lives. The flame of their friendship would
remain, but it flickered. Horace and Daisy were not all that sad
because there came a time when black-and-white intimacy needed
to diminish.

Directly after Willow's debut, she was courted by her escort,
Jefferson Templeton, a nicely cut fellow in his late twenties.

Willow had lived in the comfort of a white mansion, inherited
her father's lawyering mind, and dared dream bright dreams.

Wise old Laveda realized Jeff Templeton would be as much as
Willow could hope for. A single black girl was the lowest coin in

the Republic. Willow's gifted mind was rented by white law firms, but never mentioned.

Slowly but surely, ambition oozed from Willow in the face of grim reality and she gave up her dream.

The Templeton family, named for their former owners, were stalwarts in Baltimore's black community, building on a skill learned in slavery. The family patriarch, Josh, had become a master leather craftsman on a large horse ranch. His work was so fine that owning a "Templeton saddle" became like owning a rare orchid. An entire generation rode to the hounds with their white asses bouncing up and down on their Templetons.

Old Josh was clever, making enough prized saddles to be able to build a small leather factory that crafted a full line of tack, harnesses, running martingales, and farm leather.

Jefferson and his three brothers inherited a rare enterprise. The money came mostly from white folks and Jeff knew how to josh with them and let them believe they had outfoxed him.

But Jeff and his brothers still had one foot stuck in slavery, as would his entire generation and generations to follow. The barking hound was never far behind and life meant getting through without pissing off the white folks.

Ned and Pearly Green waited anxiously at the farm gate. They could hear Jeff Templeton's wagon chiming before they saw it, and their hearts ran fast.

How long had it been? Four years since they had last seen Amanda Kerr. Ned tugged the rope and the gate swung open and Jefferson lifted the women down.

They stared.

Pearly had shrunk some. Her face was clear, saintly, and beautified by life on the Eastern Shore. Ned's hair was all white, and though he was bent, he was still a power of a man.

They came together and held their girl wordlessly and tight.

"My, my, you has done some growing up," Ned said.

And they jabbered atop of one another up the path to the house.

It would take time before Amanda would be able to clearly pick up the lingo, cadence, and slang of their language, but it carried a melody of joy and relief.

Pearly had once been a domestic slave at the Virginia end of the shore and had become one of those Southern chefs of legend.

The big kettle hung in the fireplace bubbling with Pearly's crossbreed of gumbo and bouillabaisse, with every creature of fin and shell from the bay represented.

They set around the fireplace and passed the jug, nipped and whistled as the bite went down to their shoes. Thanks to Charlie Bugg, the village's modest still escaped unraided.

Pearly lit her corncob pipe and cleared the side table of photographs. Out of nine kids, six had survived and grown up and left, except for Ulysses, who pretty much ran the farm now. He had been named after General Grant, who sent a federal battalion to guard the Eastern Shore and keep it in the Union. Ulysses had his own cabin, which included Sugar, a sassy, bossy wife.

"Anyone know that Amanda is back in Nebo?" Jefferson asked.

"Nobody but family," Ned answered, "but everyone sure going to know by tomorrow unless we put some shoe polish on her face."

They prattled back and forth. Amanda accepted the warmth of her welcome, able to speak after a time.

"My father knows I'm in Nebo. On the way here, the trip was so dizzying I didn't have much time to think. I realize now that coming here could put you all in danger. I'll stay for a day. Put me in a safe place tomorrow so I can think it through and find somewhere—"

"Daisy said your father wouldn't send anyone to Nebo after you," Willow said.

"Laveda told me you was going to be safe here," Jefferson added.

"Lord, Lord, Miss Amanda a runaway!" Pearly said.

"Mr. Horace has really been put in his place," Willow said.

"Please, please," Amanda said, "my heart is so full, I can barely speak."

"Amen," Pearly said.

"But you don't know Horace Kerr like I know Horace Kerr. He's capable of anything," Amanda continued.

"Well, *I* know Horace Kerr," Ned said. "He been in Nebo— what, three times. Fourth time I saw him at the Wyman Landing, coming to fetch you. You know, Amanda, we got to learn to read a white man's intentions real quick. Your daddy's a bully, but he rarely been called on it. Well, he's been called on it now and he ain't going to bully us."

"I wouldn't put it past him to try to burn you out after I leave," Amanda warned.

"Remember old Sheriff Charlie Bugg?"

" 'The Big Mosquito'?"

"Me and Willow went around to see him yesterday," Ned said. "Nothing sets foot in this county without him knowing, and if they try to come for you, got to remember half the old people in Nebo was runaways at one time or another. We know the places and the routes to the places and our hound dogs can smell a nasty white posse ten miles away."

Pearly went to the organ and pumped it as Ulysses and his wife, Sugar, entered. Ulysses was as massive as Sugar was tiny. He went clear shy at the sight of Amanda, lowered his eyes, and held out his hand. Amanda gave him a mighty hug while Sister Sugar's eyes widened at the sight of the snow princess.

Willow and Amanda lay on their backs on the four-poster bed in Veda's cottage staring at the timber rafters. It was no cropper's cottage but a jewel of taste and manner.

Amanda spoke of the clash with Horace and worried about what might follow.

"Ned's pretty certain about Sheriff Bugg," Amanda said.

"He should be. Nebo has made him rich. He owns the cannery in St. Lawrence, so the men here fish up nice blue crabs and the women pick them and pack them. He pays a good price but takes a very good commission on everything. Everyone knows that Charlie's niggers are under his protection."

"Don't say it that way."

"'Scuse me, his colored folk are very Christian and peaceful. Nothing and no one moves into this county without Charlie Bugg knowing it."

"You hate him?"

"He's the best we can do. He doesn't go back on his word and that's fine with Ned and the elders. Ulysses is very shy, always been, but he's a strong boy and he'll be on the council someday."

"He and Sister Sugar make some pair."

"He doesn't hear a word she says. You heard her sing. Almost makes up for her talking."

"No kids yet?"

"I don't think they can."

Willow was being grim. Amanda tickled her hard.

"That's a little something you got around your waist. Anything in the oven."

"No, just a spread from sitting and reading contracts. I think little Matthew will be enough for us."

"He's gorgeous."

"All little chocolate drops and pickaninnies are gorgeous . . . until they take their first walk alone."

"You and Jefferson all right?"

"It's hard not to love Jeff Templeton," Willow said. "And Mama sent me off with the right words."

"Which were?"

"Don't marry up with a man with the idea you're going to change him. This is not a generation for black men. Jeff is great at what he does and can hardly keep up with his orders. A lot of white people would like to go into partners with him and his brothers. Jeff just wants to stay small and safe. I'm being a real bore."

"Yes, you are."

"I just get weary of the everlasting moral malnutrition," Willow said.

They were quiet. Often the quiet spells were as good as the talky ones.

"What happens after your month here with Zachary?" Willow asked at last. "You're flirting with losing your head."

"The only thing I'm going to lose, I want to lose so badly I can hardly stand it."

"The two of you never made love?"

"Silly, isn't it?"

"That's crazy. When you leave Nebo, what then?"

"We don't know."

"Shit!"

"I just feel the same about Zach as you do about Jeff. I'm not going to change Zachary O'Hara. The Corps has been good to him and he's dying to pay his dues. He'll be going to a new post. He wants sea duty. It's a Marine badge of honor. I can't follow him on sea duty and he'll probably be gone at least a year, fifteen months."

"Jesus, baby," Willow said. "You going to marry?"

"Can't without permission and that's Father's last line of defense. Zach will be long gone by my twenty-first birthday. I'll never go back to Inverness. I'll wait for him, someplace, maybe start a small academy."

This time Amanda received the tickles and tickled back, and they tickled and tickled until they were breathless and flopped.

"I felt so much love tonight," Amanda whispered.

"Ned says it's got to do with your hugs. You hug from head to foot."

"You're a silly billy, Willow."

"While we were waiting for you to get here, Ned told me about the first time you came to Nebo. We were nine or ten. Ned was sitting on a stump sweating. The drought was wilting his stunted corn and sorrows had all started to pile up. Losing his kids to the world and the earth was cruel and he was all but broken. He said you came up to him and wiggled up on his lap, put your arms around his neck, and laid your head on his shoulder and told him, with nary a word, that you understood how sad he was. And you knew why he was so sad and it made you sad as well."

"If Ned only knew how cold, how cunning, how manipulative I

can be. I have inherited my father's habits and a great deal of his bad intentions," Amanda said, "but the moment Zach touched me at the casino I was unable to resist him any longer and the rest of it didn't matter. All I want is to love him."

Willow wanted to say that she wished she was able to love like that and she wanted to say she was glad Amanda had become a compassionate woman. She had once thought Amanda would never find someone she loved more than Amanda.

. . . but Amanda was so tired. She peeped out a tiny snore, curled into Willow's arms, and slept.

❦· 39 ·❧

THE CRÈCHE

Several Days Before Christmas—1891—Baltimore

It had been an excellent year for the Kerr Shipyard, yet Horace was not content. The first trials and shakedown cruise of the *Vermont* were highly successful. It was perhaps the finest warship ever built in America. It was a powerful announcement to the world of America's new might: a ten-thousand-ton warship. As the year came to a close, every dry dock was laying new hulls and every inch of Dutchman's Hook buzzed with activity.

The nation was tied together by rail and great riches were steaming in from the West and down the Mississippi. America clung to a national dream of a canal through the isthmus and a two-ocean navy.

Then came disturbing news. The navy had made the decision to build a battleship on the West Coast. One could call that progress, Horace supposed, but it was ridiculous as well. How the hell are those people out there going to cast fourteen-inch guns? Or the new steam turbines? Or all the electrical equipment? A California-built battleship would take some of the luster from the great yards at Newport News and Brooklyn, to say nothing of Dutchman's Hook.

Horace's dream of bottling up the Chesapeake was put on hold. Did he even want the monopoly now? Those sons of bitches in Washington were talking about antitrust legislation, the first step to choking off the great industrialists!

What was the use of taking over the Constable yard anymore? Could there even be a merger without the marriage of Amanda and Glen Constable? Hell! It all had to do with Amanda's flight. That awful night she left Tobermory.

With all his plans of all the years, an alignment had finally been set for continuity and industrial power that would put him among the mighty.

Now he didn't know if he even wanted the fucking Chesapeake.

. . . enough of that.

The Christmas ritual was upon him. Horace Kerr would again play his role of noble benefactor. No Scrooge, he. On with the show!

Dutchman's Hook was trimmed up in ribbons, and Horace, acting like an eager candidate for office, made a round of the yard, pumping hands with the sauerbraten, spaghetti, and pork-and-beans workmen. Envelopes, a bonus of two to four days' extra pay according to rank, were passed out, and kegs of beer uncorked, and everyone doffed their hats.

The foremen and shop bosses, all called by first name, pocketed five days' pay as bonuses. They got rum. The main gates were locked against a demonstration by temperance screechers.

Who says you can't toast the Lord on his birthday!

In the meeting hall in the executive building, the architects, engineers, office staff, and titled managers received baskets that included cheese from Luxembourg, English tea biscuits, jellies and jams from Maine, and Scotch whiskey.

And for their children, a Santa Claus with sacks of little wooden livery vans, popguns, rag dolls made by a black community's old folks—an annual goodwill purchase—and bags of candies. Peppermint stripes drooled sticky off happy little chins.

Due to the influx of female office workers—most of whom were unmarried—brought in to use the new writing machines and such, the Pinkertons kept a wary eye on the backside pinchers and those making too many trips down the hall or too many trips to the punch bowl.

It was a wonderful party.

Horace was still gimpy from his sail to Immigrant Reef and leaned on a cane, with Daisy attending him closely.

When they reached their carriage and tucked in, they scarcely spoke all the way into Baltimore.

During the past few years, there had been an explosion in the uses of electricity. Inverness was the first of the Baltimore mansions to illuminate its grounds. Each season now, Kerr engineers enhanced the spectacle, lighting up the place with its own generators and drawing common folk from all over the city. They came by trolley and walked six blocks up Butcher's Hill.

Nice Christmas touch, the folks from downhill able to share the lights with those living uphill. Crowd control was in place; white people came through the main gate and walked the circular driveway into the blaze of lights. Blacks came through a side entrance.

A rotating bandstand erected by the great pine tree had orchestras from the Peabody Conservatory, the symphony, the Salvation Army, and the U.S. Army, Fort Meade, backing choruses from Protestant churches.

. . . and around to the enormous west lawn and living crèche with camels from the Baltimore zoo, live Josephs, Marys, and Wise Men. Baby Jesus was a doll.

The cast changed hourly.

Those on the "list" gained entry to Inverness itself, to the foyer where Horace had planned earlier to hang the finished portrait of Amanda.

On this first night, the heads of charities, orphanages, churches, and hospitals all gratefully accepted envelopes from the Kerr Foundation.

Tomorrow would come upper-midlevel city and state officials. Republican ward bosses, prominent citizens, and upper-midlevel businessmen.

And the night after, the elite!

Horace did not throw the switch this year, passing the honor to one of his vice-presidents. He was alone, in the dark, in the master's quarters, hit once again by that dull tingly pain. He stretched out on the chaise, unpeeled a cigar, and felt about the nightstand for the lamp and matches.

He could hear the lead trumpeter of the Baltimore Symphony splay the chilled air with angelic notes followed by massed choruses.

God, he wondered, how can you be so cruel? Why should any man, much less a good man like himself, be made to bear such suffering? Was he an incarnation of . . . not to think of such things, Horace.

Daisy no longer shared his bed. Her room, however, was close at hand.

"Horace?"

He grumbled weirdly.

"It is time for you to make an appearance," she said.

Daisy turned up a lamp and saw him on the chaise trying to scratch a light from a match. There! The cigar was up and burning.

She came closer. He looked ghastly.

"I won't be able to come down tonight. Make excuses that I . . . am indisposed . . ."

"What is it, Horace?"

"Indisposed. Come back when the circus is over."

"I'm getting the doctor."

"No, no, no. Joy to the world. Just say I got ahold of some bad oysters. That will keep them laughing."

"I'll send someone in to watch you and I'm calling Dr. Owens."

"No, not Owens. I feel a bit tingly in my left arm and I seem to be foaming when I speak. I've had one of these a few days ago. A small stroke, I'd say. Comes and goes. When the house is cleared call that Jewish doctor at Johns Hopkins, Goldberg or Goldstein . . . Goldman. It's about time I got something back for my donations . . ."

"You shouldn't be smoking," she said, reaching.

"Will you do as I say! For God's sake, woman, let me enjoy my cigar!"

♦· 40 ·♦

THE HORSE MARINES

December 27, 1891—the Naval War College

Zachary O'Hara sat on the side of his cot, pitched over, and fell on the blankets and pillows arrayed on the floor to catch him. He had trained himself to come awake an instant before he crashed and was able to break the fall, somewhat.

He lifted his head and tried to read the clock, but the eyes were too sore. An icy shower did him no good at all, was more like a herd of pounding buffalo.

Zach picked up the pillow and blankets, tossed them on the cot, curled up fetal-like, and spun into an annoying half consciousness. Now then, where were we . . . ?

CONCLUSION/RECOMMENDATION #103
 RIFLE CALIBRATION
  The assault Marine must land, penetrate, form a perimeter, and dig in against a counterattack. He must prepare to fight

twenty-four hours or more before expecting supplies and reinforcements. With orders to secure territory until relieved, there is no provision for retreat or defeat.

Marine assault gear should top out at a hundred pounds. More weight would slow his speed, drain his stamina, and hurt his efficiency.

THEREFORE: Kit, rifle, and belts of assault team should carry a trenching tool, poncho, toilet paper, bandages, bayonet, water, and ammunition for twenty-four hours of continuous combat. (Niceties—rations, soap, blanket, toothpaste, etc.— will come in later.)

The Marine must be a superior marksman and equipped with the most accurate rifle of the lowest caliber that retains stopping power.

Such a rifle should be between .25 cal. and .30 cal.

The point is: Because of his mission, he cannot expend ammo carelessly. He should not be ordered to come ashore with a fifteen-pound rifle that uses .45-cal. ammo.

With a nine-pound rifle and smaller-cal. ammo, the Marine can come ashore with 35 percent more ammo and a gain in accuracy of at least 50 percent.

Beyond 400/500 yards a modern Krag-Jorgensen rifle will double the accuracy . . .

The Marine will . . . the Marine will . . . over . . . time . . .

That was when Zach tumbled off the edge of his bed, showered, and plunged into a whirling dream of hell on earth until a persistent knock sent him crookedly to the door.

"There is a telephone call for you in the duty office."

Telephone call! Energy from God knows where flooded into him.

Zach patted himself down. He was in skivvy drawers. He found his bathrobe and the key to his room, stepped into the hall, and locked the door.

"Stand guard on my door until I return. Sensitive information."

"Aye, aye, sir."

Into the duty office he blundered. The chief on duty rang the switchboard.

"Naval War College."

"BOQ, my party is ready."

"It will take me a minute to reconnect."

The chief gave up his seat and the phone and retreated from the room.

"Lieutenant O'Hara."

"This is Willow. I'm in Baltimore. I just got back from a Christmas visit."

"She all right?"

"She's fine. How you doing, Zachary?"

"Oh, I'm rolling along real well. Finishing up on time, so I ought to be coming down after the first."

"You sound miserable," Willow said.

Zach balked.

"No, I'm . . . I'm . . . Christ, Willow, give me something to hang on to!"

"Amanda has always been aloof from the idea of loving a man. The way she loves you is beautiful, and very frightening. When you come to Nebo it could be the only time you ever have together. You know that."

"I know."

"Neither of you is ever going to get over it."

"I know . . ."

"Don't end up dying there together."

"It's crossed my mind."

"Hers as well. I don't want any Romeo and Juliet bullshit," Willow cried.

"Thanks, Willow. Happy New Year now. Bye."

"Bye, Zach."

"Waiting, are you waiting?" the switchboard asked.

The duty chief reentered.

"Let me give you a hand back to your quarters, sir."

"Appreciate that, Chief, but first can we get a call through to the barracks in Washington?"

"Should have no trouble getting a line this time of night."

"Get me Major Boone."

"Marine barracks."

"Major Ben Boone, please."

"The major left yesterday, sir."

. . . hello . . . hello . . . are you waiting . . . ? are you all right, Lieutenant . . . ? no, we turn right here . . . there's your room . . .

Zach fished the key out of his robe . . . the chief and the petty officer helped him in.

"I'm fine, I'm all right. Thank you."

. . . Jesus H., Ben's been haunting the halls of the War Department in endless meetings, their communiqués and calls had to be read between the lines . . . Ben said he had never mentioned or heard the word *Japan*. Did they get it?

Zach balanced on the edge of his cot and pulled the writing table up to him.

"Where were we . . . conclusion one hundred and three . . . rifle calibration . . ."

He no longer had the strength to grip the pen or keep his eyelids open. Harpies inside him shrieked for sleep.

"Where were we? Think maybe a little five-minute pick-me-up nap."

He came out of it fighting to awaken and heard the count of ship's bells. Eleven in the morning! The night had fled. Zach bolted upright. The room was an ugly gray. Outside the window, the weather muffled up, nasty.

Ben! He's left Washington and never contacted me!

All right, man, he commanded himself, get your shit together in rapid order.

Fortified by six hours' sleep, he cleaned himself up and made his room shipshape and had a tray brought in from the officers' mess. By noon he returned to "Random Study Sixteen." Two hundred pages coming to an end. Too late? Never mind, keep working on it.

He poured in bitter coffee, shook his aching hand, and pushed on to the final recommendation.

CONCLUSION/RECOMMENDATION #105

ALTHOUGH great similarities make the Anglo-American alliance possible, we have enormous differences regarding Britain's imperial role and America's future role in the coming century.

The British empire came into being through naval power with a minimal number of home troops and modern arms to conquer an overmatched adversary. Once in power, the British mastered the principle of "divide and rule" by putting native troops into British uniform.

Their imperial expansion was based on ancient principles of invasion, rule, and exploitation.

The British soldier in the colonies is apt to act superior, imperious, and fortified with the righteousness of his God.

The American "empire" was gained through internal expansion, the use of slave labor, and dismissal of the Indian.

America's future role as a world power is not for the conquest of territory but for commerce with sufficient naval power to keep her shipping lanes open and her advance bases protected.

We will certainly choose the wrong side at times and be called into combat or have to impose stern measures, but the ROLE of the Americans and the American psyche will enable us to befriend native populations. Guided by propositions of equality and basic decency, our garrisons could become welcomed.

The United States Marine Corps has established itself as the American gold standard. The Corps is a state of collective willpower. When we depart a post, we will leave the footprint of democracy.

"Random Study Sixteen" was writ. Two years, even more, had been compressed into seven months, but to what avail? Unprinted, shelved, never to see the light of day?

To beat the fists against the walls in frustration? Amanda. Your man is so down. I'll be long gone when that terrible war against the Japanese must be waged. What can be more bitter now than to prophesy unheard?

Fuck them all. Give me a command aboard a battlewagon squiring drunken sailors to the brig . . .

. . . so . . . the Marines will parade until there are three or four of us left and then the barracks will be turned over to the secretary of agriculture and the ground ripped up and planted with an experimental crop of turnips.

Major Ben, get back up here and let's cry in our beer, together. Come on, Ben, let's get the fucking deal over with.

Zachary trudged over to the office, three flights up, and dialed open the safe. He took "Random Sixteen" out, added the final sheets, and tied them all together in wide red ribbon, then locked the safe.

It was only two-thirty in the afternoon. Where was Ben? No need to hurry, Ben, nothing to celebrate.

Come on, O'Hara, stop feeling sorry for yourself. You're bleeding all over the place. Cheer up, you're going to see Amanda soon.

Let's see. A little horseback ride in the nippy air would bring me around. He left a note for Major Ben as well as a message at the desk and returned to his quarters for some heavier clothing.

Zach got along well with Bountiful, a fine old ceremonial beast. As they trotted out of the stable, a first little snow was piddling down. Zach was saluted through the guard post and rode onto the path that circled the island.

Bountiful was very happy for the stretch. Horse and rider made down a short bluff to the big eucalyptus tree where he and the major usually rested on their morning drill.

Zach dismounted and pressed his forehead against the horse's neck and explained to the animal why he was so screwed up and watched their breaths crisscross. He dug into his jacket—

"Ahoy!" a voice sounded.

Christ, now I'm hearing things, Zach thought.

"Ahoy! Ahoy! Ahoy!"

"Yo! Over here, Major!"

Ben's horse skidded down the bluff, half blinded by the snow.

He came alongside and leaped from his saddle onto Zach, taking them both to the ground.

"We got them!" Ben shouted, taking off his campaign hat and slapping it on Zach, back and forth. "We got them! We got them!"

On their feet, they stomped out a Cherokee war dance, howling like wolves. Zach leaped up, grabbed a branch of the tree, and did a backflip off it.

"We got them!"

They hollered and beat on each other until they fell into each other.

Ben related his titanic struggle in meeting after meeting. One by one, he convinced the navy into his camp, even Chester Harkleroad.

"It was tough-titty treading all the way. They couldn't envision the landing boat, they couldn't envision turning over command at the water's edge. They were shitty. As the days wore on, they began to realize what we were driving at. Never used the word *Japan* once, but the line of logic was so pure no one didn't get what we were driving at."

The unfinished "Random Sixteen" became the great whisper into their ears. Zach fired a hundred questions and Ben went over it all again.

"I've finished 'Random.'"

"How about that! What day is this, anyhow?"

"Not sure. It's after Christmas and before New Year's."

"So, happy New Year."

"Happy New Year, Major Ben."

They banged on each other a few more times and drank the sweet wine of victory.

"Ben, when the Corps selects a commander, you're going to have to let me brief him, page by page and conclusion by conclusion."

"That won't be necessary, Zach. You're taking them down there."

"Yeah, sure I am and U. S. Grant is a Mexican admiral."

"It's your command. First Rovers—Fleet Marine Force."

"Okay, funny, funny, funny. Knock it off."

"Zachary O'Hara was the only name seriously proposed or considered."

Zach blinked. The snow lifted and the sun gave off enough warmth to sparkle up the ground. He slid down the trunk of the eucalyptus tree with his back holding it up. He became light-headed.

"My command! I've dreamed of this since I was six years old."

"You've written the text, and now you're going to prove some things in the field. We've obtained undivided attention. You're going to show them how it works."

"Jesus Christ," Zach said.

"I can't get you Jesus, but the Gunny wants to go down to the Amnesties as your top kick."

"And to think, this morning I didn't even want to wake up."

"Getting you to Newport has been like hitting the inside of a straight flush—it's totally natural for you to follow through commanding the First Rovers."

"First Rovers, Fleet Marine Force. It's my command. I was born to take this command. Born to it."

"Won't be all that easy, Junior, so don't fuck it up."

"I was put on the doorstep of a Marine barrack the day after I was born. I'll know how to take care of my men."

"So you will, Skipper."

They clinked imaginary glasses and drank an imaginary drink.

Zach became quiet, then said, "Did you ever have to give or take orders that were dead set against your principles?"

"I know what you're getting at. I've been on the guard detail when there was a strike at a factory, and one in the coal mines. Being a strikebreaker, escorting scabs through the picket line, was terrible. Fortunately, we never had to open fire on anyone."

"Da didn't like strikebreaking duty, either."

Ben was quiet for a time. "I was a horse Marine," he said.

"I didn't know that."

"At the end of the Second Seminole Rising, we ran them down in the Everglades. Caribs . . . Seminoles . . . they weren't savages."

The sun cruised so nicely they wished they had brought a picnic, or at least a bottle. Ben seemed distressed about the Seminoles. Whatever happened in the Everglades, he wanted left there.

"We all have a dirty secret," Ben said. "You got one?"

That startled Zach. "Don't think so," he muttered.

"We've all got a dirty secret. I was liaison to the army before the Civil War. At the time there wasn't much of a military presence in Washington, couple companies of Marines at the barracks were about it. I got a whiff of some secret orders. The Marines were to be dispatched to Harpers Ferry, where John Brown was holed up, and bring him in, dead or alive. Some of my family had been lynched for moving runaway slaves on the underground railroad. John Brown was our high lord of abolitionists. There was a good chance I'd be ordered to take a company to Harpers Ferry. I got myself a forty-eight-hour pass and blew town before orders came down."

"That was over thirty years ago," Zach said. "How does it play out with you now?"

"I'd have the same problem today. As long as you are in the Corps, that number is going to come up and tear your guts out. It's a hard moment."

"I'll be ready."

"We know you will," Ben said, fishing around in his pocket. He came up with a pair of captain's bars and put them in Zach's hand.

"You'll have to have some rank in the Amnesties."

When Zach took the silver bars, he realized how much heavier they were than the rank he was wearing now. The step beyond. Zach sequestered his joy and the unreality of it.

"I'm glad we've been able to come to this moment, Zach. I had some twinges of doubt when you got that letter from Amanda."

"And you were worried that I wouldn't come back from my leave?"

"I was. Not now."

"Maybe I do have a dirty secret," Zach said suddenly.

"You'll come back. You're a war lover, like your old man."

"I'm not a war lover."

"In order to defend what we've got, every generation has to ante up war lovers."

"Ben, was there really a Yolanda?"

"Sort of. There's always a Yolanda but the memory gets mistier with age. And if it wasn't Yolanda, it was Cassandra or Miranda and Sally Anndra—"

"Or Amanda."

"Or whoever is standing on the dock waving farewell to her Marine."

"I hear you, clearly."

"You're going to be in the Caribbean for several months before there is a public announcement. No wives, no camp followers. We hope we don't have to keep you there that long, but you have to make a two-year commitment."

"I figured. Anything else?"

"You've got the gist."

Ben patted himself down, hunting for tobacco. "Shit! I was in such a hurry to get out here to see you with everything, I forgot my friggin' pipe and tobacco."

"Stand at ease, the day may be saved," Zach said, digging into his jacket. Two apples for two great horses. A pack of cigarettes down at the bottom.

"You smoking now?"

"I used to carry them for, you know, Lilly, when we strolled on the beach after the weather changed, and a good Marine always has . . . *matches!*"

They surrounded the cigarette to cut off the breeze. Ben lit up, drew, and gave a nice long "ahhh."

"Damned, it's nice out here," he said, puffing contentedly, then sizing up the brand. "Real elegant smoke. Probably some crap for the French aristocracy put out by Barjac."

"No, she told me her brother got the tobacco in Morocco. It was too expensive to put out on the market, so he makes some up for the family and a few friends."

"Now, that is high living," Ben said.

Zachary sniffed in an aroma he'd known before. Not that he wanted Lilly, but it was Lilly's sweet scent. She would like to smoke on the way back up to her villa right before the lovemaking. She'd get heady and giggly and every so often she'd kiss him openmouthed and exhale the smoke into him.

"Sure nice out here," Ben repeated.

"Ah, let me have a puff. Stirs up a naughty memory."

Ben passed the smoke.

"I can see how you can get hooked on this," Zach said. "I'll have to make a New Year's resolution not to take it up."

Major Boone began to ascend. Zach, being the good sport, took it down to the butt. They lit another.

"Sure is nice out here." Sure was.

"Every time I stopped by this goddamn tree, I worked out a landing or a defense."

"You know, so did I."

"Okay, let's have an invasion, right now."

"Sounds great."

"Do you want offense or defense?"

"Both."

"How many troops gonna make your assault?"

"How many you want?"

"One entire battalion."

"That's more than enough. Who's the enemy?"

"Anyone who doesn't agree with us."

"The landing was sloppy. I wanna inspect them before we move inland."

"Fall in, you creatures, on the double, goddammit! Battalion formed. All present or accounted for, SIR!"

"Jesus H. Christ. Can't you people form a straight line! What the hell is this war dance they're doing?"

"They have to piss, SIR!"

"They shoulda pissed when they were wading ashore."

"In my command, SIR, no Marine pisses his pants, even when submerged."

"Order them to piss and take three steps forward."

"Cocks out, right face, PISS!"

"Downwind, goddammit! You, big jock, you're pissing on my boots!"

"Battalion re-formed and eager for combat, SIR!"

"Before we go into battle, I wish to inspect them. Have your first company take off their knapsacks and open them for inspection. What the fuck is this, pictures of naked women! And you, son, when did you last brush your teeth . . . button your fly, there, Corporal . . . your fingernails are dirty. Put him on report . . . and you, what the hell you shaking for!"

"He always does that before combat, SIR!"

"I've come a long way in my time and seen sorry-assed Marines. You sure they're not sailors?"

"They're ugly, but they're mean, SIR!"

Ben stubbed out the second cigarette butt and took a step toward Zach and pitched into his arms.

"Oh, oh," Ben said, speaking quietly into Zach's ear. "We have been penetrated by an enemy spy. Her cigarettes were loaded."

"What would that be?"

"Opium, you asshole. Anyhow, brave Marines do not buckle at the first sign of distress. Gimme a boost and I'll inspect them on horseback."

Zach threw Ben onto the saddle.

Ben started down the line, muttering and cursing, with Zach running after him.

"You are on your horse backward, SIR!"

"Like hell I am. He's just pointed in the wrong direction."

❧ 41 ❧

WINTERSET

Two Weeks Later—Nebo

Sister Sugar: *When the sun come up on Nebo . . .*
Chorus: *Weary Moses looked him down . . .*
Sister Sugar: *Over Jordan stood the promise . . .*
Chorus: *Weary Moses looked him down . . .*
Sister Sugar: *Oh my childs, I go no further . . .*
Chorus: *Weary Moses looked him down . . .*
Sister Sugar: *Josh, we take them 'cross the river . . .*
Chorus: *Weary Moses lay him down . . .*
Sister Sugar, Chorus, and Congregation:

> *In the cold, cold ground,*
> *We done set old Moses down.*
> *'Cross the river we did go,*
> *For the battle of Jericho.*

> *Lay him down! Lay him down! Hallelujah! Lay him down!*

Extemporaneous lyrics and glory-bound voices shouted out sightings of Jesus and Mary and loved ones gone. No matter how frenzied the singing and shouting and stomping and clapping became, the voices continued to blend heavenly.

On a cold, clear day like this and with an eastern wind, their singing would leap clear over to Wyman's Creek Landing, where the Quakers contemplated in the utter silence of their simple meet-inghouse.

The sea grass and swamp grass and cattails and bittersweet and bayberry were spiked up stiff from last night's ice storm and began to bend, crack, and drip, lighting billions of diamonds. The branches of the trees hung wearily under their burden.

A staccato of breaking ice popped from every direction. This was a land alone, part Maryland, part Virginia, and all of Delaware, a state of little consequence, named for Indians who were too trust-ing of the white man.

It was as though a pagan giant had turned over a humongous pot of mud, and wherever it splattered down it formed a convulsive coastline with uncountable numbers of islands, estuaries, rivers, creeks, sounds, straits, and baylets.

This entire glob of land existed as a 150-mile barrier against the Atlantic Ocean on its east. A passage in and out of the Chesapeake Bay around Norfolk's tidewater allowed ocean and bay to merge and mingle. With the James and Potomac Rivers feeding the bay and the Atlantic finding its way into the bay, one of the world's most abundant waters of marine life evolved.

The land behind the bay contained the magic nutrients to yield that imperial Maryland tobacco. With many of the plantations gone, the shore's soil was sufficient for general farming.

The black village of Nebo was pleasantly self-exiled from the mainstream and mostly concerned with getting their field crops and seafood to market and otherwise keeping clear of the white people.

The village was built on marshland, barely gripping bedrock, so its cottages were on somewhat of a tilt. In the Nebo Abyssinian Baptist Church, the steeple would virtually sway like a metronome when the congregation was in full song.

Beyond Wyman's Creek Landing, Zachary O'Hara pulled Jeff Templeton's livery van off the road and gazed at the mournful loveliness of the place.

The road was slushy and every tree crackled and dripped, animal tracks scrambled and disappeared, and the bare threads of the farmlands pocked out of its dusting of snow.

"It's enchanting," Zach said.

"It isn't too kind to visitors this time of year. We sure glad Laveda built her lodge here. Willow and I come over often as we can. Amanda is going to scream and faint dead away when she sees you. She wasn't expecting you for five more days."

"I got a grace period. Why don't I jump into the back and change into some easy clothes."

"Well now, nobody in Nebo ever seen a Marine in officer's uniform. They would be mighty pleased."

"I'll be a mess from the mud."

"Oh, Pearly and the ladies will clean your uniform, sparkling."

"Okay, buddy, you've got a deal."

"All right! Amanda's going to fly right through the roof."

The trip was a spellbinding grind.

A first touch of Nebo reached them, scent of peat and a moment, voices in song.

They entered a churchyard filled with headstones, all leaning south, bent by the north winds.

> *Oh, sweet rose of Galilee,*
> *Send thy precious love to me,*
> *Lay me down, oh, lay me down,*
> *On thy bosom,*
> *On thy crown.*

"That be Sister Sugar, Ulysses's wife. She sure sounds nice when she's just singing."

Jeff hitched the horse, then gripped Zach's arms, gave him an affectionate little shake to steady him up, and led him to the church door. When it opened a cold blast bolted in, causing everyone to turn around and look.

My God, what a handsome-looking white man! Shining head to toe like one of Jesus' saints.

Pearly stopped playing. Sister Sugar stopped singing. The place froze like a tableau.

Zach took off his hat and nodded.

Amanda, in gingham, arose and came to the center aisle, each moving toward the other until they met. He lifted her into his arms and carried her out and set her down.

The church emptied. They were surrounded by celebrants. Amanda grabbed Zach's hand, tugged him free of the welcomers, and pointed out their direction.

She turned and waved and everyone cheered and they ran off. Past Ned and Pearly's cottage to a tiny pier. The duckwalk over to Veda's was slippery and flooded from the ice storm. A small raft with a handline took them across the few feet of marsh.

With the voices zinging after them, Amanda opened the door. The lodge room was stunning with Laveda Fancy's fine tastes, acquired as the matron of Inverness. Pewter plates and mugs set on the table and a giant beaten copper kettle at the fire and a grandmother's clock of ancient vintage, and fine-cut crystal in an open cabinet, and furnishings hewn so long ago by some master Yankee craftsman, and large hand-wrought tongs that had lifted ten thousand logs.

There was a sleeping alcove with a four-poster bed covered by a Quaker quilt and a comfortable little reading nook alongside.

And Amanda's touches to make her man warm in January. By the fireplace, feather beds had been laid out and were waiting for them to crawl under and there were enough candles to light a cathedral, and arrangements of rusted leaves, some scarlet, mostly brown.

Wine from France by way of Baltimore.

A sudden awkwardness closed in, and strangely, they seemed to hold each other off at arm's length.

Zach tried to conjure up the words. "This is the most wonderful moment I've ever come upon or will ever know," he said. "I want to love you perfect. If we savage each other, it could linger bad. I don't want to screw it up."

"You're going to make me cry, Zach."

"Slow and soft," he said, "and we'll whisper to each other and stay together."

She nodded. "After their debuts, a lot of my girlfriends became engaged and married and some of them had very bad experiences, untidy and painful."

"There's something else I'd like to get over with, now. I can be here till mid-February, then I report to my new assignment. For the first several months, my whereabouts are to remain secret. I cannot tell you where and I am committed for up to two years."

She had braced for such words and now took them staunchly. Her eyes grew wide. "Are you wearing captain's bars?"

"Yes."

They held each other lightly, like dancers, and swayed together. She whirled out of his arms.

"And I've saved up something to tell you as well. I know my lover loves me dearly. We are going to be glorious together." Now she became nervous. "I have many friends among the artists, some very close, and some who have collections of salacious litera-ture . . . often illustrated. I have devoured every piece of filth I could get my hands on and you are about to collect a curious and daring woman."

Well, vintage Amanda. She rambled on.

"At first I thought I'd make a list of things to explore, then I began to realize it could be never-ending, so I thought about keep-ing a diary to recall every detail, but I'll remember what is to be remembered and until such time as I can give and receive with equal skill and ardor. I am at peace with the fact that you are experienced in these matters . . . and so forth and that you can introduce special pleasures you have experienced, but I don't want details of with whom you discovered them and I have read the Marquis de Sade, and although I want no part of pain I want you to know I have been a sophisticated reader . . ."

Zach bolted the door and she drew the curtains.

"Undress, Captain," she commanded. "I will see you buck naked now. I wish to see your cock."

"Well, it's really nothing, Amanda."

He unbuttoned and undressed down to bedrock.

"You call that nothing!"

"It's pretty much a standard issue."

"Can I touch it?"

"Well, sure, but you see these things have a mind of their own and no matter how willful a man may be, he may not be able to suppress, I mean—did your girlfriends tell you about—"

"Premature ejaculations!"

"In a situation like this"—his voice went squeaky—"if the Marine finds relief once or twice, then he should be able to settle into the same . . . mode of his lover . . . girl."

"We will go wild from time to time?"

"Depend on it."

"And new things?"

"I don't think we're going to run out of ideas."

Each square inch of the body gives off a different song. And their lips and fingers discovered them all, touching and feeling until the lover's fingernails came alive with sensation . . . lips counting eyelashes.

. . . slow it down

You gaze, so sweetly dazed. Minutes, then hours of staring, until they could read each other's prints and everything opened and welcomed them to hallelujah land.

All that night they floated on a pond of incredible calm. And became ready before daylight.

With exquisite care they mated, and even the pain of it was a hurt gladly acquired.

They were total lovers!

. . . good-bye, world . . .

"Your tummy's churning," Amanda said.

"It's just the tide changing."

Footsteps outside. They sat up in the feather beds. A firm knock.

"Who's there?"

"Ned Green."

Ned could hear them scurrying about. In a few moments they opened the door sheepishly. They could see Pearly on the other side of the creek.

"I been putting your plates at the door for four days now like you was in a zoo. You get over to the house and get some nourishment."

Ned poked his head inside and called to Pearly. "Just what I thought. There was a shipwreck and two white people was washed up on the shore. They seem in terrible shape!"

"Leave them children alone!" Pearly called.

"Notice he ain't carrying her around no more. Hell, he'd fall in the creek."

Light-headed and wobbly, the lovers faced daylight, hanging on to each other for balance. Though lust was undimmed, it was overtaken, for the moment, by hunger.

Zach devoured four slabs of ribs smothered in enough beans for a squad and a quart of apple cider and corn bread troweled with strawberry jam, and Amanda wasn't all that dainty, either. They waddled to the fireplace and curled up and cooed and listened to its crackling and heard distant voices come and go. "So they finally come out." "Sure are powerful for white folk." "Don't you be getting no fancy ideas, Ulysses Green."

By the end of the week they found themselves lured to Pearly's table at main mealtime. Folks visited them and they took walks about the fields of Nebo. Amanda taught in the classroom for a time each day, or hung about the kitchen, or brightened up Veda's cabin, or sat in the back of the Abyssinian Baptist Church holding hands with Zach and listening to choir practice.

Zach earned his keep at the boat shed, where the men repaired clam rakes and oyster diggers and mended nets and sails, sanding, caulking, and painting the hulls of the skipjacks.

Here Zach got drawn into the Nebo soft sport of arm wrestling. Everyone wanted a chance to pin that smiling white boy. Up and up the ladder the challengers came as Zach won supporters who bet their pennies on him.

Zach moved into serious competition, challenged one by one by the Nebo team (who were mighty fine baseball players in the spring and summer).

With Ulysses Green the anchor for Nebo's arm-wrestling squad, they'd not lost in years. Well, this was as far as Mr. Zachary Captain O'Hara would go. First left-handed. Then right-handed. Fourteen to nothing.

Nebo seized Zach. The church seized him. A man and a woman holding the wee hands of a child between them.

. . . one day as a little boy he stood beside his da at a pond in Central Park where a papa swan led a squad of cygnets and the mama swan tended the rear. "That's a family," Zach had said to his da, and Paddy choked up . . . even at Onde la Mer, there was a distance between Zach and the Barjacs, who were overlords at play. Not totally real, was it?

. . . Nebo was real, with the boys walking alongside Daddy, guns on shoulders, in from the hunt, slim pickings.

Women so black and beautiful that the movement of their hands with needle and thread was dance.

Well, hell, the United States Marine Corps supplied him with brothers, dozens of brothers. But not one brother of his own. It only gave him men to emulate.

Life began with a cursed bugle and cold-water shower by day and a lonely taps by night in a cot not known by anyone but himself.

Aunt Brigid gave him a place to sleep and took him to a place to kneel.

Now Amanda, now Nebo. It rushed into him and filled that barren space, this village which had taken over Amanda as a young girl.

How can lovers compare? Any two lovers who have discovered the ultimate intensity, then gone beyond, believe that they are the first lovers since time and no one has ever felt such remarkable love.

Their lovemaking, from fierce to subtle glance across the room, did not begin or end but was in motion all the time. Sometimes, barely breathing, sometimes, tied to a post, shrieking.

. . . until each knew every print . . . every scent . . every detour . . . and sight . . . and anticipation . . . and taste . . . and sweet voice and vulgar voice and places wandered into that suddenly opened a new flood of sensations.

. . . until such exhaustion left their only half-opened eyes to gaze and their ears able to hear the birds jabber.

And sleep easily.

Bold and shy, they answered the curiosities of rich minds. Bold and shy, they loved each other's raw naked beauty. Wisely, they probed not of each other's past encounters because they were not disturbed by them.

The weather had been fine for a few days. They put on mud boots and walked beyond the fences, along a creek where there was no road and it seemed that no one had ever been this way before.

An eagle graced their view, hovering on a dead limb intensely, gathering up for a swoop into a movement of trout.

Amanda and Willow had gathered mushrooms in the summer, and at times, Ned would let them on one of the skipjacks to go rock fishing. They weren't too good with the lines, but they stayed out of the way, and after a time, Ned let them steer the craft.

"That big rock over there is filled with mussels in late springtime. We'd wade out and cut them off for bait."

Amanda's eyes opened widely, suddenly. She froze and put her finger to her lips for him to be still. A low, mysterious grunting:

bup-bup, bup-bup, bupbup. She knelt, trying to stifle the sound of her breaths darting into the cold air.

The grass moved. Snake? Frog? Turtle?

As deftly as she could manage, she moved the matted grass and gasped! A henlike creature, a bird all rusty-feathered with a long beak, was startled.

It was gone!

"Did you see it?"

"Yes."

Her heart was racing as she grabbed his hand. "Did you see it? It's a king rail. Willow and I spent hours looking for one. We began to think Ned was playing a trick on us. During my last summer here, we found a nest. Ned's only seen three of them since he was born. They live deep in the marsh grass."

She said "Oh my God" several times, caught her breath, and let out a "Wow!"

"Any profound meanings?"

"I don't know. Only that it's always hidden away like a secret."

"And all secrets are found?"

"I don't know," she said. "It's kind of the way the people in Nebo live. They don't want to be discovered."

As they walked away she looked back several times and got a perfect bearing because she had something to talk about at the dinner table.

Back at Veda's, Amanda drew a map of the location and a somewhat drawing of the bird and extracted a promise from Zach to back up her discovery later, at dinner.

He stroked her face and wondered what the rail bird had told her.

One of Willow's paintings near the stairs seemed to have the same distinctive features of the field they had walked. Was that where she and Willow had found the nest earlier?

Every time Zach had looked at Willow's gauzy brushstrokes, he thought he saw a white shading in the tall grass, perhaps a figure of a woman.

"I've looked at this a hundred times," Zach said. "Is that where we were?"

"Yes, very good," she answered.

"And is that little dot over there you?"

"Yes."

It had been a very long time, close on two hours, since he had touched her and kissed her well. With one hand Zach managed a mug of tea. The other hand was filled with her breast. He set the cup aside, laid his head against her bosom, and she dropped her pen and unbuttoned her top buttons, let her dress slide down over her shoulders, and awarded him full access.

He was stricken with bliss and she enfolded him and they swayed ever so gently, for ever so long. Amanda opened her eyes. They were filling with mischief.

"I've got something to show you," she whispered. "Light up a lamp."

They went up to the loft, which served as an extra sleeping place and, more recently, as an adventurous bordello filled with wild things. A ladder lay on the floor, to a side. She told Zach to set it up by a trapdoor. He poked it hard and it swung open into a storage area.

Amanda went up and into the space with her lantern. In a few moments she handed him down three paintings covered with oilcloth.

Amanda dusted them and removed the covers. The paintings were in Willow's blurry style, of three nudes. They could not be distinguished by face, but the body of the model was unmistakable.

. . . Amanda posing topless in the same grass where they had found the rail bird. And one of her stretched on her stomach drying her hair on Veda's porch and one was the full front of a girl proud of her nakedness.

Back before the fireplace, he arrayed the pictures while she filled wine goblets.

"I've something to tell you, Zach."

"Aye?"

"Willow was my first lover."

She waited for his reaction. It was a smile.

"It's not that hard to understand," he said.

"I'd like to tell you, if . . ."

"Then, tell me."

"Will and I turned sixteen. There was no boy, not in my circles, who I wanted to escort me on my debut. That's when I ended up with that phony Scottish so-called aristocrat. There were some artist friends I couldn't take, but no one in the old-boys' crowd.

"I was not happy. My girlfriends were nailing down husbands as fast as their hammers could pound and I learned from them that first love could be foreign and frightening and cause a great deal of pain.

"That was the summer I had Private First Class Zachary O'Hara ordered by the commandant to attend a party at Inverness. And that was when you touched my breast in the garden and my life turned on that moment. I was livid when I realized I could not have you on demand. I'd never been challenged like that before or been walked away from. It was the wrong reason for falling in love with you and it took a long time to change into something decent.

"After her debutante ball, Willow was being courted seriously by Jefferson Templeton. We were going our separate ways. I demanded to be able to come to Nebo with her for a last summer.

"Willow was a fair artist, as you can see, and she began sketching me. A Jewish peddler, Jacob Nussbaum, made stops in Nebo. In his wagon he had pots and pans and old magazines and used eyeglasses and women's undergarments and secondhand children's shoes, mirrors, store candies. I loved those candies. His wife made them.

"That summer, his son, Morrie, drove the rounds with him. Can you believe Jacob's son was an art student in Boston? He was scouring for scenery to paint. Willow saw it as a chance to get free art lessons. Jacob would double back through Nebo in a week or so. Willow talked Jacob into leaving Morrie with us. He slept upstairs in the loft.

"The two of them started sketching me and I felt like a queen. Well, Morrie assured me that all students drew nude models, and after all, there are naked women hanging all over the walls of the museums. I agreed to lower the top of my dress. Zach, it was the most thrilling sensation of my life, other than you. And to make the game fair, Willow did likewise.

"Anyhow, Morrie left me all his sketches and rode off with Jacob, pots clanging. They're on a pad, tucked away at Inverness. Willow did these three of me during the rest of the summer."

Amanda stopped, anxious now that it could jolt Zachary, wrongly. He wore a smile that said mischief is mischief.

"Should I finish or just leave it?" she asked.

"As you wish."

"You're not angry?"

"I don't think so."

"I want to keep no secrets."

He leaned over and pecked her cheek.

"Willow and I had slept together since we were infants. This was the summer of our sad parting. As she painted me we grew very affectionate. We slept close and kissed and then she felt what she had painted and I did the same. We rubbed a lot and it was really good but we didn't go inside each other. Willow wanted hers for Jefferson and she would not take mine. So, that's my secret! I hope I haven't hurt you terribly."

"I love you more than I did an hour ago, if that's possible."

"Willow and I have not touched each other again. You're not jealous at all?"

"Envious, a little bit. It seems pretty natural for the two of you, and if you hadn't, maybe you'd have regretted it all your lives."

"I guess men have those feelings as well. My dear brother, Upton—"

"Men care for each other and run around bare-assed with their nothings hanging out and talk sex and women all day, but that isn't part of our world. However, I sure do understand Amanda and Willow."

That night, the greatest, most impossible fried chicken and mashed potatoes and a round of hymns and a few sea chanteys and Marine songs rang out from Ned and Pearly's.

And they found a new plateau of loving, a place of trust and truth.

As the truth made them happy, there was the first sounding of an outside world seeking them back.

Time can come and go like a bolt of lightning.

Time can be slowed to a lovers' infinity.

But time cannot be stopped.

❦ 42 ❧

TRUCE

A Fortnight Later—Ben's Cottage

Ben seemed to age before his very own eyes. "Random Sixteen" was done. All the years of pondering and collecting were now writ with a wizard's logic, ready to be tested, argued, revised, included, or discarded. This was secret for now; there were the keen hands of admirals helping guide it through the bureaucratic rapids.

The same young man who dared write the forbidden name of Japan was soon to take his men to the Amnesty Islands.

Ben could rest a bit; not too much. He had to remain on watch to protect Captain O'Hara's flanks. Seeing it unfolding was what Ben lived for.

And Christ Almighty, only a year ago it was never going to happen. Zach took the material and made it sing and dance and show a fearless face.

What shithouse luck, Hillbilly Ben! He dozed in his great chair, contentedly, and didn't try quite as hard to stop the old bones from cracking. Sleeping in the daytime. Lord, what next? Ben wondered. Maybe he'd court a lady for a last fling before a last fling before a last fling. Who was available but a few itchy, out-of-bounds wives?

How about that music teacher, Miss Florence What's-her-name? She was giving off some powerful looks across her piano, accompanying that violinist, What's-his-name.

Ben dozed. Nice to doze without guilt.

A knock on his door had the authority of a silver knob at the end of a rich man's cane.

"Come in!"

Horace Kerr entered and signaled Ben not to get up. He set down his top hat and cane and went directly to the liquor tray and poured himself a double.

"What are you doing up in Newport this cold-assed winter's day?" Ben asked.

"I have this and that to take care of with my brothers at Tobermory. Drink?"

"No, thanks," Ben said.

"I do not have to review," Horace began, "how long we've known each other, etc., etc." He stopped and seated himself. It was then Ben took note that Kerr had lost quite a bit of weight and sagged slightly on the left side of his face. Horace became misty-eyed.

"I want my daughter back," he croaked.

Ben resettled himself without reply.

"Please understand, Ben, that I'm not here to bark. I'm seeking advice."

"Then we'd have to leave the bullshit outside," Ben said.

"Yes," Horace answered, retreating.

"Is this visit out of love for Amanda or more commercial in nature?"

Into the rapids Horace Kerr went. "More from love than I believed possible. But there is always the gnawing matter of continuity. You know about continuity, trying to keep your Corps alive."

Ben indicated that an early drink might be in order. They tipped glasses. The room closed in as Ben probed for the precise words.

"Zach and Amanda are beyond all fear of us, Horace, and I do represent the Corps to him. The two of them, alone, are going to make their decision. You and I will have to abide."

"I am prepared to compromise," Horace said.

"They won't be seeking a compromise nor issuing threats. They are going to do what they say they are going to do."

"I feel like General Lee at Appomattox." Horace knitted his brow. "This report or monograph or study, whatever, that O'Hara has done up here at the college seems to be gaining attention in Washington. All I know about it is that it is a thesis on future marine and naval warfare. Confidentially, Navy Secretary Culpeper and Commodore Harkleroad called me in. I'm laying the hull for the *Georgia,* sister ship to the *Vermont.* They want me to change the midship scheme to make a place for a forty-man Marine contingent. Ben, I'm not trying to bleed you for information, just putting two and two together."

Ben smiled.

"You have the reputation of being untouchable, Ben. Now O'Hara's name is floating around among the top brass as your protégé."

Ben hid his face in his drink.

"You have Porter Langenfeld's attention," Horace said.

"High time."

"This work. Is O'Hara some kind of genius?"

"No, he's not a genius."

"What is he?"

"Intelligent and organized, works beyond human capacity, finds his line of logic, and builds his case with clarity, but there's more. He's got the balls to walk into twelve-inch guns without backing down. If his name is on it, you are getting the truth."

"And the truth?"

"Amphibious warfare, fought correctly, will require casualties, and that's not in the American lexicon."

"A twenty-four-year-old Marine captain who won't bullshit. That's a hell of a piece of personnel for the Corps. Don't lose him. Where are you sending him?"

"Somewhere," Ben answered.

"Committed mission?" Horace asked. "For how long?"

"Up to two years."

"Wives?"

"No."

Horace heaved a sigh.

"Does Amanda know?"

"Only that he'll be gone for a long time."

"What do you think they're going to do, Ben?"

"I suppose their first rush of being together has settled in. Reality of the future has to be hovering around them."

"They won't try anything desperate, will they?" Horace asked.

"There's a chance, Horace."

They spoke now with great frankness of the unspoken things. As a Marine's wife, Amanda would enter a life filled with loneliness and often fear, and at the expense of her own gifts.

As for Zachary O'Hara, no matter how he tried to split himself in half, both Amanda and the Corps would stand to lose.

Now Horace moved in on what his creative mind had worked up to.

"He'd make an extraordinary executive in industry. Isn't that right, Ben?"

"You want your daughter back. I want my Marine."

"But if we all agree, he should serve out this mission. Two years is not all that long to wait. He will be a great executive, and still a boy."

"What about his tainted ancestry?" Ben asked.

"God willing, he'll agree to a quiet conversion. There are lots of Presbyterians from Ulster with Irish names. O'Hara could well be a Protestant. It will be a hard sell in the banking community and among my peers, but a sane answer to all this. There are bound to be some Catholics breaking through into the hierarchy soon."

Ben sat back and studied a master of conspiracy in his illuminating moment.

"Let's see if I've got this right," Ben said. "First you dangle a high position before his eyes with the delicious promise of a partnership. Then they separate for two years. You pray, in a Protestant manner, that Captain O'Hara gets so caught up with his mission and his life that he will recognize the futility of marriage. During his absence, you can work on Amanda, say she is abandoned, Zach is never coming back . . .

"Or!" Ben went on. "He comes back and they marry. And you've got what you want anyhow."

"It's all rather decent, isn't it!" Horace protested.

"Suppose she is pregnant now?" Ben asked pointedly. "You going to put a bastard in the mix?"

"Ben, don't get out of hand. That was very nasty."

Time for a topper.

Horace sighed sadly.

"If Amanda is pregnant, we could arrange an elopement and marriage and have that documented so that when he ships out she can return to Inverness and possibly arrange an annulment. In that way the boy . . . the child, would be legitimate and even have his name changed to Kerr. Or, on the other hand, if Amanda insists, she can wait for O'Hara to return."

Ben's heart cried. But Horace was off and running to the music of his own voice.

"I have lost my great dream, anyhow, if Amanda doesn't marry Glen Constable. There will be no merger, no monopoly of the Chesapeake. In order to expand and buy Constable's option on the tidal basin, I'd have to make a public stock offering. That would mean bankers on my board of directors, stockholders screaming at me, government regulators crawling through my books . . .

"Of course I don't have room to build another rowboat at

Dutchman's Hook and there is a nice flow of navy contracts for the next decade, but Jesus, the navy is going to build a battleship on the West Coast, without my bid, in order to save that voyage around Cape Horn. What the fuck do cowboys and miners know about forging fourteen-inch guns? Where will they get them done—at some Indian reservation?

"So, if worse comes to worst, O'Hara will return in a few years and become a director at Dutchman's Hook, even though it portends a bitter struggle with my own class. I can only pray that Amanda has had her fill of him in Nebo. However, to cover all bets, I should present them with my offer, should I not? What?"

"Absolutely."

"They won't receive me in boogeyland."

"That would be awkward."

"Perhaps, well, you know, you do have a powerful influence on O'Hara," Horace hinted.

"No way."

Horace Kerr tottered. He wanted to ask Ben to write his own ticket, any ticket. The problem was that there are some sorts you simply can't do business with.

"Why don't you write your daughter a letter," Ben said.

"Will you see that she gets it?"

When Major Boone became Uncle Ben, he knew he'd put his foot in it.

Did Horace Kerr realize he'd met his match in these two people?

"I'll see to it."

That damned tick overtook Horace's left eye, again.

❧ 43 ❧

THE LETTER

A Week Later—Nebo

The day after Sunday church, they awakened to a mood that had drifted into Veda's lodge. The fog outside somehow had found its way in and diffused throughout the room. Amanda was tight and Zach was tight, responding to each other's affection with some stiffness. Nor could naughty whispers lighten them up.

Was it something the preacher had said at church, or was time on everyone's mind? Their friends looked at them fairly hurting, like taking a step back and shaking their heads and lowering their eyes before those poor kids.

Zach went to the boat pier, working mucky on shoring up a pair of sagging pilings. Ned picked it up, quicklike, and when Ulysses came bubbling down the duckboard, he threw a glance to his son to indicate that Zach was in a mood.

The village wondered how long it would be before Zach and Amanda bent.

Amanda snapped string beans in the kitchen. Pearly shuffled about moaning low some sorrowful song and it annoyed Amanda, as if it were the only damned song she knew.

Even though the sun burned the fog off by noon, seemed like the whole of Nebo was still engulfed.

Enough string beans.

She chopped at the collard greens.

"Damn!"

Amanda dropped her knife and sucked at the finger she had nipped.

"You'd think they'd know how to sharpen a knife down at the boat shed."

"Ain't nothing wrong with that knife," Pearly said.

Amanda caught her breath, rocking on the stool, as though she'd just run a long distance.

"It's okay, baby girl," Pearly said touching her shoulder. Amanda threw her arms around Pearly and rested her head in that old flat place and stifled her sobs quickly.

"It's okay, baby girl. Now, now. You two been so brave, we've all been wondering when the fears would start to take over."

Amanda held on until she stopped reeling, said she was all right, and tried to jack up a smile.

"I told myself not to start counting days and we've tried so hard but so that—"

"Amanda, when you talk that fast, the end of what you're saying overtake the front of what you're saying and it sure comes out confusing."

Amanda toughened. "I'll be all right, now."

"Anything in particular you'd care to let me know?" Pearly asked.

She thought about it a moment and shook her head and attacked the collards again.

"Pearly?"

"Yes, baby."

"Is there a ghost in Veda's cottage?"

"Everybody in Nebo got their own special ghost."

Someone's been in there with us for the last two nights."

"It's just the world calling you back."

"No, it's a ghost with a voice and I know Zach hears it. He wakes up suddenly and puts his hands to his face and gasps. He never says anything, but I feel his sweat when he lies back down and I can hear his heart pounding."

"Here, let me cut these greens, you're making a mess."

"I'm dog tired," Amanda said. "I spend the nights watching him, listening to him breathe. I'm going to excuse myself. I have to set a fire and have some hot water for his tub."

"You better rest some."

"I will. I'll curl up in the loft and take a nap. It's nice up there."

Pearly went to the cup nook, took a waiting envelope, and handed it to Amanda.

"This come early. Sheriff Bugg delivered it, personal. Folks are knocking at the door . . . knocking at the door."

Amanda stared at the envelope, knowing Horace's perfect flaring handwriting.

For Miss Amanda Blanton Kerr. Personal. Hand-Deliver to Ned Green.

She hesitated, fingering it, turned it over to its seal, and there was written *I Implore You to Read This.*

"I'm going. If Zach stops by, tell him I'm napping in the loft and there is hot water on the stove by the tub and—"

"You better get some sleep, baby, you look like hell."

It was dusk. Zach's footsteps outside brought her to a half-conscious state, fighting her way out of a gray third of a hard dream. She sat up groggy in the loft as he opened the door downstairs.

"Amanda?" he called.

Before she could answer, she was shocked by his scream. "Amanda! Amanda!"

She could watch him through the railing, staggering, hit by a sudden rush of terror.

"Amanda!"

She did not answer, but waited, watching him fall against a wall. "Leave me alone, Da!" Zachary screamed.

And she waited till he quieted.

"Is that you, sweetheart?" she called down.

Zach groaned with relief.

"What are you doing up in the loft?"

"Taking a nap. There's hot water on the stove. I'll be right down."

"All right . . . all right. I'll take care of it."

He drew the curtain to the tub alcove behind him and, in time, came out, a little melted and calm, and he dressed wordlessly.

She sat before a mirror and brushed her hair.

The grandmother's clock chimed fading and squealy like baby birds in a nest squawking for food. Amanda went to the clock and opened the cabinet to reset the weights.

"Let the damned thing run down. I'm sick of hearing it," he snapped. After a moment: "Somehow I was startled when you weren't here. The cold at the pier went right through me, today. Sorry. Since when have you napped in the loft?"

"I like it up there. I feel safe, like a rail bird. No one can see me."

"Sorry," he repeated. "Sorry about my rotten mood."

"This is going to be painful enough without us turning on each other. We're going to have to get through these next days together," she said.

He kissed her well, not desperately, but soothingly and comfortingly. "I must tell you something that I should have told you our first day in Nebo, but I was leery of saying anything that could upset that moment," he said.

"Then?"

"I'm not much of a Catholic but I believe in God and God had something to do with us coming together here in Nebo."

"Very much."

"From the first time we made love, I knew that if you con-

ceived, I would take it as a message from God and resign from the
Corps without a backward glance and spend my life loving you and
caring for our family."

"I've always known that, Zach. But if we haven't conceived, is
it likewise a message from God?"

He was silenced.

"I've been fawned over all my life and that doubles as a curse,"
she said. "If you're fawned over, you also become the target of
many hateful stings of envy. I built a space between myself and
everyone else in order to protect myself and I played it very
haughty. Willow was the only person to ever become a soul mate.
All of the rest were under my control and some were afraid of me.

"And along came Zachary O'Hara, who was not going to serve
the princess nor do her bidding. Therefore, I had to subjugate you.
When you so rightly saw through my scheme and refused to escort
me to the Constitution Ball, my rage at your rejection could have
burned down a forest. I have inherited from my father the nature of
imposing authority and could stand anyone down, including my
father."

She took the crystal top from the carafe and poured them wine.

"I wanted to hate you and hurt you last summer in Newport.
However, when I hissed out my letter of dismissal to you, it
brought me no solace. From the moment you took to Lilly, I knew
no sleep without torment and I was determined to hate you more,
until that day at the casino.

"You closed the curtain of our booth and gripped my arm.
Well, Zachary, I received my message from God and it was orgas-
mic. I told God that I would settle for this month in Nebo and I
also told Major Ben I would do nothing to make you leave the
Marine Corps. I thought I could trick God and become pregnant so
it would be your honorable decision to resign from the Corps and
not mine. But God didn't buy it. I'm not pregnant."

Amanda took up the letter from Horace.

"This came early. It is from my father." She broke the seal and
read in a shivery voice.

My Beloved Daughter, Amanda,

   Life shall remain unbearable for me until you grant me peace through your forgiveness.

   I have wronged you and I have wronged Zachary O'Hara in a nefarious manner.

   I will accept whatever decision the two of you make with no further high dudgeon on my part.

   I have come to learn that Zachary is an outstanding young man with a brilliant career ahead.

   If you wish to marry, I will not withhold my approval. If you feel it wise to wait, I shall wait with you.

   When Zachary deems that his military service is completed, I shall welcome him as my son-in-law with an eye to him becoming in the future the director of Dutchman's Hook.

   Arrogance yet exists in us strongly from the time of slavery. The class system continues to linger, but I shall work ceaselessly for Zachary's acceptance and recognition. I do this with the same passion that you have for your work in women's education.

   Yes, I have laid myself bare, so let us not dillydally. I respect the fact that he is a Roman Catholic and I certainly shall honor his decision not to convert. But please find this reasonable: The only thing I ask is that your offspring be raised in a Protestant manner. I cannot sign over my grandchildren (I thrill at that word) to the Roman clergy and still win over my establishment. I live as, and need to continue being, an industrialist. These are the facts of my life and I cannot change the order of things.

   If, God forbid, you and Zachary decide to go your different ways, you must return to us. We are what we are, family.

   Your loving and sorrowing father,

                                 Horace

Raised as a princess, the princess knew how to read between the lines.

It was her father, all right. Once he got a wedge in, he'd get over his newfound humility in short order. The letter was pretty to hear, but inside lurked a thousand greedy, air-sucking tentacles.

Yet.

Amanda could not dismiss it out of hand. There was a desperate chance that it could help her keep Zachary.

"He's offering you the empire," she said, not believing the sound of her own words. "He knows how strong we are, together."

Zach paled.

"Father's new light-of-day bluff should be called. And you and I together, solidly bound, can change a lot of things at Dutchman's Hook."

"And turn Inverness into a house of joy," Zach said.

"If this is not the end of the line for us, Zach, then we are going to have to fight like hell."

"Starting life in a conspiracy."

"Zach, we can do it!"

"And while we're at it, change the direction of the stars. The only ship I want to build is a flat-bottomed, steel-skirted boat thirty feet long that can land a platoon of Marines with a measure of protection."

The letter seemed to turn dirty in her hands. Horace Kerr's words were encrusted in lies. He'd never change, and Zach was shaken and she became shaken.

She put it in the fireplace and let its evil smoke stream up the chimney.

"For God's sake, man, please just let me be a Marine's wife!"

"Just as you would hate yourself for taking me to Inverness, I'd hate myself for taking you into the Corps."

There, it was said, cold, point-blank.

She wanted to argue that she'd make it work, to come with him when she could, to hell with the stings of the navy and Marine wives, and when he was away, start up a small girls' academy, and bear it when he was gone because it would be pain worth bearing, or, even if he went into combat, *I could raise the children,* and the more she argued with herself, the blacker the horizon appeared.

What? Bust his career up because he'd spend his married nights longing for her and erode his function as a commander?

And you, Amanda, how long will you live in the shadows of fear and loneliness before you turn old? If I love him as I must love him, I must let the man go or tell the kids, your daddy is gone, he's a Marine and he loves you very much, but Daddy is very important and we must hold up our end of things.

"The glass slipper doesn't fit, no matter how I try to squeeze it on my foot," she said at last.

"I cannot fill your needs, Amanda."

"You can more than fill my needs, only you are already married, Captain."

Zach backed down on the hearth and she came within touching distance.

Voices from the Nebo Abyssinian Baptist Church, with Sister Sugar's riding above them all.

"I'll not close the book until you tell me why he has come into this place with us."

"I . . . uh, don't know what you mean."

Amanda clenched her fists and shrieked to the rafters. "Paddy O'Hara! I know you're hiding up there in the rafters! Paddy! Come down! Your son is hurting!"

"Just because I became startled for a moment when I didn't see you."

"Paddy! Tell him to stop lying to me!"

Zach came to his feet and raised his hand but did not strike her. He walked away feebly. Amanda went to the four-poster, picked up a blanket and folded it, and went up to the loft.

Zach collapsed into a big chair, motionless and mute, not hearing, not seeing, fearing the waves of fear that engulfed him.

Amanda crawled to a place where she could see down and not be seen and wrapped herself up tightly and stuffed it all down.

Come ye home,
Come ye home,
Come ye home when the cruel war is done!
Come ye home, home, home,
Come when the cruel war is done!

The grandmother's clock croaked the hour . . . and another hour, another hour, and then it became so still, they could hear each other's breath.

Now darkness outside and the fire burned low. A soggy rain tapped on the roof.

"Amanda?"

"Yes?"

"Aren't you cold?"

"Aye, I'm cold."

"I put some logs on the fire. Are you after coming down?"

"I'll come down."

He was on the feather bed as the fire flared, and had spread some pillows about to make it an easy place to talk. He patted the feather bed and she came alongside.

"I'll tell you now," he said softly.

44

THE FIFTH COMMANDMENT

February 1892—Tobias Storm's Mansion—Washington

This rite of passage gladdened the old men's hearts like no other. Now they could take off their own kits and rest easy. The mysterious force that bound them was coming to a close in a perfect circle.

Paddy O'Hara had given them each their lives, and Paddy's fine son had been nurtured. The future was now engaged by Zachary. It was a vague future, only a promise, but—in strong hands.

Tobias Storm formed up a second AMP class, then retired as a major but remained on hand as a civilian adviser. AMP's first graduates were gaining attention. For the third class, a pair of midshipmen from Annapolis as well as a pair of West Point cadets were coming to study at the Marine barracks.

Master Gunnery Sergeant Wally Kunkle's transfer to Zachary's First Rovers, Fleet Marine Force, was a hell of a way to close out his own career.

Forty years before, at the Philly Navy Yard, Paddy O'Hara had pulled a bloodied-up little street urchin from a boxing ring and given him a place in the barracks on the deck near the stove to sleep. He was the drummer boy alongside Paddy at Bull Run.

He had been a kid brother to Paddy, in a manner of speaking, standing in for the four brothers who had been lost in the Irish famine. Perhaps the Gunny was a surrogate son to Paddy until Zach was born. He burst with pride to be Zach's gunny on this important mission.

And Benjamin Malachi Boone? That peculiar piece of personnel was accomplishing what he had been ordained to accomplish. Although sixty-five years stared at Ben, there was no retirement parade in view.

Rumor had it that the new commandant would be a full colonel. If so, Ben, the senior major in the Marines, would be promoted to lieutenant colonel and stationed in place to protect the flanks of Zach's mission to the Amnesties.

Zach was their pride.

When the front-door knocker was heard, their three faces smiled. What a hell of a picture the lad cut.

Toasts.

And came time for them to catch their breath.

Ben had a big surprise. The army had set up a warehouse in Colón, Panama.

"We don't know what the political situation will be when we build that canal, so they're loading supplies in for future use. It could be that a rebellion has to be staged in Panama to snatch the isthmus away from Colombia, or there could be a strongman at the head of Colombia who wants to play ball, or there could be some kind of democratic movement, or we may make a deal with banditos in the hills to guard our passageway. Whatever the event, arms to support whoever will be ready in Panama, ha, ha, ha, ha."

Mischief of the highest order.

"In this cache, Krag-Jorgensen rifles and hundreds of thousands of rounds of ammunition. A hundred of these rifles will be 'borrowed' and sent to you. It could be ten years before the army even knows they're missing."

"Hey, we'll drink to that!" So filled they were with their own glee that they had not noticed that Zach appeared to be ill. The Gunny saw it first.

"You all right, Captain O'Hara?"

Zach studied the patterns of the rug, then looked to one another and they grew apprehensive. Zach took an envelope from the high cuff of his glove and handed it to Major Ben.

"What's this?"

"My resignation from the Corps," Zach answered.

"What the fuck did you just say?" Ben asked.

"I am resigning. It is within my purview."

Tobias cleared his throat. "We Wart-Hogs were known for our pranks in the past."

Zach did not answer. Each man reacted, stunned, puzzled, in dread.

"I love you people," Zach rasped. "I love the Marine Corps. I love her more."

"Jesus Christ!" Tobias cried.

Ben came nose to nose with Zach and Zach stared dead ahead, unblinking.

"You don't know the seriousness of what you're saying, Zachary. The admiral-in-chief of the United States Navy and the commandant of the Corps handpicked you. If you don't take this command, there can be only one deduction, that the author of 'Random Sixteen' doesn't have enough belief in his words to stand behind them. 'Random Sixteen' will be impeached, trashed."

"Indeed"—Tobias entered the fray—"you'd be branded as a coward in Marine's clothing. You shock me, Zachary."

"I realized that this moment would fall heavily on you," Zach said.

"Maybe you think my time in China was a big gas. I've got a hundred stab wounds in my back and two thousand nights of long-ing to come back to my country. Maybe you think I didn't freeze my nuts off in Alaska. You have been singled out, spoon-fed, and coddled by the Corps since you were born. Thank God Paddy O'Hara isn't alive to see this moment."

Zach continued to look directly ahead with the passionless face of a tin soldier guarding a national monument. "I know this is hard to take," he managed.

"Hard to take! This is a big-time fucking!" Tobias retorted. "Can't you see what's been done for you? You have been given a chance to change the way the world thinks. No one has that kind of chance. Change the way the world thinks."

Gunny watched this lashing and remained silent. In a long moment, Ben and Tobias caught their breaths.

"A dog ran over the trolley tracks and the front wheels cut off the tip of his tail, so he turned to see what was happening and the back wheels ran over his head. Don't lose your head over a little piece of tail," Tobias preached.

At last the Gunny spoke up. "Tell them why, Captain O'Hara."

Zach faded. "I'm done in," he said. "I have nothing left to give the Marine Corps."

"Nothing left? You haven't even worked up a sweat!" Tobias said.

Ben beat his fist on the desktop, his face filling with horror. "Oh, my God," he said.

"I'm done in," Zach repeated.

"It's all so fucking clear," Ben said. "In the back of my mind I've always had fears about this guy. Look at him. He says he's done in. Zachary O'Hara has used you and you and me and the Corps and everyone in his life and every day of his life to pull the con of the century. Zachary O'Hara knew from the day he was born that the Corps was there to serve him. This guy has the brain and the looks and the big name. His life has been a clever, stunning charade. This boy is slick."

Ben filled his mind to overflowing with Zach's treachery and he reeled between disbelief and rage.

"His tactics began the day he enlisted, with great fanfare and, oh yeah, the tears over his father's grave. Well, let's put Little Precious on guard duty at the Washington barracks. He's about the biggest showpiece the Corps has left. And we three. Get him into AMP. We owe his daddy! And brilliant young Zachary swoons us into a commission and swoons me into taking him to the War College. That was his dirty plan. Newport. Playing the brokenhearted fool, he cruised subtly and with the sly glance and the wispy touch until every virgin heiress on Mansion Row was in heat. You should have heard the phone calls I got begging me to bring him to their parlor.

"George Barjac pleaded with me to talk Zach into the tobacco business and was ready to throw Lilly into the bargain. But Zachary didn't want to get involved in a setup with too many sons and sons-in-law.

"And, oh yes, Admiral-in-Chief Langenfeld was ready to swap a battleship for this . . . this piece of shit. Having surveyed the situation, no way Zach O'Hara would spend two years in a Caribbean shithole."

"You're yellow! You're a coward!" Tobias roared.

"Having brought the Princess Amanda to her knees, begging and crawling, the two, so, so much in love, have a plan to cut the balls off Horace Kerr. Our man has found his big ticket. Now, to get out of the Corps before his beautiful scheme collapses. Gentlemen, I give you the new tycoon, the master of Dutchman's Hook and his blood-drinking wife a-weeping and a-wailing o'er the old man's grave."

"Do I have permission to leave?" Zach asked quietly.

"Bastard!" Ben cried, throwing his fist. Zach turned his head so the blow glanced. Tobias backed up against the door and threw the bolt.

"You have broken the Fifth Commandment to love your father!" Tobias cried.

"That's enough, both of you," the Gunny said. "The Fifth Commandment doesn't say anything about loving your father. It says you will honor your father."

"Don't get cute, Gunny," Ben warned.

"Zachary O'Hara has given his life to defend Paddy's honor and the honor of the Marine Corps."

Tobias was about to come on shouting when Ben held his hand up, trying, trying to get into what the Gunny was saying.

"What are you talking about?" Ben rasped.

"I was at Paddy's bedside as he lay dying. A day before he got away, he asked me to take his confession and he told me everything."

"No! You be quiet!" Zach demanded.

"Sorry, sir," the Gunny answered.

"I did not know you were aware of it, and I command you to remain silent," Zach said.

"Sorry, sir. We have to deal with it now."

The Gunny had puzzled the accusers into silence.

Zachary continued to protest weakly as the Gunny pressed him down into a chair.

"I've watched Zachary O'Hara bear it year after year in silence. He wrote the book on courage."

45

HELL'S KITCHEN

1884—New York

Had Paddy O'Hara remained in Ireland under livable circumstances, he would have become a self-ordained clan chief as powerful as the priest.

He was of great strength, a boy like a man, working the fields with his da and brothers from a tender age. No man dared challenge him, even as a teenager, lest he get starched.

There was a learning side to him. When a traveling bard or illegal hedgerow teacher came to the village, he'd slip off to the hidden classroom to fill a longing. As the sole member of the family and village, including the priest, who could read and write English, he got to read the viscount's dirty edicts aloud as well as quote a line from Shakespeare.

Paddy was fifteen when the Terrible Hunger struck and over those years he buried his mother, father, two sisters, and four brothers, victims of starvation and disease. Two other sisters died at sea fleeing Ireland on a famine death ship.

When it was done, only himself and his older sister Brigid had survived.

The two of them landed in New York in 1852 into a chaotic scene. The Irish shanties of New York, tin and clapboard shacks with yards that held a chicken or two, were cluttered up along the Hudson River at midisland, then segued into tenement up to Seventh Avenue near Times Square.

New land, old story of survival. Immigrants were dumped at a fort, the Castle, at the bottom of Manhattan. No one forgot their first night in America, sharing the place with hundreds of cats and the devastating smell of cat urine.

The Germans had come from higher social orders—tradesmen, craftsmen, stone masons—and even the Italians had seen great art and had a true cuisine, giving off vast aromas.

Every waterfront dumped coolies. The Chinese banded together in mysterious alleys of high suspicion.

Already they were stepping off boundaries of ethnic enclaves; Germantown and Chinatown and Little Italy, and the blacks fleeing north jammed the Upper West Side in Harlem.

For the Irish it was picking shit with the ducks, shoveling holes and ditches. Their place was a bawdy land near the bottom of the pole.

The first Irish immigration, a generation earlier, had come to build the Erie Canal. They had improved their lot very little.

The coming of the young Irish women fleeing the famine gave a first true grace to their community. In the eyes of affluent New Yorkers, the Irish women spoke a variety of English, were severely Catholic, and thus honest, and were of special value to those who could afford a nanny or domestic. The Irish maid, snippy, clever with words, and an independent breed, formed up strong sisterhoods at the local parishes, able to pick off the best of the lads, get them out of ditches, and settle them into the misery of the married life, so long avoided in their ways.

Brigid O'Hara was such a domestic. Although she never married, she placed herself well as a head maid of the second floor in a

Fifth Avenue mansion owned by German Jews. The Germans were inclined to be demanding and stingy but capable of loyalty to those loyal to them. Further, they were nowhere near as class-conscious as the newly rich Americans.

For Paddy O'Hara, choices were simple. He replaced the neighborhood gang leader. In a year or so Paddy was on the well-worn path that ended up in the state penitentiary at Ossining.

Fortunately, Paddy caught the eye of Corporal Gilligan, the local Marine recruiter who trolled Hell's Kitchen for prospects. That day Paddy took the oath was a grand day for himself, and for the Marine Corps as well.

In a manner of speaking, Paddy O'Hara was born to be a Marine. Of obvious value, he did well at a time when promotions in the Corps were rare. In a matter of a few years, he was a ser-geant in the detachment at the Philadelphia Navy Yard.

The soft side of Paddy was never far behind. The death of his family brought on an abstruse search to replace them, and in the Corps, he found some of it.

A little brother came to him in the person of Wally Kunkle, a boy who lived as a sewer rat and fought for pennies at the yard. The day Paddy carried the battered boy out of the ring, took him to the barrack, and mended his wounds was the beginning.

Wally was taught to read and write and ultimately got sworn in to the Corps as a drummer boy at the age of thirteen.

During the Civil War, Paddy saved Wally's life at Bull Run and again at Fort Sumter during the creation of his legend.

The war done, Marines went to faraway posts, but the friend-ships stood firm, particularly those in the special order of the Wart-Hogs.

Peace brought Paddy into contact with his softer side again. He had risen to top major and was one of the most honored Irishmen in New York, useful for ceremonies and recruiting. The recruiter was himself recruited.

Brigid pulled him by the ear to church for Sunday mass, where he was introduced to Maureen Herndon, recently out of County Meath, and a member of her staff at the mansion.

The great warrior melted, and after a proper courtship, they married and left church under a canopy of drawn sabers.

Unknown to either, Maureen had contacted the consumption, a scourge of post-famine Ireland. She was soon with child and the illness raced into her lungs as she gave her entire strength to her pregnancy.

Maureen died three days after Zachary was born.

Never was a man so crushed as Paddy. The sweetness fled. Giving his son to Brigid to raise, he sought duty in places far away, where he could drink, fight, and fornicate. For over four years he evaded the child. Then Brigid tired abruptly, wore thin, and her own demise could clearly be seen.

By command of the commandant, Paddy was awarded the highest enlisted rank, sergeant major of the Corps. The commandant suggested he take care of his son, who had spent his first five years in Hell's Kitchen.

Zachary proved hardly a trouble. Marine wives on base mothered the lad even though he preferred to fend for himself. Father and son lived together in a civilized manner, enjoyed the ceremony and color. As long as Zachary was a little Marine and so long as he stayed clear of Paddy's moods, it went smoothly.

But not inside them. They seemed on good terms at times, then Paddy would go into a long and brooding silence that shut out the world, including his son.

Zach never knew if he was truly wanted.

The place they seemed to come together was in Paddy's moments of pride over his son becoming a self-taught scholar and a voracious reader.

They were friendly indeed, later sharing the end of a bar, but untouchingly so. Zachary did not fear his father or back away from a point he needed to argue. He was proud of Paddy O'Hara, but he was not his father's satellite.

Going their opposite ways except when they needed contact, they established separate lives and a kind of mutually agreed-on friendship.

By the time of Paddy's retirement, with the vice-president in attendance, Zachary was in total comfort in the Marine atmosphere.

Paddy O'Hara's return to Hell's Kitchen with his son had obvious rewards. With few Irish heroes to celebrate, Paddy O'Hara's Saloon became an instant shrine.

Paddy proved not much of a businessman but of enormous value to Tammany Hall and the rising Irish politicians. This was the ward central, where deals were cut and palms were greased.

Within the hallowed halls, Paddy's Medal of Honor and ten other citations for bravery were encased in glass, along with his sword and pistol and a battle flag from Fort Fisher.

The man had pissed more beer in the ocean than most breweries could make in a week. He was a deserving icon and could spend out his days being the object of worship.

Paddy had a decent flat over the bar and grew friendlier to his son. He had free access to every vaudeville, play, and musical in the city.

Fact was, Paddy was growing dependent on Zachary. And that was fine. Zach carved himself a space in the storeroom adjoining the bar, a mat on the floor, reading lamp and a square of wood to write on. From this vantage he could keep an eye on his da, lend a hand at peak hours, help shut down, sweep the sawdust, and now and again get into the singing with those fine Irish voices.

Zach kept an eye on the register and moved into taking better care of the books. And better care of Paddy, who became more and more permanently engaged in greeting and missed the good solid meals, and often ended up in his bed snoring with one shoe off and one shoe on.

Zachary dearly missed the Corps, where footsteps clicked smartly and did not stumble, and all was bright and shined up and crisp, with no slobbery bragging of men who used the bar stool as their stage.

They'd never smell ale on a parade ground or know the exultation of exhaustion at the end of a three-day forced march.

It was a foul place, Hell's Kitchen, and though he was becoming
his father's keeper . . .

Well, then, girls took his mind off the work and study load.
Zach was fancy company, with vaudeville tickets and sweet talking
learned from his books. But Zach was counting days after his sixteenth birthday. In just two years, he was going to be able to enlist
in the Corps.

Oh, for the clean barrack floors and starched shirts and orderly
manner of life, where men got along with one another and need
not scratch eyes out or spit teeth from a split lip.

You see, he did not find it in the gangs. The young thugs were
fiercely jealous of him and of his da's fame. The older crowd in the
saloon reminded Zach on a daily basis that he'd never measure up
to his da as they patted him on the head.

He was a loner walking the streets of the strange neighborhoods but sure enough of himself to go where he wished, and soon
knew how to draw smiles from the Greeks and the Poles.

He wandered into the upper reaches of the West Side, where
those odd folk, the Jews, had set down. He could sense their old-
country privations.

Story after story of massacres of Jews in the Pale gave a growing sense that there would be floods of Jewish immigrants in the
next years.

The other face of Harlem, the black continent, was crowding up
with former slaves or the children of former slaves fleeing the South.

The songs of the neighborhoods, the Irish and Italian tenors,
and the longings sung from the rickety Negro churches to the
strange wail of the Jews, had a harmonious meeting place in street
after street. After all, they sang of the same thing.

This burgeoning place was a strange place of villages, toiling,
sweating, aspiring side by side there to serve the comforts of an
exploding middle class and upper middle class and upper class and
upper upper class.

Zach pondered. Could such a place ever sort itself out? It was a tinderbox on the borders but never quite burst into the all-consuming flame. Gangs and riots were softened by a promise of plenty as the cultures seeped from neighborhood to neighborhood.

For the Irish, down the social ladder, there was always hostility against the blacks, who they feared were after their jobs.

When summer's heat and wet crushed the city or there was an economic slump or a killing or a political fucking, black and Irish tensions went to the brink.

What happened that night at Paddy O'Hara's Saloon was bound to happen.

The Galway Brewery down by the river was a prime supplier for the midtown, West Side bars, restaurants, and gardens.

Its teamster corps was solid Irish, driving livery vans artistically decorated with posters of current events and solid horses sporting chimes and plumes.

A Galway teamster was no small measure of a man. Indeed, each beer wagon had a helper, always a black man, who did most of the heavy work, rolling the kegs in and taking the empties away.

Paddy O'Hara's Saloon was on the route of Tommy Bannon, whose horse was in far better shape than Tommy himself. After twenty-five years of draying, he was drowning in the sorrows of life as well as drowning in the other stuff that surely wasn't holy water.

Tommy, though, was a respected man. In the early days, he had gained prestige as one of the first teamsters and purveyors of Galway beer. Add that to a fine singing voice and jolly manner.

However, his family grew larger and larger and his fine singing voice went croaky over the years. Often, these days, he dozed in the driver's seat. Though past his prime, he could still be a fine show.

The owners of Galway Brewery, the Mulcahy brothers, had sentimental loyalty to anyone who had come from their county in the old country. They turned their eyes away when, again and again, Tommy fell off the wagon and had to dry out at the Angels of Mercy.

Tommy's helper, an elderly Negro, certainly past fifty, known only as old Henry, had been on the job eighteen years. When Tommy fell ill, Henry ran the route, earning an extra twenty-five cents a shift. In the past few years, old Henry drove the route, often as not.

When Zachary knew Tommy Bannon was down, he'd often hitch on with Henry and help him run the route. Henry was not only amusing to banter with but had a terribly keen mind in sorting out the confusion in the city. They became like pals, the first black person Zachary had ever really known. On the route, Zachary got a firsthand view of the general abuse a Negro bore in an ordinary workday.

It annoyed Zach and puzzled him. Would America implode before it could become cities without boundaries?

It was a scorcher, the most brutal and suffocating heat wave in twenty years, some said. The July evening had driven everyone to the rooftops and fire escapes gasping for breath, and the fire hydrants below opened, dousing the kids, and movement slowed to a shuffle.

When out of Long Island, a beedler of a thunderhead of lightning and rain roared onto Manhattan like a prayer answered from the Almighty.

Breath-saving, lifesaving, cooling, the storm dumped and hovered. People stood there on the sidewalks pointing their mouths up like fish drinking and doused themselves to the bone.

It made for a horrendous mess out on the streets, mixing up horse shit on the cobblestones and turning them snot-slippery. Iron wheels spun and horses lost footing. On the unpaved streets, vans went down nearby, hub-deep in mud. It was fun for the kids, but hell on wheels for the teamsters.

Paddy O'Hara's Saloon had been drunk near dry before the storm, and the afternoon delivery was nowhere in sight.

The first street out of the Galway Brewery was an uphill affair. Wouldn't you know, the wagons were loaded to the gills and man, beast, and wagon struggled to get to their routes. Deliveries ran later and later. A busted axle at the gate and flying barrels made life no easier.

Tommy Bannon generally fell sick with one thing or another when it stormed. The brewery became more short of men as crews had to go out and help crippled wagons.

Bucking it alone, old Henry left Galway overloaded for the thirsting bars, three hours late, pulled by an intemperate horse.

At Forty-fourth and Ninth Avenue, two companies of fire wagons raced down the street in an opposite direction, answering an alarm. Henry veered out of their way and slammed the curb, tipped, and dumped.

As the storm headed for Jersey, a midnight crowd jammed the saloons to overflowing. Paddy O'Hara's ran stone dry and was deserted as though a bill collector had entered the place.

Paddy O'Hara was annoyed. Along with the heat and a dry saloon, he'd lost a goodly sum in the poker game he ran in the cellar. Paddy, who could outdrink any man in the bar, hit the hard stuff in his anxiety.

And that damned bloody sharp pain tore through his stomach. Of late, the pain seemed to visit on a daily basis or more. At first, Paddy ignored it, then drank to smother it. With all the crap going on, it hit him bad, this night.

Knowing the saloon business from his vantage point in the storeroom, Zachary stayed in place to put things in order later.

The saloon was quite well trashed up and would stay so until the morning cleaning crew. Zach nodded off for one of his patented twelve-minute naps as his da emptied the registers and fumed over the pain in his belly.

Paddy finally heard the iron rims of wheels and clip-clopping hooves of an unsteady horse and was all but snorting fire when old Henry entered.

For a moment, a sense of pity overtook Paddy at the sight of

Henry, drenched, yellow-eyed with exhaustion, and in fear of a tongue-lashing.

"It was a mess out there tonight, Mr. O'Hara, sir, worst I ever seen in eighteen years. I come straight to you soons I could and skipped all the other bars."

"A lot of fucking good that's going to do now. I lost a fucking fortune tonight."

"Truly sorry," Henry said, glancing hungrily at a badly picked-over free lunch counter. It had been a long, grueling day and he had not tasted a bite for twelve hours.

Paddy always saved the leftovers for Tommy Bannon and Henry. Henry had his own tin plate and tin water cup behind the bar near the free lunch table. It was often his one solid meal of the day. At times, Paddy let old Henry clean the mess at the free lunch table, wrap the scraps in butcher's paper, and take them home.

Paddy set Henry's plate on the counter. "All right, fix yourself a plate." There weren't too much leavings, but Paddy took some bologna from the cooler and added it.

Paddy calmed a bit, looking at a creature more miserable than himself. "Henry," he said, "you're the only one that really gets a free lunch. There is no such thing as free lunch. Why? I'll tell you. Any Irishman will spend ten times more for what he's drinking than what he does eating."

Famished and light-headed, old Henry shoveled bologna and sardines and onions and carrot sticks and soda bread into his face with his fingers, munching with few teeth and drooling down his chin. Ugly sight, Paddy thought. Thank God they ain't in the Marines.

"So when is Tommy coming back on the route?"

Henry wiped his mouth with the back of his hand, asked for water, and went at the rest of the plate.

"Mr. Tommy has been sick for several days."

"He's always sick when it rains," Paddy said.

"I mean double sick, sir. Mr. Hogan, the dispatcher, went and seen him at the Angels of Mercy Mission and Mr. Tommy's missus and kids was all wailing over his cot. Mr. Hogan told me I was to do the route until they decided to break in a new man. Sir, can I have the rest of those leavings?"

Hogan, the dispatcher, was a bloody Ulsterman and suspected of not being of the true faith. Paddy didn't trust Hogan.

"Henry, there's been talk."

"Concerning which matter?"

"They say Hogan is going to get rid of Tommy and give you his route."

"I never heard nothing about that, sir."

"Fuck you didn't. Hogan told you to be real quiet about it, didn't he? Someone overheard him talking to you about it."

"That's not true, Mr. Paddy."

"Yeah, man, you'd be the one nigger teamster they could get away with, and then, more nigger drivers. The brewery would save a fortune."

"No, sir, no, sir."

"You're a liar, Henry."

"I ain't lying to you."

Paddy O'Hara shrieked as fearsome pain, like a bullet, ripped into his stomach and he wobbled and doubled over, made cries like a woman giving birth. He looked up at Henry through maddened eyes.

Paddy's hand wrapped in natural movement about the bar blackjack, a sap of lead pellets covered in leather. No man in Hell's Kitchen was so accurate and devastating in its use.

Gagging in pain, Paddy's left hand grabbed Henry and lifted him off the bar stool and pulled him over the bar, and the right hand lashed out, bashing the sap into Henry's head, shattering the edges of Henry's temple with a single blow. Henry puked. His eyes nearly popped out as Paddy lined up a second blow.

"No, Da, no!" Zachary's voice shouted from the opened store-room door.

Old Henry did not require a second blow.

Paddy O'Hara, renowned for his lightning thinking under fire, let Henry fall to the floor and turned his back to Zachary.

Within a minute, Paddy ditched the blackjack, snatched a bottle of rum from the bar, smashed its bottom, and pulled the jagged edge over his own face, ripping his skin, and he punched himself hard in the nose, turning his face gory.

He knelt alongside Henry's body and wrapped Henry's fist around the broken bottleneck, then looked up to Zachary standing above them.

"The son of a bitch tried to kill me!" Paddy cried.

God be thanked that Commissioner Andy Burke was in a card game at the Hibernian Club a few blocks away. Andy Burke was familiar with and on top of these circumstances. It was very late and the street was quiet.

The commissioner shut the saloon down tight against curiosity seekers and, God forbid, a wayward reporter.

The ambulance and a doctor arrived with no bells. It backed into the side alley and whisked off quickly with the dead man's body.

Paddy was cleaned up, his cut taped closed.

"Not too bad, you'll need a few stitches," the doctor, a stitch master, told him; otherwise he was fine and lucky.

Paddy was helped to a table.

"What happened?" Burke asked.

"He come in very late and must have been drinking up a storm, probably had a shot at every bar he delivered. I fixed him something to eat, but he was raging, cracked off a bottle, reached over the bar and cut my face, and bashed my nose as well. I pushed him off me. He was so drunk he fell off the stool, cracked his head on the corner of the bar, then hit it again on the foot rail, wedging in his face."

Paddy stopped, aware that his son was standing close by, listening.

"Did you see it, Zach?" Andy Burke asked.

"No, he didn't," Paddy answered quickly.

"Zachary," the commissioner said, "you wait now over in the ladies' parlor. I'll be with you later."

Burke ordered a cop to help Paddy up to his flat, where the doctor would stitch him up.

It was half four and dawn peeking through when the commissioner was satisfied with the cleanup and found his way into the ladies' drinking parlor, where Zach sat in a booth in a stupor.

Burke was a steadying sight, great muttonchop sideburns, top-of-the-line bowler, a diamond stickpin in his cravat, a man as dandy as his reputation.

He set a bottle of Paddy's best Scotch whiskey on the table and invited himself to a glass and ran through his notes.

"Can we have a little talk now, Zachary?"

Zach mumbled.

"Here, take a couple of sips, won't hurt you any."

Indeed, it helped.

"I realize this has been a traumatic experience for you, but as you know, it is not an uncommon occurrence. We like to close the report quickly on these barroom incidents. Not that anyone gets too upset when Irish brawl with Irish, but when you start mixing the races, particularly the niggers, it can be like lightning on a short fuse, if you get my meaning."

Zach nodded.

"You often rode with old Henry?"

"Yes, sir."

"We don't have a complicated case. In that you are the only possible witness, your statement will close the matter and spare us a coroner's inquest. So, you came out of the storeroom to see what the ruckus was all about and you saw your da kneeling by old Henry."

Zach just stared down.

"Then you could smell Henry, reeking from rum. Your da said Henry was a master at sneaking booze from his deliveries and stealing off the free lunch table. I'm sure every bartender of Eighth Avenue will confirm that."

Burke waited.

"I read myself to sleep," Zach said.

"You slept? With this heat, through the storm, no beer, and a hundred Irishmen needing a drink?"

"I often nod off no matter how loud things get. I sort of sleep with one eye open."

"So the saloon emptied, and later on, Henry comes in dead drunk and mad and you kept sleeping."

"I didn't see Henry come in."

"Indeed. What woke you up?"

"My da had a fierce stomach pain and shrieked to high heaven." Zach broke into a sweat and took another nip at the whiskey. "It gets blurred," he said.

"You have to corroborate your da's story. Henry was on the floor and your da was kneeling over him. You never saw any blows struck."

"Old Henry was Temperance. He never drank," Zach rasped. "I saw what happened."

"He was at Henry's side, right?"

"No, sir."

"Go on."

"I awakened by Da's scream. He was reeling around gagging and all doubled over. It sometimes annoyed Da the way Henry ate with his fingers, sometimes half starved. Da come out of his pain raging and hit Henry," he said, and pointed to his temple. "You've seen how fast he is with the blackjack. Split the man's skull."

"You liked old Henry?"

"Aye."

"Paddy told me you oftentimes walk around in Harlem, totally without fear."

"Aye."

"What attracts you?"

"I never understood why the Irish, with our own desperate and tragic history, don't have a penny's worth of compassion for black people."

"Indeed, Zach, keeping the niggers down is a high priority. It is going to remain that way until our people feel they are first-class

Americans and not threatened. Maybe one day down the line, when we've made our way in as equals, our fears will diminish."

Zachary knew what was coming and felt trapped and horrified. Burke flipped his notepad closed.

"If that is your story, then there will be a formal inquest, son testifying against father. The penny press will distort this into a monumental scandal. It is not even August yet and this city will boil over. We can't pass it off as a common barroom brawl. Paddy O'Hara is a great hero to us. His Congressional Medal of Honor tells the Irish they can rise and achieve and be proud and respected as Americans."

In that moment, Zachary thought of running without stopping, clear to the Mississippi.

"Paddy's had a hard life, what with the famine and digging his family into the ground and the butchery of the Civil War, and just as he was looking at a moment's peace, he lost your mother."

"They say I look like her."

"Aye, that's true."

"And I've seen him look at me a thousand times and in that instant he saw her, but it was only me, who had killed her."

"So here we are," Burke said. "Your father is a great man with common flaws. He lost his head for one moment of his life, because he has the cancer."

The unspeakable word had been spoken.

"How can you know that! No doctor has told him."

"I've seen too much of it, Zach. He's a powerful man, but he'll have to give in and learn it from a physician soon enough. They'll juice him up and keep him going for a year or two."

"He shouldn't have!"

"But he did," Burke said. "Consider the race riots. Consider the rest of your own life after you send your da to die in prison. You hear me, boy. The fall of such a hero will humiliate the United States Marine Corps, forever, and the Irish community will never live it down."

"I want to see a priest!"

"No. Either way you choose, you've a burden on you for the rest of your life. What will it be, Zachary? You either bury the lie in old Henry's coffin or you rat on your father."

February 1892—Tobias Storm's Mansion—Washington

As Gunny Kunkle related the story and Zachary told the ending himself, he felt a lovely lightness coming over him as the demon fled his body.

Tobias Storm and Ben Boone were chalky numbers, close-eyed, ashamed.

"I was allowed to join the Corps underage so my da could live to see me sworn in."

"I gravely misunderstood," the Gunny said. "Paddy was near gone when he told me and I should have come to you a long time ago, but you were already an elegant Marine while he was still alive. When we were on post together in Florida, I never saw a young lad cut his corners so square, so sparkling, so smart and on top of things as you. Even as a private, I knew you were heading for the top, so I let it ride, never realizing your terrible burden for eight years."

Zach was calm, his face whipped by the winter winds of Nebo, his eyes bright.

"The lie wasn't buried in old Henry's coffin and didn't have to wait till Halloween to come out of the graveyard," Zach said. "I had the obnoxious grace to attend Henry's funeral. And I believed the only way to get it out of my system was to become a Marine's Marine. But it doesn't go away. The more perfect I tried to become, the more I realized I was feeding the lie. I felt I existed mainly to keep the lie fed."

"Paddy loved you. You've got to know that. I was at his side when you were born."

"Da loved me when I was born and I loved him the moment he died. It was all the time in between that was the problem. I loved the Corps and that's all I've wanted from life. When I lived in Hell's Kitchen, I longed for the Corps. But then the lie dragged my soul down so badly I was never at ease inside the Corps. I had two masters and one of them was killing me and not letting me serve how I wanted to serve."

Tobias got enough of a grip on himself to awkwardly extend his hand.

Zach shook it.

"We all go off with some secret or lie never properly attended to," Tobias said. "But this is not your burden to carry alone, anymore. It's a matter I share with Amanda and you and the Gunny. It's my responsibility as well, and you have to know you did the only thing you could do. Paddy and the Corps owe you."

If Ben Boone knew of tears, he would have spent them now.

"I didn't believe my own words when I chewed you out," Ben said.

"I know."

"I always had the fear of you leaving the Corps, and when you told us, it broke my heart."

"We're fine, Ben," Zach said.

"Your old man laid it on you and so did I. I saw the way you handled the project and I made you feel you had to be our savior, the indispensable man, and I wrung 'Random Sixteen' out of your guts. You are more than free to resign, but don't get tangled up with any guilt. There are many good men who can take the mission and get it done. Lieutenants Kirkendahl and Maynard from your AMP class. Captain Coleman and Captain Ward are real works in progress."

"Go off with your lady love. You need to be free," Tobias said.

"Aye," the Gunny agreed.

"Why the hell didn't Paddy ask your forgiveness?" Ben asked.

"Of course he did. Or at least that's what he wanted to do. Maybe that's why he followed me to Nebo. Paddy wasn't much for passing out affection and my aunt Brigid was much the same.

"I was never close to a family. The Barjacs were astonishing, but I wasn't or couldn't be part of them. Every evening in Nebo, I'd quit my little job at the boatyard, wash up at the pump, and cross the duckboard bridge to Veda's.

"And she was there waiting, standing in the door, and wouldn't let me in without paying her a hundred kisses. That's what people do, kiss each other at the door.

"And morning came without the sound of reveille. And I'd listen to the first birds of the morning chatting it up. I could go through an entire day, taking orders from no one. I never felt a weight of orders and discipline because the Corps was my life, but then I found there is another life. How wonderful to hold Amanda through the night. What a wonderful way to live.

"One day, near the end of my furlough, she wasn't waiting at the door. She was up asleep in the loft, and when I didn't see her, I panicked. She knew and she demanded that my da and I have it out, there and then."

"So you're going to build the navy a few ships, are you?" Tobias said.

"No, and as far from it as we can get," Zach answered. "As soon as I get my discharge, we are booking a boat for England and staying with her brother until we can collect our wits. From there, the Channel ferry and then through France by barge and rail to Italy, then Greece, and an old slow freighter around the Mediterranean to Egypt, then through the Suez Canal to the Orient, and in a year, more or less, we plan to debark in San Francisco. California will surely have something that will appeal to us."

Zach took the captain's bars from his pocket and offered them to Ben. "Put these on the right pair of shoulders," he said.

"Keep them. Show them to your grandchildren, someday."

✺· 46 ·✺

O'HARA'S CHOICE

That Evening—Prichard's Inn

From her room upstairs, Amanda could see Zach enter the hall, and she was waiting at the top of the stairs. No dainty stuff here now. They came together like two hot winds. He kicked the door open and tossed her into the deep, inviting feather bed and leaped on her. She tickled him and he crashed onto the floor and crawled away and she caught his foot and he went flat and she pounced.

Circled, they did, around the bedposts, panting and grabbing enough clothing to tear off each other.

She doused him from the water pitcher and he wrestled her, using quite a bit of strength now, and pinned her to the floor and she screamed and swung at him and whacked him good. Mr. Prichard was starting to wonder if they were not engaged in an all-out naval battle. As the purveyor of Marine farewell parties and one-night stands, he knew to furnish his rooms with tasteful but party-worthy furnishings. A total bash-in would cost a Marine not more than ten or twelve dollars.

She tickled him again and tried to crawl off on all fours, and that's how he caught her.

"Take your boots off, you savage!"

They locked in, the pair of them, till even the Marine boy's strength was gone and they both keeled over quivering.

He helped her back onto the bed as best he could and collapsed beside her.

"Oh God, that was wonderful!"

"You are hereby declared a Wart-Hog," he said.

After a time.

"I resigned."

"How did they take it?"

"Very bad at first. The Gunny had always known about that night. My da told him before he died. The Gunny told them today and they sent me off with Godspeed."

"Poor baby, you must be done in," Amanda said.

"Don't fret, I'll catch you again later."

"How long before we're free to go?"

"They'll push it through. No more than a week or so. The commander at Quantico has granted me nightly leave off the base. We're well set up here."

"I went to the shipping office. I've a list of all the spring sailings. We'll book a grand ship and marry at sea in the captain's cabin and have a huge wedding party in the ballroom with two hundred total strangers."

Zach propped on his elbows, put a pillow against the headboard, and sat against it, sullen.

Amanda realized immediately. She closed her eyes and recited firmly: "We will not let my money come between us. I have instructed my mother and the Blanton family lawyers to sell back all my stock in Dutchman's Hook to my uncles. The funds will go into a trust for that future girls' school, and I'll establish it in a place where black girls can study as well. There is some Blanton money, enough for a blowout of a journey and to start up a life in California. I want you to handle the money together with me."

Zach mumbled.

"Then we'll burn the damned stuff and take a train to California," she said.

"You make me love you so much," he whispered. "We'll go by boat."

Well into the night, after the bar closed downstairs, Amanda slept, at last, but there was no sleeping for Zachary. He marveled at what he saw in the dim light, traced over her body so that she smiled in her sleep.

That was the last of Zach's memory.

Grumph. Captain O'Hara's pillow was wet with his sweat as though his face had been caught in drying cement. "On your feet, goddammit, Marine," Zach grunted to himself. He dragged himself up, whereupon he supported two of the four bedposters.

His memory failed as to who had collapsed from lovemaking first. There was still half a night left and she was even more beautiful than before.

The immediate situation called for fresh air and a rasher of bacon. Zach followed himself down a set of swaying stairs. Mr. Prichard nodded almost bashfully as Zach bumbled his way outside, attaching himself to the fence. Between gasps of pain and gasps of wonderment, Zachary O'Hara near broke into tears at the thought of his new life. For the hundredth time, he assured himself that in order to purge his da's secret, he had made an honorable decision to leave the Corps. Yet something annoyed him. Perhaps it was just touchiness. She seemed to have things so well planned out—where they would sail, where they would land, and how they would live thereafter. He'd given it all to her, but somehow a bit of a nasty urge crept in from Amanda's vibrancy.

A distant sound.

Zach heard something from the direction of Quantico. The horse Marines were not in a class with the army cavalry, but, by God, they had their own prance and smell. The oils and liniment they mixed were different from the army stuff and . . . What the hell, I don't smell anything.

Colors! Little Zach O'Hara was whisked from his feet to his da's shoulders as the color guard lowered the standard and that certain stillness followed by an instant of grace. Da's eyes met those of his son. They said nothing, but Zach always remembered the smell of saddle soap and the liniment on Da's hands as the last of the horsemen trotted by.

This time the stairs got him and he was out of it as he hit the pillow.

He felt over the bed. Amanda was not there. Zach bolted up, then saw her sitting across the room. The basin was filled. He dunked his face, cleared his head, and saw her dressed and sitting there.

Zach scratched his belly and cracked his back and allowed himself a huge "phew."

. . . then noticed Amanda had not budged in her seat, her back erect and she was dressed to go.

He knew the next five minutes were going to be the worst of his life.

"I know you are leaving me," she said. "We are not going off together."

Zach stood up, shocked.

"What the hell is coming off!" he demanded.

"You tell me," she said.

"How can you know something like that when I don't know that myself?"

"Oh, I've known since I rushed past you when you were guarding the secretary of the navy's office, over four years ago."

"You're thinking like a crazy woman. Paddy O'Hara no longer has his hold on me," Zach cried. "We can live the life we're both hungering for."

"All I really begged of God was for us to have our time in Nebo." The words stuck, trying to find their way out of Amanda's wavering voice. From the first night at Nebo, the game had changed forever. Not only had she conquered this grand fellow but more. Now she'd carve him into the perfect cavalier, walking one step to her rear, and after one month or two or three, he would begin to lose his steel and would submit, always submit.

Amanda had bedeviled herself into believing that their union was equal, but it never had been so since the first day in the secretary of the navy's office. Amanda's will was insatiable. It was like her to be so. No kind tears for the Marine Corps now. She'd won the field.

"I'm going alone," she said tersely.

The pallor of the moment lingered. Zach tried to come to her but was unable to move.

"Come on, Zach," she cried. "Lift me up in your arms and carry me away."

"I can't," he cried. "What the hell's the matter with me?" He was still unable to move; her command flooded him. "You are dismissing me," he said.

Her answer: "Or are you dismissing me?"

"Why," he cried, "why, why, why?"

"You've drunk your fill from the most potent cup of all. You are smitten by the aphrodisiac of a patriot. That is how men like you come about."

Their time was done.

"What will you do?"

"I'll cry for a year and a day or however long it takes, and then I'll wake up one morning and it will be different, and I'll get along and see what there is. I'll make out fine. I'll live a worthy life."

He dared gaze upon her and he gave her the softest of smiles, and she smiled as well.

"Good-bye, then, Captain O'Hara," she said, and went on her way.